FIRST TIME
Lucky

LONI HANSEN

This book is a work of fiction. Names, characters, places, assumptions, and incidents are either the product of the author's imagination or are used fictitiously. Any resemblance to actual persons, living or dead or otherwise, events, and locales is entirely coincidental.

FIRST TIME LUCKY
Copyright © 2023 by Loni Hansen
Portland, OR

All rights reserved. No part of this book may be reproduced, scanned, distributed, or used in any manner without written permission of the author except for the use of brief quotations in a book review. For more information, or to obtain permission to excerpt portions of this text, please contact the author: lovelonihansen@gmail.com

First edition May 2023

ISBN 978-1-954815-08-7

Cover Design by Kristin Erickson

To my first, my favorite, my forever.

MAKE A WISH AND BLOW

Colette

Colette Harris poked at the hot pink fondant bow tie wrapped around the thick chocolate shaft. If not for the words *Make A Wish and Blow* scrawled in white frosting across a pair of substantial balls, the cake might easily have been mistaken for a rocket ship. Or a mushroom. Maybe a sad ferret.

Honestly, a sad ferret cake would have made more sense considering Colette was turning thirty today, and the last time she'd seen anything resembling a penis this up-close and almost-personal was when she walked in on her roommate screwing the drummer of an Irish punk band. Her *college* roommate.

She couldn't believe an entire decade had passed since that night. She would never forget how horrified she'd been, how hot her cheeks flamed, when the drummer, a red-haired, green-eyed hunk, stopped mid-thrust, rose to his knees on the top bunk, and looked over his broad bare shoulders at Colette standing open-mouthed in the doorway. He flashed her a sparkling, wicked grin, seeming to feel no shame about being caught *in flagrante delicto*.

His erect penis, which was darker than Colette thought a penis would be, and fatter, too, was on full display, and she hadn't been able to stop staring.

"Aye love, want to join?" The drummer's voice rumbled in a way that made her burn even hotter and turned her insides to molten liquid.

Pathologically unable to be cool, Colette had stuttered a pathetic excuse and fled. Her roommate's flirtatious giggles and the deep bass growl of the drummer chased her down the empty hallway, haunting her to this very day.

She could have done it then. Popped her cherry once and for all. But she really hadn't wanted her first time having sex to be as part of a threesome. Now she wished she had done it. At least it would have been a typical college experience. Okay, slightly atypical. But at least she wouldn't be turning thirty today, still very much and pathetically a virgin.

How had she let this happen?

Ten years gone, and the only other dicks she'd seen had been in photographs or on television or in anatomy textbooks, which didn't count as actual, real-life penises. Now, thanks to Mallory, her legal assistant and the only person at the office who remembered today was her birthday, Colette could add this chocolate penis cake to her ever-growing list of not-real penises she'd seen over the past three decades of a very chaste life. Perfect.

Mallory snickered as she pointed to the punny message frosting the cake balls.

"Get it?" The twenty-three-year-old made a crude gesture with her hand and pressed her tongue against the inside of her cheek, making her light-brown skin bulge.

"Yeah, funny." But Colette's tone implied the opposite.

"You don't like it?"

"No, I do. It's great, Mallory. It's nice of you to remember."

Because except for her best friend Brooke—who'd sent a quick 'It's your birthday, bitch! This is your year! Drinks on me!'

text that morning on her way to another audition—no one else had. Not that she was expecting much, but she usually at least got a cheesy e-card from her mom and Geoffrey, or a quick phone call from her little sister who was always either leaving an airport or arriving at one. *Can't talk long, just wanted to say happy birthday, I love you, don't forget to pluck your chin hairs!* It was nearing 6:00 PM and Colette's phone and email had been oddly silent. So, the cake was a welcome, if slightly inappropriate, gesture.

Mallory crossed her arms over her ample chest and pushed her glossy red lips into a pout. "You're not mad, are you? It was this or a My Little Pony cake."

"Wait," Colette said. "You found a bakery that sells kid cakes and dick cakes in the same window?"

A teasing smile played over Mallory's mouth. "It was most definitely not a kid's cake. That pony was hung."

Colette choked on a startled squawk.

Mallory snorted when she laughed, a quirk that made her a favorite around the office. That, plus she was smart, hard-working, ambitious, told good stories, and brought homemade tamales to work every Monday. In some ways, Mallory Soledad reminded Colette of herself when she was starting out as an entry-level legal assistant—eager to learn, putting in long hours, wearing her hair in a messy bun shoved through with pencils.

In other ways, they were nothing at all alike.

Mallory was the office flirt. Her skirts were always too short, her tops too tight, her make-up too heavy. And her stories, while entertaining, almost always revolved around sex. Every week, a new man or woman. Mallory liked both and had no problem sharing her very vigorous love life with anyone who would listen. Fresh out of law school, Mallory was still learning what was an appropriate conversation for the workplace and what was better suited for happy hour.

This cake, for instance, was a classic example of Mallory's

playful exuberance getting ahead of her common sense. But since it was Friday, and her birthday, Colette dropped the lecture.

"I like it," Colette repeated as Mallory perched herself on the leather armchair angled in front of the mahogany desk. "I really do. It's not exactly work appropriate, but it looks delicious."

She raised her eyebrows suggestively, and Mallory burst into laughter again. Her hiccupping giggles were contagious, and it took only a few seconds before Colette was laughing along with her.

A knock on the closed office door interrupted their fun.

Colette swallowed her laughter. In a panic, she scanned the room for some place to hide the vulgar cake, but nowhere seemed suitable. She was a minimalist with interior decorating and there was only the desk and a couple of chairs filling the space. No filing cabinets, no tall plants, not even a bookshelf. Mallory certainly wasn't helping. She was laughing so hard now that tears streamed down her face.

"Crap." Colette reached for the plate as the door opened.

And that's how she ended up holding a dick in her lap when Scott Campbell, the son in Campbell and Sons, and her new boss, stepped into the room.

Scott's dark, bushy eyebrows shot up, and a mischievous smile twisted his mouth when he saw the cake in Colette's lap. Her cheeks grew hot, embarrassment spreading like wildfire across her skin.

Until last week, she and Scott were both junior attorneys and had spent plenty of late nights and long lunches together, writing briefs, filing paperwork, and rehashing whatever trashy dating show was trending. But Scott had been promoted to partner just last week, so technically he was her boss now, and everything about this penis cake situation screamed sexual harassment lawsuit waiting to happen.

"It's my birthday," she blurted out because someone needed to say something.

"Happy birthday," he said without breaking eye contact. "Go on then. Take a bite."

This sent Mallory into another fit of gasping laughter.

Scott reached behind him to close the office door. "Please tell me Barb in HR isn't invited to this party."

Scott Campbell was a good-looking man. He was a few years older than Colette, with a square jaw and regal forehead. He wore his rusty-brown hair short on the sides, long on top and tousled to create a perfect, just-got-out-of-bed look. His nose bent slightly to the left, which actually made him more attractive by the very nature of its imperfection. His hazel eyes reminded her of agates, and there was something dangerous about the way he allowed them to roam over anything and anyone he wanted.

There was no shame in those eyes, no flicker of embarrassment or hesitation. *Wolfish*, Colette thought when Scott bit his lower lip and asked, "Do you think you can handle all of that?"

As he moved closer to the desk, his eyes grazed over Colette's mouth, then roamed over her chest before finally landing again on the penis cake still resting in her lap.

Mallory stopped laughing long enough to say, "Maybe just the tip."

Colette shot her assistant a poisonous look. This stopped being funny the second Scott knocked on her office door. Except Scott was now laughing with Mallory. The two of them giggling like a pair of horny teenagers. Minds in the gutter, both of them.

Scott took the cake from Colette, set it on the desk, and cut a small sliver from the left ball. He popped the bite-sized slice into his mouth and chewed for a minute, acting like he was a judge in a cooking competition.

Finally, he said, "Well, ladies, that's the first time I've ever eaten a dick. Do they all taste that sweet? Because if they do, please tell me why every girl I'm with always complains about giving head?"

Mallory sputtered, pretending offense, but then playfully swatted Scott's thigh. "Sounds like you're just hooking up with the wrong girls."

He swung his hungry grin over to Mallory. His eyes swooped up and down the length of the younger woman, taking in her generous curves and the sloped vee of her cleavage rising above her lacy, low-cut top. He stuck his thumb in his mouth, then his forefinger, slowly licking off the chocolate cake crumbs. Mallory held his gaze as she ran her tongue over her bottom lip.

Colette cleared her throat. "Was there something you needed from me, Scott?"

The connection between Scott and Mallory broke, but the sexual tension in the room still crackled. Except now his hungry gaze was back on her. He loosened his tie. The sleeves of his suit jacket tightened around his biceps.

"It's Friday," he said. "And it's your birthday."

Colette tapped her finger on the day planner open in front of her. "Yes, I'm aware."

"Don't be a smartass, Colette." He closed her day planner. "I came to see if you wanted to join me for happy hour at Gardenia's."

A small wine bar across the street from their law offices, there were dozens of places just like it across Los Angeles. Dim lighting, cozy seating, open ceilings that forced you to talk louder than you normally did, candles on the tables, bottles of wine lining the walls—Gardenia's was nothing special, but it was convenient.

"To celebrate your birthday, of course," Scott added, smiling wider.

Colette stared pointedly at him. "You didn't even know it was my birthday until you walked in here, did you?"

He looked like he wanted to argue, but then gave a small shrug. "No, you're right. I was being selfish and thought we could celebrate my promotion."

"Let's do both." Mallory hopped up from the chair, excited to make Friday night plans. "But Gardenia's…? It's a little stuffy, isn't it?"

"It's for old people, she means," Colette said.

"I just mean it doesn't really give off great birthday vibes," Mallory countered. "It's where you take clients out to lunch or make business deals or buy your mistress dinner."

She wrinkled her nose and stuck out her tongue.

"She's not wrong." Scott turned his easy grin onto Colette. "Gardenia's is more of an 'it's Wednesday and I've got nowhere else to go' spot."

"I know a great place." Mallory dug her phone from her pocket and jabbed at the buttons. "It's near Brand and Wilson. It's a dive."

"Mallory…" Colette hated dive bars. The last time she went to one, she almost didn't make it out alive, but Mallory waved her hand, cutting off Colette's protests.

"You'll love it. Trust me." Mallory frowned at her phone. "We have some time to kill, though. Doors don't open until nine."

"Food first?" Scott suggested.

The two of them made plans without her, talking about which In-N-Out served a better Animal Style. Every word oozed innuendo, and their bodies tilted closer, and Colette felt a flicker of unexpected jealousy. She couldn't tell if she was jealous because it was her birthday and she didn't feel like she should have to compete for attention with someone as beautiful as Mallory, or if seeing Scott flirt with Mallory was making her realize how much of an idiot she was for thinking there might be something more than friendship between them.

But as they were leaving, as Scott helped Colette put on her jacket, his hand lingered at her waist, then slipped lower until his pinky finger brushed her ass. Low and soft against her neck so only she could hear, he said, "You look hot in that dress."

Her skin flushed warm again as she felt a rush of possibility swiftly followed by a sinking feeling in the pit of her stomach.

Scott's hand stayed firmly on the small of her back as they walked to the parking lot. Maybe she hadn't mistaken the spark between them after all, and maybe something interesting was going to happen between them tonight. But instead of just enjoying Scott's attention, Colette did what she always did when she started feeling anxious about something. She made a pro and cons list in her head.

Pros of going to the club with Scott Campbell:
1. He has a great body and looks like he'd be an excellent dancer.
2. He said you looked hot.
3. It's a better way to celebrate your birthday than what you originally planned, sitting at home by yourself eating takeout Thai food and watching Ten Things I Hate About You for the twelfth-millionth time.
4. It will give us a chance to discuss the latest episode of Trash Island.
5. Free drinks. Probably.

Cons of going to the club with Scott Campbell:
1. He's your boss.
2. You shouldn't get drunk in front of your boss.
3. Remember the part about how he's your boss now?
4. Alcohol makes you act like a bitch.

Stop. Enough was enough. No more lists.

Lists were nothing more than security blankets to calm her nerves. They were for twenty-something Colette, scared Colette. And as of this morning, that timid girl was gone, replaced by a thirty-year-old, goddamn grown woman who was perfectly capable of making decisions without seeing her options listed in two neat columns.

In the time it took to walk off the elevator and cross the lobby, Colette Harris decided that this would be the year she finally stopped overthinking her entire life and started living it. She knew what she wanted. Now all she had to do was reach out and take it.

So, okay, Scott was her boss, technically, but he hadn't been her boss for long, and yeah, that could make this complicated, but the thing was, Colette didn't want a relationship; she just wanted someone to screw her brains out.

And Scott looked like a man up for the challenge.

He smelled like sandalwood and soap, and when he opened the car door for her, his eyes dipped to her breasts for the second time that day. The look he gave her was more than the flirtatious glint he gave Mallory. Scott Campbell looked like he wanted to devour her.

Colette wasn't sure she wanted to be devoured—yet—but she did want to stop being afraid all the time. She wanted to stop making lists. She wanted to go to a dive bar with Mallory and Scott on her birthday, get drunk and dance without worrying about how awkward it might make things at work the following Monday. More than anything, Colette Harris wanted to stop being the uptight virgin who never had any fun. And if Scott's lust-filled, sidelong glances were any indication, tonight just might be the night everything changed for her.

She'd been avoiding this long enough. Thirty years, to be exact. But it was her turn now, her chance to get lucky. All she had to do was not blow it.

Or maybe that's exactly what she needed to do.

She laughed out loud.

"What's so funny?" Scott took his eyes off the slow-moving LA traffic to caress her with his hungry gaze.

In the backseat, ignoring them completely, Mallory sang along with the pop music playing through the speakers.

Colette shook her head and rolled down her window. "We left the cake on my desk."

"The cleaning crew's going to have fun with that."

Scott's laughter sent a rush of heat racing up her spine, making her bold. She reached over and settled her hand high on his thigh. The smile he gave her in return told her everything she needed to know about the direction this night was headed.

FOR A GOOD TIME CALL

Colette

Scott's hands were in Colette's hair, on her hips, caressing her arms, cupping her breasts. Breasts he hadn't stopped staring at since they left the office four hours ago.

Scott, Colette, and Mallory had wasted almost two whole hours at In-N-Out, dithering over fries and milkshakes, then they did shots at a Chili's down the street before ending up at Giggles, the dive bar Mallory couldn't stop raving about. Honestly, it was less divey than Colette thought it would be. The dim lights and flashing strobes, along with the crush of bodies writhing on the dance floor, hid whatever less than savory aspects might have existed in the light of day. If Mallory hadn't called this place a dive, Colette wouldn't have been able to tell what kind of bar it was—besides a popular one.

Throbbing music blasted through hidden speakers. Scott moved his body in rhythm with it, grinding against Colette, keeping their bodies close with his hands around her waist. He danced her toward a wall, pinning her against rough brick and shoving her legs open with one knee. His fingers traced the pale soft skin of her inner thigh, already slick with sweat even though they'd spent barely thirty minutes on the dance floor.

His hands moved higher, fondling the line of her underwear. He pressed his mouth to her neck, teeth bared against her flesh, tongue darting, tasting her, as she tipped her head back, opening more of herself to him.

As his fingers explored, she bit down on her lip to keep from moaning his name. There was pleasure in being wanted like this —he couldn't keep his hands off her—but also, she was feeling a little self-conscious about letting such private things happen to her body in such a public place. *Look around, love, no one's watching. No one cares.* The voice in her head sounded like the Irish punk rocker she should have let take her virginity when she had the chance.

Scott bit her neck hard enough to hurt, but she liked the sting. The flash of pain was like a reprimand, a reminder to pay attention. Colette arched against him, feeling his erection through his jeans. He pressed back against her, murmuring words in her ear too soft to mean anything.

People danced around them, grabbing, gyrating, tipping drinks to their mouths, spilling half onto the floor and half down low-cut blouses and over fancy, strappy shoes. Strobe lights flashed red and orange and green and white, making the entire night seem unreal, like she was in a movie.

Scott rocked his hips against hers in time to the music. His fingers slipped under the elastic band of her underwear, breaking her Hollywood spell.

She wished she'd thought more about ending up in this position when she got dressed this morning. She would have picked something sexy and red, not her ratty, but comfortable beige cotton briefs. Colette grabbed Scott's wrist and moved his hand back to her breasts. He didn't seem to mind. He was too busy feeling the music, feeling himself, feeling her.

She closed her eyes and tried to lose herself again in the pleasant buzz of alcohol, the steady beat of the music, the intoxicating gyration of Scott's hips because even if this was a bad idea, and of course it was–sleeping with your boss never ended well for anyone–it was her thirtieth-fucking-birthday. And it was about damn time she let loose and gave a hot man permission to touch her the way Scott was touching her right now.

They were both adults who knew exactly what this was: fun with no strings attached. She could do that, if he could. And she had no doubt he could. A man his age, nearing forty, and not married? Yeah, Scott Campbell did casual hook-ups like it was his damn job.

"You're so fucking hot." His words were whiskey-scented and warm against the curve of her neck. "What is this? Lingerie?"

He plucked at the thin strap of the mint green sundress she was wearing. Earlier at the office, she'd worn a jean jacket to make the skimpy number more work-appropriate, but she had left the jacket in the back of Scott's car when they got to the club.

Scott nibbled her clavicle, working his way to the tops of her shoulders and slipping the strap off. Like her, Scott had stripped down after they left the office. He lost his dress shirt and tie, leaving him with a tight undershirt and ass-hugging, dark-washed jeans that showed off his muscles and left little to the imagination.

Colette traced a finger over his taut stomach, wrapped her arms around his waist, and cupped his firm butt, pulling him closer.

"You like that?" he murmured against the ridge of her shoulder.

The two gin and tonics she drank when she got here buzzed fire through her veins. She rode that perfect line between sober and sloppy. The silky sundress slid pleasingly over her skin as Scott rubbed against her. He licked his lips, then took her mouth in his, biting, nibbling, and she felt irresistible. This was it. Tonight was the night she was finally getting laid.

"I'm so hard." Scott moaned in her ear. "Touch it."

He grabbed her hand and moved it to his crotch. He was steel and stone, nothing like the chocolate birthday cake. She imagined putting her mouth around Scott's shaft, then spreading her legs wide and taking him in; she wondered if it would hurt. Some of her friends said it did, others said it didn't. Either way, she wanted to get it over with. She was wet just thinking about what Scott could do with her. To her.

Keeping his hand circled around her wrist, he pulled her away from the wall. "Come with me."

He led her off the dance floor toward the bar, which was good because she wasn't ready to give up her buzz. Too sober and all her common sense would come rushing back and she'd remember how bad of a plan it was to have meaningless sex with a coworker, not to mention your boss.

Bad—she was a very bad girl. And bad girls didn't leave the club alone with nothing to show for it but sad, damp, raggedy underwear and resignation that in another year, she'd still be a virgin. Bad girls weren't virgins. Bad girls lived life on their own terms. They didn't wait for dicks to be offered. They went out and took the dicks they wanted.

As Scott moved her deftly through the crowd, Colette looked for Mallory. In a dark corner on the other side of the club, the younger woman danced with a man in a tight black tank-top. Tattoos covered his arms and shoulders. He looked strong enough to lift and spin her above his head if he wanted. Their faces and bodies mashed together, moving in a slow, erotic sway, and it looked like the man was pushing his hand up her skirt.

Colette was seconds away from breaking free of Scott and crossing the room to intervene, when Mallory threw her head back with a delighted laugh and arched her hips toward the tattooed man. Her skirt slipped high on her thigh, and she grabbed his wrist, pulling him closer so he could finger the cute pink thong she wore underneath. Of course, *her* underwear was cute. Mallory probably always left the house wearing cute underwear because she was the kind of woman who didn't wait—she knew what she wanted and she went out and found it. Like tonight, in this club. She wanted that tattooed Neanderthal, and he looked more than happy to oblige.

The man buried his face in Mallory's cleavage. Colette looked away before she saw too much. She needed to face her assistant on Monday morning without thinking of her getting laid in the middle of a crowded club.

Scott put his hand on Colette's back and nudged her away from the bar toward the bathrooms instead. As the crowd broke apart to make space for them, he put his mouth to her ear. "You look like such a slut in that dress. God, I need to be inside you right fucking now."

He squeezed her ass to get her to walk faster.

He was drunk. They both were. Him more than her. If they were sober, none of this would be happening. She wanted this to be happening. Right?

Yes.

No.

Definitely yes.

Hell no.

Abso-fucking-lutely yes.

She'd been wanting something like this to happen with Scott since she started at Campbell and Sons five years ago. Though, how could he have known that, when all she'd ever done was put out friend vibes? But now, here they were at a loud, sweaty club on her thirtieth birthday, revved up from their bodies rubbing, teasing, and *yes, please, yes*. He pressed his erection against her as he moved her through the club, and it was obvious he wanted this as much as she did.

But as soon as they reached the narrow hallway with the flickering pink light and the condom dispenser hanging on the wall, as soon as he pushed her into one of two unisex bathrooms, the alcohol haze faded, and she started second-guessing herself.

The lock clicked into place. The sound of it was like a thunderclap, breaking Colette from the frenzied excitement she felt out on the dance floor.

This was different. This was serious. This was actually happening.

This was her and Scott alone in the bathroom, apart from prying eyes.

Scott grabbed her around the waist, lifted her onto the edge of the sink, tugged her underwear down to her ankles, and shoved his face between her legs. His mouth found her warmth, and he began lapping her up like she was the most delicious thing he'd ever tasted. Her legs tingled. Her head fell back. Her eyes fluttered shut.

Music pumped through the thin walls. Scott's tongue moved with the rhythm of it, the same way his body moved against hers on the dance floor. His hands rubbed her thighs, squeezing. Her breathing quickened as he flicked his tongue over her clit. He knew what he was doing. God, did he know what he was doing. She felt herself tipping over the edge, but before it happened, she opened her eyes to sneak a look at Scott, and that's when she noticed the graffiti on the wall for the first time.

Someone had taken a black Sharpie to the whitewashed brick and drawn a naked woman on all fours. A stick figure man with a rocket ship penis entered her from behind. Another stick figure man shoved his squid-shaped penis into her mouth. Two wads of pink bubblegum were stuck to her breasts, presumably acting as nipples. Beneath that, in purple Sharpie, someone had scrawled *For A Good Time Call* along with a phone number Colette doubted was still in service.

There were other things on the wall. Brown and red stains of unknown origin. More gum in a variety of colors. Band stickers.

Graffiti that made as much sense as the woman and her stick figure men. A used condom lay crumpled on the floor next to the trash can.

And just like that, like a popped balloon, Colette felt the entire night, and her chance at getting lucky, deflate. Scott's hands were on her breasts again, but now they just felt clumsy. His tongue was too rough. He was trying too hard.

Instead of pleasure, panic bloomed in her brain.

What the hell am I doing here?

THE UPTIGHT VIRGIN

Cỳỳỳỳỳỳ

Colette

Colette didn't want her first time to be in the bathroom of a dive bar propped on a disgusting sink that other people had most certainly had sex on before her. In all the years she'd imagined popping her cherry, there was quiet music playing in the background and a bed and sometimes candles, but definitely no Sharpie women on the walls being double-teamed by giant pricks.

But she didn't want to be a virgin anymore, either. She was so tired of it. Tired of telling men on the third or second or even first date that she'd never had sex. Tired of the looks they gave her when she told them—like they couldn't decide whether to laugh or feel sorry for her. Tired of them coming up with some excuse to leave early and then ghosting her. The worst time was when her Tinder date offered to pay for a male prostitute. He didn't want to be her first, but he was happy to have sloppy seconds. She didn't want to find herself in the same spot next year, another year older and still unfucked.

She tensed, gripping the sink, and shifted her weight. The porcelain was too cold. The faucet jabbed into her back. Scott lifted his head from between her legs. His lips were slick, glistening. He had the taste of her in his mouth, and she put that in the pro column.

Pros of having sex with Scott in a seedy bar bathroom:
1. Scott clearly knows what he's doing and seems to like what he's tasted so far.
2. You're both pretty drunk and probably won't even remember this.
3. But if you do remember, it would make a pretty juicy story to tell Brooke later.

Cons of having sex with Scott in a seedy bar bathroom:
1. STDs. Really, diseases of any type.
2. You're both pretty drunk and probably won't even remember this.
3. It's gross, right? People shit in here.

"What's wrong?" Scott asked.

Colette couldn't tell how long he'd been staring at her like that. His penis was still ready to go, pushing against the seam of his pants, so she couldn't have missed more than a few seconds.

"Are you...?" He stopped and tried again. "Look, are you sure you want to do this? We don't have to. I just thought... With that dress, the way you were dancing... You were giving off all the right vibes. But if this isn't what you want—"

"No. Yes." She giggled. She actually giggled. Like a horny co-ed. Who the heck was she trying to be?

Because that was the problem, wasn't it? Casual, divey, bathroom sex with her boss? This wasn't her. Buttoned-up, follow the rules, teacher's pet, good girl Colette Harris wouldn't be caught dead in a club like this, in a bathroom with a man like Scott, with her underwear pulled down around her ankles.

She shoved him away and hopped off the sink, bending to pull her underwear up and wiggling to get it over her hips. Her skirt glided down to mid-thigh, and already she breathed easier, knowing she was less exposed.

Scott stared at her with a confused wrinkle across his brow. His pretty hazel eyes crackled with a familiar anger, the fury of a man who thought he was getting laid, but ended up going home alone. She slipped past him to get to the door, where she fumbled with the lock.

"I'm sorry. I can't. I—" She shoved open the door and fled with no explanation.

"Colette, wait!" Scott called after her.

She rushed through the club, shoving people aside to get to the front door. In the ten minutes she and Scott had been in the bathroom together, even more people had jammed their bodies onto the dance floor. The music, which before sounded bouncy and bright, now felt frenzied and panicked, grinding through the speakers like twisting metal. Colette slammed her hands over her ears. She couldn't hear herself think. She could barely breathe. The air was thick with body spray and sweat, booze and sex. She needed to get out of here.

In her rush, she bumped into the back of someone.

The woman yelped, "Watch it!" And splashed part of her drink onto the man standing in front of her. But the man just laughed as he wiped the vodka or rum or whatever from his face, seemingly unbothered by the sudden inconvenience.

"I'm sorry," Colette mumbled, trying to sneak past them, but the man grabbed her elbow.

He pulled her close in a way that felt intimate rather than aggressive. Even in the dim lighting, she noticed the twin dimples creasing his cheeks, the rugged scruff shadowing his chin. His eyes sparkled like she'd told the funniest joke in the world, but in the strobe lights, she couldn't tell if they were blue or green, black or violet. His hands were rough with callouses and his fingers were strong. She couldn't twist free of him.

"Where are you off to in such a hurry, beautiful?" His voice was as playful as the curly twists of auburn hair that fell right at his jawline. "The fun's just getting started."

He reached for the woman who'd spilled her drink—a leggy blonde in a shimmering, silver dress—and wrapped his arm around her, too, so now he held both women, one on each side. He nuzzled his nose against the blonde's neck, then turned to Colette and tried the same.

"Get off me, asshole." She pushed against him, trying to wiggle from his grasp.

His biceps flexed as his arm tightened around her waist. He was strong—strong enough to hurt her if he wanted to, though he didn't seem interested in that.

"Hey, calm down, pretty." His laugh was soft, teasing. "Don't get your panties in a twist. I just thought you, me, and my friend here could have a little fun tonight, that's all. You seem like a girl down for a good time."

His eyes raked over her in a possessive way. A shiver of anticipation rolled through her, which she quickly shoved aside. Whoever this guy was, he was clearly a cocky prick who thought he could get any girl he wanted with his rough hands and cute smile. Maybe grabbing a stranger in a club like some hungry caveman made some women cream their panties, but it had the opposite effect on Colette.

"Don't tell me to calm down. And don't call me girl," she hissed. "If you don't let go of me this instant, I'll slap you with a sexual assault lawsuit so fast you'll see stars."

His eyebrows shot up, but his smile didn't fade, and he didn't let go of her. "As long as you're the one doing the slapping, I'm game."

She shoved him again, harder, and this time he let go of her at the exact moment her hands pressed against his ribs. The force of her push, combined with his sudden release, sent her stumbling backward. She tripped into another couple. A drink sloshed down the front of her dress. Boozy, ice-cold liquid seeped between her cleavage. People dancing nearby turned to stare and roll their eyes at the sloppy, drunk girl. Colette muttered her apologies, not bothering to explain she wasn't that drunk because they wouldn't believe her, anyway.

The caveman wouldn't stop grinning at her, lust in his eyes, and something else—something Colette could only describe as surprised delight. Though it could have just as easily been the angle of the lights, making his eyes dance in strange ways. They were several feet apart now with bodies quickly filling the space between them, and even though it made no sense, and she was probably imagining it, the way he looked at her made it hard to turn away.

His eyes fixed on her face, like she was radiant, unexpected, the only person in the room who mattered, the one he would be stupid to let walk away. Even the leggy blonde couldn't capture his attention anymore, though she was doing her damn best, grinding on his leg and flinging her hair in his face. After what seemed like an eternity, but was probably only a few seconds, the man broke the spell by lifting his hand to his lips and blowing Colette a kiss.

Colette scoffed in disgust, spun away from him, and marched out the front door. Unbelievable. Who did he think he was? He had no right to grab her the way he did. To suggest a threesome. That was what he'd suggested, wasn't it? Maybe he just wanted to dance. No, there was definitely lust in his eyes, a desire to see what was hiding beneath her dress. Now she remembered why she'd stopped coming to places like this. The presumption. The awkwardness. The agony of not knowing how your night would end, or whose bed you were going to wake up in the next morning. No thank you very much.

The heavy door thumped shut behind Colette, and the music faded.

She sucked in a deep breath that smelled of car exhaust and fried food. Not exactly fresh, but at least it wasn't sweaty bodies and regret. She dug her cell phone from her bra and texted Mallory that she was getting an Uber home.

Mallory texted back immediately.

Mallory: Everything ok?
Colette: Just tired. U ok? I can stay if you need me.
Mallory: Go. I found a big strong hunk to take care of me tonight.
Colette: Be careful.
Mallory: Ok mom.
Colette: Text me when you get home.

Colette opened the rideshare app. They were charging surge prices, and the waits were over an hour long because of course they were. It was midnight on a Friday in Los Angeles. What did she expect?

Historically, her birthdays had always been disasters. It was stupid of her to think this year would be any different.

She walked away from the club, not wanting Scott to follow her outside and find her alone in the dark, feeling sorry for herself. She didn't want to have to explain anything to him, either. A groan rose in her throat at the thought of seeing him on Monday.

She could quit. She could call Human Resources first thing Monday morning and just quit. Sure, she'd be leaving a good-paying job she actually enjoyed, and she'd have to dip into her savings while she looked for a new one, and Mallory would be pissed, but all of that would be better than having to tell Scott that the reason she'd left him so unsatisfied in the bathroom of a seedy club on her birthday was because she was still a virgin.

A loud motor revved in the distance. A few minutes later, a slick, red motorcycle roared past, with two people riding on the saddle. They both wore helmets, but the woman's long, blonde hair stuck out the bottom, fluttering like gold ribbons. Her silver dress was starlight against the man's black leather jacket. With the skirt pulled high around her ass, her legs looked even longer than they had in the club.

As they drove past, the man turned his head. The face shield reflected the streetlights, making him look otherworldly, but Colette could picture him perfectly. That teasing smile, the rugged angles of his cheekbones, the glint in his eyes that made her feel like he was peering straight into the center of her. He lifted one hand to blow another kiss before twisting the handlebar and zipping around the corner, engine roaring.

Standing on the corner, in her sleeveless dress, bracing herself against the chill night air because she was too stubborn to go back into the club and ask for the keys to Scott's car so she could get her jean jacket, the thought crossed Colette's mind that it could have been her on the back of that bike. If she wasn't so uptight and self-conscious all the time, overthinking every little thing, she could have been that bad ass bitch speeding off to some high-rise apartment to have her brains fucked senseless by a cute guy she would never have to see again.

Now, *that* would have been a spectacular end to her thirtieth birthday.

FIRST TIMERS CLUB

Chat Room

NotSoDirty30 (posted 2:16 am):
I almost lost it in the bathroom of a club tonight. With my boss. We were both drunk, way too drunk to be doing what we were doing. At the last minute, I pushed him away and ran off. I'm not crazy for leaving, am I? Did I do the right thing? I didn't want my first time to be in a bathroom stall. Or when I was too drunk to remember it in the morning. But part of me thinks I should have just done it and gotten it over with. What the hell am I waiting for? #beingavirginsucks

SexIsOveR-rated:
You did the right thing. Club bathroom? Gross. Who knows what diseases you might have caught?

cherrybomb:
I don't know, sex in a public place with your boss—that's like all my fantasies rolled into one. I would have jumped at that opportunity. #wishIwereyou

2Hawt2Handle:
A sex club? Freaky.

HappilyNeverAfter:
It was probably a dance club.

2Hawt2Handle:
Whatever. Throbbing music, pulsing lights, clothes still on—sounds hawt to me. Ha!

LoveConnection (Admin):
Sounds like a nightmare. Give me roses and silk sheets and jazz playing softly in the background.

cherrybomb:
#sovanilla

Shakespeare-N-Love:
You should have done it. Like you said, just get it over with. Your first time's going to be shitty no matter what you do. So who cares if it was a less than ideal situation? A dick in the hand is worth two in the bush.

2Hawt2Handle:
I think you mean the other way around. Hahaha.

TheBoyNextDoor:
That doesn't even make sense.

2Hawt2Handle:
But I bet you laughed.

HappilyNeverAfter:
Who says the first time has to be shitty?

2Hawt2Handle:
Literally everyone.

HappilyNeverAfter:
I disagree. I think the first time can be romantic, thoughtful, sweet.

Shakespeare-N-Love:
Good luck with that.

cherrybomb:
Whenever your cherry pops @HappilyNeverAfter, however it happens, we look forward to hearing ALL those juicy details.

HappilyNeverAfter:
You might be waiting a while… #prayingforamiracle

IN THE WRONG BED

TRISTAN

Despite spending most of last night drowning his liver in whiskey sodas and vodka shots, Tristan Walker woke up feeling pretty damn good. He stretched his naked body beneath soft, sky-blue sheets that smelled like mountain spring detergent, the same kind he used with his laundry. He wasn't surprised. From the moment he saw the woman at the club, he knew they were meant to be together. He rolled over to kiss his Sleeping Beauty awake and froze.

The woman of his dreams was a brunette with freckles splashed across her shoulders and a nose too big for her stern face. The woman lying beside him was a blonde stranger with a heart-shaped face and a perfect tiny nose, rosy cupcake cheeks and lips too plump to be natural. The woman beside him now was not the woman of his dreams, and definitely not the woman he remembered leaving the club with last night.

Somehow, he'd ended up in bed with the wrong person.

Shit, shit, shit. How did this happen?

He slid one leg off the bed, then the other, moving as slowly as he could. If the blonde woke up, she'd ask him to stay for breakfast. And if she asked him to stay for breakfast, she'd want to talk. And if they talked, eventually he'd have to admit he didn't remember her name. Or anything else about her. Including whether they'd had sex last night. Maybe they were too drunk. That had never stopped him before, but there's a first time for everything, right?

He found two torn condom wrappers on the floor next to his shoes, then leaned over and peered into the trash can beside the bed. They definitely had sex last night. Twice.

Tristan grabbed his pants off the floor and pulled them on, followed by his shirt and shoes. He found his leather jacket draped over the back of an overstuffed armchair in the living room, along with a silver dress that had gone limp and lost its earlier shine. As he pulled his jacket on, he brushed his fingers along the hem of the dress, and tried to remember. The woman of his dreams was wearing something green that looked more like a nightgown than an actual dress. He closed his eyes, trying to bring her face to the forefront of his mind, but it all turned into a blur.

He could have sworn he danced with her, left with her, held her in his arms all night.

A sharp pain, the beginning of a nasty hangover, jabbed his temple. He checked to make sure his phone, wallet, and keys were in his pocket, then slipped out the front door without saying goodbye to the stranger he'd actually spent the night with. Easier for them both if she woke up to find him gone.

He went in circles for a while, passing identical apartment stoops, an empty pool, a laundry room, and a small courtyard strewn with patio furniture and thorny bougainvillea before finally stumbling his way into the parking area. Sunlight splashed through a row of palm trees, turning his small headache into a raging one. The sign posted by the front gate read *La Traviata*. A steady flow of traffic moved along the four-lane road on the other side of a stucco wall, delineating the apartment complex from public property. There was a McDonald's on the far corner, a Starbucks across the street, palm trees as far as the eye could see.

Tristan could have been on any street in any neighborhood in Los Angeles County right now. Hell, he could be in Orange County even. Or, God forbid, Riverside. He shuddered and scanned the parking lot for his bike.

The red Ducati leaned on its kickstand near the front gate. It was parked at a drunken angle, not in an actual parking spot, but on the sidewalk, blocking the mailboxes. He didn't remember driving it over the curb. He didn't remember driving it at all. But he was here, wasn't he? And so was his bike. He doubted the woman he woke up next to this morning would even know where to put the key, let alone how to steer the damn thing, so he must have been the one who brought them here.

Good job, buddy, a familiar voice in his head scolded him. *You could have gotten yourself killed.*

"Bring it on," he muttered.

He grabbed one of the helmets teetering precariously on the leather seat, jammed it over his head, and hooked the other on the bike behind his left leg.

The voice turned serious. *Trust me, Triscuit. You don't want to be dead. There's a strict no boning hot chicks policy in heaven.*

"Who says I'm going to heaven?" Tristan rubbed his temple.

His headache was nearly unbearable now, a knife stabbing between his eyes and shooting pain down to his jaw. So much for waking up and feeling good. He needed the ocean. Salt water was the best cure for a hangover. Salt water, cold beer, and fish tacos —and he knew where to get a hefty dose of all three.

He pushed the bike off the sidewalk and swung his leg over. God, he loved this bike. It was curvy in all the right places and a perfect fit between his thighs. Better than any woman. Well, the woman of his dreams could be better, but he'd never find out, would he? There were almost 4 million people living in Los Angeles city limits, millions more spread out through the county, and tourists moving through every week in hoards. It would be a minor miracle if he ever crossed paths with the brunette from the club again.

Tristan turned the key. The motorcycle purred to life.

He looked at the street, then back at the apartment complex. Hell. He had no clue where he was or how to get to the ocean from here. He pulled his phone from his jacket pocket to google directions and saw he had sixteen missed calls all from the same number.

He stifled a groan as he listened to the last voicemail left less than fifteen minutes ago. His mother's voice was frantic.

"Tristan? Pick up, pick up." She forgot sometimes that voicemail was nothing like the clunky tape deck answering machines of her youth. "Why aren't you answering your phone? I need you. Where are you?" She screamed something incomprehensible to whoever was in the room with her. Then she said, "Tristan, please, as soon as you get this, come over here. It's your father. He's done it again. That son of a bitch has cheated on me for the last time."

The call ended. Tristan scrolled through the fifteen other voicemails, deleting them all without listening to a single word. They'd all be some version of the one he already listened to–his mother screaming her head off, paranoid and needing him.

This was the last thing he wanted to deal with, but if he ignored her, she'd keep calling and leaving these desperate messages. She might even call the police and report him as a missing person. Hell, after sixteen unanswered calls, she'd probably already filed a report. She'd always been overprotective, but her anxiety had gotten so much worse since Troy's death.

Maureen Walker lived in a near-constant state of red alert—more than simply preparing for the worst to happen, she expected it. Every single second of every single day. And if there wasn't a real emergency for her to get worked up about, she'd make one up.

Tristan pulled up google maps and watched the blue dot pinpoint his location. He was still in Los Angeles. Thank God for small miracles. He shoved the phone in his pocket, bent over the bike, gunned it out of the parking lot, and sped toward the Pacific Coast Highway.

PEAS IN A POD

Tristan

Tristan heard his parents screaming at each other as soon as he pulled into the driveway of their Malibu mansion. One of the top floor windows hung open. Clothes drifted from it, swirled, and landed in heaps on the neatly trimmed lawn. Expensive Italian suits, cashmere sweaters, silk ties, leather shoes—nothing was spared. Maureen Walker was a raging dervish, appearing at the window for a brief second to throw out more clothes before disappearing again. Her voice, like a crow's, scolded and clamored.

Tristan caught only snatches of her words.

"I've given you thirty years…"

"After all this…"

"How you treat me…"

His father roared back, "Maureen! Enough! This is ridiculous!"

The clothes spilled faster, littering the yard like so many

autumn leaves. Otto Walker's color palette never strayed far from brown, umber, burgundy, and mustard yellow.

Tristan parked his Ducati near the garage and hurried into the house. "Mom?" His voice echoed through the expansive foyer. "Dad?"

Gripping the banister for stability, he rushed upstairs, skipping every other step. Their voices grew louder when he reached the landing.

"That watch cost me five thousand dollars!" his father screamed.

"You should have thought about that before you screwed around with that fake plastic Barbie who calls herself an actress."

"How many times do I have to tell you, Maureen? Ivy and I are not screwing around. Give me that. That was a gift from Steven Spielberg."

"Maybe I'll keep it then, and why shouldn't I? If I remember correctly, he gave it to both of us."

Tristan walked into his parents' bedroom to find them wrestling over a crystal paperweight shaped like a skull. His father was twice the size of his mother, a hulking gorilla next to her delicate sparrow frame. Definitely not a fair fight. But what Maureen lacked in strength, she made up for in sheer tenacity. She gripped the paperweight with talon-like fingers, yanking and thrashing, refusing to let go. Otto, too, refused to let go, but he made little effort to pull the skull away, which he easily could have done if he'd wanted to.

He noticed Tristan standing in the doorway and exhaled with relief. "Tristan. Thank God. Tell your mother to stop acting crazy."

"Crazy? I'll show you crazy, you philandering son of a—" She yanked hard on the skull.

At that moment, Otto let go. Maureen flew backward, bumping into the corner of a dresser. The lamp sitting on top crashed to the floor. Maureen let out a high-pitched wail that reminded Tristan of an ambulance siren. But she'd won. She clutched the crystal skull against her chest. Her pale cheeks burned crimson; her eyes sparked with a wounded rage. Smudged mascara streaked her face. Her ginger hair sprang from her ponytail in a frantic mess.

The last time Tristan saw his mother this distraught was at his older brother's funeral last year. With arms outstretched, Tristan rushed across the room to comfort her. "Mom? Did you hurt yourself? Are you all right?"

She whimpered. "How can I possibly be all right? It's ruined. Everything is ruined. You." She jabbed her finger at Otto. "This is all your fault."

Otto shook his head. "Maureen, please. You know I would never—"

But Maureen interrupted, turning to her son to explain. "I saw him, Trissy. I drove all the way to his office to bring him lunch and you know how much I hate driving, but I thought it would be a nice thing to do. For my husband." She spat out the words. "His assistant said he was meeting with a client, but I'm his wife, so I didn't think it would be a problem to interrupt." Laser-beams shot from her eyes as she turned her heated gaze back onto Otto. "I'm your wife."

"Maureen, I told you, she was just running lines for an audition. Nothing happened."

"And she needs to be half-naked to run lines?" Her penciled-in eyebrows arched high enough to need their own air traffic control tower. "She needs to be sitting on your lap to really get into character? Is that it? Is that how auditions work these days, Otto? Because I'll tell you, when I was trying to break into this business, I never had an audition like that. Never."

Tristan eyed his father with suspicion.

Otto Walker was a successful and sought-after talent agent. He had enough high-profile clients to never have to worry about money for the rest of his life, even if he retired right now, but he liked to work. He also liked pretty women. Even though he didn't need to sign new clients, he had a weakness for busty blondes fresh off the train from Iowa, saucy red-heads with big personalities, and coy brunettes with expensive shoe habits.

Maureen had been a client of his decades ago. He got her one job—a commercial for hemorrhoid cream—before knocking her up and deciding to finally settle down as a family man.

Maureen had always been prone to jealousy and suspicion, and Tristan couldn't blame her. Otto was a rich, sixty-year-old man with a full-head of natural hair, a home gym and a personal trainer; and he worked in a business overflowing with good-looking, young women eager to replace Maureen as the next Mrs. Walker. It wasn't much of a stretch to imagine the trouble Otto Walker might get into all day at his downtown LA office.

At least once a year, Maureen threw a tantrum like this one, a big blowout that usually ended with Otto renting a private jet to Paris or taking her on a sunset cruise to Catalina on the family yacht. There was something about the theatrical nature of these fights that made Tristan wonder if his mother enjoyed them, if she started trouble on purpose for the extra attention.

But something about today's fight felt different.

Otto's clothes had ended up on the lawn before, but only the pieces he rarely wore. Never anything that he actually liked, never his entire closet, never his expensive jewelry, never the memorabilia and art pieces he seemed to treasure more than his actual family. Maureen's eyes were hard as flint, without their usual playful sparkle. Her body was rigid. Her jaw trembled. She scrunched her face to stop from crying. Maureen Walker, so careful with her facial expressions for fear of worsening wrinkles, looked like a crumpled paper bag.

She glared at the movie prop still clutched in her hands and a shadow passed over her face. "Yes," she mumbled to herself. "Maybe I will keep it. In fact, maybe I'll keep everything."

When she looked up at Otto, her chin tilted with new determination. "I'm done, Otto."

"I'm glad you've come to your senses." He reached out to her, but she put her hand up to stop him from drawing her into a hug.

"No," she said, sternly. "I mean, we're done. This. Us. Our marriage. It's over."

"Maureen, come on, sweetheart." Otto Walker didn't look at all surprised by his wife's pronouncement. He'd probably heard these same threats more than a dozen times in their thirty-year marriage. "Let me make you a Manhattan and call over to Foster's, see if I can get us a table tonight."

Tristan knew his father well enough to bet there would be a tennis bracelet or emerald ring involved in this reconciliation too. But Maureen didn't accept his peace offering. She put the crystal skull onto the dresser, walked into the large closet, and returned with a suitcase, which she threw at Otto's chest. "I'm giving you an hour, and then I'm calling the police."

Otto grunted as he caught the suitcase. He stared at his wife in a daze. Tristan had been alive on this earth for twenty-eight years and twenty-two of those he'd lived under his parents' roof. In all that time, he'd never once seen his father speechless.

"Mom…" Tristan stepped forward, wanting to steer this fight in a new direction. "I don't think you need to call the police."

"How can you possibly know what I need, Tristan?" She directed her venom at him now. "You're just like your father. The two of you are a couple of peas in a pod. Sleeping with whatever bunny hops into your bed, not caring about the other people in your life or who you might be hurting."

Tristan felt the sting of truth in her words. Anger flared in his chest, as did the desire to defend himself. Yeah, he fucked around. He'd already slept with three different chicks this week, and four last week, and okay, so he didn't call them when he said he would, but he was nothing like his father.

He wasn't married.

He wasn't in any kind of committed relationship at all. He wasn't cheating on anyone when he slept with the women he slept with; he wasn't being unfaithful or breaking up any happy homes. And he told the women up front, before he ever got their clothes off, that he wasn't interested in anything serious. Not in dating, not in friends with benefits, certainly not in marriage. The women Tristan brought back to his bed knew exactly what he was and wasn't offering before they said yes.

But his mother wouldn't understand the difference.

Maureen opened the dresser drawers and flung even more of her husband's clothes onto the floor. Otto scooped the clothes into his arms, but didn't start packing. He was obviously still dazed by Maureen's pronouncement. Their marriage had never been perfect, but for all their bickering, Tristan believed his parents truly loved one another. And he believed his father was telling the truth about not sleeping with anyone else. This time, at least.

He picked up one of his father's shirts and a pair of pants. "Mom, if you would just calm down for half a second, I think you and Dad could work this out."

Maureen threw a handful of black t-shirts at Tristan's chest. "Don't you dare tell me to calm down!"

A memory from the club last night flashed through Tristan's mind. The loud music and strobe lights. The blonde rubbing against his leg, but he only had eyes for the brunette with the freckles and mint-green dress. He'd seen the brunette shoving her way through the club before she bumped into them. Tristan wouldn't admit it, but he might have nudged the blonde into the other woman's path just so he could have an excuse to talk to her.

She looked so determined to leave, a panicked expression on her face, utter horror, as if this perfectly normal club was Dante's second circle of hell. He knew exactly how she felt. But instead of being polite and treating her with respect the way his mother had taught him to treat women, he grabbed her. He put his hands on her when clearly that was the last thing she wanted, and he knew better. But alcohol turned him into an idiot, a cocky bastard with half a brain. He groaned silently to himself, remembering that he'd asked her if she wanted to join him and the blonde for a threesome. An entire list of other, better questions ran through his mind now that it was too late to ask them.

Are you okay?
Do you need me to call you a cab?
Can I get you a drink of water?
What's your name?

He'd behaved exactly like his mother accused him of behaving. Like a heartless, self-absorbed prick.

His parents' bedroom suddenly felt too crowded. Tristan's palms started to sweat. He didn't know why he was even here, how his parents' fucked up marriage was any of his business. They had sorted it out before, they could sort it out again. Without him.

Tristan backed toward the door.

"Where do you think you're going?" Maureen asked.

"Leave him out of this, Maureen." Otto tossed the suitcase onto the bed, unzipped it, and began folding his clothes inside. "You want me gone? I'll go. You don't have to turn everything into a goddamn soap opera."

Maureen let out a frustrated howl, stomped into the bathroom, and slammed the door.

Otto smoothed a pair of trousers and laid them inside his suitcase. He gave Tristan a wary glance over his shoulder and said, "Sorry you had to see that, son. Your mother and I, well, it's complicated. But I'm sure everything will be back to normal in a few days. She never stays mad at me for very long. Do you need anything? Some cash?"

Otto reached for his wallet, but Tristan waved him off. The only thing he needed was to get the hell out of this house.

The ocean was turquoise and expansive, an inviting shimmer of diamond-studded water. Tristan followed the curve of the highway south until he reached his favorite beach—a tucked-away cove surrounded by sandstone cliffs that felt private despite the mansions looming nearby.

He parked his bike on the street and walked down a set of rickety wooden steps to a narrow beach. He was the only person here and took full advantage of that, stripping down to his boxer-briefs and slipping into the waves. The ocean took him in, rocked him, and cooled his flushed skin.

It was August, but this was still the Pacific, and while the water temperature was bearable, it wasn't exactly pleasant. He swam straight out from shore, taking long, fast strokes to warm his blood and prevent hypothermia. As the breakers rolled in, he ducked under the bigger waves, swimming with his eyes closed for a few seconds before pushing to the surface again on the other side.

After a few minutes, he was no longer thinking about his parents' fight or the dumb things that came out of his mouth last night at the club, the beautiful brunette who might have been his perfect woman but whom he'd never see again. It was just him and the waves, the burn of salt, the rhythmic swell of the tide, his body slipping through the water, his arms pulling him farther and farther from shore.

At some point, he stopped swimming and flipped onto his back. The sky stretched above him, a dizzying blue.

What are you doing, Triscuit? His brother's voice rode in on a wave.

"Floating."

No, you idiot. I mean, what are you doing with your life?

A wave splashed over Tristan's face. He sputtered on the salt water, then kicked his feet and swam toward shore. So much for peace and quiet.

Tristan might be a lot of things—selfish, cocky, listless, apathetic—but he wasn't crazy. The voice he sometimes heard in his head didn't actually belong to his dead brother. It was Tristan's own Id or Ego or whatever, pretending to be his dead brother to get him to make better choices. The angel on his shoulder, his conscience, his very own wise-cracking Jiminy Cricket. The fact that it was his brother's voice made it that much harder to ignore.

There were surfers gearing up on the beach when Tristan returned to shore. He recognized one of them, a woman he'd slept with before. For whatever reason, he could never remember her name. It was something bohemian, like Adele or Avery or Aspen.

She waved and smiled brightly at him as he emerged from the ocean. He walked toward her, not bothering to grab the clothes he'd left in a pile by the stairs. Her eyes skimmed across his broad shoulders, down his six-pack abs, lingering on the vee of his hips and the bulge in his boxer-briefs. Her smile twisted into a playful smirk.

As she wrestled her light brown hair into a tangled ponytail, the sheer white shirt she was wearing lifted to reveal a black thong bikini and an ass juicy enough to bite into. A thin layer of sand coated her tan skin. Her bright blue eyes were the color of the waves and the sky and the amulet hanging between her perky breasts.

"Hey, you. Long time, no see." He pulled her in for a hug. His cock stirred.

She hugged him back, holding him close, slipping her hand down to cup his balls, and whispering in his ear, "I was hoping to find you here. My van's parked out on the street, if you want to…"

The next thing he knew, she was pulling him by the hand and they were running across the sand, up the wooden staircase, to a white camper van with dark-tinted windows and a bumper sticker that says **Have a Good Time All the Time**.

As soon as the van doors closed, she pulled off his underwear. He tugged at her bikini bottoms, then reached behind her back and untied the top. The flimsy cloth floated off her breasts. He palmed one, rubbing his thumb over her nipple, and slid his other hand between her legs. She rocked against him, moaning. He pressed his mouth to hers, and she opened her lips wide for him, flicking her tongue out to meet him halfway. She tasted salty and a little fruity.

She grabbed his shaft, then let go, teasing, and fell back on the sheepskin blanket that covered the hard mattress of her camper van. She spread her legs and lifted her eyebrows in a tantalizing question. Her bush was natural, a light brown that matched her hair, and Tristan had the sudden desire to bury his face in it. But she handed him a condom and gestured for him to hurry and put it on. As he tore open the wrapper and pulled it over his hard cock, she touched herself, moving her hand in slow circles, biting her lip as she watched him. He entered her quickly, pushing, pumping. She bit his earlobe, raked her hand down his back, moaned, and growled. "Fuck, yes, you feel so good. God yes, fuck me harder."

Her legs rode up his torso. Her eyes closed. The amulet around her neck bounced against her breasts. Her mouth opened in wild abandon as she got closer to climax, screaming, "You're a god! Ride me, daddy!"

Tristan realized she didn't remember his name any more than he remembered hers. Now that he thought about it, he wasn't sure they'd even exchanged that bit of personal information the last time they fucked in her van like this.

She grabbed his ass, squeezing hard, and the pleasure of it coursed through him. He came with a jolt, and she moaned in delight, clenching tight around his shaft. After a long moment, she relaxed and melted away from him with a contented sigh.

He pulled out of her, took off the condom, and tossed it into a trash can before pulling his boxer-briefs back on. They were still damp and ice cold from his earlier swim, but he couldn't exactly walk out of here naked. He wished he'd grabbed the rest of his clothes before he left the beach, but she was so insistent, and his dick had run ahead of his brain. Again.

The surfer girl tied up her bikini top and pulled on the bottoms. She smiled at him. "We really should stop bumping into each other like this."

She winked, then shoved him from her van and locked the door behind them both. He was about to ask her what her name was, like a gentleman, and if she wanted to go grab some fish tacos and brews at the food cart down the street, but she bounded away from him toward the staircase, calling over her shoulder, "See you out there?"

He nodded, even though he didn't have his surfboard today and had no intention of getting back in the water.

He wanted to wait a few minutes, to let the surfer girl get down to the beach and into the water before he went to get his clothes so they didn't have to do that awkward small talk thing, but an older woman in a lime-green tracksuit walking her Yorkie past the van stopped and glowered at him. She looked mean enough to call the police on him for indecent exposure. Tristan covered the half-boner tenting his boxer-briefs and hurried away from her.

He skipped down the wooden staircase to find his clothes. The surfer girl was pulling on her wetsuit when he hit the sand. She didn't even sneak a glance in his direction as he pulled his t-shirt on and slid into his jeans. Her total attention was on the ocean and the breaking waves.

That's it? His damn brother's voice nipped at his heels as he pulled on his leather jacket and hustled back up the staircase to his motorcycle. *This is how you want to spend the rest of your life? Fucking strangers who don't give a damn about you?*

Tristan scoffed at his brother's judgmental tone. It wasn't like giving a damn ever made anyone's life better. Just look at their parents. They were prime examples of how giving a damn made things worse.

Give someone your heart, and it was only a matter of time before you ended up broken.

SECOND FIRST IMPRESSIONS

Tristan

Tristan dragged a pillow over his head, trying to drown out the shrill chirp of his cell phone. What kind of monster called before the sun came up? The ringing stopped. For half a second. He flung the pillow across the room, grabbed his phone off the nightstand, and groaned.

He thought about letting it go to voicemail, but he knew his mother would keep calling until he answered. Or she'd send the police over for a welfare check. He answered with a terse, "What's up, Ma?"

"I'm leaving your father for good this time, Trissy," she said without preamble. "I mean it. I've forgiven him more times than the Lord requires of me."

"Please tell me you're not still mad at him." A yawn snuck up on him, muffling half the sentence. "The two of you have had fights like this before, and you always kiss and make up."

"Not this time. I swear, Trissy, I'm finished with that man's nonsense. He's screwed around behind my back for the last time."

The loft Tristan's father bought for him when he graduated college four years ago overlooked the Santa Monica Pier. Tristan stared out the window at the Ferris wheel, a gray skeleton against a gray dawn rising above a gray ocean. It looked apocalyptic and matched his mood. He rolled his back to the window and switched the phone to his other ear.

"I'm meeting with a divorce attorney today," Maureen said. "He's supposed to be one of the best in the state. He represents all sorts of high-profile clients. Abigail recommended him."

Abigail was Maureen's best friend, a prattling bimbo who thrived on gossip, boxed wine, and other people's drama. She'd been married and divorced six times and was currently on the prowl for lucky number seven. Tristan wouldn't be surprised to learn Abigail was pushing his mother toward divorce so she could dig her perfectly manicured claws into Otto as her next husband.

"Are you sure about this, Mom? Divorce is a big step."

"You don't think I know that? Of course, it's a big step. I know it's a big step. That's why I need a big lawyer."

"Have you thought about counseling?"

Maureen squawked a laugh. "Oh, is that how this works? You can suggest counseling to me, but I can't suggest it to you."

"It's different, Ma," he muttered.

After Troy, Maureen pushed Tristan to talk to a therapist about his feelings. As if talking about the loss would somehow lessen the pain or make him forget. Tristan wasn't against counseling; he was just against the kind that tried to make you feel better about losing the most important person in your entire life.

"With you and Dad, there's actually something worth fixing," he said.

"Not anymore, there's not." She didn't sound sad about it, just resigned. "Anyway, I didn't call to get your permission. I called because I need a ride."

"To the divorce lawyer?"

"Please, Tristan. I'd ask Abigail, but she has Pilates."

"I don't think I should take sides."

"You're not taking sides. You're helping your mother get to an appointment." Maureen's voice softened. "You know how much driving rattles my nerves. The last time I was behind the wheel, I killed a cat."

"I thought the last time you were behind the wheel was when you drove to Dad's office."

"Yes, that's right. I killed the cat on the way home." Her voice sounded strangled. She let out a hiccuping sob. "I just can't do it, Trissy. Please. Don't make me do it."

"I don't know, Ma. I don't want to be caught in the middle like this. You could get an Uber?"

"What's an Uber?"

"Mom. You know what Uber is. Fine," he said. "What about a taxi? You know how to call a taxi, don't you?"

"Yes, I know how to call a taxi, but I don't want to take a taxi. It's going to be a very emotional day for me, and I don't want some random turbaned stranger staring at my snot bubbles and handing me curry-scented tissues while mascara runs all over my face."

"Mom, don't be racist."

Maureen sighed, and even though Tristan couldn't see her, he knew she was pouting.

She threw one last Hail Mary. "You're my only option, Trissy. And besides, it's not like you have anything else to do. Unless you found a new job that I don't know about?"

He resisted the urge to hang up on her and instead asked what time she wanted to be picked up.

"Oh, Trissy! I knew I could count on you. Unlike my ungrateful ogre of a husband."

His mother had a flare for the dramatic; she could be nosy and overprotective, and obnoxious with her love, but in her heart, she was a good woman who deserved to be happy. Tristan wanted his mother to be happy. Even if that meant getting out of bed three hours earlier than he normally did, three hours earlier than any sane person would.

"I don't want to get stuck in traffic," she said, adding just before he hung up, "Don't forget to bring coffee! Tall, non-fat, no-foam, oat latte. Extra caramel drizzle. Love you!"

They'd been waiting in the lobby of Campbell and Sons for almost fifteen minutes, ten minutes past Maureen's scheduled appointment time, with Maureen's foot bouncing impatiently, her sighs growing louder with each passing second, when the door between the lobby and the offices swung open. A woman rushed into the room with a panicked look on her face and a file in her hands. She wore sensible black heels, sheer nylons with a dark seam up the back, a tight black skirt that brushed at her knees, and a satin red blouse with a flouncy bow around the neck like she was a present waiting to be unwrapped.

Tristan's mouth dropped into his lap. He couldn't fucking believe it.

It was her. The brunette from the club.

There had to be hundreds, if not thousands, of divorce attorneys in the greater Los Angeles area, and his mother picked the one where the woman of his dreams worked. What were the odds? One in a million? More than that? Impossible odds. Nothing he would place money on. And yet, there she was, standing in front of him with calves that would look damn good wrapped around his waist and a tender neck he wanted to suck and soft curves he wanted to lose himself in and full lips he wanted to taste.

She was more buttoned up than she had been at the club. Her straight brunette hair had been tamed, pulled into a simple bun that sat low against the base of her skull. She wore less makeup, too, showed less skin, and fucking hell, that was working for him. Because even though his mother was sitting right next to him, he felt himself getting aroused.

"Maureen Walker?" The woman read from the file she was carrying. Her voice was pleasant, though a little nervous, but filled with none of the combativeness he remembered from the club.

She smiled when she looked up, revealing a smudge of lipstick on her teeth.

Tristan's heart fluttered in his chest.

Keep it in your pants, Triscuit.

"We're so sorry to have kept you waiting. I'm Colette Harris." She offered her hand to Maureen, who shook it with little enthusiasm and extra disdain.

Colette Harris. Colette Harris. The name sank deep into Tristan's bones. He would have waited hours longer if asked, as long as in the end, Colette Harris was the woman walking through the door.

But when her gaze shifted to him, that adorable, lipstick-smudged smile vanished. She took a startled step back and dropped her hand before he could take it. Too bad because he would have loved to find out if her hand was as soft as it looked.

She obviously recognized him. And was surprised to see him again, too, though clearly not happy about it the way he was. Her eyes, chocolate brown edged in gold, traced up and down the length of him. The corner of her mouth twisted into a grimace. The ease and warmth she exuded when she first walked into the lobby vanished, replaced with that stiff, defensive posture he remembered from the club. She pushed her shoulders back and swallowed hard, like she was keeping herself from saying something she'd regret.

She cleared her throat. "Right this way, please. We can talk in my office."

She led them through a maze of hallways to a door with her

name on it. She entered, holding the door open for Maureen, but stepping away just as Tristan was about to enter. The door swung and almost hit his nose, but he caught it in time. She glowered at him as he stepped into her sparsely decorated office.

He ran his fingers through his hair, trying to make his bed-head look less messy-lazy and more messy-on-purpose. He hadn't bothered with his appearance this morning, and now he wished he had. What did he care about making a good first impression with some smarmy old gold-digging, marriage-crushing lawyer? If he'd known that smarmy lawyer was going to be Colette, he would have gone to the barber for a trim and shave. He would have at least worn his nice jeans, not these raggedy ones with the holes in the knees. He tugged on his t-shirt, one he'd pulled from the top of his laundry pile that smelled strongly of sweat and sunscreen.

He had nice clothes, expensive clothes, clothes that made him look like he had his life together and was capable of treating a woman right. Clothes that didn't make him look so much like a jobless beach bum, which was exactly who he was right now, sure. But in his experience, women like Colette—powerful women, professional women—preferred a man who had his shit together. If he had known he would see her again today, he could have at least made it seem like he did. At least he wasn't wearing flip-flops.

Colette walked behind her large mahogany desk and gestured for Maureen to sit in one of the two leather chairs angled to face her.

Maureen clutched her purse against her pleated beige skirt and shook her head, confused. "There must be some mistake. I had an appointment to meet with Archer Campbell."

"Yes, that's right." Colette sat and crossed one leg over the other. She leaned her elbows on her desk, smiling patiently at Maureen. "Unfortunately, Mr. Campbell was called away on an urgent matter. I'll be taking over for him, but I can assure you, Mrs. Walker, that I'm well-qualified for the task."

Maureen's face pinched even tighter, like she was sucking a sour candy. "Are you his assistant?"

"I'm an attorney with the law firm," Colette said. "I've worked alongside Mr. Campbell for over five years now, and I'm certain you'll find my qualifications for this case more than acceptable."

She talked so primly, sat so straight—it was driving Tristan crazy.

If it were just the two of them alone in this office, he'd lock the door, rip that flouncy-ribboned shirt right off of her, bend her over that ridiculous mahogany desk, and bury himself inside her warm center. He'd find out exactly how prim she would act when he was railing her against that tidy stack of paperwork.

His mother ruined his office fantasy by saying, "You look like you're still in college."

Maureen made it very clear she didn't mean that as a compliment.

Colette's cheeks brightened to a rosy-peach color, and she squeezed her fingers together.

"It's a divorce, not a trillion-dollar business deal," Tristan said, pulling up one chair for his mother and sitting in the other. "How complicated can it be?"

Maureen heaved a sigh, but sat down.

Colette glared at him. Her gaze turned softer when she looked at Maureen. "Now, Mrs. Walker—"

"Maureen is fine, dear. I'll be using my maiden name when this is all over."

"Okay, Maureen, your... Who is this man to you?" Colette flicked a distracted wave at Tristan. "If he's your new boyfriend, that's going to make things more complicated."

"Excuse me?" Maureen's neatly drawn eyebrows arched high.

Tristan disguised his laughter by coughing into his fist.

Colette shifted in the chair, her cheeks turning even redder than before.

Tristan realized she was the type of person who couldn't hide her thoughts even if she tried. Every feeling was expressed in the fine contours of her face. This was part of the reason he noticed her at the club. Because she looked like she was having a terrible time. She was the only person there not faking. The club was clearly not her scene, and it showed in the desperate way she scanned the crowd looking for the exit. When he grabbed her around the waist, anger flashed across her cheeks, and he felt himself falling head over heels for a woman he didn't even know. In a world filled with plastic knock-offs, here was the real deal.

"I just…" Colette stammered. "If he's your new boyfriend, we might have a problem because it makes you less sympathetic—"

"Well I never!" Maureen leaped from the chair. "Not that it's any of your business, young lady, but this man is my son, not my boyfriend."

Colette's mouth dropped open in stunned horror. Her eyes widened with panic.

Turned out Tristan didn't have to bend Colette over the desk to see her lose her cool. She was managing just fine on her own.

"I'm so sorry, Mrs. Walker, Maureen." She rose from her chair and stretched out her hands in a placating manner. "Of course, he's your son. It's obvious to me now. The age difference should have been my first clue."

Her face went stark white as she heard the words out loud and realized she was making things worse, not better. Her mouth opened and closed like a fish gasping for air. "Again, Mrs. Walker, that's not what I meant, or rather, it is, but it's not important and, fuck, I don't know what I was thinking. Please, sit back down. Let's try this again."

Maureen's coral-colored lips pinched to a thin line at the highly unprofessional curse word Colette probably didn't even realize she'd said out loud, but her eyes glittered with amusement.

Tristan's mother had always enjoyed watching younger women trip over themselves to make her happy. She liked when someone other than her played the fool.

"I'd like to speak with your superior," Maureen finally said.

"Oh, I don't think that will be necessary." Colette rushed to the other side of the desk, as if planning to physically keep Maureen from leaving her office.

"Oh, yes, I'm afraid it will be very necessary." Maureen tilted her head to one side, eying the younger woman with contempt.

"Mom, let it go," Tristan said, trying to diffuse the situation. "She was giving you a compliment."

Colette twisted her hands together. Her eyes had gone watery like she was on the verge of tears. "I truly am sorry, Mrs. Walker. I didn't mean to cause any offense. I just want us all on the same page."

"Well, we certainly are now," Maureen said. "It's clear from this interaction that Campbell and Sons is not a good fit. I'll be looking elsewhere for a divorce attorney, thank you very much."

"You don't have to do that," Colette said. "There are other attorneys here who can handle your case. It doesn't have to be me. But I assure you, Campbell and Sons is the best firm in Los Angeles."

Maureen peered down her nose at Colette. "It seems we have very different definitions of the word 'best.' Let's go, Tristan."

She spun on her heels and marched out of Colette's office.

Tristan lingered in the doorway.

Colette glared at him. Her face was as red as her shirt now and he had a feeling that as soon as he left and this door closed, she'd collapse behind that enormous desk, bury her face in her hands, and cry. He hated that he was the reason she was so upset, but he couldn't exactly wrap his arms around her or kiss her tears away. She was a complete stranger. He remembered what she said in the club about slapping him with a sexual assault lawsuit and almost laughed out loud. Hearing him laugh was probably the last thing she needed right now. Instead, he offered her a half-hearted apology.

"Sorry about all of that." He waved his hand at his mother's retreating figure. "I can try to talk her into coming back, if you think it will help?"

"Don't bother," she muttered, leaning against the edge of her desk.

His eyes roamed down the length of her legs that were now stretched out in front of her. What he wouldn't give to peel those nylons off with his teeth.

"Is there something else I can help you with?" Her terse voice snapped him back to reality.

"Let me ask your professional opinion." He took a single step closer to her.

Walk away, Triscuit. Just shut up and walk away.

"So, what happened here today..." He ignored the nagging voice in his head and moved even closer to Colette. "The part where you asked about my mother's sex life... Is that grounds for a lawsuit, do you think?"

Her whole body stiffened, and her right hand twitched like she wanted to slap him across the face. He wouldn't mind if she did.

He leaned close enough to smell her cucumber-scented shampoo and grabbed a business card out of the holder sitting on the corner of her desk. She froze. He could tell she was holding her breath, waiting for him to take a step back. But he took his time, turning the business card over. There was nothing on the back. It was a minimalist design, just like her office. Nothing in this space revealed any of her personality.

When he finally straightened and stepped back, he brushed his arm against hers, making it seem like an accident, though it was anything but. He wasn't sure what he was expecting, but not this: a lightning bolt of electricity sparked between them. Colette seemed to have felt it too because a shiver rolled across her shoulders, and she let out a small gasp. The connection was so brief, it might have been nothing more than wishful thinking, because when Tristan turned to look in her eyes, her expression was devoid of anything but loathing contempt.

He waved the card in the air and smiled. "Mind if I take one? I don't think my mom will call you anytime soon, but I might."

She grimaced and walked around the desk, using it to barricade herself from him again.

"Take the card." She sat down and shuffled a stack of papers, pretending to be busy so he'd get the hint and leave. "But please don't call me. Ever."

"Even if I need a lawyer?" he asked.

"Especially if you need a lawyer."

He hesitated in the doorway, hoping she would look up from her papers so he could see her beautiful brown eyes one last time, memorize the shape of her lips, burn into his memory the sharp angle of her cheekbones. But she kept her head down, her voice dismissive when she said, "Close the door on the way out."

So much for second chances.

SMUDGED LIPSTICK

Colette

That was bad. That was so very bad.

Colette laid her head on her desk and groaned. She was going to get fired. As soon as Archer Campbell found out how badly she screwed up with Maureen Walker, he would send a security guard to escort her from the building.

She should have stuck with her original plan and quit as soon as she got into the office this morning. But when she passed Scott in the hallway, instead of things being awkward as hell the way she thought they would be, he'd smiled at her as if nothing had happened between them. As if he hadn't been fondling her breasts two nights ago, hadn't buried his face in her crotch, as if the taste of her wasn't lingering on his tongue.

He stopped and asked, in his most professional voice, if she was busy because if she wasn't, there were two new clients coming in this morning, and he could really use her help because his father had double-booked. One client was an up-and-coming

Hollywood starlet, and the other was the wife of a big shot talent agent. Both had money to spare, and they both wanted Archer Campbell to handle their divorces. None of the other attorneys were available, including Scott, who was dealing with his own tricky situation involving a pitcher for the LA Dodgers and his six mistresses, all who insisted he owed them child support. If Colette could take a meeting with one of the women and start the paperwork, Scott would be forever grateful to her. If she did a good job with the file, maybe she could even keep it and get the exorbitant fees and whatever percentage came in with the final settlement.

It was an offer she should have refused, but she was a greedy son-of-a-bitch just like the rest of them and had been lusting after a three-bedroom, two-bath house in South Pasadena for over six months now. She could use the extra money, and doing the boss a favor might open doors for her in the future. She picked the wife of the talent agent because, except for her best friend Brooke, she found actresses to be tiresome. She had a feeling Archer Campbell would prefer to work with the more famous client, anyway.

If she'd known the woman was bringing her son, and that her son would be the prick from the club on Friday night, the prick she hadn't been able to stop thinking about—much to her dismay—she would have definitely quit, or called in sick, or stepped in front of a bus.

Colette groaned again, remembering the way she stammered and sputtered and acted like a complete ass, sending Maureen Walker screaming from her office in a blaze of offended glory. Yeah, she was definitely getting fired.

She pulled herself upright, smoothed her hair, and readjusted the stupid floppy bow on the collar of her blouse. Her fingers lingered on the place where Tristan Walker had brushed her arm. Tristan Walker—a rich boy's name. And he was rich, wasn't he? At least, his family was. The clothes he was wearing this morning suggested otherwise, but Colette didn't pay much attention to fashion. Shabby surfer hobo could be the new Giorgio Armani, for all she knew.

She shoved Tristan Walker and his smoky-blue eyes from her mind. She had more important things to think about right now, like how to convince Scott that she deserved to keep her job after such a monumental fuck-up.

Fuck. She'd cursed in front of the woman, too, which definitely hadn't helped matters. She'd never cursed at work before. Double fuck.

She straightened her skirt and double-checked her makeup in the mirror on her way out of her office. She pulled her lips back in a grimace. Great. The entire time she'd been digging her grave in front of Maureen Walker and her hot son, she'd had a smudge of lipstick on her teeth.

A startled Colette blinked at her in the mirror. That cocky prick who thought of himself as God's gift to women? Hot? She must have been more rattled from losing the Walker account than she first thought. There was no way in hell Normal Colette would have thought a spoiled brat like Tristan Walker was hot. Even if he had that shaggy, laid-back surfer dude look she liked so much. Even if he looked strong enough to lift her onto the desk without even trying. She shook away the image of Tristan Walker pinning her to the desk. Not now. Not ever.

She rubbed off the lipstick smudge with her finger and hurried to Scott's office at the end of the hall. She tapped three times and waited for him to invite her in.

He greeted her with a warm smile. "How did it go?"

She closed the door behind her and leaned against it, staring at the vibrant-green philodendron dangling from the shelf above his head. All in one breath, she said, "I lost the Maureen Walker account."

"You... What?" His smile turned to disbelief, then frustration. "How the hell did that happen?"

"I don't know." She pushed away from the door and plopped into the chair in front of his desk. "It all happened so fast. She brought this man with her—"

"A lover?" Scott prompted and Colette felt less like an idiot because it was more common than people thought for spouses to bring their new flings along when they went to file for divorce. Colette didn't know if it was because they wanted emotional support or if they were eager to show off their new pretty young thing. Either way, it was better to leave the new boyfriend or girlfriend at home. At least until all the paperwork was signed.

"That's what I thought too," Colette said. "Turns out this time it was her son."

Scott stared for a beat too long, then he laughed. "Please tell me you didn't ask if the son was her lover?"

Colette groaned and buried her head in her hands. "That's exactly what I did. And then I made things worse by telling her I should have known better because of the obvious age difference."

Scott laughed so hard he started choking. He grabbed a coffee cup and took a sip of whatever was inside. "I'm sorry," he sputtered. "It's not funny."

"I just kept digging myself into a deeper and deeper hole until she stormed out and said she was going to hire a different firm entirely." Colette lifted her head and stared at Scott. "I'm sorry. I tried to fix it. I told her there were other attorneys she could work with at our firm, but she wanted nothing to do with me, with us, after I basically called her a tired, old hag."

Scott smothered another laugh. He pulled on his tie. "Try not to beat yourself up too much. We've all done it."

"Archer's going to kill me, isn't he?"

"He definitely wouldn't risk his reputation with something as base as murder," Scott teased.

"Fine, but he's definitely going to fire me."

"I'll tell you what." Scott stood and came around to her side of the desk. He perched on the arm of her chair and tugged on the floppy bow on her blouse, which was more decorative than utilitarian. "Come to dinner with me tonight, and I'll forget how badly you messed up today. Depending on how the night goes, I might even forget to tell my father you were involved with the Walker account at all."

"That doesn't sound strictly above board," she said.

"Yeah, well, we weren't strictly above board on Friday night either."

His gaze fell to her lap, and his tongue darted across his lips. Heat rushed to her center, her body responding to what she knew Scott could do with that tongue. She learned her lesson on Friday and threw away her ratty, but oh-so-comfortable beige underwear. Today she was wearing a brand new, lacy, red thong that rode up her ass crack in a way that should be illegal, but at least if Scott were to strip off her skirt and tights right now, she'd be wearing the kind of underwear someone who was always ready for sex wears. No more virgin underwear for her. Sexy thongs only.

She leaned close to Scott, but not too close. This was still a professional office, and he was still technically her boss, but clearly what happened between them on Friday night hadn't scared him away completely. Maybe there was still a chance for something to happen between them. Only this time it would be on her terms—preferably a dimly lit room with silk sheets and Lana Del Rey crooning in the background.

"Dinner sounds nice," she said, batting her eyelashes.

Scott caressed her arm in the exact spot where Tristan Walker had touched her, and her mind flashed to the two of them alone in her office, the way he leaned over her, so close they could have kissed. He smelled like sea salt and sun and man sweat. The look in his eyes as he reached around her was intense, like he wanted to put his hands on her, grab her, and carry her away. He'd settled for her business card instead, but when he'd straightened, his arm had brushed hers and something had sparked between them.

Hadn't it? A snap like a firework in her chest that she quickly tamped down because she could never, not in a million years, not with a self-centered, cocky, prick of a spoiled man-child like Tristan Walker.

But her heart fluttered even now, remembering how he'd lingered in her doorway, as if he couldn't bring himself to leave her, as if he had something more to say. She wondered what would have happened if she'd looked up at that moment. Would she be leaning too close to Tristan Walker right now? Flirting with him instead of Scott? Making dinner plans that would end up with her on the back of a motorcycle zipping through LA with the wind in her hair and the motor humming between her thighs?

"I should get back to work." Colette stood up too quickly, bumping against Scott awkwardly as she tried to maneuver out of the chair. "I have another appointment coming in at ten-thirty."

"We're still on for dinner tonight, though, right?"

She couldn't exactly turn him down now, not after she'd already expressed interest. She smiled and nodded. He told her the name of the restaurant, nowhere she'd ever heard of, and said the reservations were for eight, which seemed late for a Monday night dinner and a little presumptuous considering she'd just now agreed to go with him, but she shrugged away her misgivings. It was nice that he was so organized. She didn't have to think about it; all she had to do was show up and—what was it Scott said? Something about seeing where the night took them. She swallowed down the sudden lump in her throat and told Scott she couldn't wait.

As she hurried back to her office, she texted her best friend, Brooke.

Colette: Are you busy right now?
Brooke: Just finished with an audition. Want to meet up for coffee?

Colette: Calamity Janes?
Brooke: There's this new hipster place down the street I'm dying to try.
Colette: I'm having a really crappy day.
Brooke: Fine. Calamity's. See you in 15 min.

BETWEEN A RUT AND A HARD PLACE

Colette

"You're making a bigger deal out of this than it needs to be." Brooke Abbott stirred soy creamer into her black coffee. "Scott's cute, right?"

"He wouldn't be out of place at a Hemsworth family reunion." Colette poured milk and sugar into her coffee and scanned the menu, even though she knew before she sat down what she was going to order.

The server, a young, Black man with chiseled features and a dyed-blond faux hawk, returned to their table. He was much too good-looking to be working at a greasy diner like Calamity Janes, but Hollywood was a fickle mistress and he had bills to pay the same as anyone. The crooked badge pinned to his chest told them his name was Quint.

Before Colette could open her mouth, Brooke flashed the man a bright smile and said, "She'll have the Denver omelet. No onions, no ham, no peppers."

"So… A cheese omelet?" Quint didn't look amused.

Colette rolled her eyes and passed him the menu. "Yes, a cheese omelet, please. With wheat toast. Thank you."

Quint lifted his eyebrows at Brooke, who waved her hand over her coffee. "I'll just stick with the swill."

He shook his head and went to give Colette's order to the kitchen.

"Great," Colette said. "That guy's probably going to spit in my food now."

"You know he won't. You're their favorite customer." Brooke scanned the empty diner. "You're their only customer most days. How does this place even stay open?"

"It gets busier at lunch." Colette felt oddly protective of her little hole-in-the-wall diner.

"I've met you here at lunch plenty of times before, too, remember?" Brooke frowned at a strange stain on the table and shifted her arm away from it. "Busy is not the adjective I would use."

"Well, I like it."

When she was a kid, her mother would bring her and her brother and baby sister here for breakfast. Sometimes it was their only meal of the day, and the diner's owner, Jane Freeman, always made sure they walked away with full bellies, even if Mom came up a few dollars short on the check, which she often did. Jane Freeman sold the place to her son ten years ago and moved to Florida. Luckily, her son changed nothing. The menu stayed the same. The music from the jukebox played the same 1950s bopping swing songs and the old western movie posters, though more faded now, still hung on the walls. The one behind the cash register was signed by John Wayne. For the past twenty years, Calamity Janes had been Colette's sanctuary, especially on days like this one, when her chest felt tight and her mind wouldn't stop racing.

It might not be the hippest restaurant in Los Angeles. It wouldn't even crack the Top 100. But the food was reliable and filling, and the prices were reasonable, cheap even, and no one rushed you to eat faster so they could seat the next customer. Whenever Colette slid into the squeaky, purple vinyl booth, the knots in her back loosened and she started feeling like herself again.

Her mother used to say, *Nothing bad can happen when you're at Calamity Janes.*

"I thought thirty was going to be your Big Year." Brook interrupted Colette's wandering thoughts.

"It is my Big Year."

"And yet, we find ourselves back at Calamity Janes when we could be at that hip new brunch place down the street. They're supposed to have the best smoothies in the city."

"I don't like smoothies."

"Have you ever even had a smoothie?"

"Of course I've had a smoothie."

"When? Where?"

"I don't know. At Jamba Juice or something."

Brooke laughed and shook her head. Her dark brown hair fell in thick, gorgeous waves around her shoulders. Blonde highlights added dimension and shine and brought out the turquoise flecks in her blue eyes. Since she dropped out of law school six years ago to pursue acting, she had been cast in more than one shampoo commercial. She called gigs like that her bread and butter, because even though she hadn't pulled any big television or movie parts yet, she was doing well enough with smaller parts and commercials that she didn't need to take on a second job like most of the other actors in Hollywood.

"How did your audition go?" Colette asked her. "What was this one for? A pilot on CBS?"

Brooke waved a finger. "Don't change the subject. Dinner with your boss. Is it happening?"

"I already told him yes," Colette said. "I can't exactly back out now."

"You mean you don't *want* to back out."

"What's the difference?"

"You could back out if you wanted to." She reached across the table and tapped Colette's phone where it rested beside her elbow. "Text him right now and say you're coming down with a cold or something. Or why not just tell him you changed your mind and the dinner's off?"

"I can't do that."

"Why not?"

"I'll get fired."

"So what? Then you sue for sexual harassment."

"I'm not going to sue for sexual harassment."

"And he won't fire you." Brooke pursed her lips in that smug way when she knew she was right about something. "I don't understand what the problem is, Coco. From what you've told me, Scott's a hottie, and he's clearly into you. For fuck's sake, you already let him go down on you in a nasty-ass club bathroom. That can't be any worse than dinner and a nightcap at his place after. So what's holding you back, really? You do want to get laid, right?"

"Yes, but—"

"Yes *and*," Brooke interrupted. "See, that's always been your problem. You're constantly giving yourself excuses and reasons to say no when what you really need is to say yes, yes, yes!" She pounded her fists on the table and threw her head back in a perfect imitation of Meg Ryan in *When Harry Met Sally*.

Their server, Quint, reappeared at their table in the middle of Brooke's fake orgasm. He set the omelet down in front of Colette, but he was staring at Brooke, fixated. When she finished her theatrics, she smiled at him and flipped her hair over her shoulder. A spark of energy passed between the two of them.

Colette ignored them and cut into the omelet. The cheese was the wrong color, white instead of orange.

"What's this?" Colette stabbed some omelet onto her fork and sniffed it. "It's not cheddar."

"Yeah," Quint said with a shrug. "Cook's trying a new cheese. Gouda or Camembert, something from France, I don't know."

"It's supposed to be cheddar." The fork clinked against the side of the plate as she set it down.

"It's cheese, Coco." Brooke rolled her eyes. "Just eat it."

"Thanks." Colette gave Quint a stiff smile as he walked away, but she didn't eat the omelet.

Brooke stared at her.

"What?"

"I love you, Coco. We've been friends for a long time. You're like a sister to me. So when I say this, you know I'm saying it because I love you. And I want you to be happy." Brooke pushed Colette's omelet out of the way and grabbed hold of her hands. "Darling, Coco, my sweetest Colette. You, dear, are in a rut."

"I just like things a certain way, that's all." Colette tried to pull her hands away, but Brooke refused to let go.

"Sounds like a rut to me." Brooke said.

"Are you saying I'm boring?" She couldn't believe she was having to defend her life choices to her best friend.

"I don't hang out with boring people." Brooke squeezed her hands and flashed her a smile. "I'm just saying that if you want thirty to be your Big Year, you're going to have to do Big Things. Scary things."

"I went to a club Friday night," Colette pointed out. "You know how much I hate clubs."

"You just haven't been to the right one." Brooke finally released Colette and gestured to the untouched omelet. "You're never going to know what you actually want from this world until you try things you've never tried before. Take a chance, Colette. Go out to dinner tonight with your boss and if he wants to take you home after, then you go and you get your damn V-card punched. Maybe without the pressure of your first time hanging over your head, you'll finally loosen up a bit and start to enjoy your damn life."

"I enjoy my life just fine. Thank you very much."

"You work, you go to the gym, you eat the same thing every day, you go home to an empty bed." Brooke listed the tasks off on her fingers. "Then you wake up and start all over again in the morning. Is that really how you want the rest of your life to be? Scheduled and predictable?"

"I have two hours blocked off every Saturday for life's little surprises." Colette meant it as a joke, but Brooke rolled her eyes.

Colette spread butter and a thin smear of strawberry jam on her toast. She bit off a corner, spraying crumbs across the table when she said, "I'll have you know I find my routine very comforting."

"Your routine is what's keeping you trapped."

Brooke rummaged through her purse for a compact mirror. She checked her teeth, fluffed her hair, and smeared a fresh layer of pink balm over her lips. She snapped the compact mirror shut and scooted to the end of the booth.

"I've told you my opinion," Brooke said. "I think you should go out with your boss and let him fuck you senseless. But if you need to make one of your lists to convince yourself, by all means. I won't stop you." She stood and did a quick scan of the diner. "I need to freshen up. I'll be back in two shakes of a lamb's tail. Don't have any adventures without me."

She blew Colette a kiss and walked toward the bathrooms.

As much as Colette hated to admit it, Brooke had a point. She had been in a bit of a rut lately. And by lately, she meant her entire life.

She could blame it on her ambitions and career goals, the fact that it took discipline and a strict schedule to get through law school, and now those habits were deeply ingrained in her psyche. Or she could go further back and blame her mother, who divorced Colette's father with no back-up plan, no job, no savings, nothing but a minivan and whatever clothes they fit into three suitcases.

Those were lean years, chaotic years—living out of the car or cycling through cheap motel rooms, standing in line at the food bank, missing school, getting robbed, falling asleep to the sound of her mother sobbing. Those were the years when Colette realized nothing in life was guaranteed. If a person wasn't properly prepared, it could all fall apart with the snap of a finger.

Things got easier after Colette's mother met and married Geoffrey, a tech millionaire who took care of her and her kids in a way Colette's father never did. But even though they were in a much better place, the panic was just starting for Colette, who worried their comfortable life with Geoffrey could be snatched away at any moment. Nothing and no one was safe. So she soothed herself with lists and calendars and organized binders. She took comfort in seeing her days spread out before her with no surprises. Knowing exactly what was coming next kept her from spinning out of control. All these years later, she still fell back on routines and lists. It had kept her safe for this long, hadn't it?

Her life was scheduled, yes. It had to be to get everything done. But predictable? 'Make out with boss at club' hadn't been written into her weekly agenda. Neither had 'Insult a new client and lose a big account.' Also not on her calendar for today? 'Let boss take you out to dinner and punch your V-card.'

A pros and cons list would help, but instead of making one about Scott, her mind circled back to Maureen Walker's shaggy, surfer bum son.

Pros of tracking Tristan Walker down and giving him a piece of your mind:
1. It will feel good to bring him down a peg. His ego's not doing him any favors.
2. It would be very unpredictable of you.

3. You can finally stop thinking about him.

Cons of doing anything at all involving Tristan Walker:
1. It's a waste of time. He's never going to learn.
2. He'll just make you feel stupid again.
3. Knowing your luck, he'll probably try to kiss you.

The place where his arm brushed hers still tingled. Against her better judgment, her body responded to Tristan Walker this morning in her office in a way it had never responded to a man before. Not even to Scott when he was between her legs at the club. With Tristan, it had been different. Instead of immediately wanting to pull away or crack an awkward joke, she'd wanted to lean into him. She'd wanted more of him pressed against her, more of her tingling. Too bad he'd opened his mouth and ruined everything.

Colette salted and peppered her omelet. It was here. And she was hungry. She might as well try it. But the cheese was too cloying, not at all balanced with the eggs, and her stomach twisted in rebellion. Shoving the plate away, Colette looked around for Brooke. Her friend had been gone a lot longer than she normally took to freshen up.

A few more minutes passed. Colette scrolled through her phone, reading through the comments people had left on her post in the First Timers group last night. She glanced up every so often to check for Brooke or their server, Quint, who also seemed to have disappeared. Finally, Brooke came out of the hallway where the bathrooms were. She skipped to the table with flushed cheeks and messy hair, her lipstick wiped clean. As she slid into the booth, she took her compact out of her purse again and used the small mirror to reapply her lipstick and tame her wild tresses.

A few seconds later, Quint slinked out of the same hallway Brooke had just come from. He adjusted the diner apron wrapped around his waist as he set a check on their table without looking at Brooke and then walked to the kitchen.

Colette stared at her friend, but Brooke refused to look at her. She frowned at her reflection in her compact and plucked at her eyebrows.

"I can't believe it," Colette said, holding back laughter. "You fucked our waiter, didn't you?"

"I couldn't help myself." Brooke snapped the compact closed and tossed it into her purse. "Did you see his eyes? How he looked at me? Did you see his ass? Yum."

"I don't get it. How do you do it?" This wasn't the first time in their friendship that Brooke had disappeared at a restaurant for a quickie with a perfect stranger. "How do you go from meeting someone to banging in a bathroom in less than ten minutes?"

"First, it was the employee break room, not the bathroom." Brooke's eyes sparkled with excitement. "Second, and what I keep telling you, Coco—sex is easy. Just spread your legs and moan."

She opened her mouth in an expression of pleasure and gripped the table like she was about to come right then and there.

An elderly couple eyed both women with disdain.

"Knock it off, Boo Boo. You're embarrassing me." Colette flipped over the check. "He could have at least comped our meal after having his way with you."

Brooke pressed her fingers to her chest in mock horror. "Who do you think I am? A common whore? I pay for all my meals, sweetheart. I'll pay for yours, too."

She reached for her purse, but Colette waved her off. "I've got it. Save your money for a smoothie."

They walked out of the diner arm in arm. Colette leaned her head on Brooke's shoulder. "So? Was he any good?"

"You know I don't fuck and tell." Brooke kissed the top of Colette's head. "I'll tell you what. Call me tonight after you finish screwing your hot boss and we'll compare dick sizes."

Colette choked on a laugh. "I really don't think that's going to happen."

"Which part? Screwing your boss? Or telling me about it while he's in the shower washing off your sweet juicy cum?"

"Stop." Colette shoved her away.

"I'm teasing, you know I am." Brooke pouted. "But you will call me? If anything interesting happens?"

"If he hasn't completely blown my mind and left me undone with his enormous cock, then yes, I'll call you."

"That's the spirit." Brooke pulled Colette into one last hug, then climbed into her BMW.

"Good luck!" she shouted out the window as she drove away. "And remember, sex is fun!"

THANKS, BUT NO MORE DICKS TONIGHT

Colette

Sex is fun. Sex is fun. Colette repeated the words Brooke yelled to her outside the diner until they lost all meaning. What is sex? What is fun? What is *is*?

Oh God. She was completely freaking out, and she still had all of her clothes on. So did Scott. They hadn't even been seated for dinner yet.

This date was going to be a complete disaster.

If it even was a date.

Scott leaned against the wall in the crowded restaurant entryway and scrolled through his phone, not even looking at her. A small frown tugged his lips. Okay, not a date. Just business. Colette could handle that. Business casual, just friends, talking shop—these were all things comfortably inside her wheelhouse.

She should have clarified before they left the office what exactly the plan was for this evening, but she'd been distracted by the rambling message Tristan Walker left for her when she was at Calamity Janes with Brooke. She listened to the voicemail five times, but couldn't figure out exactly what the man wanted. It sounded like he was trying to apologize except he never actually said the words 'I'm sorry.' And every sentence ended with an upward inflection, like he was asking a question even when he clearly wasn't? After the third time listening, she was pretty certain he was slurring his words. Figured a guy like that would be drunk by noon.

Colette buried herself in work and forgot about Tristan and her date—or not date—with Scott until Scott appeared in her doorway asking if she was ready to bounce. She stared at him like an idiot until he broke the silence. "Dinner? Are you still in? I made reservations at Blue Samurai for eight. Remember?"

The little green clock on her desk that looked like a retro radio box told her it was a quarter to. No time to go home and change into something sexy. No time to freak out about whether she had lipstick on her teeth or if she needed to shave her legs. No time to call Tristan Walker back and chew him out. No time to ask herself why she was even thinking about Tristan Walker and sex in the same breath. Scott swept her out of the office and into his Porsche and then they were at the restaurant where the hostess apologized, but they were clearing their table now, it would be a few more minutes, and thanks for your patience.

Scott shoved his phone into his pocket and turned his attention on Colette. His arm snaked around her waist and he nuzzled her neck. "Maybe we should have ordered take out. I could be eating sushi off your naked body right now."

Colette laughed too loudly and side-stepped away from him, pretending to look for the hostess. "Was that us? Did she call your name?"

Scott's nose wrinkled in confusion. "I didn't hear anything."

"It's so loud in here." Colette scanned the dimly lit restaurant. With tall ceilings and an open floor plan, the place sounded like a school cafeteria. But candles flickered on tabletops, and everyone looked like they were going to prom. Well, not Colette. Colette was dressed like a schoolmarm, but Scott didn't seem to mind.

He moved close to her again. One hand rested on her back, while the other creeped up her leg, exploring the hem of her skirt. So, this was definitely a date. And they were definitely headed toward her cute red thong ending up in a ball on Scott's bedroom floor.

She closed her eyes and took a deep breath. It didn't have to lead there if she didn't want it to. She was in control of this situation.

Her brain started to list out the pros and cons, but she shoved the bullet-points away. Thirty was her Big Year. Big Years meant Big Risks. Big Risks, Big Rewards. She couldn't help but glance at Scott's package, which for now was safely tucked inside his pants. Though it was hers tonight, if she wanted it. All she had to do was spread her legs and moan, right? Brooke made it sound simple enough.

"Scott?" The hostess scanned the small entryway filled with people. "Your table is ready."

Scott pressed Colette against the leather couch in his high-rise apartment. He kissed slowly and generously, like he had nothing else on his mind but her. He nibbled her lip. His hands slid up her hips, rocking her lower on the cushions.

"Dinner was good," she murmured. "Thank you."

"You said that already." His voice was low and husky. He tasted like sake and soy sauce.

She kissed him back and her hands slid up his chest, feeling his muscles beneath his white undershirt. The flaps of his dress shirt fluttered around her. She fumbled with the buttons at first, but figured it out eventually. The sake she had at the restaurant made her feel light and buzzy around the edges. She was going to do this. She was really going to go through with it this time. There was no reason not to.

Sexy man who seemed very into her. *Check.*

Sexy red underwear. *Check.*

Sexy cool downtown apartment with no roommates or parents to burst in on them at any moment. *Check.*

Sexy leather couch. *Check.*

"I love these tights, but they're coming off."

Scott pushed up her skirt and tugged on the waistband of the tights, yanking them down to Colette's knees in a rush, then switching it up again and going slow. He scrolled his fingers down her thigh, behind her kneecap, slowly peeling the tights off her right leg, then her left. He followed his fingers with his lips, kissing her feet, ankles, calves, knees, until he got to her inner thigh where he lingered, breathing in her scent.

Colette's skin flushed with pleasure. She ran her fingers through his hair as Scott moved his mouth closer to her pussy. As he pushed aside the slender scrap of fabric that was really more for looks than anything else, she tensed and pulled him out from between her legs by his hair.

"Ouch! What the hell?" He sat up, rubbing his head.

"Sorry." Colette smiled at him shyly. "Ticklish."

"You weren't ticklish at the club on Friday night."

He grabbed her legs and pulled her onto his lap. Her knees splayed open over the top of him. His hard cock pressed against his dress pants.

"Feel that? You like that, don't you?" With his hands around her waist, holding her still, he ground against her.

The rubbing sent a flare of pleasure through her core. And she wanted to relax into it, into him. He knew what he was doing. She should just let him take control and show her what she'd been missing all these years. But her mind latched on to the bare windows spanning the entirety of one wall.

"Can anyone see us from here?" She hopped off Scott's lap,

smoothed her skirt down, and shimmied over to the windows, pretending it was the view that had pulled her away from Scott, not her nerves. Fake it until you make it, right?

Los Angeles glittered in the distance. Colette had never seen the city like this before, stretched from the edge of the mountains to the edge of the sea, a sprawl of gold and red and sparkle and white; it was beautiful. And her first thought, rising with no coaxing or permission on her part, was, *I wonder what Tristan Walker is doing tonight? I wonder which of those lights belongs to him?*

Behind her came the clinking sound of a belt being taken off, then the slough of pants hitting the tile. Before she could turn around, Scott was there, pressed against her, pinning her to the glass. "Don't worry, babe. We're too high up. They couldn't see us even if they wanted to, and trust me, they want to because we're about to put on one hell of a show."

He wrapped his hand around her throat from behind and pushed her head up. She gasped, and he mistook her surprise for consent. He spun her around, his hand still clasping her throat. He'd stripped down to his underwear. His cock strained against the fabric. His eyes were dark with lust.

He shoved her against the window and pushed up her skirt. Cold glass caressed her bare ass cheeks. His fingers pushed aside her thong and separated her folds, searching for her wetness, her warmth, her swollen desire. But there was no desire. Not anymore. The pleasure she had been feeling on the couch vanished the second he put his hand around her throat. She thought she wanted him to take control, but now that he was doing it, she was terrified.

"Wait." She choked out.

He backed off as soon as the word slipped from her mouth.

"I've got condoms, if that's what you're worried about." He ran his finger down the silk sleeve of her blouse and laughed. "How are you still wearing all your clothes?"

He grabbed for her shirt, trying to pull it over her head, but she ducked away from him, moving away from the window, away from the couch and into the kitchen where there was nothing comfortable to have sex on and plenty of knives within reach. Not that she would even—never—but it was nice to know they were around. Just in case.

In case what? Brooke would scream at her right now if she knew what Colette was thinking. *You're going to do what to this perfectly nice—not to mention sexy—man who wants to screw you like you've never been screwed before? You're going to stab him? Cut off his dick? He's the one who should be terrified of you. Crazy bitch.*

Scott pulled his pants back on and followed her into the kitchen. His dick was still hard, tenting the fabric as he reached past her to grab two stemless wine glasses from the cabinet.

"I think we could both use a little more wine." He popped the cork from a cabernet and filled the glasses halfway.

"We drank an entire bottle of sake at the restaurant," Colette reminded him.

"Yeah, but you still seem a little tense." He flashed her a weighted smile as he handed her the glass.

She tipped it to her mouth and swallowed half the wine in two gulps.

Scott raised an approving eyebrow. He shifted his body to be close to her again, backing her against the sharp corner of a countertop, his hands braced on either side of her in a trap made of flesh and bone and curly, blond arm hair. She was wrong. There were plenty of places in this kitchen for a person to be properly screwed.

As if he could read her thoughts, Scott took their wine glasses, set them to one side, and grabbed her around the waist, hoisting her onto the countertop. He spread her dangling legs and gave her a wicked grin that she recognized from the club.

Before he could go any further, Colette shouted, "I'm a virgin!"

She slapped her hand over her mouth, but it was too late. The words were already out there, and once blurted, she couldn't take them back.

Colette knew exactly what was going to happen next. She'd seen this play out half a dozen times over the past fifteen years, give or take. Every time she told a guy the truth, it all went sideways. The guy got mad, and Colette went home humiliated, still a virgin, and convinced there was something wrong with her. Something broken. Something not worth loving. But a small part of her hoped that tonight would be different. That Scott would be different. That he wouldn't care, or rather that he would and instead of freaking out about her confession, he would take her by the hand, lead her back to the couch, offer to make her a cup of tea, and ask her to tell him her story, the whole of it, the reasons why and why not, and how he could make her comfortable. But hope, that cruel bitch, apparently had made other plans tonight.

Scott stared at Colette for half a beat, then laughed. "Hilarious. Jesus Christ, you really had me there for a second."

"I'm not kidding. I've never had sex."

"With men?"

"With anyone?"

He stepped back. "You're bullshitting me."

"I'm not. I'm a virgin. I'm sorry, I should have told you." She still didn't understand this part of herself that felt the need to apologize and make excuses to men who didn't deserve it.

Scott's eyes narrowed to hard, angry slits. "You sure as hell don't act like a virgin."

This pissed her off. She crossed her arms over her chest and her feet at the ankle. "And how is a virgin supposed to act, exactly?"

He made a 'duh' face. "Like a virgin. Pure, innocent, virginal. It's right there in the goddamn word. You're not supposed to let guys feel you up in clubs or shove their tongues inside your pussy."

"Your tongue was not inside my—"

"It sure as fuck was." He spun away from her, digging his fingers into his hair. "Goddamn it. What the actual fuck. You're too old to be a virgin."

He kicked a plastic garbage can that was sitting next to the sink. Colette slid off the counter and stomped into the living room to grab her tights off the floor. "There's no expiration date on my coochie, you idiot."

"I'm not the idiot here, Colette. For fuck's sake. I can't sleep with a fucking virgin."

"Why the hell not?"

"Because I'm not sixteen anymore, that's why the hell not. I'm a grown man. I want someone who knows what they're doing."

"Well, good, because I didn't want to sleep with you anyway."

"What? You've been throwing yourself at me ever since we started working together."

"I've been throwing myself at you? You're the one putting your hands all over me. You're the one who invited me to that god-awful club on Friday."

"Fuck!" He slapped his forehead. "That's why you ran out on me? Because you're a goddamn virgin. I thought you were on your period or something. Jesus fucking Christ. And I invited you out to Gardenia's. The club was all Mallory's idea."

"Whatever. It doesn't matter. I'm not sleeping with you. Not now. Not ever."

She shoved her feet into her sensible work shoes and, clutching her tights to her chest, marched to the front door. Before she reached it, Scott grabbed her elbow and spun her around.

"You're a cock tease. You did this on purpose." His voice was low and menacing.

She struggled to break free, but his grip was too strong. He rocked his hips against hers. His dick was still hard, and he pushed it against her crotch.

"Do you do this with all the guys?" He hissed the words through clenched teeth. "Act like a little slut, lead them on, let them get a taste and then cut them off before they have a chance to get their dick wet? Is that what gets you off? Giving perfectly nice guys blue balls? Laughing in their faces as you sashay your perfect little ass out the front door?"

Scott wasn't the first guy to say something like this to her. A guy she went on two dates with in college locked her in his car and refused to let her out unless she gave him a blow job. Luckily, she had her cell phone with her. The second she started dialing 9-1-1, the door locks clicked open.

"Perfectly nice guys don't hold women in their apartments against their will," she said in the same voice she used with her clients' unruly ex-spouses when they were trying to get more than their fair share, simply out of spite.

Scott let go of her and stepped back so fast you would have thought she'd kicked him in the nuts. She grabbed her purse that was sitting on the entry table, stuffed her tights inside, and ran out of his apartment. To her relief, he didn't chase after her.

She jammed the elevator button, but when the doors didn't open right away, she crashed through the door leading to the stairwell instead. Scott's apartment was on the top floor of a very tall building. Six floors down, and she was wishing she'd waited for the elevator. By the time she finally reached the ground floor, her calves and glutes were on fire, but at least that made up for the fact that she skipped the gym tonight to hang out with Scott.

Her stomach knotted as she replayed what had happened in his apartment. Why did she open her big fat mouth?

Because she didn't actually want to have sex with him, that's why.

Pros of sleeping with your boss...

At this moment, Colette couldn't think of a single one, but her cons list was a mile long.

Cons of sleeping with your boss:
1. He'll have seen you naked.
2. He'll be constantly undressing you with his eyes at the office.
3. He'll want a blow job under the desk.
4. Someone will find out.
5. People will call you the office slut.
6. It won't work out and you'll break up.
7. Break ups are messy.
8. Things will get awkward.
9. Everyone will know your personal business.
10. You won't be able to sit in meetings together without thinking about all the dirty things you did together.
11. You'll probably get fired.
12. You'll definitely get fired.

She could go on, but why bother when the only con that mattered was this one: Scott Campbell was a grade-A asshole. She stood outside his apartment building disoriented, trying to remember where she'd parked her car. Then she remembered with a groan that Scott had driven them to the restaurant and then to his apartment. Her car was still parked in the lot at the law firm, much too far to walk.

After she ordered an Uber, she texted Brooke.

Colette: Sex is not fun. Sex is terrible.

It took a minute before Brooke texted back.

Brooke: Oh babe, what happened? Pencil dick?

Colette: No. Well, maybe. I don't know. We didn't get that far. I got scared and told him I was a virgin.
Brooke: You didn't.
Colette: Not on purpose. It just sort of came out.
Brooke: I assume since it's barely 930 and you're texting me, that he didn't take it well.
Colette: He. Did. Not.
Colette: Can I come over?

It was another minute before Brooke responded.

Brooke: Sorry, Coco. I'm entertaining.

It was the word Brooke liked to use instead of booty call.

Colette: That guy from Calamity's?

Brooke sent a winking kiss emoji.

Brooke: What can I say? I've got the sauce. Call you tomorrow?
Colette: Have fun. Don't do anything I wouldn't do.
Brooke: Oops. Too late. Twice.

Brooke sent a peach and eggplant emoji, which made Colette laugh. She could always count on Brooke to make her feel better, even when she was at her lowest, and tonight was definitely the worst she'd felt in a long time.

Colette stared at the Uber app, watching the cartoon car get closer to her location, urging it to hurry. When it finally arrived, she let out a sigh of relief that the driver was a woman. She just couldn't deal with any more dicks tonight.

FIRST TIMERS CLUB

Chat Room

NotSoDirty30 (posted 10:45 PM):
Am I the only one who self-sabotages? Tonight, for example, this hot guy takes me out to a really nice dinner. Really nice. We're having a good time. The conversation is interesting. Then we go back to his place and I'm definitely thinking tonight is the night. This is it. He's into it and I'm into it. Or I thought I was into it? Until we get to the part where our clothes are on the floor and my brain completely freaks out! What is wrong with me??? I'm a 30-year-old woman who can't look at a penis without screaming and running in the other direction. Am I broken?

SexIsOveR-rated:
Penises are pretty scary.

TheBoyNextDoor:
You want to talk about scary? Have you ever seen a vagina?

SexIsOveR-rated:
I have one. So. Yes.

LoveConnection (admin):
Oh sweetheart, you're not broken. None of us are. We're just waiting for our perfect match.

2Hawt2Handle:
Sorry @loveconnection. No such thing. Soulmates? Perfect match? No thank you. It's all bullshit anyway. You're telling me that with almost 8 billion people on this planet, there's only one perfect person for you?

LoveConnection (admin):
That's not what I said. I think a person can have multiple matches in their lifetime. What I mean is that sometimes we self-sabotage because the person in our bed isn't the person our heart wants. Let alone needs.

cherrybomb:
Or sometimes you just want to fuck someone so badly, they can smell your desperation a mile away and decide you're definitely not worth the hassle.

2Hawt2Handle:
Try deodorant?

HappilyNeverAfter:
I completely understand @NotSoDirty30. I do the same thing. Why can't I just shut off that part of my brain and let myself have a good time?

NotSoDirty30:
Everything was going fine until I told him I was a virgin. It was like I told him I had leprosy or a tail or something.

cherrybomb:
Why bother telling him at all?

NotSoDirty30:
Honestly? It just slipped out. It was like a part of me felt bad not telling him, like he had this right to know that he was about to have sex with someone who's inexperienced. Or maybe @loveconnection is right and the subconscious part of my brain knew exactly how he would react, and I blurted it out so I wouldn't have sex with someone who turned out to be a complete a**hole.

LoveConnection (admin):
That makes perfect sense. You were testing him. You wanted to see if he was worthy of your vulnerability. It sounds like you found out he wasn't. Trust me. The heart is smarter than the brain with these things.

cherrybomb:
I don't get it. Women have it so easy. You could pop your cherry anytime you want. All you have to do is lay back and let it happen. Men are expected to know what they're doing.

HappilyNeverAfter:
What about porn?

2Hawt2Handle:
#yesplease

HappilyNeverAfter:
No, I mean, what about the standards men expect women to uphold because of the porn they watch?

cherrybomb:
The standards are there for men, too, not just women. But think about it. Virgin women are prized possessions in some places. Virgin men are just losers.

NotSoDirty30:
Well, I'm definitely feeling like a loser tonight, so it's not just men.

HappilyNeverAfter:
Would anyone ever be interested in doing an in-person meet up?

2Hawt2Handle:
Ooooh, like an orgy? We can all pop each other's cherries and then we don't have to worry about this anymore.

cherrybomb:
#virginorgy

HappilyNeverAfter:
Haha. But no, that's not what I meant. Just like for coffee. I like the chat room but sometimes I think it would be easier to talk face to face about some of these things.

TheBoyNextDoor:
I thought the whole point of this group was anonymity. It's easier to talk about this kind of stuff when I'm not looking someone in the eye.

LoveConnection (admin):
The point is to support one another as we move past our insecurities into a deeper place of self-love, self-worth, and connection. We're here to learn from one another and try to build more meaningful relationships.

2Hawt2Handle:
I'm only here because I thought it would be a good way to get laid.

cherrybomb:
It's not a bad idea. Why don't we pair off and sleep with each other? Just get it over with like @2Hawt2Handle suggests.

TheBoyNextDoor:
I'm not doing that.

SexIsOveR-rated:
Hell no.

2Hawt2Handle:
It was a joke.

cherrybomb:
Don't back down now, @2Hawt2Handle. We were really on to something!

HappilyNeverAfter:
Well, if anyone ever wants to meet up for coffee #notsex—send me a message!

LoveConnection (admin):
One last piece of advice before I sign off. This is for you @NotSoDirty30, but applies to the rest of us too. One day someone will come along who makes you want to run to him, not away. You'll know when it's right. Your heart will tell you. All you have to do is be brave enough to listen.

NotSoDirty30:
Thanks @LoveConnection. I really hope that turns out to be true. Otherwise, I'm dying alone.

HappilyNeverAfter:
You won't be alone! The First Timers will always be here for you!

cherrybomb:
#virginsforlife

IT'S JUST LUNCH

TRISTAN

Let me ask your professional opinion...
Tristan should have kept his mouth shut.
When you asked about my mother's sex life...
And the award for worst pickup line goes to...
Is that grounds for a lawsuit, do you think?
Tristan buried his face in his pillow and let out a strangled scream. Idiot. Idiot. Idiot.

He didn't know why he'd said any of that to Colette Harris. He wanted her to know that he remembered her from the club, but he could have said a hundred other, less snarky things. "You look pretty in red, but I like you better in green." Even something simple like, "Hey, I saw you at Giggles on Friday night, didn't I? Sorry, I acted like a jackass." Even that would have been a thousand times better.

But no. He said the first thing that came to his mind and, if she didn't think he was a jackass before, she certainly did now, because it was definitely a jackass thing to say and he felt like a jackass having said it. He groaned again and rolled over.

Sunlight filtered through his windows. Almost noon on a Thursday morning and he was still in bed.

Living the dream.

"Shut up." He covered his face with his pillow again.

He was never stepping foot outside this apartment. He'd have everything delivered. Groceries, beer, girls. The world didn't need him, and he had no use for the world. At least, not a world where Colette Harris thought of him as a self-centered prick with nothing but sex on his mind. But how could he not have sex on his mind when it came to Colette Harris?

She was the most beautiful woman he'd ever laid eyes on. And she was an enigma. She clearly hated dance clubs and threesomes and random guys with bad pickup lines. That much he knew. He also knew she worked as a divorce attorney and—he tried to think of something else, but all his mind could come up with was the lipstick smudge on her straight teeth, the dark seam of her tights climbing up the back of her calf, the pucker of her pink lips when she frowned at him. He wanted her to frown at him again, or smile, or make literally any face as long as she directed it at him.

Oh, for fuck's sake.

Why was he getting so worked up over a woman he didn't even know? A woman who clearly didn't like him. And someone he was definitely never going to see again. He threw off the covers and stumbled to the bathroom to splash water on his face.

You could see her again if you really wanted to, Triscuit.

He dried his face on a towel and walked into the kitchen.

Colette Harris' business card taunted him from the fridge door, where he stuck it three days ago when he was feeling more optimistic. He called her office as soon as he got home on Monday and left a rambling voicemail apology. Three days had passed, and he still hadn't heard from her. He took the card off the fridge, crumpled it in his fist, and dropped it into the garbage bin.

Then he fried an egg and ate it on a piece of sourdough toast with half an avocado.

Since when did you become such a hipster, little brother?

He wondered how Colette liked her eggs. Stop. Enough mooning over Colette Harris. There were a thousand other more interested and easy fish in the sea. Certainly, he could find one up for anything, a hottie who could purge from his mind the sound of Colette's angry voice telling him off and the image of her ass in that tight skirt.

He grabbed his phone off the counter where it had been charging all night. Since he last looked, he'd received two texts and one voicemail. One text was from his friend Nick.

Nick: Joshua Tree this weekend?

Tristan shot him a quick text back with a thumbs up and picture of a cartoon man climbing up a cliff.

Tristan: Rock and roll.

The second text was from his dad. His mom left the voicemail. He listened to that first.

"Trissy, it's me. It's your mother, Maureen." She sounded even more frazzled than usual. "I found another lawyer, but they're telling me I need to provide documentation of our finances for the past seven years? Or the entirety of our marriage? I'm not sure which. I showed him my credit card bill, but he says he needs bank accounts and retirement stuff and I don't know what else. Your father handled all of that. He has a guy, a tax guy, I think. Maybe I should call him? Do you know what his number is? Oh,

Abigail's here. We're doing a little retail therapy today and we'll probably end up at the spa. So, if you're planning to come by the house, don't come by until later this evening. Oh! Come for dinner, love. I'll have Laurie make us your favorite pot roast and potatoes."

Tristan stopped eating red meat five years ago, partly on a whim and partly because his idiot friends dared him to. He never started up again after realizing he didn't miss it. His mother knew he didn't eat red meat. He must have told her a hundred times before.

Tristan made himself a strong cup of coffee before reading his dad's text.

Dad: Hey, son. We need to talk about the apartment and your mother. I'll stop by at 11:30 today with bagels. See you then. Dad.

Tristan glanced at the microwave clock. "Shit."

Punctuality was Otto's middle name. He'd be there in ten minutes, which meant Tristan needed to be gone in nine.

He yanked on his favorite pair of Levi's and the first t-shirt he could find in his closet. He didn't look at what it was, just pulled it over his head, grabbed his leather motorcycle jacket, helmet, keys, wallet, phone, slipped on his boots, and ran out the door. Mid-turn of the deadbolt, he stopped, flung the lock open, and went back inside, rushed into the kitchen where he plucked Colette's business card out of the trash and stuffed it, still crumpled, into his pocket.

Tristan paced in front of the office building, trying to decide what to do next. Go inside and take the elevator to the law offices of Campbell and Sons and ask for Colette directly? Pretend to be an interested client? Or sit on the park bench and wait for her to come outside? Because she had to come out eventually, right? For lunch, or when she went home for the day. Was she even at work today? He scanned the parking lot but had no idea what kind of car she drove. Damn it.

However it happened, whether he went inside to find her or waited out here, she was going to take one look at him and think he was a stalker. Because he was definitely acting like a stalker.

He didn't understand what was going on with him. This woman who had probably forgotten all about him the second he walked out of her office had him all tied up in knots that he couldn't seem to untangle, no matter how hard he tried. He had never been so confused about what he wanted in his entire life. He should leave before she saw him. No, he should call her and tell her he wanted to take her to lunch. Before he could change his mind, he pulled his phone and her business card from his pocket.

He skimmed the four texts his dad had sent in the past ten minutes.

Dad: Hey, son. I'm here. I'm at the door.
Dad: Hey, son. I've been knocking for a while. Are you awake?
Dad: Hey, son. We really need to talk. If you're home, answer the door.
Dad: Hey, son. I guess I missed you. Okay, call me as soon as you can. It's important.

Tristan texted his dad a quick message so he would stop worrying.

Tristan: At the doctor. I'll call you when I'm done.

Colette Harris walked out of the office building right as he hit send.

Tristan stuffed his phone in his pocket, struck by the horrified realization that he was a complete idiot with nowhere to hide. He should have never come here. Of course Colette Harris wouldn't want to see him. She made that perfectly clear three days ago after the fiasco that was his mother's appointment, after she didn't return his sloppy, apologetic phone call. She was going to think something was wrong with him, that he was a total creep. He ducked his head and started to slink toward his motorcycle, but it was too late. She'd already spotted him.

"You." Her lip curled like she smelled something foul. "What are you doing here?"

She scanned the parking lot like she was looking for someone. "Did your mother come back to talk with one of the other attorneys?"

Hope lifted her voice. Tristan hated that he had to be the one to crush it.

"Ah, no. She's, um, I don't know. I just came by to see if you wanted to go to lunch?"

She blinked, confusion rippling over her face. "What?"

"Lunch." He mimed eating a sandwich. Stupid. He shoved his hands in his pockets. "I know this great taqueria close to here."

"You're joking, right?" She laughed. The sound made his pulse race.

"No joke," he said with a smile he hoped was disarming. "Just tacos."

"I don't think so." She shook her head and dug into her large shoulder bag, looking for something.

Of course she wasn't going to make this easy on him. He wouldn't be this smitten with her if she did.

Get it together, Triscuit. Sheesh. Smitten? What are you in middle school?

She could probably smell the desperation wafting off him. Be cool. But she was wearing knee-high gray socks and a black skirt that stopped at mid-thigh and that slip of nude skin between the two was doing things to his manhood, making him want to get down on his knees and beg. He'd never begged for anyone. He wiped his mouth, afraid he was drooling, but thank God, his hand came away dry.

"Look, I know I was a complete asshole to you at the club last week," he tried again.

Her eyebrows arched. "Understatement of the year."

"In my defense, you spilled your drink on me first." He teased her.

The corners of her mouth twitched, but didn't lift into a full smile. "In my defense, you were standing in my way."

"Fair enough." He spread his hands open at his sides. "I should have realized you were a VIP with better places to be and cleared a path."

"Exactly." The smile flickered across her face so quickly he almost missed it.

But it was enough for him to keep pushing.

"So let me make it up to you," he said. "Let me buy you lunch."

He could see her thinking about it, doing whatever mysterious calculations women do in their heads when trying to decide if a man was safe or not. He tried to look as casual and non-threatening as possible, relaxed even though his heart was slamming against his ribcage, even though he had a sudden, strong, caveman-like urge to lift her over his shoulder and carry her somewhere private with a door that locked.

"I don't know." She stretched the words in a way that made it seem like she might say yes, but then she shook her head. "No, it's not a good idea. I don't have a very long lunch break and you're a client's son."

"Technically, she's not your client anymore." Dumbass. Why did he have to remind her?

She looked crestfallen. Red bloomed high on her cheeks. "Right. Anyway. Nice seeing you again, I guess?"

She stepped around him, and Tristan did the same stupid thing he'd done in the club: he grabbed her arm. "Wait, please."

Her eyes locked onto his, and he fell into the spirals of golden brown. He couldn't look away even if he tried. He noticed subtle changes in her face. Pupils widening, her nostrils flared. Her lips parted ever so slightly as she took a sharp breath. He wasn't holding on to her tightly. She could slip away easily if she wanted to, but she didn't. Instead, she slid her hand over the top of his, her fingers resting gently against the back of his hand. Sparks rushed up his arm.

"Colette?" A man's voice boomed across the parking lot, breaking the delicate connection building between them. "Is everything all right?"

Colette dropped her hand and stepped away from Tristan. A look of horror spread over her face as the man walked over to them. Whoever this dude was, he definitely dressed and strutted like a stuffed-shirt, pompous asshole.

"Is this man bothering you?" the pompous asshole with the purple silk tie asked Colette. He rolled up the sleeves of his dress shirt like he was planning to fight Tristan.

Tristan's hands curled into fists. Bring it on, asshole. He was more than happy to knock this prick down a peg.

He's got fifty pounds on you, Triscuit. Look at the size of those biceps.

Scrappy always beats strong.

Who the hell told you that bullshit?

Tristan stepped forward because if this was going to go down, he would need the element of surprise to win. He'd need to throw the first punch, but Colette grabbed his elbow and laid her head on his shoulder, and all that cocky macho bullshit drained from his body. He turned into a puddle on the concrete.

"He's not bothering me. He's—" She squeezed Tristan's arm. "He's taking me to lunch."

The pompous asshole's mouth dropped open, and he sputtered out a few words that Tristan didn't hear because there were birds singing in his head, like he was in a freaking Disney movie.

Colette pulled on Tristan's arm, dragging him away from the sputtering, pompous asshole. Under her breath, she asked, "Where's your car?"

He pointed at his Ducati parked under a small tree.

"Absolutely not." She exhaled a puff of air and tossed her head. "We'll take mine."

Turned out that hers was a rust bucket. A turquoise Chevy Aveo with only one hubcap. The passenger door groaned like a dying goose when he opened it and the seat cover was torn, but Tristan wasn't about to complain. He didn't care what Colette drove as long as she took him with her.

"Who was that guy?" Tristan asked as they pulled out of the parking lot.

"What guy?"

"The guy with the tie. The one you're clearly running away from?" He rolled down the window a few inches.

"I'm not running." But she glanced in the rearview mirror like she was expecting to see the pompous asshole following them.

"You work together?"

She nodded. "Where are we going?"

"Is he a Campbell or a Son?" Tristan leaned forward and flipped on the radio. It was tuned to a classic rock station, and he nodded approvingly, turning up the volume so he could hear the music above the traffic noise.

"Son," she said. "You know it's not polite to touch someone else's radio without asking, right?"

Tristan grimaced and snapped the radio off. "Sorry."

"That was a good song." She reached for the knob and wailing electric guitars filled the silence.

She tapped her thumbs on the steering wheel matching the beat and turned to him with an impatient look on her face. "Now, will you please tell me where we're going?"

HOT ENOUGH TO MELT

TRISTAN

Eddy leaned out of his food truck and bumped Tristan's fist. "Hey, man. How's it hanging? Haven't seen you in an age. You leave town or something?"

"Nah, man." Tristan patted his stomach. "I've been around. Just trying to watch my figure."

Eddy tilted his head back, laughing. "Mick Jagger physique over here worrying about a couple of tacos? Pshh. You still climbing?"

Tristan shrugged. "Now and then."

"Then you can eat all the damn tacos you want." Eddy took a pencil from behind his ear and pressed the tip to a pad of paper. "The regular today?"

Tristan turned to Colette, who stood to one side with her arms crossed over her chest, looking like she'd rather be anywhere else with anyone who wasn't him. Oversized sunglasses hid her eyes, but she bit the corner of her lip and shifted nervously from one foot to the other. She looked as nervous as a bunny rabbit, and he fully expected her to take off running back to the car. They were at least ten miles from her office building, where his motorcycle was still parked. A long walk if she ditched him.

"What kind of tacos do you like?" he asked.

She scanned the chalkboard menu. "Carnitas are fine."

"Two?"

She nodded. "And a Coke?"

"You heard the lady," Tristan said to Eddy, who gave him a wink.

"Carnitas and chapulines coming right up." Eddy plunked a glass Coke bottle onto the window shelf and popped off the top. He handed it to Tristan, who handed it to Colette, who took a dainty sip.

Eddy disappeared from the window to make their tacos.

While they waited, Tristan stood close to Colette with his hands shoved in his pockets and his tongue tied in knots. Now that they didn't have the radio to distract them, he was at a loss about what to say to her. He'd never not known what to say to a woman, and it was sending him into a spiral. The longer the silence stretched, the more his mind raced to find something interesting to say. But he kept coming up blank.

This was a bad idea. She clearly only agreed to go to lunch with him because she didn't want to talk to that guy from her office. She didn't seem at all interested in getting to know Tristan better. And he couldn't blame her since he acted like a total prick in their previous two interactions. Which made him even more desperate to change her mind.

He cleared his throat.

She exhaled an impatient sigh.

Cars passed on the street, and Tristan noticed a VW Beetle, a vintage model with a surf rack and painted sunshine yellow. Without thinking, he bumped his fist lightly against Colette's arm and said, "Slug Bug yellow."

A startled yip escaped her.

"What the hell was that?" She rubbed her arm.

"Oh shit. I'm sorry." Tristan cringed.

He hadn't hit her very hard, nothing compared to how he and Troy used to wail on each other's arms anytime one of those stupid cars passed by, but he'd still hit her.

You really have a death wish, don't you, Triscuit?

"It's, uh, it's a habit," he rushed to explain. "Didn't you ever play that game as a kid?"

She stared at him like he'd lost his damn mind. And he had, if he thought punching her in the arm was going to make her like him.

Eddy interrupted at that point to hand over a paper bag filled with tacos. "Don't stay away so long this time, okay, bud?"

Tristan promised and grabbed the bag and a handful of napkins.

There was a park across the street. Kids screamed on the playground. A group of teens bounced a basketball around a court that had hoops but no nets. Tristan found a picnic table in some shade and separated the carnitas from the chapulines.

Colette unwrapped one of her tacos, frowned at it, but took a bite. As she chewed, her face and shoulders relaxed a little.

"This is delicious," she said.

"Best tacos in LA." He bit into his first, enjoying the crunch and acidic flavor of lime.

"You seemed pretty friendly with the owner," she pointed out.

"I used to come here like twice a week."

"Do you work around here?"

"Something like that." He shrugged and took another bite.

It was Troy who worked a few buildings down from Eddy's taco truck. Troy and Eddy who used to climb together on Sundays. Troy, who introduced Tristan to chapulines. His brother was the last thing he wanted to talk about right now, though. Sob stories about dead brothers didn't exactly make good foreplay.

Colette seemed to pick up on his reluctance because she changed the subject.

"What are chapulines?" Colette frowned at the taco in his hand.

"Want to try it?" He held it out to her, but her nose wrinkled in distaste.

"I want you to tell me what it is first. Because I'm pretty sure that's a cricket leg?" She jabbed her finger at a bit of insect dangling from the corn shell.

"You're right. It's toasted grasshoppers. A Oaxacan delicacy." Tristan pulled the leg out and popped it into his mouth.

A shudder rolled through her. "What does it taste like?"

"Kind of smoky, a hint of lime." He took another bite, making a big deal out of chewing it, like he was sipping fine wine instead of munching grasshoppers. "Really, it tastes like whatever sauce it gets cooked in, and Eddy's sauce is a revelation."

"That's quite the Yelp review."

He held a freshly unwrapped taco out to her. He could see her thinking about it, but in the end, she shook her head. "I can't get over the thought of those little bug legs getting stuck in my teeth."

"Oh, God." He stared at the taco with pretend horror, then flashed his teeth at Colette. "You have to tell me. As an attorney, you've sworn never to tell a lie."

"You're mistaking attorneys with Pinocchio. Or George Washington." But she laughed when she said it and a wrinkle creased the bridge of her nose.

It was the cutest thing Tristan had ever seen.

"Your teeth look fine," she said.

"No bug legs? You promise?"

"No bug legs." She made an 'x' sign across her chest. "Cross my heart."

She finished her second taco and sat sipping her Coke and scanning the park. Her eyes followed the bustling movements of nannies and moms pushing strollers, men and women jogging on their lunch breaks, pigeons fluttering and cooing in a fountain. The sunlight brushed copper highlights into her dark brown hair. Somehow in the past few minutes she'd grown even more beautiful, which Tristan didn't think was possible. He realized this was the first time he'd seen her somewhat relaxed. How much more beautiful might she be, he wondered, if she let go of her inhibitions and actually allowed herself to have a little fun?

"Are you in a hurry to get back to work?" He crumpled the empty taco wrappers and tossed everything into a nearby trash can.

"Why?" Her eyes narrowed on him with suspicion. "What did you have in mind?"

"How about dessert?"

"Do you ever eat anything normal?" Colette gave Tristan's bone marrow and blackberry ice cream cone a skeptical side-eye.

"Do you ever eat anything interesting?" He shot back, arching his eyebrows at her plain vanilla scoop.

They walked along the Venice Beach Boardwalk, trying to avoid bumping into the large crowds of people strolling and shopping and skating. It didn't matter if it was a holiday weekend or the middle of a random Thursday afternoon, Venice Beach was always a madhouse.

"Don't these people have jobs?" Colette glared at a tanned, muscled gym rat who bumped into her elbow because he was looking at his phone.

The bro didn't even apologize. He spun away from Colette and kept walking with his eyes still glued to the screen. Tristan was about to go after him and demand an apology, but Colette darted her tongue out to catch a drip of ice cream and he forgot all about the guy.

It was hot today, and the ice cream melted faster than they could eat it. Colette scraped her long, pink tongue over the vanilla drip running down the cone. Tristan wanted to be that cone. She caught him staring.

"What? Do I have something on my face?" She wiped the back of her hand over her mouth.

They kept walking, licking their separate cones. Every time Colette darted her tongue out, Tristan felt a shock of wanting spark through him.

"I can't believe you talked me into playing hooky," she said.

"I didn't talk you into anything," he said. "I just asked nicely."

"I needed this." She tilted her head back to soak up a ray of sun.

She had left her gray blazer in the car when they parked in front of the ice cream shop. Her sleeveless blouse billowed around her curves. The freckles on her shoulders looked like chocolate sprinkles, and he wanted to taste her.

"Do you like being an attorney?" Tristan asked the most boring question he could think of to distract himself from the curve of her neck, the pale, soft skin he'd like to sink his teeth into, the freckles he wanted to trace with his tongue.

"It's interesting work, and it pays the bills." She popped the last of her ice cream cone into her mouth. "So, yes. I guess I do like it."

"Divorce is interesting?" He didn't mean to sound so harsh about it, but he kept thinking of his mother throwing his father's stuff out the window, the anger in her eyes as she ordered Otto out of her house and out of her life for the last time.

The skin on Colette's shoulders flushed a bright pink. "No two divorces are ever the same, which makes it interesting. It's hard, too, though. Dealing with all the intense emotions that come with a dissolution of marriage."

"It sounds like a nightmare. All that squabbling over some stupid pots and pans."

"With broken hearts, pots and pans aren't just pots and pans. They're symbolic of everything the couple's losing. But you're right, things can get really messy. You wouldn't believe the trivial trinkets people fight over when their relationship is ending."

"You might be surprised."

She shot him a horrified look. "Right, your parents are going through it. I'm sorry. I don't mean to be insensitive." After a brief pause, she asked, "Has your mother found another attorney?"

Tristan tossed the rest of his uneaten cone into a trash can as they walked past, his appetite gone. "She does this all the time, you know. Threatens to divorce him. Eventually she takes him back."

"Has she ever gone to an attorney before?"

The question stung like a slap. So did his answer. "No, she hasn't."

Colette's silence spoke volumes.

"I don't get it," he said, hearing the anger in his voice, but doing nothing to calm it. "Why would you want to be a part of a couple breaking up? Take my parents, for example. They've been married for over thirty years. They should be seeing a marriage counselor, not signing retainers."

"Maybe they *have* seen a counselor."

He snorted in disbelief.

"You're their son. They might tell you a lot, but they're not going to tell you everything." Colette's voice was gentle. Her hand brushed his arm, and a shock sparked through him.

He stopped walking. They stood in the middle of the boardwalk, facing each other. She looked at him, not with pity, but with understanding.

"My parents divorced when I was ten," she said. "And it was a shit show."

She laughed, but he could tell it was a wound that still cut deep. Her eyes darted to the ground, then back up to meet his. He stepped closer and tangled his fingers in hers, fully expecting her to pull back, but she didn't. She tilted closer. The corners of her mouth lifted in a broken smile.

"My mom, she didn't really have the support she needed. She just knew she wanted out, so she left. She took me and my brother and sister with her, but she didn't have a job or any savings, and no one was there to help her or tell her the right way to do things. My dad—he's a prick. He was so angry with her for leaving that he sold everything. The house, all the things we'd left behind. He moved and didn't tell us where he was going. He took all the money, everything, cleaned out the joint accounts. She should have gotten half. More than half if you count child support. Anyway, if she'd had an attorney, or even just talked to one for twenty minutes, she could have avoided so much pain and hardship. We all could have." She laughed again, that same heartbreaking sound that made Tristan want to hold her in his arms and never let go.

Then she seemed to remember who she was talking to—a man she barely knew. One who had accosted her in a club and left her drunken voicemails. She uncoupled their fingers and took a small step back, shaking her head.

"I'm sorry," she said in a rush. "That was a lot to dump on you."

"It's all right."

"I got through it. So did she. We all did. It took time and work and faith and resilience and a bit of luck, but eventually we all landed on our feet. It would have been nice to have someone to keep us from falling in the first place, though," she said. "So I guess that's why I went to law school. Why I chose family law. Yes, I'm helping people navigate the end of a relationship, which can be very difficult. But I'm also helping to usher them onto a new life path, one that might lead to better days. And that's what keeps me coming back. That hope. Knowing I might help a woman, or a man, step onto that new path with confidence rather than fall flat on their face and break something on the way down. Maybe it's stupid, but I like to think I'm helping the people who come into my office."

"When you put it like that, you're a goddamn saint." He kept his voice low as he reached for her, wanting to pull her to him again, to feel her skin on his.

But she spun away from him. She was a fast walker, one of those people who swung her arms and kept her eyes straight ahead, blazing a path through oblivious tourists. He hurried to catch up and soon matched her step for step.

"What about you?" she asked. "What kind of work do you do that lets you traipse around the city midday on a Thursday?"

"I'm kind of in between jobs right now."

It wasn't a total lie. But it wasn't exactly the truth. Tristan was fired from his job at the climbing gym six months ago when he showed up to work blasted out of his mind and dropped a kid on belay. The kid was fine. Tristan caught him before he hit the mats. Kid probably had the best damn time of his life flying like that, but the kid's mother was so worked up she almost busted a spleen. His manager, who endured twenty minutes of screaming and lawsuit threats, didn't appreciate Tristan's mellow attitude and fired him on the spot.

Tristan hadn't bothered looking for a job since. He hadn't even updated his resume. Dad's generosity paid for the apartment, and his mom gave him more than enough cash every week to pay for his bills and a semi-extravagant lifestyle. If extravagant was eating out every night and buying hot girls drinks at the club. An ex-girlfriend called him spoiled once and he couldn't argue with her. He wasn't going to tell Colette any of this, though. Not after she just poured her heart out to him about her hard-scrabble childhood.

They walked for a few minutes without talking, then Colette

inhaled sharply and asked, "Does your girlfriend know you took me out to lunch today?"

"My girlfriend?" He sputtered a laugh. "I don't have a girlfriend."

"That girl at the club? The one in the silver dress? You aren't together?"

It impressed Tristan that Colette remembered what the other woman was wearing because he sure didn't. But was that jealousy in her voice? The hint of possessiveness?

"We met at the club that night," he said. "We were just dancing."

"Oh." There was a hint of relief in her voice, then the nervousness returned. "Did you sleep with her?"

He barked out a laugh.

She stopped short and shook her head. "Sorry, you don't have to tell me that."

Her eyes were wide, doe-like. He stepped toward her and tucked a loose strand of hair behind her ear, making sure his finger brushed her cheek. "Would you be mad if I had?"

Her jaw twitched. "You can do what you want. I don't even know you."

"Yeah? Well, maybe we should change that."

Something flickered in his peripheral vision, then someone shouted, "Watch out!"

Tristan barely had time to react. The rollerblader careened straight toward them, his arms spinning wildly, the look on his face one of pure terror. At the last second, Tristan grabbed Colette around the waist and swung her out of the rollerblader's path, narrowly avoiding a catastrophic collision.

Colette gasped in surprise as Tristan pinned her up against the stucco wall of a nearby shop, his broad shoulders protecting her from the out-of-control skater, who bounced between groups of people, trying desperately to stay on his feet.

Her laugh was soft, trembling. "That was close."

"Good thing I was here." His breath moved the fine hair framing her face. "It would be such a shame for your perfect body to suffer even a scratch."

She laughed again, a breathless sound, and stared at him with her lips slightly parted.

Colorful graffiti spanned the length of the wall behind her, but she was the brightest spot. The peach skin. The rosebud cheeks. The brown freckles. The turquoise blouse that made her golden eyes pop. The vibrant red of her lips. She should be in a gallery.

He traced one finger along that narrow, exposed slip of skin between her skirt and her knee-high socks. She sucked in a sharp breath. Her eyes were bright with wanting. Her chest rose and fell as if she'd been running. Tristan was breathing hard too.

"God, you're beautiful," he whispered.

His fingers twisted in her hair as he cupped her face and leaned in for a kiss. She arched toward him, meeting him halfway. Their lips touched, and she melted against the wall. Both of her hands pressed against the concrete as if she needed the support to keep from sliding into a puddle at his feet.

He felt her trembling as he pushed her mouth open with his tongue, as he tasted her for the first time. The sweetness of vanilla lingered.

Her tongue met his, and his knees went weak. He braced one hand on the wall by her head. With the other, he caressed her jaw, pulling her closer, kissing her deeper. She let out a quiet whimper, and his whole body lit on fire.

Oh boy, Triscuit, the voice in his head taunted. *You're in trouble now.*

BOARDWALK STATE OF MIND

Colette

Colette lost herself in the kiss.

Tristan's fingers tangled in her hair. He moved his hand over her face as his tongue probed hers. His breath was warm and sweet. His broad shoulders blocked her view of the boardwalk, making it seem like they were the only two people in the world. When he nudged her legs open with one knee, when his finger traced over the exposed skin of her thigh, her whole body ignited. She'd never been kissed like that before, never lost herself so completely in someone else's touch.

Her mind hummed with all the dirty things she wanted Tristan Walker to do to her.

Rip her blouse.

Suck her tits.

Turn her around.

Fuck her hard against this wall.

How was this happening? Did he drug her ice cream? Or was she so basic that one chivalrous act could bring her to her knees?

Speaking of knees. She would get down on her knees for him if he asked, suck him off in this bright sunshine with the whole world watching. An image flashed through her mind of the two of them speeding away on his motorcycle, her arms wrapped around his chest, the hum of the engine awakening the beast between her legs. Another image quickly followed: Tristan sweeping her off her feet and tossing her onto an enormous bed covered in satin sheets. He hovers over her, spreads her apart — Colette shoved Tristan away, breaking off their kiss.

"I'm sorry," she panted. "I can't — This isn't — I have to go. I have to get back to work."

He kept her pinned against the wall with his arm braced near her head. His brow furrowed as he bit his lower lip, like he was trying to figure out her whole deal. He searched her face, and she hated the way it felt like he was looking inside her, like he could see every hidden part. She dropped her gaze to the sidewalk, where some parasailing pamphlets and an empty paper coffee cup skittered in the breeze.

Tristan grabbed her chin and tilted her head up again. "Hey."

His eyes were the color of the ocean and deep enough to drown in.

"That was good, right?"

His voice wobbled with an uncertainty that Colette hadn't heard from him before. Every word until now had been self-assured, to the point of conceited. But there seemed to exist another, softer Tristan hiding beneath all that hotshot bravado. A man with insecurities like everyone else who hadn't been expecting to have his entire world knocked off-kilter by one stupid kiss.

"I mean, it wasn't just me," he pressed her. "You felt that too?"

He leaned in for another kiss, but her heart leaped into her throat and her head spun. Before, she wasn't thinking anything at all, and now she was thinking too much.

She needed space to breathe and quiet to hear her thoughts above the pounding of her heart. And she needed him to stop staring at her like that. Like he wanted to be her everything. It was making her dizzy.

She sidestepped around him, narrowly avoiding the second kiss, and stepped into the flow of people moving along the boardwalk. The sun shone brilliantly, and the world shimmered in Technicolor. She marched toward the street where she'd parked her car.

"Colette, wait!" He raced after her.

She lengthened her stride.

He grabbed her hand to slow her down.

"Look, thanks for lunch, but this isn't going where you think it's going," she said in a breathless rush.

"And where do I think it's going?" His eyes scraped down the length of her.

If he was this hungry when she had clothes on, imagine how ravenous he'd be when she was naked. Where the hell had that dirty little ditty come from? She shook the thought away and shook off Tristan's hand too.

"I'm not like that girl in the club you were with last week."

"Oh, are you two friends?"

"What?" She jerked to a stop, and he ran into the back of her. She whipped around to glare at him. "No. Of course we're not friends."

"Then how do you know what she's like?"

Colette folded her arms over her chest. "I just mean I'm not going to sleep with you."

His eyebrows darted up, and a playful smirk toyed on his lips. Lips she wanted to kiss again, despite herself.

"I wasn't even thinking about that." A wicked glint flashed in his eyes. "But now that you mention it—"

She let out a groan of frustration and spun away from him,

continuing her furious march to the car. He was laughing when he caught up to her a second time.

"Come on, Colette. I was only teasing you. You don't have to sleep with me." His pause was weighted and drawn out before he added in a husky voice, "Not today anyway."

Was this what a heart attack felt like? Pressure in her chest. Numbing in her arms. Her jaw clenched so tight her teeth might crack. Her heart pounding and pounding, slamming against her ribcage like a kick drum. Dots of light exploded in her peripheral vision. The smell of cotton candy drifted from somewhere nearby. She felt herself tip forward.

Tristan grabbed her around the waist. "Whoa there."

He cradled her against his chest, holding her upright. Concern etched his features as he peered into her eyes. "Are you okay? It looked like we lost you there for a second."

His arms around her were warm and strong. She felt his heart beating, pounding as hard as hers.

"Too much sugar," she whispered.

"You're not diabetic, are you?" He smiled.

She shook her head and tried to laugh, but it came out as an awkward sputter. "I'm fine. I'm sorry. I just got dizzy for a second. It's nothing."

She untangled herself from him, but he kept one hand around her waist, as if afraid she might faint again. Oh my God, she fainted. Not quite, but close enough. She would not have considered herself a swooner before today, and yet that's exactly what she'd done.

Tristan was still smiling at her. How could she possibly sort through her million and one racing thoughts with him staring at her like that?

"I really need to get back to the office," she said.

"Well, you're my ride," he said. "So I guess I'm going wherever you're taking me."

Colette's cheeks warmed at the innuendo. She walked away

from him, hoping he wouldn't notice how flustered he made her. When they were almost to the car, she dug her phone from her pocket and texted Brooke to find out if she was home.

Colette: SOS.
Brooke: Come over. I'll chill the rosé.

There was a stack of work waiting on Colette's desk, but no way would she be able to focus on any of it. Not with the memory of Tristan's lips burning against hers. If it wasn't for needing to drop Tristan off to get his bike, she would have gone straight from the boardwalk to her best friend's apartment.

As she turned into the office parking lot, Tristan said, "I think I should get your phone number."

"You have my phone number. You took my business card, remember?" She pulled up alongside his bike and put the car in park, but left the engine running.

"No, I mean, your cell," he clarified.

"What would you need that for?"

"In case I want to ask you out again." He sounded so nonchalant about it, but there was an eager gleam in his eyes that made her heart flutter.

Colette stared at the phone in his hand and wondered how many women's numbers were already stored in that little black book of his. Feeling bold, she rattled off her number and watched him type it in. As soon as he hit save, she realized two things. First, she'd had no urge to make a pros and cons list before giving Tristan her number, even though she definitely should have made one because cons would have outweighed pros and she could have avoided her second problem, which was that she had absolutely no clue what she would say if he made good on his threat and actually called her.

"This was fun," he said as he got out of the car. Before he closed the door, he winked at her. "Let's do it again soon."

THERE ARE ALWAYS CONS

Colette

Colette poured herself a second glass of wine, but when she went to top off Brooke, her friend waved the bottle away. "I've got an early audition tomorrow."

"Another sitcom?" Colette asked.

"A movie." Brooke flashed her straight white teeth in an excited smile, but then shook her head. Her loosely gathered topknot trembled. "No, I can't talk about it. I don't want to jinx it."

Brooke had always been superstitious with auditions. She never told Colette any details about the projects until she knew one way or the other if she'd gotten the part.

"Besides," Brooke said. "We're talking about your man problems. Don't try to change the subject."

Colette groaned and sucked down half the wine she just poured.

"It's simple," Brooke said. "Do you like him?"

"I don't know him."

"You spent all afternoon with him, didn't you?"

"Yes, a couple of hours, but that's not long enough to really know a person."

"It's about twice as long as I spend with the guys I bring home."

"Yeah, but you're—" She cut herself off before she said something she'd regret.

"I'm what? A slutty whore with no morals?" Brooke had an unnerving habit of lifting only one eyebrow in a way that made her look like a very judgmental—and very sexy—librarian.

"That's definitely not how I would describe you." Colette grabbed one of a dozen throw pillows scattered around the living room. She clutched it in her lap, soothing herself by smoothing the crushed red velvet up and down, petting it like it was a toy poodle.

"You know me," she said. "You know I've got these stupid hang ups and I can't just jump into bed with someone the way you do."

"You can. You just don't want to."

"And that makes me an uptight bitch, I know."

"That's definitely not how I would describe you." Brooke scooted closer to Colette so their knees touched.

They sat together on the lambskin rug with their backs leaning against Brooke's avocado green couch. Brooke's apartment was small, a one-bedroom with thin walls and bad lighting, but she made the best of it with her keen sense of style. The decor was a mix of art déco and old Hollywood, glamorous and decadent but not over the top. Etta James sang sultry blues in the background, her voice crackling through the speakers of a refurbished record player. Candles flickered on side tables, making the room feel cozy.

"Let me say this a different way." Brooke sipped her wine before continuing. "He was nice to you, right?"

"Surprisingly, yes."

"And he seemed interested?"

"I mentioned the kiss, didn't I?" Colette had unloaded the entire story on to Brooke within seconds of entering her apartment. It took her a full glass of wine to get through all the delicious and terrifying details, and then she'd reached for the bottle to pour another and asked Brooke what the hell she was supposed to do next.

Brooke's nose wrinkled. "You said he kissed you like he was a drowning man and you were oxygen. Which, again, I don't know what that means, but I'd say he's definitely interested. Okay, so he's nice, and he seems into you. And he's cute."

"Ugh." Colette finished her second glass and reached for the bottle. "If you like the shaggy, just rolled out of bed surfer look."

"I mean… It's top five for me so, go on. I think you also said something about ocean eyes?" Brooke wiggled her eyebrows. "And he caught you when you were fainting—"

"I didn't faint."

"Swooning, then. It doesn't matter. He caught you in his arms like a goddamn superhero."

"So he's strong. So what? I run marathons."

"You ran one marathon." Brooke wagged her finger in the air. "Ten years ago."

"Well, I'm signing up for another."

"When?"

"I don't know. Let me see…" Colette grabbed her phone and googled the dates of the next LA Marathon.

"You're changing the subject again." Brooke snatched the phone from her hand and hid it behind her back. "So, Tristan Walker—goddamn, that's a stud's name if I ever heard one. He's nice. He's into you. He's cute. He's strong. He's rich."

"We don't know he's rich."

Brooke's eyes popped wide. "Oh my God, I thought you knew."

"Knew what?"

"Who he is."

"He's an egotistical mama's boy who thinks he's God's gift to women. That's who he is."

"He's Otto Walker's youngest son." Brooke said the name like Colette was supposed to know who she was talking about.

Colette shook her head. "Who the hell is Otto Walker?"

"Only one of the hottest and most sought-after talent agents in the business. Or he used to be." Brooke twirled her finger around a strand of hair that had slipped free of her bun. "He's represented so many really famous people. Molly Ringwald. Kathleen Turner. Jon Cryer. Rob Lowe for a hot minute. Now he mostly works with a lot of B-list, TikTok, up-and-coming YouTube stars like Baby Cherry, Jonesie Tomisina. People like that."

"Who?" Colette had never heard either of those names. And TikTok was for bored and lonely teenagers, wasn't it?

"It doesn't matter," Brooke said. "The point is, Tristan Walker is a golden boy with daddy's money to burn and he's into you. So, what's the problem again?"

"Do I need to remind you?"

"The virgin thing." Brooke sighed and rested her head against the couch. "I don't know how many times I have to tell you it's not that big of a deal before you believe me."

"It was a big deal to Scott."

Brooke's face twisted in disgust. "Scott's a douche."

"Who's to say Tristan won't act the exact same way when I tell him?" Colette frowned at her third glass of wine. The rosé was starting to taste bitter. Or maybe it was imagining Tristan's reaction when he found out she was a virgin that was putting her off.

"Don't tell him," Brooke said bluntly.

Colette rolled her eyes. "Sure, like he won't know the second he spreads my legs."

"How would he know?" Brooke challenged her, but Colette

felt stupid answering because she didn't actually know whether a guy could tell. The movies and books made it seem like it would be obvious to anyone who tried to put his dick inside her, but movies and books were wrong about so many things. Why wouldn't they be wrong about this too? But she would bleed, wouldn't she?

Brooke spoke into the silence. "Listen to me, Coco. I've slept with plenty of guys like Tristan, and trust me, unless you come right out and say it, he won't be sitting there analyzing or inspecting you or trying to figure out if you feel different from the hundred other women he's slept with. He's just going to be thinking about how hot your bod is and how he can get his nut off inside you."

Horrified, Colette pressed the pillow to her face, muffling her voice, when she said, "No. Ew. Gross. Maybe I should become a nun."

"That is the last thing you want to do." Brooke pulled the pillow from Colette's face. Mischief glinted in her eyes and twisted the corners of her mouth. "Trust me. You want this man to fuck you."

"I do?"

"After how you described that kiss? A very chaste, very public kiss? You said it melted your bones. Isn't that what you said?"

"I said it melted my brain—but yeah, whatever, same thing."

"Imagine what it'll feel like when he's kissing you in private." Brooke's eyes glittered as she laughed. "Kissing your privates in private is what I mean."

Colette thumped her with the pillow.

Brooke grabbed the pillow and chucked it across the room. "This is your Big Year, remember?"

"Yes, because you won't let me forget."

"Tristan is the perfect man to lose your V-card to," Brooke said. "He's hot. He's experienced. He'll treat you right. And if he doesn't, you call me immediately, and I'll take care of it." She cracked her knuckles.

"Thanks, Boo Boo." Colette leaned her head on her friend's shoulder.

"I'm serious, Coco. I like this for you. It makes sense." Brooke leaped to her feet. "Let's make a list."

Colette frowned. "A list?"

"One of your pros and cons thingys. I'll get some paper." Brooke ran out of the room and returned a few seconds later with a pink notepad and a purple pen with a fuzzy turquoise ball bobbing on the eraser end. She plopped down on the rug beside Colette again. "Okay, let's go. Pro: he's fucking hot."

"Con," Colette said, adjusting her legs to a more comfortable position. "He's practically a stranger."

"Actually, that's going in the pro column." Brooke wrote it down before Colette could argue.

"How is that a pro?"

"You don't want your first time to be with someone you actually like," Brooke said. "Trust me. Just get this awkward one out of the way and then you can fall in love."

"You said it's going to be fine. Good even."

"It will be. Probably." Brooke made a face. "I don't know, Coco. I don't remember. My first time was so long ago and maybe it's different when you're sixteen and having sex for the first time versus thirty and having sex for the first time, but just in case, let's go with the theory that it's always going to be awkward as fuck to fuck for the first time and so you should do it with someone you don't have to see again if you don't want to."

"So… Not my boss." Though she made fun of it tonight, she was still reeling from the humiliation over her failed date with Scott. They'd been avoiding each other in the hallways at work, which was manageable so far but didn't seem like a good, long-term solution.

"There's another one for the pro column. Tristan is not your boss." Brooke jotted it down.

"What about cons?" Colette grabbed the list from Brooke. "You didn't even make a column for cons."

"Because there are none." Brooke snatched the list back and ripped off the top sheet. She folded it in half and stuffed it into the side pocket of Colette's purse, which was sitting on the couch near her head.

"It's time for my beauty rest." Brooke stood up and kissed Colette on the top of the head. "You know where the extra blankets are if you need them."

Brooke blew out the candles as she walked into her bedroom and closed the door.

Colette poured a fourth glass of wine for herself and curled up on the couch with her feet tucked under a knitted blanket. She took the folded slip of paper from her purse and smoothed it onto her lap. Brooke's handwriting looped playfully across the pink scrap of paper.

Across the top scrawled the words: *Pros for Fucking Tristan Walker*

Underneath was an extensive list, some added without Colette's approval.

1. He's hot AF.
2. He's a stranger, so you never have to see him again after he pops that cherry.
3. Ocean eyes.
4. ~~*Good kisser*~~ ~~*Great kisser*~~ *Fucking fantastic brain melting kisser.*
5. He's not your boss.
6. You finally won't be a virgin anymore. (Hurrah!)
7. He's rich.
8. He knows famous people.
9. He's experienced, so you can let him take the lead.

11. Strong arms.
12. Cute ass.

Colette had said no such thing to Brooke, and though the point was technically correct—Tristan's ass was pretty cute—she didn't know how it fit into the pro column exactly. Something firm to grab onto, she supposed, and her chest flushed at the thought. She pulled the blanket up around her chin and finished scanning the rest of the list.

13. Can probably get us into cool parties.
14. He's definitely not going to be a stage 5 clinger.
15. Good sex + no strings = perfect fuck buddy

At the bottom of the paper, Brooke scrawled: *Really, Coco, you've got nothing to lose here except your virginity. And you don't want that anymore anyway, right?*

Colette let her mind wander back to the boardwalk, to when Tristan swept her to safety from the out-of-control speed skater. She could still feel the rough stucco pressing against her arms, the thrust of his hips into hers, his hand grabbing her face, his mouth finding hers, the way they fit, how she hadn't wanted him to stop. She was getting turned on just thinking about it. The damn butterflies in her stomach were as big as cranes now and while she could blame part of that on the wine, she knew most of it was because of Tristan.

Brooke was right. If Tristan Walker could make her lose her mind over a simple kiss, imagine what he could do to her behind closed doors.

But of course, there were cons. There were always cons.

The pros filled up the entire front side of the paper. Colette flipped it over to write on the back.

Cons of Fucking Tristan Walker:

*1. He's been with other women who knew what they were doing.
2. You don't have any clue what you're doing.
3. STDs???*

Colette scratched this one out the second after she wrote it down. They'd obviously use condoms.

*3. ~~STDs???~~ You'll have to shave your legs.
4. You won't be a virgin anymore.*

She stared at the last thing she'd written. It was a repeat of what Brooke wrote on the pros' side, but it belonged in both columns.

Colette didn't want to be a virgin anymore, but she'd also been one for so long that she wasn't sure who she would be on the other side of this. Would she morph into some kind of horny sex goddess like Mallory and Brooke? Or would she pop her cherry and then go another fifteen years without seeing another dick?

She did her best to not let her virginity define her. It was not, in fact, her entire personality, but it was a significant portion of it. And even though she had never said it out loud to anyone, not even Brooke, she was scared, terrified really, of letting go of this part of herself that had been with her for so long. Would she like the person she became? An even more terrifying thought flitted through her mind: What if she had sex and absolutely nothing changed?

She stuffed the pros and cons list back inside her purse and took out her phone.

Four months ago, when she was bored and frustrated and surfing the internet, asking Google stupid questions like "can cobwebs grow inside a woman's vagina?" and "how old is the oldest living virgin?", she stumbled across a private group who called themselves the First Timers. Out of curiosity, or because she'd had one too many Kentucky mules, she asked to join the group. She had to answer a few questions first. It was one of the weirdest applications she'd filled out in her life.

Are you over 18? Yes.

Do you believe that if people have sex before marriage, they're going to hell? Oh, fuck no. Hell is Puritan patriarchal bullshit.

Do you want to lose it? I've been trying… And failing.

When it comes to your first time, what are you most afraid of?

She'd hesitated over that last question before finally typing in her honest answer: *I'm afraid of losing control.*

The admins approved her request within minutes.

She lurked for weeks, scrolling through old posts and trying to figure out who exactly made up this group of First Timers. Mostly, they seemed like supportive and kind people with one thing in common: they were all older virgins who didn't want to be virgins anymore. One member liked to use the term Bad Virgins to describe the people who joined the group.

Every so often, a red flag popped up. One time, a new member asked an established member if he could pay her $1,000 to swipe her V-card. Within the hour, he'd been kicked out of the group. It was that, plus the continuously supportive comments that flooded in whenever someone posted about something they were struggling with, that finally convinced Colette to stop lurking and start taking part.

She pulled up the group chat now and scrolled through the new posts.

BoyNextDoor, whose avatar was a black guitar, had just posted about a bad Tinder date.

She grabbed my junk under the table. I jumped so hard I spilled wine all over her dress. The dry-cleaning bill was over $100. FML.

The comments were already pouring in, ranging from sympathetic to hilarious. One member asked, *Yes, okay, that sucks. But how was the food?* Colette started to type something in the comments, but a text popped up on her screen, distracting her.

Tristan: Lunch again tomorrow?

She hesitated, trying to decide if responding right away would make her seem too eager. Though in a scenario like this—where Colette was trying to play sex kitten, who knew exactly where she wanted him to put that dirty tongue of his—was eager bad or good? Her fingers hovered over the phone. Sex kitten? Did that mean she was going for it? She was actually going to say yes to fucking Tristan Walker? Only if he wanted to fuck her back.

Her fingers fumbled over the screen.

Cunt.

She erased her mistake and tried again.

Clit.

Damn it. Fat fingers. Nervous fingers. She took another sip of wine and typed slower.

Colette: Can't. Sorry. I'm in court all day.
Tristan: Hot. Free for dinner?
Colette: Sure. But I'm picking the place this time.
Tristan: I can't wait to see what you choose. I'm sure it'll be an adventure.
Colette: How do you feel about Medieval Times?

He didn't text back for a few minutes, and she was certain she'd blown her chances with him. What kind of nerd suggested Medieval Times, even in jest? She laughed at her stupid pun to keep herself from screaming in frustration as she stared at her phone, waiting for him to text back. Minutes passed. Great. Fastest rejection of her entire life. She hadn't even taken off any of her clothes this time.

Her phone vibrated, making her jump. She held her breath as she read his text.

Tristan: Honestly, I think it's a tourist trap, but I'm happy to be your knight in shining armor for the evening.

Before she even finished reading this text, another popped up on the screen.

Tristan: I can't promise I'll protect your honor tho.

INNUENDO BY CANDLELIGHT

Colette

Colette read Tristan's text so many times over the next twenty-four hours that at some point the words stopped making sense.

Her honor? Did he know she was a virgin? How had he found out? Who had told him? Had he somehow stumbled into the First Timers chat? That seemed unlikely, and anyway, she wasn't using her real name and her avatar was a cartoon version of Elle Woods and Bruiser from the movie *Legally Blonde*. A little on the nose, sure, but there were thousands of women lawyers in the greater Los Angeles area. Some of them were probably even virgins too. There was absolutely no way he could have discovered her real identity from the group chat alone. So they must have a mutual friend in common. Or he was psychic.

Brooke's text popped onto her phone ten minutes before the judge reappeared.

Brooke: Stop freaking out. He's referencing medieval times. You know how maidens are definitely always virgins, and the

knights are definitely always showing up to save the day and slay those pesky sex dragons?
Colette: What the hell is a sex dragon?
Brooke: Fuck if I know, but you're getting me one for Christmas.
Brooke: BTW why didn't you tell me your kink was Robin Hood?
Colette: More like Heath Ledger circa 2001.
Brooke: Fuck yes. King. I would have let that man put his jousting stick anywhere he wanted. Be still my beating heart. RIP.

Colette snorted a laugh and her client, an uptight woman with her hair in a chignon and one too many diamond bracelets glittering on her wrist, glared at her. The judge's chambers opened, and a gray-haired, Black woman with a serious expression and billowing robes settled onto her bench. She slammed her gavel once, calling the court to order.

Colette tucked her phone inside her briefcase. Dreamy actors and sex dragons would have to wait.

During their half hour lunch break, somewhere between scarfing a sandwich from the deli across the street and organizing her paperwork for the afternoon portion of the trial, Colette texted Tristan the address to Gardenia's, which was across the street from the courthouse.

It was no Medieval Times, but at least they'd be able to have a halfway decent conversation without having to shout the whole time, and the air wouldn't reek of horse shit.

In the end, she was glad she picked some place close because, thanks to an embittered ex-husband and a judge who seemed to really enjoy sorting people's dirty laundry, the case ran long. By the time Colette finally left the courthouse, she was already ten minutes late and didn't have any time to change out of her court attire—a black pantsuit with a rose-colored blouse underneath and sensible, low-heeled slingbacks.

In her car in the parking lot of the restaurant, she discarded her jacket, then unbuttoned the top three buttons of her blouse, allowing the silky fabric to splay open, revealing the lacy edge of her bra. She shook her hair out of its barrette. It was a tangled mess, but maybe her date would be too busy looking at her cleavage to notice. Her date. She almost laughed. Sex date was more accurate since this relationship wasn't going any further than a one-night stand. If it even got that far. She applied a layer of lip gloss without looking in a mirror, fluffed her hair one last time, and walked into Gardenia's.

Through the crowded restaurant, Colette spotted Tristan at a cozy table for two in the back corner, where he scrolled through his phone while he waited for her. She told the hostess her party was already here and wove her way to the table.

Tristan rose from his chair when he saw her approaching. His eyes flicked up and down the length of her appreciatively, lingering on her breasts for several seconds before moving back to her face. He looked good, too, in a pair of dark jeans and a heather gray sweater that fit him perfectly. His hair was pushed back from his face, but a piece of it kept slipping loose and falling over his temple.

He smiled and stepped forward to give her a quick hug. She breathed in the salt breeze scent of him, reminding herself to relax. They were here to have dinner and drinks. This was a date, and she'd been on plenty of dates before. There was no way she could mess this part up. She didn't have to think about the sex part until later. She didn't have to think about it at all tonight if she didn't want to. *You're in control*, she reminded herself, and sat down in the chair he'd pulled out for her.

"As I'm sure you've noticed, this is not Medieval Times." She smiled. "But I can promise you the food is better."

"Honestly, I'm a little disappointed." He stayed standing beside her chair.

"Oh?" She lifted the napkin off the table, shook it, and spread it across her lap.

He leaned over and pressed his mouth close to her ear. The scruff of his five o'clock shadow tickled her skin as he whispered, "I was really looking forward to pillaging your castle."

Goosebumps rose over her entire body. She was glad for the dim lighting so he wouldn't see her burning red cheeks or the mottled flush of embarrassment spreading across her chest. His fingers brushed the length of her arm as he moved away from her and returned to his seat.

"So." He picked up a menu like nothing had happened. "What's good here?"

Colette grabbed the other menu and used it to shield her face until she could get her emotions back under control. Pillage her castle? Sweet Jesus, she was in trouble. Whatever pretense she might have had earlier about this being nothing more than a casual date flew out the window along with her composure the second Tristan's lips drew close to her ear. His breath, warm and inviting, had unraveled her before the sexual innuendo ever slipped from his mouth.

She was having sex tonight.

With the man sitting across from her.

Fuck it.

This was happening. She was going to fuck Tristan Walker. She'd decided. Her body, at least, seemed on board, with every nerve ending tingling and heat warming between her legs, turning her into a puddle with the slightest touch. And if she kept repeating it to herself, maybe her mind would get on board too.

I'm going to fuck Tristan Walker tonight. He's going to pillage my castle.

But first: scallops.

"I think the crab cakes are pretty good too," she said, lowering the menu and offering him her best come-hither smile. "See? I eat interesting things sometimes."

"I bet you do." He folded his hands under his chin and eyed her like she was the appetizer.

Colette cleared her throat and picked up a thicker menu. "Should we order wine?"

"I already did."

The server appeared as if by magic with a bottle of red Colette knew was expensive because she'd had clients order it for her after successful settlements.

Tristan tasted the wine and nodded his approval. The server filled their glasses and left the bottle on the table. "I'll give you two a few more minutes to decide," he said, and left them alone again.

"So, did you help anyone step onto a new path with confidence today?" Tristan twisted his wine glass.

He didn't seem to be making fun of her. She shifted in her chair and reached for her glass.

"Actually," she said. "Today I just helped a bitter, rich woman exact revenge on her cheating ex. She spent over half a million fighting the settlement and walked away with a set of Corning Ware you can buy at Goodwill for five bucks and a classic Mustang that doesn't even run."

"Ouch." Tristan winced.

"Yes, but seeing the expression on her ex's face when the judge ordered him to hand over the title of his precious baby was worth it to her, I guess."

Tristan slumped back in his chair. He frowned at his wine, twirling the stem so the burgundy liquid sloshed inside the glass. The divorce conversation clearly made him uncomfortable, probably because he was thinking about his parents' impending break-up. But even without the personal connection, the fastest way to kill a date was to talk about bitter divorces and broken hearts.

Colette changed the subject before Tristan spent the rest of the night sulking. "What about you? Save any damsels from rowdy roller skaters today?"

That seemed to be enough to shake him from his funk. He lifted his eyes to her again, a sly smile tugging on the corners of his mouth. "Not yet, but the night's still young."

"So if you weren't out playing Superman, what did you do today?"

"I went climbing with some friends."

"Like rock climbing?"

He nodded.

She sipped her wine and studied him.

"What's that face?" he asked.

"What face?"

"The one you're making with your nose all scrunched like something stinks. I know the wine's delicious, so it must be the rock climbing. You don't like rock climbing?" He arched his eyebrows in a challenge.

"I've never tried it."

"Well, see? How can you decide if you like something or not until you actually do it?"

"I'm not sure I agree with that philosophy."

"Then tell me." He reached across the table and took her hand. "How do you decide what to like?"

Under the table, his knees touched hers. If she tried shifting away, he found her again, keeping this point of connection between them constant.

She took another sip of wine, stalling for an answer. "Well, I suppose I just look at whatever it is and try to decide if I'd like it or not based on past experiences and research."

"Research?" He ran his thumb over her knuckles. "What kind

of research?"

"I don't know. I read books. Or watch documentaries. Listen to other people's first-hand experiences."

He was looking at her like she was growing a second head out of her shoulders.

"What? Is there something wrong with that?" She tried to pull her hand away, but he gripped it tight.

"It's not wrong," he said. "It's just a very safe way to live."

"I like safe."

"I'm not safe, but you like me."

"I'm actually still in the research phase," she said, surprised at the subtle flirtation in her voice and the way she leaned closer to him, exposing more cleavage.

"Is there anything I can do to move the process along?" Under the table, his hand slid over her knee. Above the table, his eyes dipped to the soft rise of her breasts.

"I suppose letting me talk to a few of your ex-girlfriends is out of the question?"

He laughed, a loud, bold sound that caused a few heads to turn. But he didn't pay them any attention. He was completely fixed on her. His hand slid higher up her thigh. Heat flared between her legs, spreading to her center, giving her a preview of where tonight could be headed if she let Tristan take the lead.

His thumb brushed the crease of her thigh.

"God, I wish you were wearing a skirt," he said in a rough voice.

She exhaled a soft pant and bit her lip, regretting her choice to wear the more sensible pantsuit for her day in court. If that judge hadn't wasted so much time, Colette could have changed into a slinky dress, and Tristan's thumb could be playing with the seam of her underwear, feeling her wetness, making her wetter with his skin on hers. Who even was she right now? This was so not like her. But something about Tristan made her want to throw all caution to the wind. Forget safe. She wanted to know what it felt like to have Tristan thrusting dangerously inside her.

She imagined them sweeping the place settings off the table and going at it like horny baboons right there in the restaurant in front of all these fancy-dressed people. Tristan seemed to read her mind because, with his thumb still caressing her inner thigh, he leaned his head close to hers and said, "Hey. Do you want to get out of here?"

He must have misread her hesitation, thinking she was going to turn him down, because he quickly followed up with, "You can say no. I won't get mad. It's just, it's kind of loud in here, and I can't stop thinking about taking off these very silky but very frustrating pants."

He blushed when he said it, which was so damn cute Colette almost climbed over the table to get to him.

Instead, she frowned at the menu. "We haven't eaten."

Not that she was hungry, not for food anyway.

"We can order takeout," he suggested.

She nodded and removed the napkin from her lap, dropping it onto the table. "Let's go."

Tristan flashed her an eager grin and reached for his wallet to pay for the wine.

This was happening. Tristan had invited her back to his place, and she'd said yes, and when they got there, all she had to do was relax and enjoy herself. All she had to do was say yes. Yes, yes, yes. She imagined herself throwing her head back and pounding the table as Tristan fucked her senseless. She could do it. She would do it. She reached for her phone in her purse to text Brooke about the details. Well, not all the details, just the important ones. Like where she was going and who she was going with and oh, by the way, when you see me tomorrow, I won't be a virgin anymore. She texted an eggplant and peach emoji and hit send.

A shadow fell across her screen. Colette looked up, expecting to see their server, but finding Scott Campbell looming over their table instead. His eyes darted between her and Tristan and the look on his face was one she'd seen a hundred times before on the faces of clients going through a nasty divorce.

Shame. Hurt. Hostility. Fury.

His jaw was set. His fingers clenched around a high ball of scotch.

"Well, now, don't the two of you look cozy?"

Colette could tell by the hard edge in his voice that he'd come over to their table with one thing on his mind: he was pissed and looking to start a fight.

YOU'RE INVITED

Colette

"Scott?" Colette scooted her chair back an inch. "What are you doing here?"

He swirled his drink slowly as a cruel smirk played over his face. "I heard you won in court today. This is where we come to celebrate, isn't it?"

His eyes skimmed over Tristan, who looked completely baffled and more than a little perturbed at the untimely interruption. Scott ignored him and turned to smile politely at the couple sitting at the next table over. He reached for an empty chair. "Anyone using this?"

He grabbed the chair before they answered and dragged it to a spot at the table beside Colette. "You two don't mind if I join you for dinner, right? I wasn't interrupting anything important?"

Tristan's mouth popped open, like he couldn't believe anyone could be as stupid as this guy butting in where he clearly wasn't wanted.

"Bro," Tristan said flatly. "We're on a date."

"A date? Wow." Scott pretended to be impressed. He swiveled his gaze to Colette. "You sure move on quickly, don't you?"

"Scott, please. Just leave us alone." She fumbled with the buttons of her blouse, suddenly self-conscious of her exposed cleavage.

"What are you talking about, dude?" Apparently, Tristan's surfer bro voice came out when he was upset. "Colette? What is this asshole talking about?"

"She didn't tell you, dude?" Scott mimicked Tristan's tone. "We were hot and heavy for a while. Just last week, actually. Yeah, that's right, bro. This chick really knows how to string a guy along. Isn't that right, hot stuff?"

He reached under the table and squeezed her knee.

Colette flinched away from him, knocking her elbow against the table with the sudden motion and tipping over the bottle of wine. Tristan caught the bottle before any wine spilled and set it right again.

"Dude. You need to leave," Tristan said to Scott. "Now."

Scott laughed and lifted his hands in a pacifying motion. "Okay, okay. Don't get your panties in a twist. I'll go. I don't need this kind of drama anyway."

He rose from the table like he was about to leave, but at the last second, he turned, bent his mouth to Tristan's ear, and in a voice loud enough for Colette to hear said, "But I feel like I should warn you, this bitch is a cock tease. She'll toy with your balls, let you go down on her all damn day, but when it comes to getting some for yourself, you better set your expectations real low. She's a virgin. A dry cunt virgin. So yeah, sorry *dude*, but the only thing you'll be banging tonight is your own hand."

Tristan leaped to his feet, rocking the table. A water glass toppled. He grabbed Scott's shirt collar and shoved him back. "What the fuck did you just say to me? Are you fucking kidding me with this shit, you prick? You talk this way in front of a lady? I should call the fucking cops."

The whole restaurant had gone dead silent. Everyone stared at the two men grappling in the corner. Scott's mouth twisted into a bemused snarl. Spit flew from Tristan's lips. Red flushed up his neck, spreading into his cheeks. He cocked one arm, his hand turning to a fist.

Colette watched, horrified, unable to move. Her ears were ringing. Her eyes had gone tunnel-vision. She knew she should leap to her feet and stop the two men from fighting. Or try to. She should say something, but her mouth refused to open. Her legs refused to work. Scott's voice echoed in her head: *dry cunt virgin, cock tease.*

He'd only pretended to lower his voice when talking to Tristan. The entire restaurant had heard him say these terrible things about her.

"Get off me." Scott shoved Tristan back. "I was just trying to do you a favor. Jesus, relax. I'm going."

With a final smug glance in her direction, Scott stalked away from them.

Colette buried her face in her hands. She wanted to crawl under the table and disappear. Everyone in this bar knew she was a virgin now. Everyone, including Tristan.

He touched her elbow. "Colette? Are you okay? Who was that guy? And what the hell is his problem? Fucking asshole. Just ignore him. Hey, don't cry. Guys like him don't deserve your tears."

But her eyes were dry. It was the breathing part she was having trouble with. That and she couldn't stand the feeling of everyone staring at her, their eyes pricking at the surface of her skin. She bolted up from her chair, knocking Tristan out of the way, grabbed her purse, and fled the restaurant.

She was halfway to her car when Tristan caught up with her.

"Colette! Wait!" He grabbed her arm and pulled her to a stop. "Why are you running away? What the hell was that guy talking about in there? Do we need to call the police?"

She shook her head and kept walking toward her car. "No, it's nothing. Just ignore him."

"Is he your ex or something? Please, Colette, talk to me." He stayed close to her side, matching her pace. "Don't let that jerk-off ruin a perfectly good night."

A laugh blasted from her mouth. "Is that what this is? A perfectly good night?"

"I thought so." He sounded hurt. "I mean, that's definitely the direction we were headed in until that weirdo crashed the party."

He grabbed her hand, not pulling her to a stop this time, but threading his fingers through hers as they walked. "So your crazy ex-boyfriend wanted to stir up trouble. So what? Forget him. He's clearly missing half of his brain. We were leaving anyway, remember?"

He drew her close, nuzzling her hair. She pushed him away because she needed space to breathe.

When they reached her car, she focused all her attention on trying to find her keys inside her purse. Why did she have such a big bag? What could she possibly need to carry around to justify a bag of this size? For Christ's sake, she wasn't Mary Fucking Poppins—practically perfect in every way, who was absolutely getting fucked by that hot chimney sweep.

"Crap!" Colette shouted when her hand scraped through her purse for the fifth time and came up with nothing. "Where are my keys?"

A jingling sound drew her attention.

"These keys?" Tristan rattled them in the air near her face. "You dropped them when you were hauling ass out of the restaurant."

"Thank you." She snatched them from his hands, turned to unlock the car, then turned back around to squint at him. "Why are you still here?"

"What do you mean? We're going back to my place, remember?"

"That's still happening?" She shook her head. "Even after what you heard in there?"

A look of amusement darted across his face. "All I heard were the rantings of a raving lunatic. What I can't stop thinking about is the way you were looking at me across the table and the way your leg felt under my hand."

He stepped close to her and ran his hand up the inside of her thigh the same way he had when they were in the restaurant. His touch made her weak, took her breath away, but she closed her eyes and forced herself to resist him.

"I'm not like that," she said. "I'm not that girl in the restaurant, I mean. The one who flirts and bats her eyelashes and lets a man feel her up under the table."

He leaned closer. His thumb moving ever closer to her most sensitive center, and even though it was through her pants, she lit on fire for him and her whole body shuddered.

"I'm a virgin," she blurted, then immediately regretted it, but he already knew anyway. No thanks to Scott. "That raving lunatic wasn't wrong. I probably won't fuck you tonight. I mean, I was planning on it, but now everything's kind of ruined and I know I shouldn't care and we should just go back to your place and fuck because it's not that big of a deal but—"

She took a breath, and he kissed her. Slow and deep and lingering, but with no tongue. His hand was still on the inside of her thigh, but lower down now, at the midpoint between her knee and hip. He squeezed her leg gently. When he eventually broke away from her, they were both panting a little.

He pressed his forehead to hers. "You know I don't care that you're a virgin, right?"

"You don't?"

"No. I really don't. I used to be a virgin. Everyone did."

"Yeah, sure." She laughed. "You probably lost it when you

were like thirteen? Fourteen?"

He scoffed. "Excuse me, but I'll have you know I was nineteen when I first slept with a woman."

"Nineteen? Isn't that pretty old?"

"Look who's talking." But he said it with a gentle smile as he grazed his knuckles over her cheek.

Colette sighed. The fight-or-flight sensation she felt in the restaurant was draining out of her now. She wasn't in the mood to go home with Tristan anymore; she was sure that if she tried, this night would turn into an even bigger disaster than it already was. But she no longer wanted to crawl under the car to get away from him, and that felt like progress.

"Can I ask you something?" Tristan traced his finger down her arm.

She nodded.

"Is your virginity something guys give you shit about a lot?" That a man would be angry to discover the woman he was about to fuck was still a virgin seemed to baffle him.

"Well, it's not like I've told a lot of guys," she answered. "One or two. Well, three with Scott. But I'm not going up to random guys on the street and asking them if they want to fuck a virgin."

He laughed. "So, it's not a very scientific sample."

"No, but from my experience, at least the times that I've tried to have sex with a guy or it was going there or whatever, and I stopped it, they freaked out. The nice guys just ghost me. The jerks…" She waved her hand toward the restaurant. "Well, you saw what happened."

Their bodies were close enough she felt him tense.

"Piece of shit." He looked over his shoulder. "I ought to go back in there and break his nose."

"He's not worth it," she said.

He turned back around and smiled at her. "You're absolutely right. Why waste my time on him when I have you right here?"

He bent over her and placed small kisses along the curve of

her neck. When he reached her jaw, she grabbed his face and pressed her mouth to his. She prodded his lips open with her tongue, unable to figure out if it was his chivalrousness that turned her on, his desire to protect her honor, or that he'd followed her out of the restaurant, worried about her, when he could have just bailed. Either way, in this moment, she ached for him. She arched her hips so his hand was between her legs again. He moaned and rubbed his thumb slowly against her.

"For fuck's sake. These pants of yours are killing me," he murmured. "When can I tear them off you?"

His words were a cold bucket of ice water dumped over her head, a reminder of how buttoned up and uncertain she was. Her body clearly wanted Tristan. But her heart, her mind? They weren't as sure.

She pressed her hands to his chest and pushed him away. He didn't resist.

"I can't. Not here. Not like this. Not in the parking lot. Not tonight. Not after—I'm sorry—"

He placed a soft kiss on her lips. "You better not be apologizing to me."

"But you want to have sex with me?"

"Of course I do. You're hot as hell, Colette. And I think I'm even kind of starting to like you too."

"Words every woman waits her whole life to hear. 'I think I'm even kind of starting to like you.' Gee, thanks."

"You heard the first part, right?" He laughed. "Where I said you're hot as fuck?"

He brushed a ribbon of hair from her face and dropped a sweet kiss on the tip of her nose. Then he rocked away from her and settled his back against the side of the car so they were standing shoulder to shoulder.

After a few seconds of silence, he asked, "Are you one of those Christians or something? Waiting until you're married?"

"No, nothing like that. It's just — It's a long story."

"I look forward to hearing it." He rushed to add, "Whenever you're ready, of course. You don't have to tell me a damn thing right now. And you don't have to sleep with me either."

"I don't?"

"I mean, I'd love it if you do, but no. Not if you don't want to."

"I want to..." The words jammed in her throat, and she started over. "I think I want to. Maybe not tonight, but soon? Shit, I don't know what I want."

"You don't have to figure it out right now," he said, dipping his head toward her. "But you need to know one very important thing."

"Oh? And what's that?"

"If you decide to come home with me at some point, you should be damn sure it's what you want." His voice rolled slowly and sensuously over her skin. "Because once I get you in my bed and start showing you all the ways I can make you feel good, you're not going to want to leave."

Heat burned through her whole body. Her knees went weak, and she was glad for the car to hold her up.

"How about I make you a promise?" He planted gentle kisses on her skin again. One at the end of each sentence, like he was sealing the promise between them. "For as long as we're still having fun doing whatever it is we're doing, I won't pressure you. I won't ask. I won't beg. But I won't let you forget that I'm here. If you want me to be your first time, I'm all in for that. If you don't, if you just want to make out on the couch and get all hot and heavy with our clothes on, I'm cool with that too."

His thumb brushed the long curve of her neck, tracing over where his lips had been.

"For how long?" she whispered.

"What do you mean?"

"How long would you let me string you along like that?"

"I prefer to think of it as extended foreplay." His hand

dropped to her breast, cupping it and letting the thumb graze the nipple through her bra.

Her breath caught, and she angled her body toward his. He moved his hand to her waist, drawing her close.

She tilted her head so she could look him in the eyes. "What if I never want to have sex with you?"

"That would be a tragedy because you're so damn beautiful, and I bet you feel like heaven." He clutched her against his chest for a second as they stared into each other's eyes. Then he shrugged and, without letting go of her, said, "But I'd get over it. Contrary to what you may have heard, not every woman I meet in a club ends up in my bed."

"I don't want a boyfriend," she said, abruptly pulling away from him and shoving the keys in the car door. "So you don't have to worry about me getting all clingy and going fatal attraction on you if we end up sleeping together. That's not what this is. I don't want a relationship. I just want to get laid, and you seem to know what you're doing, so that's all this would be."

Before she could get the car door open, he stepped up behind her, grabbed her waist and pressed his whole body against hers, rocking his hips against her ass, burying his face in her hair. His voice was a low growl that sent a thrum of electricity through her.

"I'm happy to be your one-night stand, if that's what you want," he said. "This thing between us doesn't have to be anything but sex. Whatever you want. You just say the word, and I can be inside you before you even realize your pants are off. Or…" He spun her around. His hands stayed on her waist. In the faded half-light of the evening, his eyes glittered with desire. "Or we can take our sweet time."

Before she knew what was happening, his mouth was on hers, demanding, but not forceful. Urgent, but not frenzied. His tongue danced against hers, moving in ways she didn't know were possible, and her mind flooded with images of his tongue moving like that against other places on her body. She moaned and rocked against him. His hand slid up her ribcage and brushed the sides of her breast, and she shivered in delight. Maybe tonight would be the night she lost her virginity after all.

She was on the verge of changing her mind about going home with Tristan when he broke away from her and took a step back. He stared at her with a stupid grin on his face.

She stared right back at him. "Why are you looking at me like that?"

This was it. This was when he changed his mind about her and decided she wasn't worth the trouble.

"I was just thinking," he said, stuffing his hands in his pockets and rocking back on his heels. "If I'd known I wasn't going to get laid tonight, I would have worn more comfortable underwear."

Her mouth dropped open, then she laughed.

"Now you have to tell me what kind of underwear you're wearing," she said.

His smile turned sly. "Wouldn't you like to know? Goodnight, Virgin."

He blew her a kiss and started to walk away. He went only a few steps before stopping and turning around again. With his hand still stuffed in his pockets and the shadows playing over his face, he looked suddenly bashful.

"Hey," he called to her. "Are you busy this weekend?"

She took a step toward him, closing the distance. "Not really. Just planning to do some laundry and catch up on trashy reality television. Why?"

He looked up at the sky and then back down at her with what she would have sworn was a nervous glint in his eyes. He had the look of a man who was about to go out on a limb and was afraid of falling flat on his perfectly chiseled face.

"This is going to sound crazy," he said. "But just hear me out, okay?"

FIRST TIMERS CLUB

Chat Room

NotSoDirty30 (posted 8:15 PM): Need advice! A guy I barely know asked me to go with him to Joshua Tree this weekend. We've hung out twice. And while there's definitely some intense physical chemistry happening between us, and I think I want him to be my first time, I'm not 100% sure that's where this is going. I'm worried that if I go with him this weekend, I'll be sending the wrong signals. Help!

HappilyNeverAfter: Go! You should definitely go! Your first time could be in a tent under the stars! How romantic!

SexIsOveR-rated: Is this the same guy from your last post?

NotSoDirty30: No. Different guy. I'm not a glutton for punishment.

cherrybomb: Too bad. Being punished is hot. #glutton

SexIsOveR-rated: How the heck would you know anything about being punished? #gluttonforvirginity

cherrybomb: Ever heard of a little thing called porn? Haha. I also have a very excellent imagination.

NotSoDirty30: Unlike Asshole #1, Joshua Tree guy actually didn't treat me like a freak when he found out I was a virgin.

HappilyNeverAfter: And he didn't run?

NotSoDirty30: Nope. I think it actually might have turned him on.

cherrybomb: #virginsarehot

HappilyNeverAfter: Good for you! Sounds like you might have found your Prince Charming. I think you should definitely go. #sexunderthestars

cherrybomb: Yes! Go out and get dat ass!

Shakespeare-N-Love: I agree with @HappilyNeverAfter and @cherrybomb. You should go on the trip, see how this plays out. Besides, it's about damn time someone in this group got laid!

cherrybomb: Here's what you're going to do. You're going to drive out to the desert with this hottie and you're going to smoke some weed and do some mushrooms and drink some booze and look up at the stars and have some slutty, hot fun!

LoveConnection (admin): A reminder @cherrybomb that we don't slut shame in this group. This is your first warning. One more, and I will remove you from the group.

cherrybomb: I wasn't shaming. I was using it in an empowering sense. Like, Go on girl, get yours! We need to take that word back anyway and redefine it.

LoveConnection (admin): Perhaps, but this is not the forum. That word can be triggering.

cherrybomb: Fine. Go Sex Goddess go!

NotSoDirty30: So, I'm going?

SexIsOveR-rated: Might as well give him a chance.

HappilyNeverAfter: Definitely you're going.

Shakespeare-N-Love: Follow your heart and you will never be lost.

cherrybomb: What are you still hanging around here for? Don't you have some sexy lingerie that needs packing?

A SUITCASE FILLED WITH LINGERIE

Tristan

Tristan glanced at Colette who had one arm floating out the window of the Jeep Wrangler soft top he'd rented for the weekend. She looked beautiful in the golden light, with the sepia hills rolling behind her. Her chestnut hair, which was pulled back in a high ponytail, fluttered in the wind. With her owl-eye sunglasses and red silk scarf tied under her chin, she looked like a classic movie star, a woman who deserved to be worshiped and fawned over and taken care of. He had the sudden urge to pull the car over and bury himself inside her right there on the side of the highway with traffic zooming by and the radio blaring. He wanted to hear her scream his name.

He released a slow breath and returned his gaze to the road ahead. Maybe this trip had been a bad idea.

Ever since finding out Colette was a virgin, Tristan hadn't been able to stop thinking about it. About her. About peeling off her clothes and exploring the body underneath, taking his sweet time with her, opening her legs and her mind to the possibility of what sex could be if she relaxed and let herself have a good time.

It wasn't the virginity part that was turning him on so much. Okay, that was a lie. The virginity part was pretty hot, but more than that, it was Colette herself, that she'd chosen him, trusted him for some inexplicable reason to be her first time.

Don't get ahead of yourself, Triscuit. You haven't made her come yet.

The stupid voice in his head was right. She'd said yes to the trip, not to his dick. Not yet, but a lot could change in forty-eight hours away from the city, under a brilliant blanket of desert stars with coyotes howling love songs in the background.

Since when did you become such a sappy romantic?

He turned to look at her again and caught her staring. She blushed and her smile was shy. He reached across the seat and squeezed her knee. Her blush deepened as she turned to look out the window, but she let his hand stay and even covered it with hers, stroking his knuckles tenderly. Her relaxed mood was a stark contrast to an hour before when she'd showed up outside his apartment complex with two oversized suitcases and a large shoulder bag.

"You know we're only going for one night, right?" He'd stared pointedly at her bags. "And I definitely can't fit all of that on my bike."

The horrified expression on her face made it seem like he'd just asked her to climb into a den of hissing rattlesnakes.

He laughed. She crossed her arms over her chest, her initial terror turning to stubbornness. "I'm not setting foot anywhere near that death trap."

"Good thing I rented us a Jeep then." He tilted his head to the vehicle parked at the curb.

Air rushed from her lungs in relief, but as she eyed first the Jeep and then her luggage, the tiniest of frowns tugged on her mouth. "I might have over packed. I wasn't sure what I would need. I've never been to the desert before."

"You haven't lived in So Cal very long then, I take it?" He picked up one of her bags and tossed it into the back of the Jeep.

"I've lived here my whole life." She lifted in the other suitcase.

"And you've never been to the desert?" He stared at her in surprise.

She offered him a reluctant shrug. "No one's ever invited me before."

"You don't have to wait for an invitation to do something, you know." He stepped forward and slipped his arm around her waist. The oversized, sage-green shirt she wore like a dress felt as soft as it looked. "Sometimes you can just go and do something because you want to. Because it's fun."

"Going to the desert by yourself doesn't sound all that fun to me."

"That's because you've never been." His fingers toyed with the leopard-print belt around her waist. "Stick with me. I'll show you just how fun the desert can be."

"Hmmm, I bet you will." It didn't sound like she believed him.

He had the next forty-eight hours to change her mind about the desert. And maybe about her virginity, too. But he wasn't going to force that conversation. If she wanted him, he was here. And if she didn't want him? If nothing happened on this trip, if their kisses remained chaste and their hands stayed above the clothing? It surprised him to realize that he would be fine with that too. He just wanted to spend time with her, to discover what she loved and what she hated, to hear her talk about her hopes, her dreams, her disappointments, what made her mad, what made her cry, what made her laugh.

God, he was turning into a hopeless romantic, wasn't he?

They hadn't had sex. He hadn't even seen her with clothes off.

Even so, she was doing things to him, turning his insides all squishy and soft, making his head spin and his heart race. He found himself wanting to laugh for no reason, open his mouth and belt out a song. It had been so long since he'd felt anything other than numb.

Ever since his brother's funeral, Tristan had been moving through the world in a daze. He felt wrapped in thick fog and nothing and no one had been able to reach him. And now here was Colette, a ray of light piercing the haze, and he wanted more of that light, that heat, more of her. He knew he was treading into dangerous territory.

Colette made it perfectly clear she wasn't interested in a relationship with him, and honestly, he wasn't sure he wanted one with her either. A virgin might be good fun for a minute, but then what? What came after? He could imagine her regretting her choice and getting angry with him for pressuring her, even if he'd done no such thing. He could imagine her getting too attached, going fatal attraction even though she promised she wouldn't. He could imagine her being jealous if she ever found out the high number of women he slept with before her—he'd stopped counting after one hundred. One or both of them could end up with broken hearts.

But maybe they wouldn't. Maybe they could live happily ever after. Not that he'd ever believed in that fairy tale before, but maybe with Colette… Maybe.

Talking in the Jeep with the soft top rolled down proved impossible. Whenever one of them tried to say something, the wind snatched the words right out of their mouths. Colette smiled and gave a *what-can-you-do* shrug. Tristan smiled back, turned the radio up, grabbed her hand, and drove a little faster.

When they finally pulled up to an elegant stucco ranch house surrounded by cactus and artfully placed rocks, Tristan was kicking himself for not renting a quiet sedan for the weekend. After two hours of traffic noise and the screech of classic rock, he was ready to take Colette into a quiet room somewhere and—he let his mind drift to the dirty things he wanted to do with her, the dirty things he wanted to whisper into her ear.

Two other cars were already parked out front. Techno house music blasted through the open windows of the desert cottage. Voices shouted and laughed over the music. Colette gave the house a nervous look. She twisted her hands in her lap, fussing with the strap of her shoulder bag.

"Don't worry," Tristan said, hopping out of the Jeep. "They're chill. They love everyone."

"No, it's not that." Colette unbuckled her seatbelt. "It's just, it's a house. I thought we'd be, I don't know, camping or something."

"Are you disappointed? Because I'm sure one of these assholes brought a tent, and we could set it up in the yard."

"Not disappointed." She grinned. "Relieved."

She dragged one of her suitcases from the back of the Jeep, but Tristan grabbed her waist and pulled her toward the house instead. "Beers first, unpack second."

Tristan followed the voices to the back of the house where the kitchen opened onto an inviting outdoor patio space complete with grill, tiki bar, luxurious patio furnishings, and a hot tub. Four people sipped beers together in a loose circle on the patio. Three were guys Tristan had known for most of his life, his brother's friends who had let him tag along with them on their many outdoor adventures. They were good dudes, but he hadn't seen much of them over the past year. They reminded him too much of his brother.

The fourth person was a blonde he didn't recognize, a woman with sea glass green eyes and a compact climber's body. She had her arm threaded through Carlos's, her head leaning casually against his shoulder, her long, thick hair cascading down his large biceps.

When Tristan appeared in the doorway with Colette at his side, the group stopped talking and turned to stare. For the briefest second, Tristan thought about turning right back around and dragging Colette out of there. They could get a private hotel somewhere else, maybe go to San Diego instead, anywhere but this desert with these people, this place that had taken so much from him. But then Nick Stathos, the one who had set up this entire trip, stepped forward and scooped him into a bear hug.

"My brother," Nick whispered against Tristan's neck. "You made it. It's so good to see you."

The other two guys, Carlos and Jacob, joined in the hug, squashing Tristan in the center, slapping his back, going on about how it had been too long and if they didn't know any better, they would have thought he was trying to avoid them.

"But who's this?" Nick broke away from the group hug and approached Colette, who lingered in the doorway, looking uncertain.

"This is Colette," Tristan introduced them. "She's a friend from—" But he couldn't think of a good way to explain how they knew each other. This is my mother's divorce attorney, well not anymore, but for like a half second she was, and oh I didn't tell you? Yeah, mom and dad are getting divorced. Surprise.

"We met at a taco truck." Colette swept in to save the day. "He was trying to convince me that chapulines are the next big thing."

"She refused to try them," Tristan interjected.

Carlos and Jacob both groaned in disappointment and then started arguing about whether chapulines were better covered in hot sauce or chocolate.

"Anyway," Tristan said to Nick. "She's never been to the desert, so I invited her to come. I hope that's okay?"

Nick was a good-looking guy, a blend of Japanese on his

mother's side and Greek on his father's. When he smiled, dimples formed in his cheeks, disarming anyone who came within a foot of him, including Colette, who didn't seem to mind one bit when he scooped her into a warm embrace. He didn't hold on to her nearly as long as he'd held on to Tristan, but when he pulled away again, she was blushing and breathless. Tristan felt a flicker of jealousy, which was stupid because Colette wasn't his girlfriend, and even if she was, Nick was gay.

He tamped down his inappropriate caveman instincts and took the beer Carlos offered him.

"The more the merrier." Nick grinned at Tristan. "As long as you're okay sharing a bed because we only have the three bedrooms and we're already doubled up in the other rooms."

Carlos offered Colette a beer, and she took it, tipping it to her mouth like she hadn't had anything to drink in days.

Tristan's mouth dried up, and he couldn't figure out how to answer Nick. He needed to be cool and casual, but his thoughts were tripping a mile a minute thinking about Colette under the sheets with him, her long bare legs brushing against his. He tipped his beer to his mouth and gulped greedily, buying himself time.

When Tristan invited Colette on this trip, he hadn't been thinking this far ahead. The invitation was spontaneous, blurted out in a moment of excitement. Sleeping arrangements never even crossed his mind. Maybe they'd be setting up that tent after all. He glanced at Colette, worried she'd be upset that he hadn't told her they might share a bed, but she was far from mad. She smiled warmly at Nick and then, surprise of all surprises, winked at him. "We can double up, no problem."

The ease with which she said it sent Tristan's pulse jumping.

But he echoed Colette's cool tone as he said, "Yeah, no big deal."

Nick clapped his hands once, then pulled a fresh beer from the cooler and cracked it open. "Great. Your room's the last one on the left. Finish your beers and let's pack up and head out. We're wasting daylight."

Colette leaned close to Tristan and whispered, "Where are we going?"

"Rock climbing." He clinked his beer bottle against hers and walked out to the driveway to get their bags.

She trotted after him, protesting. "I don't know how to rock climb."

"First time for everything," he said with a sly wink.

He loved how he made her cheeks flush like that, how the bridge of her nose wrinkled like she was holding back a sneeze.

"Don't worry." He pulled two of her bags out of the back of the Jeep, set them in the dirt, and then reached for his backpack. "I won't make you do anything you don't want to do."

Their fingers brushed as he handed her a suitcase. Their eyes met and a spark of desire flickered in her gaze. He stepped closer, but before he could put his arm around her waist and draw her in for a kiss, the front door opened and Carlos and the blonde stumbled out laughing, playfully shoving each other.

"Hey, Triscuit!" Carlos called out to him, using the nickname Troy had given him as a kid.

Tristan cringed at the way it sounded coming out of Carlos's mouth—grating and unnatural. But he didn't tell him to knock it off. Tristan wasn't the only one who'd lost someone important, and this weekend was all about remembering the good times. Keep it light, keep it easy, don't get in a fight with his brother's best friend over something as small as a stupid nickname.

"Sara's got an extra harness for your girl," Carlos said, smacking the blonde's ass before shuffling her off to one of the other cars to get the gear.

Tristan waved his thanks and reached to pick up a bag.

"You can't seriously be expecting me to climb," Colette said as they carried their luggage into the house.

"Like I said before, I'm not going to make you do anything

you don't want to do," Tristan replied, struggling to get the bags down the narrow hallway to the last bedroom.

"The more you say it, the less I believe you." She brushed past him as she entered the room, rubbing her body against his in a way that felt deliberate.

He followed her inside, where they stared a moment at the queen-sized bed that took up most of the space. The tension in the air between them grew thick, nearly unbearable. Finally, Tristan couldn't take it anymore. He leaned over and pushed on the mattress, breaking the uncomfortable silence. "It's a solid mattress. Not too springy. That's good. I hate springy. But listen, if this is too much for you, we can sleep head to toe. Or above the sheets, below the sheets. I can even sleep on the floor."

"Or we can just both sleep in the bed like normal people and see what happens," she said, and the suggestion in her voice made his knees weak.

He slid behind her, wrapping his arms around her waist before dipping his head and kissing the curve of her neck. Colette hummed and leaned back against him. Her voice vibrated to his core and he couldn't help himself—he wanted her, and he wanted her to want him. His hand ran up the side of her thigh, pushing the hem of her shirt dress higher.

"You can't wear this climbing," he murmured against her skin.

"No?"

"Not unless you want everyone staring at your ass." He cupped his hand around one of her cheeks. She was plump, smooth, and he felt himself stirring, hardening quickly. If he wasn't careful, he was going to be a goner for her before they even started.

"What should I wear?" she asked in a breathy voice. She hadn't moved away from his hand, but she seemed to tense up.

He couldn't tell if she was excited or nervous, probably both, but he had promised they didn't have to do anything she didn't want to do. So, with some reluctance, he moved his hand off her ass and back to her waist.

"Jeans are fine," he said, still pressing delicate kisses to her neck.

"I think I have some jeans in here somewhere." She moved away from him to grab the suitcase. She fumbled with the zipper for a second, then flipped open the top. Her eyes popped wide with panic as she tried to close it again. "Oops, wrong one."

But she hadn't been fast enough and Tristan had seen the lacy lingerie neatly folded inside. He reached over her and opened the suitcase again, pulling out a slinky black number that was more ribbon than cloth.

He rubbed the silk between his fingers and smiled at her. "You definitely can't climb wearing this."

"Don't laugh." She grabbed the lingerie from his hands and stuffed it back into the suitcase.

"I'm not laughing." He grabbed her around the waist and pulled her against him. "It's hot that you brought lingerie. I can't wait to take it off you."

She bit her lip and peered at him shyly. She seemed to be waiting for him to do something or say something, but he couldn't figure out what. She inhaled deeply, and then he felt her hand pressed against his erection. The one he'd gotten touching her ass. The one that had gotten even stiffer at the sight of the lingerie. She was touching him through his jeans, just holding him, not even stroking, but it was enough to make his breath catch in his chest.

"Is this for me?" Her voice was husky and low, taunting him.

He grabbed her head and pulled her to his mouth. She rubbed him through his jeans. He moaned against her. The thought darted through his mind that the bedroom door was hanging open, and she definitely would not be into that. Taking her with him, not wanting to pull his mouth from hers even for a second, he twirled them toward the door, reaching with one hand to push it closed. She squealed as he danced her around the room, and his cock responded to the sound, pushing hard against his pants.

As the door was swinging shut, Nick's voice called down the hallway, "Okay, lovebirds, let's go! The rocks are calling our names! Canoodling can wait until after dark!"

With a gasp, Colette broke away from Tristan. She stared at him with a stunned look on her face. He grinned at her and gestured to a suitcase. "Jeans, t-shirt, a jacket in case it gets cold. You have five minutes, then we're leaving without you."

He left her alone in the room to change. After he closed the door, he leaned against it to catch his breath. When his boner stopped throbbing and the blood had returned to his brain, he walked outside to where everyone else was loading up the cars with climbing gear. Nick gave him a knowing glance and a thumbs up. Tristan ignored him.

He squinted at the washed-out blue sky stretching above them where the sun hung hot and heavy. There was entirely too much daylight left, a full afternoon and evening to get through before he would have Colette all to himself again.

"Make yourself useful, bud." Nick shoved a coil of rope into Tristan's arms. "Put this in the truck. I've gotta grab the cooler."

Tristan had been so distracted thinking about sharing a bed with Colette, he'd forgotten the real reason they were all in Joshua Tree this weekend. As he stared at the rope in his hands, his mouth went dry and fear spiked in his chest.

"Everything okay?" Colette's voice cut through his panic.

She stood in front of him, studying his face carefully. She had changed into a faded pair of jeans with holes in the knees and a white t-shirt that dipped low in the front, revealing the peekaboo edge of a hot pink sports bra.

He forced a smile. "More than okay. I was just thinking about that little black number waiting for me back in the room."

Her eyes narrowed. He could see her thinking about whether

to call him on his bullshit, and it unnerved him that she had seen so quickly through his lie. He was grateful when she decided not to push. She played along instead, arching her eyebrows and quirking her lips into a flirtatious smile, dragging one finger down the length of his bare arm. "If you're lucky, maybe you'll get to see the red one too."

A horn blared. Someone shouted for them to hurry. Tristan hesitated. Colette grabbed his hand and, ready or not, pulled him to the car. They piled in with the rest of the group and gear, and then they were speeding toward the rocks.

Halfway there, Colette leaned close to Tristan and whispered in his ear. "You don't have to do anything you don't want to do."

THE HARDER THEY FALL

Tristan

Colette was halfway up the granite wall when Tristan's panic returned with a vengeance. His vision narrowed. Every muscle in his body tensed. Sweat slicked over his palms and no matter how hard he gripped the rope, he could feel it slipping through his fingers. It was going to happen again. She was going to fall and it would be all his fault. He was going to kill her the same way he'd killed his brother. He'd made a terrible mistake bringing her here.

Through the hum of panic, he heard someone calling his name.

"Tristan? You all right, buddy?" Nick stood right next to him, but sounded a million miles away. "You got this?"

Tristan blinked sweat from his eyes and focused on Colette, who was still on belay, testing her feet on a thin ledge, reaching for a jug to pull herself up a little higher. She was fine. She was safe. He was holding tight to the rope. The knots were secured. He'd double-checked, triple-checked them. He swallowed down his fear. The worst thing he could do right now was panic. She needed him to be alert. She needed him to catch her should her grip fail or her toe slip.

"I'm good," Tristan said to Nick.

"She's doing great up there." Nick stayed close to Tristan's elbow and the rope keeping Colette safe. "For a noob."

Tristan nodded, but his throat was too dry to speak.

They picked a beginner route to warm up on, a blob of a rock with plenty of jutting hand and foot holds. As easy as climbing a ladder. Colette agreed to try a route only after everyone else had taken a turn and after Tristan promised nothing could go wrong, not with him on the other end of the rope. *Don't worry, I'll catch you if you fall. But you won't fall.*

Of course she could fall. Why had he promised her she wouldn't? People fall. It was a universal truth Tristan knew all too well.

"It's good to see you happy again, man," Nick said, keeping his head tilted back, watching Colette's progress. "Troy would be proud of you."

Hearing his brother's name pushed Tristan over the edge. The tentative hold he had on reality snapped and swept him backwards in time to a year ago when he and Troy and Troy's friends came out to this same park to climb. They were on a different rock formation that day, but it wasn't far from the one they climbed today. Not even a half mile from where he stood. If he turned his head just right, he could see the looming silhouette, the sheer granite face taunting him. His brother's voice echoed off the rocks. "Falling!"

Not his brother's voice, Colette's.

Colette was shouting, "Falling!"

She hadn't fallen yet, but her legs trembled, and Tristan could see her fingers slipping from the rough handholds. All she had to do was lean back into her harness, and he could lower her to the ground. Before he could call up instructions, she let out a yelp and let go.

The rope ran a few inches through Tristan's hands before he stopped it with the brake. Momentum combined with slack sent Colette swinging into the rock face. Instead of kicking her feet out to slow her fall, she curled into a terrified ball and slammed full force into the rock. For a second, she hung slumped in the harness, not moving, not talking, not doing anything, and Tristan's chest constricted with panic.

No, no, no. This couldn't be happening. Not again. Damn it! How had he let Nick talk him into coming along on this stupid trip?!

He swallowed the stone in his throat and called up to her, "Colette? You all right up there?"

Still curled into a ball, she swung on the end of the rope, her hands clinging tightly to the line running into her harness. That was a good sign. If she'd been knocked out, she would have gone limp like a rag doll.

"Colette?" He tried again.

Her voice was mouse-like and trembling. "Can I come down now, please?"

A large section of her hair had fallen loose and blocked her face. So he couldn't tell if she was crying or laughing or plotting to kill him once her feet were back on flat ground.

He instructed her to hold on to the rope, sink her weight into the harness, and hold her feet out in front of her so she could push off the rock if she needed to.

"I'm going to lower you all the way down. Trust me, okay? I've got you." The words tasted sour.

When her feet touched earth, she let out a shout of relief and began scrambling to unhook herself from the harness. Tristan moved to help her. "Are you okay? Are you hurt?"

Blood streamed from a cut above her right eye. He winced at the sight.

"Is it that bad?" She lifted her hand to inspect the cut.

"Don't touch it." He worked at the knot in her harness to uncouple her from the rope.

Nick strode over to them. He let out a low whistle. "Damn, I knew we should have stopped to rent helmets. Stupid Carlos was supposed to bring them."

He shot an angry look over his shoulder to where Carlos, Jacob, and Sara were working on a more challenging route on a different section of the rock. Then he turned back to Colette and leaned close, lifting her hair from her face so he could see the cut better.

"It doesn't look too bad. It's just bleeding like a motherfucker." Nick smiled at her and thumbed over his shoulder. "There's a first aid kit in the car. Don't worry, we'll get you cleaned up and have you back up on this rock in no time."

"Absolutely not," Tristan said.

Colette held onto his shoulder as she stepped out of the harness.

"Don't be a baby, Triss," Nick said. "She got a slight bump on the head. It's no big deal. We've all climbed with worse."

"I'm not putting her back up there." Tristan unbuckled his own harness, stepped out of it, and kicked it to one side. "We're both done."

"We haven't climbed Cyclops Rock yet." Nick frowned.

Tristan's mouth went dry. He stared at his brother's best friend. Maybe he hadn't heard him right. "Cyclops? You want to go up Cyclops?"

When Nick nodded, Tristan lost his cool. He threw his hands in the air and shook his head. "There's no way in hell. No way, man."

"That's the whole reason we came out here, remember?" Nick dug in, stubborn as he always was. "To honor Troy. Cyclops Rock at sunset. You agreed to do this with us."

"I agreed to come on this trip," Tristan said. "I agreed to

climb, but you never said anything about Cyclops. Why the hell would I get back on that death trap?"

"You know what Troy always said. Falling is inevitable, but unless you're dead, you damn well better get back on your feet, dust yourself off, and clip in." Nick slapped Tristan's shoulder, and Tristan nearly buckled under the force of it. The irony of Nick's words, how he seemed completely oblivious to Tristan's grief, didn't help.

"It'll be good for you," Nick said. "It'll be good for all of us. It's been a year, Triss. We can't let that rock intimidate us anymore, right?"

"Un-fucking-believable." Tristan shrugged away from Nick. "Do what you want, but I'm telling you, the two of us are done. We'll be in the car."

He grabbed Colette's hand and led her toward the main path that would eventually take them to the parking lot.

Colette didn't say a word to Tristan until she was sitting in the back of Nick's SUV, and he was hovering over her with a cotton swab and hydrogen peroxide.

As he dabbed at the skin around the cut, she asked, "Who's Troy?"

It was a simple question, and one with a simple answer, but he said, "No one you need to worry about," and turned away from her, pretending to need a fresh cotton ball. Really, he just needed a minute to swallow back his tears. He was trying to impress her, not make her feel sorry for him.

He poured more hydrogen peroxide onto a clean cotton ball, then moved her hair from her face so he could get to the cut. "Hold on to something. This is really going to sting."

LUCKY

Colette

I almost died a virgin. The entire ride back to the rental house, these words kept playing on repeat in Colette's mind. When she'd felt herself slipping off that rock, when the rope pulled taut and sent her swinging into the granite slab, her life flashed before her eyes. And what a short, sad, lonely life it was.

She touched the bandage Tristan had so carefully placed over the cut on her forehead. He'd been so gentle with her, so kind, checking to make sure she wasn't in too much pain. He kept apologizing too. *I should have never invited you. I should have never convinced you to try climbing. It's not safe. You could have been killed.*

But she wasn't. That's what she kept thinking as she watched the sun dip below spiky Joshua trees, the sky a watercolor painting of orange and red and shadows. She had a pounding headache and a copper taste in her mouth, but she would live. She was never slipping her legs through another climbing harness or scrambling up the side of a cliff face, but she would live. She had taken a nasty fall and lived. Not everyone got so lucky.

Colette reached for Tristan's hand across the backseat of the SUV and squeezed it. He squeezed back. A tingle ran through her. Every touch, every breath, more exciting than it had ever been because today was the first day of the rest of her life. She had escaped death, and she knew exactly how she wanted to celebrate.

Back at the rental, Tristan's friends cracked open beers and fired up the grill. They clamored about their climbs, describing each move in excruciating detail, even though they'd all been there, watching from the front row. Colette couldn't tell if this was how they always acted, or if they were being extra obnoxious because Tristan had bailed on their original plan to climb Cyclops Rock. Nick was the loudest, trying to draw Tristan into the conversation even though Tristan was clearly not interested.

"You should have been there, Triss," he said as he chopped onions to sauté. "Jacob did this insane heel hook to get over the crux. He was a monster out there."

"And remember that dyno on Big Bertha?" Carlos let out a low whistle. "You want to talk about beast mode. That man does not quit."

The onions sizzled when they hit the hot pan.

Tristan drained his first beer and grabbed a second, but said nothing in response to Nick and Carlos's back and forth bragging. He'd been especially quiet since his fight with Nick back at the park, answering only when someone addressed him directly. And sometimes not even then.

Like when he was cleaning up Colette's cut, and she asked him about Troy. He'd shut her down even though she could clearly see that Troy had been someone important to him, someone he cared about deeply.

She stayed close to him as he moped around the house. Anger radiated from his tense shoulders, and the more he drank, the more tense he got, until Colette worried he was going to erupt. She sank down onto the couch beside him, letting their knees bump.

"You okay?" She kept her voice low so no one else would hear. "Do you want to drive back to LA tonight?"

Some of the tension in his shoulders disappeared as he studied her. He wasn't completely relaxed, but he looked less like a volcano now, which was progress. He held up his almost empty beer—his fifth, if Colette was counting right—and shook it. "Probably not a good idea."

"No." She relaxed against the couch, tucking her feet underneath her. "Probably not."

"But I wouldn't mind putting space between myself and these assholes." He jerked his thumb toward the kitchen where Nick, Carlos, Jacob, and Sara were doing tequila shots.

"Well, we have our own room, remember?" She raised her eyebrows suggestively. "With a lock on the door and everything. We could just tell your friends we're tired and want to go to bed early."

When the words left her mouth, she waited for the hiccup of panic, but it never came.

"Are you suggesting what I think you're suggesting?"

She crawled her hand across the cushion and placed it on Tristan's knee.

"What about your head?" He peered at the bandage.

"It's fine. It doesn't even hurt anymore." She brushed her fingers over the cotton tape. "Not much anyway. You'll just have to be gentle with me."

His eyes bugged out a little, and then a smile warmed his features. She liked it when he smiled at her like that.

"You have no idea how gentle I can be." He swept her hair back from her neck and placed feather-light kisses on her skin.

"Not too gentle, though," she said a little breathlessly. She kept expecting the sharp knife of panic to slice through her desire and send her running in the other direction, but so far, the only direction she wanted to run was straight into Tristan's arms.

He rose, took her by the hand, and led her toward the bedroom.

"Start dinner without us," Tristan shouted to his friends in the kitchen.

They whistled and hollered in response. Colette's cheeks burned. The old Colette would have changed her mind. But this new version of herself, the one who had skimmed so close to death, didn't care that she was about to lose her virginity in a house full of strangers. She didn't care if they heard her moan. She didn't care if they teased her later. She didn't care about anything except Tristan.

She wanted him, and she wanted him now.

When the door shut, Tristan pushed her against it and kissed her hard. She fumbled her hands behind her back until she found the lock and clicked it into place.

Tristan's mouth was hungry for hers, his tongue parting her teeth. He kissed her like a dying man, as if this was the last time he was ever going to kiss anyone ever again. It was intense. A little too intense. Colette laid her hands on his chest and whispered against his seeking lips, "Gently, remember?"

"I'm sorry," he said in a breathless rush. "You're right. You're hurt, and I'm going too fast, and I… It's just… You're beautiful." His eyes skimmed over her curves, drinking her in. "So beautiful. And you smell like summer. And life is too fucking short."

He pushed off the door and turned away from her, but not before she saw the look in his eyes switch from passion to pain.

"Do you want to talk about it?" She trailed after him.

"About what?" He sank onto the bed, stretched out on his back, and tucked his hands behind his head.

"I don't know. Whatever's got you looking sad like that." She sat on the bed near him.

"Come here." He grabbed her and pulled her down so she

was curled up against his side, resting her head in the crook of his shoulder. "The only thing I want to talk about is about how I can get you out of these clothes."

His hand slipped down to her waist and tugged on the loop of her jeans.

Colette's heart hammered so hard she was certain he could hear it echoing in her chest. Now that they were here, alone in bed, she wasn't sure what to do. It was a different feeling than the times she'd tried to have sex before and couldn't. She wanted Tristan. Her whole body hummed for him. She just didn't know what to do about it—like the actual logistics of sex. Did she take off her clothes first or wait for him to rip them off her? Did she have to say the words, "fuck me, please," or would he just know? The other times she'd come close, like with Scott, it was the men who'd been the aggressors, who'd tugged at her clothes, placed their hands wherever they wanted, moving so quickly she'd barely had time to catch her breath or really decide what she wanted. That had been part of the problem, she realized. Those men had never given her brain a chance to get used to the idea, but with Tristan, things would be different.

In the parking lot outside Gardenia's, he'd said he wouldn't pressure her and he wouldn't beg. If they were going to do this, Colette would need to be the one to make the first move.

Shadows filled the room. Neither one of them had bothered to turn on a light, but there was enough light coming in through the window from the patio, which was ablaze with twinkle lights and a crackling campfire, that they could see the shape of one another in the dark.

Colette traced the outline of Tristan's jaw with the tip of her finger. He turned to look at her, pulling her a little closer against his body.

She nibbled his earlobe and whispered, "Let's play a game."

NEVER HAVE I EVER

Colette

Their faces were so close that Tristan was little more than a blur, but Colette could tell he was smiling by the way his eyes crinkled. He said, "Yeah, okay, I'm in."

"Never have I ever gone skinny dipping," she said.

He laughed, and her head bounced. "How is this going to work if we don't have any booze?"

"Instead of drinking, you have to take off a piece of clothing."

He shifted his arm out from under her, rolling so that instead of her head resting on his shoulder, they were lying face to face, with their noses almost touching. A smile played on his lips. "All right, but I'm not sure this is going to be an even playing field."

"We'll see." She plucked at the sweater he was wearing. "Never have I ever gone skinny dipping."

He stared at her and didn't move.

"Wait," she said, unable to keep the surprise from her voice. "Seriously? You've never been skinny dipping?"

"I may have a tiny case of ichthyophobia."

"I hope it's not contagious."

"It's an irrational fear of fish," he explained. "Don't laugh. I'm not afraid of them all the time, just when I'm in open water. I'm terrified they're going to swim into whatever small orifice they find."

She didn't laugh, though his explanation was baffling. "You surf."

"I wear a wetsuit most of the time and, if not, then swim trunks or boxers. Always swim trunks or boxers. Never naked. My turn." He traced his finger up her leg, sending a jolt of pleasure through her. "Never have I ever kissed a man."

"Hmmm, that feels like cheating," she said, but she peeled off the lemon-chiffon cardigan she'd been wearing to fend off the chilly desert night air.

Then it was her turn again. "Never have I ever had sex."

"Look who's cheating now." He laughed as he peeled the gray cashmere sweater over his head.

They were both in t-shirts and jeans now, but Colette had an advantage in that she was wearing a bra and underwear, and Tristan was just wearing underwear. Unless he wasn't. Her skin flushed at the thought and at the way Tristan was tracing his finger down the length of her arm, tickling her elbow.

"Never have I ever worn a suit to work," he said.

"Does it count as a suit if you're not wearing a tie?"

"Yes." He tugged on the collar of her shirt. "Take it off."

She sat up, stripped the shirt over her head, and laid back down beside Tristan, who let out a satisfied moan as his eyes traced over her bare shoulders and down to her cleavage, which looked especially ample lying in this position. He bit his lip and ran his finger between her breasts. Her breath hitched in her chest and her body ached for more, melting under his touch.

"This is nice," he murmured and then began kissing her collar bones, moving his way down to her cleavage.

She reveled in his attention for a few seconds, then pushed

him playfully away. "We haven't finished the game yet."

"Sorry, I got distracted." He nipped at her skin.

She swatted his ass. He grabbed her wrist and held it on his firm buttocks, staring her down, daring her to move. "I think it's your turn."

"Never have I ever eaten grasshoppers," she said.

He released her hand, and the shirt came over his head. She ran her hands over his hard pecs and toned stomach, enjoying his athletic build and the fine layer of reddish-blond hair growing on his chest.

Tristan interrupted her exploration of his body by brushing her hair back from her forehead to inspect the bandage. "Never have I ever cracked my head open on a rock."

She pretended to be offended, but moved her hands to her pants and unzipped them slowly. Tristan bit his lip as she shimmied out of the jeans and tossed them to one side. His breath came quicker now, excitement coloring his cheeks.

"These are cute." He touched the tiny red bow on the top of her polka-dot underwear.

They weren't the sexiest pair she brought on the trip, but they were cute, at least. And they matched her red lace bra. Tristan couldn't take his eyes off her. He ran his finger over the seam of her underwear. The growing bulge in his jeans was visible even in the dim light.

With her mind fixed on getting him out of those pants and hopefully winning the game, she said, "Never have I ever seen a guy naked."

"Come on." He groaned. "This isn't fair."

She laughed and twirled her finger at his pants. "Take them off."

He was in the middle of unbuttoning his pants when she remembered.

"Oh!" She covered her mouth with her hand.

"Oh, what?"

"I have seen a guy naked," she said. "Once in college. I walked in on him banging my roommate."

He'd gotten as far as popping the button open, but stopped as he reached for the zipper. "You saw his full dick?"

She flushed thinking about it, but nodded.

"How did it make you feel?" he asked.

"What?" She giggled uncomfortably.

"After you saw his dick." He drew his zipper down slowly. "How did you feel after? Was your heart racing? Were your cheeks flushed? Was your stomach in knots? Was your pussy wet?"

His pants were off before she even realized what was happening. He wore black boxer briefs, and his cock was bulging the fabric, hard and big enough to be intimidating. She stared at it and then flicked her eyes back up to his.

"My pussy's wet right now." The words slipped out of her mouth before she even knew what she was saying.

She clapped her hand over her mouth, stifling her horror, but Tristan smiled at her and then made a sound like he approved of her dirty mouth. He grabbed for her, but then stopped with his hand on her hip and pulled back. "Is this okay?"

"Yes," she said in a breathless whisper.

He pressed his mouth to hers, and his fingers pushed aside the thin slip of her underwear. He unfolded her and pushed his finger deep inside. She gasped with pleasure, but he tensed and asked again, "Are you sure this is okay?"

"I'll tell you," she said in breathless gasps as he moved his thumb over her clit. "If I want you to stop, I'll tell you."

She kissed him, moaning into his mouth as he fondled her. He was bringing her close to the edge, teasing, sliding one finger in and out of her warm center, then moving two inside her. It felt good, but she wanted more.

She slid her hand over his cock, and a shiver ran through her. "Tristan, I'm nervous."

He stopped fingering her and slid his hand to her waist. He nuzzled his face against her neck. "Honestly? I am too. I know I shouldn't admit that to you."

She laughed softly. "Actually, that helps me feel less nervous."

"We don't have to do anything you don't want to do."

They laid a moment, pressed together, skin on skin. Then she rolled onto her back, putting space between them. He rolled onto his back too. They stared at the ceiling.

"We still haven't finished the game." His fingers inched to find hers in the middle of the bed.

"I think it's your turn," she said.

"Never have I ever watched a woman masturbate."

She snorted a laugh. "I don't believe that."

"It's true." He sounded hurt, but when she turned her head to look at him, he was smiling. "The women I've been with were all happy to have me bring them over the brink."

"Well, I've never watched a woman masturbate before either," she said, shoving down an unexpected flash of jealousy. "So I guess both of us are keeping our clothes on."

"You've never masturbated?" he asked.

"No, I've definitely masturbated. I masturbate all the time. Okay, not all the time, but I know what I'm doing. I know how to get myself off."

"So, you *have* watched a woman masturbate." The smile on his face was wicked.

She opened her mouth to argue with him, then realized that technically, he was right.

"Sneaky little—"

He hooked one finger around her panties and tugged on them. "Off."

But instead of her underwear, she reached around and unhooked her bra. Tristan moaned his approval, cupped his hand around one of her breasts, and rubbed his thumb over her nipple. "These are even better than I imagined."

She tried not to focus on the part where he'd admitted to imagining her naked, or the part where she was almost naked now and feeling horny as fuck but also nervous about where this was headed, if she was even going to be good at any of it. She changed the subject to distract herself. "I still can't believe you've never watched a woman masturbate."

"You want to help me change that?" He scooted closer to her on the bed.

"What do you mean?"

When his eyes lifted to her face, she saw his desire burning and ready. There was something slightly dangerous about it, but she couldn't turn away. She didn't want to.

"Show me." His voice was rough and low. "Show me how you get yourself off. So I'll know how you like it when it's my turn."

She laughed softly. "I don't think—"

He took her hand and moved it to her crotch. "Make yourself feel good, Colette. I want to watch you come."

She slipped her fingers beneath her underwear. Fuck, she was so wet. Wetter than she'd ever been in her life. She slicked her fingers through the wetness and moved in slow circles, pleasure sparking through her whole body. But she stopped after a few seconds, slid her hand back to her stomach, and shook her head.

"I can't. Not with you watching. I feel ridiculous."

"I won't watch then." He rolled his back to her. "I'll just listen."

But she still couldn't. It felt too intimate. Even more intimate than sex. She was stiff, awkward, and felt herself turning inward, the way she did whenever she felt herself losing control of a situation.

Picking up on her silence, Tristan rolled over. He took one look at her and then got up from the bed. This was it, Colette thought. This was when he turned into a different man, an angry man who called her a cock tease, then stormed out of the room, leaving her humiliated and ashamed. She heard a zipping sound, then rustling as Tristan looked through suitcases. When he returned to the bed, he held two silk scarves she'd brought along for a reason she couldn't remember now.

"Close your eyes." His touch was light as he wrapped one of the scarves around her head, covering her eyes. He was careful to avoid the bandage.

"I'm putting one on too," he said. "Peek if you want."

She pulled down one side of the scarf and watched as Tristan knotted his own blindfold at the back of his head.

"Now, lie down," he said.

She repositioned her blindfold and lay back on the bed. The mattress shifted as Tristan lay down beside her. Her eyes were open, but all she could see were the edges of light, the entire room blacked out by the simple scarf wrapped around her head.

"Just breathe," Tristan said. "Breathe and let your body tell you what you want."

She felt him moving beside her and realized he was touching himself.

"Let go of the idea of what it's supposed to be," he said, panting a little. "And just enjoy the feeling of it. It's supposed to feel good. Let yourself feel good."

She slid her hand down to her underwear, slipping them off this time. She lay completely naked, blindfolded, next to a man who was stroking himself slowly. She'd never been naked next to anyone like this before. She never expected to be naked and unable to see. There was a vulnerability to it, but also thrilling freedom. She slipped her fingers inside herself and gasped with pleasure. Tristan moaned beside her and murmured her name. Her desire for him flared. She rubbed her clit, slowly at first, then faster, then slow again. She lifted her hips, writhing, moaning.

Beside her, Tristan let out a low growl. "You're so fucking hot. I can smell your pussy. I can feel it on my fingers still. Can you still feel me inside you?"

Her clit throbbed, ached. "Yes," she gasped. "Yes, I can feel you." She imagined it, his fingers first, then she imagined what his cock might feel like inside her, pulsing, filling her, taking her over the edge. She moaned his name, and her whole body came alive with the electricity of her orgasm. It was a wave that pulled her under and sucked the breath from her lungs, and when she finished, she was panting. Tristan groaned, shuddered, and went still. He was panting too.

"How was that? Nice, right?" He rolled over and his hand slid across her bare stomach, dipping lower toward her pelvis until he settled on her sharp hip bones. "It sounded like you were enjoying yourself."

"Mmmm." She had no words. When she'd touched herself before, it had always felt nice, of course it had, but it had never felt like that, like she was being cracked open, her whole body ablaze with want.

"You want to do it again?" Tristan asked, his hand working its way lower, finding the soft crease between her thigh and dragging his thumb over her. She shuddered in delight.

His cock was still hard and pressed against her leg now.

"I can't come more than once." Colette was efficient about everything in her life, including her own pleasure.

"Want to bet?" His fingers spread her open. He massaged her clit, and she felt herself rising to him, wanting more.

She reached to take off the blindfold, but he stopped her. "Leave it on."

He moved his way down her body, starting at her neck, kissing his way to her breasts where he spent a few minutes sucking and teasing her nipples. She arched her back as his lips moved down to her stomach, then traced the arc of her hips, then her inner thigh. She was almost on the edge of a second orgasm by the time his mouth finally reached her clit, and when he flicked his tongue, lapping her up, enjoying her, it took only a few seconds before she blossomed again. She let out a quiet whimper and melted into him.

He climbed back up to the head of the bed and removed her blindfold.

The world was so much brighter than she remembered. Tristan was smiling down at her, his head and shoulders haloed in a soft, gold light coming from underneath the closed door. She flicked her eyes down the length of him, bracing herself for the vision of his hard cock and hoping it didn't send her running from the room. But at some point, he'd put his underwear back on. He saw her looking and smirked at her. "Guess you've still only seen one man naked."

She swatted his arm and reached for her underwear, which were wadded up at the bottom of the bed. She pulled them on, then reached for her bra, stopped, and turned to look at him. "That was nice."

Heat rose to her cheeks as the words left her mouth, and she ducked her head, hoping he wouldn't see.

He took her chin between his fingers, lifted her face to his, and planted a sweet kiss on her lips. "It was nice. Now, let's go find something to eat. I'm starving."

He rolled off the bed. She grabbed his hand. "What about you?"

"What about me?"

"I mean, we didn't have sex. You didn't get—"

He interrupted her with a kiss. When he pulled away, he said, "I got everything I needed, Colette."

The way he said her name and the way he looked at her made her want to stay in this room with the door locked for the rest of the night, and maybe for the rest of her life. Her feelings hadn't come out of the blue, but they still surprised her.

Tristan Walker was supposed to be her first time, and that was it. A one-night affair—one time and one time only. She wasn't supposed to fall in love.

KARAOKE VIRGIN

Tristan

Colette stared wild-eyed at Tristan and shook her head. "Absolutely not. I'm not doing that. Never in a million years."

Tristan nudged the song binder across the table and tapped his finger on the cover. "You can pick a duet. Come on. There must be at least one song in here you're dying to belt at the top of your lungs."

She folded her arms across her chest and continued shaking her head. "I don't sing karaoke."

"That's what you said about coming twice in one night, too, and look how well that turned out for you." He spoke the words in a low whisper against her neck and delighted in the effect he had on her.

She shivered and her cheeks flushed pink, and it took all his willpower not to pick her up and carry her off into some dark corner and have his way with her. He could make her come again for a third time in one night, but he wasn't sure he could hold himself back any longer if he did, and he was having second thoughts about being Colette's first time.

Not because he didn't want her. Hell, he wanted Colette Harris so badly it physically hurt. No, he was having second thoughts because he was starting to think that when this was all over—whatever this even was—she was going to end up breaking his heart. Or he would break hers. She made it clear in the parking lot of that stupid, hipster wine bar that she didn't want a relationship, which was all fine and good if he could figure out how to keep his feelings out of it.

Seeing her dangle up on that rock this afternoon, then helping her down and dabbing the blood from her forehead, then masturbating together—which was one of the hottest and most vulnerable things he'd ever done in bed—all of this was making him realize he was starting to care about her. And not just pretending to care because he wanted to stick his cock in her pussy, but really care. As in, he was worried more about making her happy and comfortable than he was about whether he got laid this weekend.

Sex had never been complicated before, but he had a feeling sex with Colette was going to wreck him. And he wasn't sure he was ready to be wrecked.

"It's just one little song," he pleaded with her as he flipped the binder pages. "Four minutes and it's over."

He couldn't stop himself from making it sound dirty, couldn't stop his hand from wandering high up her thigh under the table. She'd changed into a tight, leather miniskirt that was making him regret suggesting they go out tonight. They should be alone in a room with the door locked, doing things to one another that were illegal in some countries.

The bar and karaoke were both supposed to be serving as a distraction. But the smoky lighting and background murmur of laughter, the way her hair fell in thick waves down her back, the bump of music through the speakers, and the sour tang of margaritas they were sipping, spun him into a sex haze. All he could think about was when he would get her alone again, when he would have a chance to strip her down to bare skin so he could taste her, fill her, fuck her.

Get a grip, Triscuit. It's not magic. It's just pussy.

"No one's even paying attention," he said to Colette, gesturing around the bar where nearly everyone was deep in their own conversations, ignoring the microphone.

Colette sighed and shoved the binder back to him. "Fine. I'll do it. Just this once. Because I think you're cute. But we're going up there together, and you're picking the song."

"You think I'm cute?" He feigned shyness.

"Don't push it." She flashed him a smile that set his heart racing.

Five minutes later, a young woman finished her song to a smattering of unenthusiastic applause, and the karaoke DJ called Tristan and Colette to the stage. Tristan handed her a microphone and winked. "Are you ready for this?"

She shook her head.

The song started with synthesized bass and kick drum beat, followed by a glittering, 80's pop sound that got a few whoops and claps from people in the audience. Upon hearing the first notes, Colette threw her head back and laughed.

"Oh good, you know this one," Tristan said.

"A little on the nose, don't you think?" She grinned.

Tristan lifted the microphone to his mouth as the words to Madonna's *Like A Virgin* appeared on the screen. He sang in falsetto, channeling his inner rock goddess. When the chorus started, Colette lifted the microphone and belted out the words. She didn't even need to look at the screen. She stared at him as she sang, her eyes dancing, her hips swaying to the bouncing beat. They might as well have been the only people in the bar for how much they paid attention to their audience. Tristan got so caught up in Colette's slightly off-key rendition, it surprised him when the song finally ended and patrons started hooting and hollering. He grabbed Colette's hand and dipped her into a bow.

As they stumbled off stage, she bumped against him. "Thank you. That was fun."

Back at their table, she sipped a fresh margarita, still laughing and shaking her head. "What a rush. I've never done anything like that before."

"Honestly?" He tucked her hair behind her ear. "Neither have I."

Her mouth dropped open in exaggerated surprise. "Are you kidding me? This was your first time singing karaoke?"

"Karaoke virgins, right here, folks." He raised his voice and pressed his thumb into his chest.

Colette swatted at him, embarrassed, but no one was paying them any attention. He scooted his stool closer to hers and slipped his arm around her waist. "I believe that trying new things is good for the body and soul."

"Is that right?" She cuddled against him, whispering kisses along his neck.

Just as she was getting started, she jerked back and pointed to a pool table on the other side of the bar. "Isn't that Nick?"

Tristan twisted his head to look. Nick, Jacob, Carlos, and Sara leaned on pool sticks in a loose circle around an antique-looking felt table. A pitcher of beer and four glasses sat on a nearby table. Sara laughed, tossed her blonde hair over her shoulder, and bent over the table to take a shot.

"Should we go over and say hi?" Colette asked.

The foursome had been noticeably absent from the rental house when Colette and Tristan snuck out of their bedroom two hours ago. Tristan hadn't let on, but he was glad there had been no one around to see the radiant flush Colette's double orgasms had left on her face. Glad, too, that they wouldn't have to deal with Nick's teasing.

Tristan was still pissed at them for thinking he would have

any interest in climbing Cyclops Rock this weekend of all weekends. They'd gone without him despite his protests. Even after Colette's fall, knowing she was hurt and bleeding, and knowing how upset Tristan was, Nick had taken the gear to the cursed rock, racked the carabiners and cams, waited until the sun touched the horizon, and then shimmied up to the top with the others where they poured out a beer in Troy's honor. And Nick had made sure Tristan heard all about it on the drive back to the rental house, unnecessarily describing the play-by-play, every crimp and jug and slippery toe hold. *You should have been there, man*, he kept saying. *It would have meant a lot to him.*

Dead men don't have feelings about anything, Tristan had wanted to say, but he'd kept his mouth shut.

"They look like they've got a pretty intense game going," Tristan said to Colette. "Let's leave them be. In fact, let's pay our tab and go find something else to do that neither of us has ever done before."

She raised her eyebrows with interest. "Do you have something specific in mind?"

"I might." He slid off the stool, grabbed her hand, and led her to the bar, where he paid for the drinks.

Outside, the night air was crisp and bright, the sky a blanket of stars. Rock formations and crooked Joshua trees rose from the flat desert landscape, looking like hunched giants and dancing men in the dark. Every time a car passed on Route 62, bright headlights washed over them. Tristan and Colette walked aimlessly for a few minutes, peering into the dimly lit windows of closed shops, talking about nothing important. Since leaving the bar, he hadn't let go of her hand.

They passed another bar with loud music and clamoring voices coming from inside. Colette seemed drawn to it, but Tristan pulled her away.

"What are we looking for, exactly?" she asked.

"I'll know it when I see it."

A few minutes later, they turned a corner and there it was, shining like a beacon in the night. The Vacancy sign flickered neon red. A smattering of cars were parked in the lot. A few of the windows were lit up from the inside, but most were dark.

"A motel," Colette said flatly.

"Not just any motel." He steered her away from the main office, around one row of rooms to a concrete pool surrounded by a low stone wall. "A motel with a pool."

Technically, since it was after 10:00 PM, the pool was closed for the night, but that wasn't going to stop Tristan. The main office was out of sight, and the few motel rooms that looked over the deck were dark. Tristan hopped over the wall easily and then turned back, reaching out his arms to help Colette swing over.

"I don't have my swimsuit," she whispered.

The pool glowed an inviting turquoise. Tristan walked to the edge and dabbled his fingers, testing the water temperature. He straightened, pulled off his shirt, and tossed it onto a nearby deck chair. Then he kicked off his shoes, unzipped his pants, and pulled them down to his ankles, along with his underwear. He didn't wait for Colette's reaction. Buck naked, he shoved his clothes out of the way, walked to the deep end, and dove in.

SKINNY DIPPING

Tristan

The water was colder than Tristan expected it to be. When he'd tested it with his fingers before diving in, it had felt warm enough, but with his whole body submerged, the temperature felt several degrees cooler. The water rushing across his bare skin was cold enough to shock the breath from him for a half second, but not so cold that he was worried about hypothermia. It was warmer than the Pacific Ocean, which he'd swum in many times, with the bonus that there were no fish.

He stayed underwater for half the length of the pool with his arms extended in front of him like an arrow, his legs kicking like a dolphin. When he reached the center, he surfaced.

A splash sounded behind him, then tiny waves rippled over his limbs. He turned to see Colette skimming through the illuminated turquoise. She spread the water with her hands and frog-kicked toward him, her nose and eyes bobbing at the surface like a lurking alligator. Beneath the ripples, her skin flashed pale.

Tristan moved toward her, his hands feeling for her underwater and pulling her close. Like him, she was completely naked. She giggled as their limbs tangled.

"Are we going to get in trouble for this?" she whispered.

"I won't tell if you don't." He wrapped his hand around her head and pulled her in for a kiss.

The chlorine on her lips was tangy and sharp. She threaded her leg around his. He gripped her around the waist. The water made everything feel new and otherworldly. Weightless, limitless. Every time they brushed together beneath the water, a shock went through him. He had never felt so alive inside his body. He was hard, his dick pulsing, wanting her more than he'd ever wanted anyone. Her hand wrapped around his shaft, and he almost exploded. He held himself back, though, releasing a soft moan into her mouth that she breathed in and returned to him after he pushed his hand between her legs and fondled her pussy.

Her breasts bobbed weightless in the water, sliding against the surface of his skin. Her nipples were hard, and he wanted them in his mouth to suck and tease. He guided her through the water and pushed her up against the wall. He gripped her waist and angled her back so her breasts rose like twin icebergs on the water's surface. He flicked his tongue over one and then the other. Colette giggled softly. Her legs moved up and wrapped tightly around his waist. The heat of her pussy nearly sent him over the edge again.

Before they could go any further, a blinding security light snapped on. Colette squealed and ducked back under the surface of the water. Tristan, too, shrank himself into the turquoise blue. He pressed a finger to his lips, motioning her to be quiet, even as they both struggled not to laugh.

"Who's out there? You'd better not be swimming!"

Colette clamped her hand over her mouth, stifling the laughter she could no longer contain. Tristan threaded his fingers through hers and pulled her toward the metal steps hanging over the edge of the deep end. He let her go first, enjoying the view of her supple ass as she hoisted herself onto the deck.

He clambered after her. They laughed as they stumbled around, gathering their clothes. Trying to get dressed with wet skin proved difficult. Tristan stubbed his toe against a deck chair.

"Shit!" He hopped on one foot, pulling up one pant leg as the other flapped loose.

Colette was full-belly laughing now, her arms stuck in her shirt as she tried to force it down over her head.

It was at that moment a lanky man with red hair and a full beard came striding around the corner with a flashlight in one hand and broom in the other. He shook the broom over his head, wielding it like a weapon. "Get the hell out of here, you degenerates! Can't you read the sign? Pool's closed."

Tristan finally shoved his other leg into his pants and pulled them on. He shoved his feet quickly into his shoes, grabbed the rest of his clothes and ran after Colette, who had already hopped the stone wall and was fleeing into the night.

"Goddamn LA hipsters," the man shouted at their retreating backs.

Colette couldn't stop laughing. She danced in a circle around Tristan, her skin flushed, her eyes sparking. "Oh my God, I can't believe we did that! Do you think he called the police? Could we have gone to jail? Oh my God."

She let out a coyote howl and darted away from Tristan, then darted back. Slipping her arm through his, she rested her head on his shoulder. "What's next? Climb to the top of a mountain? Play chicken on the highway?"

She spun away from him, acting like she was going to step into the middle of the road. He pulled her back. "How about some food?"

"God, yes, I'm starving."

They hadn't eaten anything with their margaritas at the karaoke bar, and they hadn't eaten the burgers Nick had been cooking at the rental house. Now that he thought about it, Tristan couldn't remember when they'd eaten last. He liked Colette relaxed, but he didn't want her reckless.

He led her to a different bar, one without a karaoke machine, and grabbed a booth in the back, far from the crowds of young people mingling near the dart boards. They sat opposite one another. When their knees bumped under the table, she smiled at him and he smiled back.

"Ever had bison burgers?"

Her nose wrinkled, and she shook her head.

"Me neither," he said.

When the server got to their table, Tristan ordered two burgers with fries.

After the server was gone again, Colette plopped her elbows on the table and rested her chin in her hands. "Well, it's not chapulines, but I think it will still probably count as the most interesting thing I've eaten in my entire life."

He laughed and sipped his water, washing the chlorine taste out of his mouth.

"Hey." Colette's face had turned suddenly serious.

The stare she gave him across the table was intense, and his stomach knotted, worried that he'd upset her.

"I just want you to know that I'm having a lot of fun tonight," she said. "Really. I haven't let myself just relax and have a good time since… Well… I guess since I was a kid? Maybe not even then." There was sadness in her laughter.

Feeling more relaxed now that he knew she wasn't mad, Tristan reached across the table and took her hand. "I'm having fun too."

"I guess I had to grow up pretty early," she said, running her thumb over his knuckles. "I was the oldest and somebody had to look out for my sister and brother. My mom was distracted with all her shit, and I never really had a chance to break the rules or let my hair down because I was too busy making sure we had money for food and gas, making sure we all got to school on time, that kind of thing." She flicked at her still-damp tresses and laughed again, the sound a little brighter than before. "I'm sorry. Wow. Am I bringing down the mood or what?"

"You're not," he said. "I like hearing about your past. I like getting to know you better. In fact, I want to know everything there is to know about you."

The second her eyes locked onto his, he realized he'd gone too far. She was going to think he was desperate, and maybe a liar who would say anything to get her in the sack.

"Everything you want to tell me," he backtracked.

Her eyes narrowed with suspicion. Then she relaxed and flopped back against the booth, sliding her hand out from under his.

"I think it's your turn," she said. "Tell me something about your past. A deep, dark secret. Your childhood wound. What made Tristan Walker the man he is today?"

Tristan laughed to disguise his discomfort.

He should have kept his mouth shut. He should have kept things light and fun and breezy. He hadn't lied to her—he wanted to know everything about her and what made her tick, what she loved and what she hated, her hopes and dreams and how she liked her coffee. But it seemed like a delicate line to tread. The more he knew about her, the harder it would be when whatever they were doing together ended.

Just as Colette was showing impatience with Tristan's silence, the server appeared with their burgers. Seeming to forget all about their conversation, she scooped up the burger and took a huge bite, spurting ketchup out the side of her mouth.

Her eyes rolled back in her head, and she moaned. "God, this is so good. I wish someone had told me years ago how good bison burgers were. Life changing. That's what this burger is."

She flashed Tristan a devilish grin and took another bite.

TELL IT TO THE STARS

Tristan

It wasn't a mountain exactly, but it was far enough away from the highway to avoid the sweeping headlights and engine sounds, and high enough to feel like if you reached, you could brush your fingers through the stars. Tristan sat next to Colette on a dry patch of scrub grass and watched her do just that. She lifted her hand over her head and spread her fingers, scraping them through the air. She tilted her head back, and her hair fell loose over her shoulders. Her mouth hung open, her eyes wide with wonder.

"I didn't know the sky could be so beautiful," she whispered even though they were alone and it wouldn't have mattered if she'd shouted at the top of her lungs. No one would have heard.

Tristan watched her watch the stars. The light of other worlds reflected in her eyes.

She said, "It feels like we're the only two people alive in the world right now," and scooted close so their hips and shoulders touched.

The trail to get to this spot had been easy to find. Tristan had been up here a few times in years' past with his brother and remembered that it started in a neighborhood south of the main highway. Once they found the trailhead, the footpath was clear of scrub and easy to follow. Tristan used his cell phone flashlight to help keep them from tripping over something or getting lost. After about fifteen minutes of a leg-burning incline, they reached the flat summit. Far to the west, the San Bernardino Valley glowed a hazy orange. Closer in, the small towns of Joshua Tree, Twentynine Palms, and Yucca Valley glimmered brighter. Still, they were not bright enough to outshine the stars.

A shiver rolled through Colette's shoulders. Tristan wrapped his arm around her and drew her close so they could share body heat. They wouldn't be able to stay out here long without coats, but he wanted her to see how beautiful it was, if it was as beautiful as he remembered.

It absolutely was.

A shooting star zipped above them, blazing bright for a second before disappearing. Colette gasped with delight. Tristan didn't believe in signs, but if he did, that would have been a damn good one. He shifted his weight to keep his legs from going to sleep.

Now or never, Triscuit.

He cleared his throat, keeping his eyes on the stars when he said, "Troy was my brother."

He felt Colette shift beside him and knew she had turned to look at him, but he kept his face lifted. He could only say this to the stars and the darkness in-between.

"He died last year." It surprised Tristan at how easily the words left his mouth. For so long they'd been jammed at the back of his throat, choking him, and there was relief in saying them. He held his breath, bracing for Colette's response.

Tristan didn't talk much about his brother because he hated the inevitable reactions. First came the shock. But he was so young! Then the morbid curiosity. How did it happen? Then the sadness. I'm so sorry. How terrible! What a tragedy. Sorry, sorry, sorry. The apologies were the worst part because no one had anything to be sorry about except Tristan.

He stopped telling people about Troy shortly after the funeral. The pitying expressions and condolences offered little comfort and served only to fuel his rage and self-loathing.

Colette was the first person he'd opened up to like this in almost a year. The first person he'd wanted to tell, but as he waited for her to say something, he worried he misjudged the situation. Misjudged her. Sure, she opened up to him at the bar about her family, but that didn't mean she wanted to know every sorry detail about his tragic life.

Yes, she does, the voice in his head reminded him.

At the bar, she'd asked him about his secrets. She'd wanted him to share something. Now he had, and now he was terrified of what she was going to say in response. He couldn't take it back, though. The words floated between them, drifting to the stars.

Her hand found his in the dark. She laced their fingers together and surprised him by asking, "He was your older brother?"

He nodded, waiting for her to ask how it happened.

Instead, she laid her head on his shoulder and said, "Tell me your favorite thing about him. What was he like?"

A lump jammed in his throat. A year's worth of words and missing the person he loved most in this world—it all came spilling out in a rush.

"He was the best big brother anyone could hope for. He was spontaneous, always looking for some new adventure, some new thing he hadn't tried yet. He took me skydiving for my twenty-first birthday. He's the one who introduced me to chapulines tacos. He would call me and say, 'Be ready in five minutes.' And I'd have no idea where we would end up, but it was always something good, something wild I could have never guessed in a million years. Once we rented paddle boards on Catalina Island and spent the whole day paddling around the entire island. We saw a pod of dolphins, and he just dived right in and swam with them." Tristan laughed at the memory. "I stood there screaming at him about sharks, and he's just splashing around with these bottle-nose dolphins telling me to stop worrying so much. Life is short. That's what he always said. Life's too short to waste time being afraid."

Tristan fell quiet. He hadn't talked about his brother this much with anyone ever. He felt both wrung out and exhilarated.

Colette's voice held the hint of a smile when she said, "It sounds like you two had a lot of fun together. You must miss him."

There weren't enough words in the English language to describe just how much he did.

"Do you want to know how it happened?" he asked.

"Only if you want to tell me."

He *did* want to tell her, which surprised him. Maybe it was the darkness, the way it hugged them close and made every word feel like a secret that wouldn't count in the morning. Or maybe he just wanted her to know this worst part of himself when there was still time for her to change her mind about losing her virginity to someone like him.

"We were climbing," he said and waved his hand in the general direction of the park where they'd spent the afternoon. "Close to where we were today."

"Cyclops Rock?" Even with the bump on her head and blood dripping down her face, she'd been paying attention earlier that afternoon.

"Yeah. It was just the two of us that day, though. The other guys, I don't know, they had to work or something, I didn't ask. Troy showed up at my apartment and told me to grab my gear and get in the car. So I did. We climbed together a lot. We trusted each other." Another lump formed in his throat, this time from fear, dread, the sour taste of his mistakes. "He trusted me."

Tristan knew Troy was dead the second he hit the ground. A body doesn't land with that much force and survive. It took him longer to understand what had gone wrong, that it was his fault his brother had died.

"It happened so quickly," he told Colette. "One minute he was halfway up the route. The next thing I knew, he was falling. He just dropped." He jerked involuntarily, remembering the sound of his brother hitting the ground.

Colette sucked in a sharp breath, and her hand tightened around his, but she stayed quiet. In the distance, a coyote yipped. Another one took up the song until they were howling together.

"It never should have happened..." But the rest of the words jammed in his throat. He shook his head, unable to say anymore.

Troy had climbed the route before. It wasn't a hard route, and Troy was a strong climber. It was a warm-up climb, the kind he could have done in his sleep. And that's where it all went wrong. Troy was overconfident in his abilities, and Tristan was complacent because his brother was like a gecko. He'd never fallen off a wall in his entire life. Complacency led to distraction. Two women were climbing together on a route nearby. They were hot. Toned and tanned, blonde-bombshells with boisterous personalities. Troy had flirted with them before tying into his harness, somehow getting them to agree to come over to the rental house later that night.

Tristan watched the women with greedy delight, only half paying attention to his brother, who was starting up the route. He was lead climbing, which meant he was responsible for fixing the safety gear into place before continuing up the rock. Tristan had him on belay, ready to let the rope out or pull it taut as the situation required.

The first part of a lead climb was always the most dangerous part, as Troy wasn't yet clipped into anything. There was nothing to stop his fall, though if he fell at this point, he was still close enough to the ground that he might, at worst, break an ankle. But Troy never fell. The second most dangerous part of the climb was when he was installing the next cam into the rock. The distance between where he perched precariously on the smallest of footholds to the point of protection below him was significant enough to cause serious injury if he fell. But as long as Tristan never let go of his brake hand, Troy was still relatively safe. Tristan could catch him. But Troy never fell.

His brother was climbing, approaching the next clip-in spot, looking strong and unstoppable as always when he called for more slack in the rope. Tristan fed the rope through his carabiner, and Troy pulled it up. He was singing a song from the musical *Oklahoma*. A hawk spiraled overhead. The women on the rock next to them were talking loudly to each other, shouting encouragement.

The woman climbing called out to Tristan. When he looked up at her, she waved.

He took his hand off the rope for a second to wave back. A second. Maybe two. Not his brake hand, never his brake hand. Still, he had one hand off the rope when Troy shouted, "Falling," which made it nearly impossible to stop what happened next.

There was a sharp tug, a shout, and then the rope was whizzing through Tristan's brake hand. He tried to tighten it, but it was moving too fast and burned off a layer of skin. The rope kept flying through his fingers as if it had no end. Eventually, it jammed in the belay device, but by then it was too late.

Tristan had left Troy with too much slack. He knew better. But his focus had been on the woman who'd waved, distracted by her muscular thighs and flexed biceps. His eyes were off his brother for less than a minute, but it was more than enough time for everything to go horribly wrong. His brother never fell, and the one time he did, Tristan hadn't been there to catch him.

He untangled his fingers from Colette's and pressed the heels of his hands into his eye sockets, trying to scrub away the memory of his brother crashing to earth, his body splayed over the rocks, broken and not moving. He shuddered a sigh.

Colette wrapped her arms around him and drew him close against her, rocking him gently. She kissed his temple.

"I'm so sorry that happened to you," she said. "I can't even imagine what it must have felt like to lose him like that."

It was a different sort of apology than he was used to hearing, and instead of the usual flash of anger, he relaxed against her and taking comfort in her embrace. He turned his face toward her. The pale light from the stars glittered on her eyelashes. He kissed her, tasted salt, and realized she was crying. Only when she reached up and brushed her thumb over his cheek did he realize he was crying too.

He pulled back quickly, clearing his throat and rubbing his hands over his face, embarrassed by his tears. He pushed up to his feet and dusted off his pants.

"It's getting late." He reached down and offered her a hand up. "We should head back to the house before they send a search party out looking for us."

She nodded, grabbed his hand, and clambered to her feet.

Tristan's eyes had adjusted to the dark, and there was enough ambient light from the stars that he didn't need the cell phone flashlight going down. He knew where he was going now. He kept a tight hold of Colette's hand and led her safely to the bottom of the hill.

It was almost 1:00 in the morning by the time they got back to the rental house. All the lights were off. Tristan had no clue if his brother's friends were in their rooms or still at the bar, and he didn't bother checking. They were adults who could look after themselves.

"I'm going to brush my teeth." Colette grabbed a small bag from her luggage and disappeared into the bathroom.

Tristan sat on the edge of the bed and kicked off his shoes. He slipped out of his jeans and took off his shirt. Down to his boxer-briefs, he laid back on the bed with every intention of getting up to use the bathroom after Colette was done with it. But the entire day—from the climbing to Colette's fall to their hot make-out session and skinny dipping adventures to telling her about Troy—all of it had left him completely worn out.

Within seconds of his head hitting the pillow, Tristan was asleep.

ONE RULE

Colette

Colette stared at herself in the bathroom mirror. Her cheeks were flushed. Her eyes glinted with excitement. She was going to do this. She was actually going to have sex. Tonight. As soon as she walked out of this bathroom. All the way sex, not just the teasing, tonguing, fingering they'd done earlier. A man was going to put his penis inside her vagina and—she burst into hysterical giggles at the ridiculousness of the whole thing. How clinical her thoughts sounded, like she was about to go in there and teach a sex education course. Like she was a robot about to run a very human experiment.

She ran her hands over her naked body.

"You are very much not a robot," she whispered to herself.

When she'd agreed to go on this trip, she'd thought of it as a vacation from her real life. Which meant real life rules didn't apply. She could be whoever she wanted to be, do whatever she wanted to do. She could climb up a sheer rock face with only a thin rope keeping her alive. She could sing at the top of her lungs in a bar full of strangers. She could skinny dip in a motel pool. She could eat a bison burger. She could hike in the dark and watch shooting stars. Her fingers brushed over the bandage on her head. This weekend, she could do anything. And right now, what she wanted to do most was fuck Tristan Walker.

Her skin was dry from the chlorine and the hike had left a thin layer of salty sweat on her bare skin. She sniffed her armpits. Not too bad, but just in case, she did a quick sink wash and then added an extra layer of deodorant. She smoothed eucalyptus scented lotion all over her body, and her own touch aroused her. She brushed her teeth, combed her fingers through her hair, then carefully peeled off the bandage.

The cut had stopped bleeding a long time ago. It didn't look all that bad, actually. Barely a scrape. She tossed the bandage in the trash and reached for the lingerie she'd brought into the bathroom with her.

It was a black slip of a thing with a gaping hole in the crotch and a bustier that lifted and squashed her breasts to pornographic proportions. It took her a few minutes to figure out exactly which hole her legs and arms were supposed to go through, but she pulled it on and squeeze it over her breasts, and when she looked in the mirror, she was struck by how utterly delicious she looked. Quite the snack.

She swiveled in the mirror, checking herself from all angles. Had her ass always been that juicy? Her boobs always so perky? There was no way in hell Tristan was going to be able to resist her. One last check to make sure there was nothing in her teeth, and then Colette flicked off the bathroom light and walked back into the bedroom.

Tristan lay on top of the bed, not moving. Gentle snores rose from his half-open mouth. He'd stripped down to his boxers, but hadn't bothered getting under the covers. He hadn't bothered turning off any lights, either.

"Tristan?" Colette whispered, feeling suddenly self-conscious and a bit stupid standing over him in her slinky lingerie.

He grunted, but his eyes stayed closed. He rolled over, snuggling deeper into the pillow.

So much for her big plans.

Colette tied herself in knots trying to get out of the lingerie. *They couldn't be serious with this stuff*, she thought when her arm got stuck behind her back. She wrenched it free. After a few minutes of battling, she finally escaped the lingerie and traded the see-through lace for a comfy cotton t-shirt. She slipped into the bed beside Tristan and stared wide-eyed at the wall.

She was the furthest thing from tired. Her mind raced, replaying all the intimate and exciting moments she and Tristan had shared tonight. Her body was racing still, too, wanting more. She'd come twice tonight but, apparently, she was a greedy little sex goddess now because she wanted to come again. She wanted to come with Tristan inside her. The pull toward him felt deeper than want, felt like need, and sharing this bed wasn't helping the situation.

She tried to draw her mind away from his broad chest and strong hands, the way he worked his fingers between her legs, the way his mouth tasted of chlorine from the pool. She shuddered with delight, replaying the moment when she wrapped her legs around his waist. She'd felt his hardness, his excitement; she'd almost had him inside her, if only that motel clerk hadn't interrupted. She giggled softly into her pillow, feeling again the exhilarating rush of fleeing the pool and hopping over the wall. Remembering the way Tristan had chased after her, grabbing her a moment and pulling her into his arms, how he'd pressed his mouth against hers with such urgency.

None of these mental replays were helping to calm her down. She was only making herself hornier. She squeezed her eyes shut and tried to think of something that didn't involve Tristan's lips.

The story he'd shared about his brother had broken her heart.

She had watched his face the entire time he was talking, watched the waves of emotion roll through him. His brother's death had shaken Tristan to his very core, and he was still dealing with the aftermath. Colette had been through her own dark valleys, but she couldn't imagine losing someone like that. She didn't have a close relationship with her siblings, but if she were to wake up tomorrow to learn they'd died in a tragic accident, the news would devastate her.

She rolled over to face Tristan, who looked almost angelic in sleep. A curl had fallen over his forehead. His cheeks were cherubic. She brushed her hand over the rise of his shoulder, not wanting to wake him but wanting to feel close to him. He'd opened up to her tonight, shared something so incredibly personal with her, and out there beneath the stars, she'd felt connected to him in a way she hadn't thought possible with someone you were just having sex with. Or were *about* to have sex with. Would have sex with eventually.

Damn it.

The fact that she was feeling protective of him, knowing he had shared something with her that he rarely shared with anyone, only made her want him more.

But not tonight. His eyes twitched beneath their lids as he dreamed about her or something else—Colette would never know.

She sighed and rolled to her side of the bed, toying with the idea of toying with herself because she really couldn't stay up all night throbbing for Tristan, wanting him the way she wanted him. She needed sleep. Her hand moved to lift her shirt, but then Tristan shifted beside her. She realized his snores had stopped, and his breathing sounded different.

He rolled toward her. His voice was so quiet she could have imagined it. "Are you asleep?"

"No," she whispered.

He slid his hand around her waist and drew her close to him.

His erection pressed against her ass. She pressed back against it. He hummed softly against the back of her neck, and the sound awakened her whole body.

Their breathing quickened, their chests rising and falling together.

His hand slid over her hips. He toyed with the hem of her t-shirt.

"You're not wearing any pants," he murmured.

"You should have seen me earlier," she teased. "I tried on one of those itty-bitty lingerie things."

He groaned in disappointment, and she felt his cock stiffen even harder against her buttocks.

"Any chance I could sweet talk you into putting it on again?" He brushed her hair from her neck and pressed soft kisses to her skin. He kept his hand firm on her hip, rocking his cock against her slowly, so there could be no doubt what he wanted from her tonight.

"I don't think so." She rolled to face him and laid her hands on his chest. "It was very complicated to get on and off, and considering what we're about to do to each other, I think we shouldn't waste time with complicated."

Dim light filtered through the window, enough to see his face in the shadows, the smirk that twisted his mouth.

"And what are we about to do to each other?" he asked in a gruff voice, drawing her hips close.

His cock pressed against her stomach. She wiggled her hand underneath the band of his boxer-briefs and wrapped her fingers around his hard shaft. He shuddered and moaned, then lunged toward her, kissing her with that same urgency from earlier at the motel pool. She pressed against him, wanting him to know that she was feeling the same desire and excitement.

After a few seconds, Tristan broke away suddenly. He was panting hard. He stared at her for a moment with something like bewilderment on his face. She moved in for another kiss, but he backed away, shaking his head. "Wait, look, Colette. Before we do this. I have to say something."

Colette folded her arms across her chest and waited.

"I don't want to be the guy who punches your v-card and leaves."

"I do," she said. "I want you to be that guy."

"Your first time should be special. It should be with someone you care about. Someone you could have a future with."

"I call bullshit," she said. "You're going to lie here and tell me every woman you've ever had sex with is someone you imagined a future with?"

"No, but you and I, we're different. I'm no good. I can't promise you tomorrow. I can't promise you anything but this, what's here right now. Tonight. That's it. That's all I have to offer. Here and now and nothing else."

"And what makes you think I want anything you're offering except this?" She stared pointedly at his dick. "If I didn't want to do this, I wouldn't be here. So, no commitment. Got it. I promise I won't fall in love. Now, please, can you just fuck me already?"

He laughed and relaxed again, drawing their bodies together.

He pressed his mouth into the curve of her neck and said, "Okay, but if we're going to do this, I have one rule."

She waited, holding her breath.

His hand slipped under her t-shirt and cupped her ass. His finger ran over the seam of her underwear. "I want you to tell me when it feels good. Tell me when you want more or less, harder or slower. Tell me when you're getting close."

"That's more than one rule," she said, breathless with anticipation.

"You're right." He laughed against her shoulder. "Okay, I take it back. Here's my one rule." He pulled slightly back so he was looking into her eyes. "I want you to give yourself over to me completely."

She sucked in a sharp breath.

"Say it." He squeezed her ass harder. "I'm not going to start until I know this is what you really want. Say you want me inside you."

"Tristan." Her pussy throbbed. Her underwear was soaked. She wanted him so much it hurt. There was no part of her that was tense, no part reluctant. She'd never felt more relaxed and more ready. Everything in her was screaming, go, go, now, now!

"I want you. I want you inside me." The words slipped off her tongue with no hesitation, and her whole body tingled at the way Tristan looked at her. Excitement, desire—he wanted this as much as she did.

"Tell me what to do." She rocked her hips against his. "Make me lose control."

IT'S SO EASY TO FEEL GOOD

Colette

"Spread your legs." Tristan pushed his hands against Colette's thighs. "Open for me, baby. Let me see you."

He licked his lips as his eyes roamed over her pussy. He slid one finger along her wet folds, opening her more, rubbing her clit until she sucked in a sharp breath, then taking his finger away again.

Colette had lost her clothes quickly. A few fumbling seconds after she'd told him she was ready, he yanked off her t-shirt and underwear and tossed them in a heap on the floor. Tristan rolled her onto her back and straddled her. His eyes grazed over her face, then down to her breasts, lingering before moving to her hips and pubic area. He pushed her open and ran his finger through her wetness, groaning like a man wandering the desert who'd just found his oasis.

He plunged his face between her legs and licked her clit, sucking, humming vibrations that rolled deep. She arched her hips with a gasp. His tongue moved with such confidence, slowly at first and then faster, harder, pulsing, bringing her right to the edge, but not over. He lifted his head and moved to her breasts. She moaned with pleasure as he sucked her nipples.

He rose again and said, "Roll over."

Before she could turn, he grabbed her roughly around the waist and flipped her onto her face. He slid his hands under her hips and lifted her ass into the air. He smoothed his hand down her back and pressed himself against her, sliding his hands around to her breasts again, fondling them, then sliding back down to her hips. His hand moved to her crotch, spreading her, finding that warm center again. This time, he thrust a finger inside her. She gasped, muffling the sound with a pillow. He thrust a second finger inside her. She moaned.

"You're so fucking tight," he said. "And you're wet. You're so wet. You're ready for me, aren't you, baby? You've been ready for me for a long time."

He rolled her onto her back again.

Then he pulled his shirt over his head and shimmied out of his boxer briefs. He stayed kneeled above her, staring at her face, watching as her eyes slid to his cock. She bit her lip. Her breath came in quick gasps now. He was rock hard, his penis standing at attention.

"You like this, don't you? I can tell by how you're looking at me. You want this inside you. You want me to fuck you so hard you lose your fucking mind? Is that what you want, baby? You want this hard cock in your sweet, soft pussy."

She swallowed and nodded. Her pussy throbbed with wanting.

"What do you want, sweetheart?" He used his knees to spread her legs and then rubbed his thumb over her clit. "Tell me what you want."

"I want you to fuck me with that huge cock," she gasped, arching her hips at his touch. "I want to feel you inside me. I don't want you to stop until I fucking come."

"That's right," he said. "Now hold on to something. I'm about to rock your world."

He grinned as he leaned over to the nightstand for a condom. After it was on, he grabbed both her wrists and jerked them above her head. She loved the feeling of him pinning her down, loved that she didn't have to think about if she was doing it wrong or right or how this was all going to end. She writhed under him, excited. The anticipation was almost too much.

"Ready?" He growled and slid into her wet folds.

A kitten-like mewl escaped her lips. His eyes found hers in the dim light, and though he didn't ask if she was okay, he could see the concern in his eyes. She met his gaze, grinned, and then rocked her hips up.

"Holy fuck," she moaned. "It's even better than I imagined. You feel so good."

He thrust inside her, moving slowly at first, spreading her wider. She felt the fullness of him, her walls clenching around his shaft, tightening with pleasure and desire. He moaned and grabbed one of her legs, lifting it up onto his shoulder so he could thrust deeper.

She whimpered and gripped his shoulders.

Fuck, he felt so good. They rocked together, riding that wave higher. He released her hands to grab hold of her breast, flicking his thumb over her nipple. The sensation sent her even higher. She let out a wild moan of desire.

"You like that?" He flicked her nipple again, and she almost came.

"Not yet, baby," he growled in her ear, moving his hand down to her ass, squeezing it and running his thumb along the seam of her thigh.

He pushed deeper inside her.

"I can't—" she gasped. "I'm going to—"

He slowed his thrusting and moved his hand to her clit, tightening and massaging, sending her straight over the edge. Her whole body convulsed. Sparks exploded around her. There was a rush of sensation through her entire body. She heard an enraptured keening sound and realized it was her. She was arched, riding the wave of pleasure, when Tristan thrust inside her one final time, then shuddered and groaned. He clutched her tighter. She felt his orgasm throbbing with hers. One last thrust, and then he folded over on top of her, panting.

She threaded his fingers through his hair.

"How was that?" he whispered.

"Oh my God." The words came out in a pant. "This is what I've been missing?"

"Fucking amazing, right?" He rolled off of her, turning to remove the condom and tossing it into the trash can by the bed.

Then he rolled back onto the bed. His cock was still semihard. He was breathing like he'd just finished an intense workout. Which, honestly, they kind of had.

Colette pulled the sheet up around her breasts and curled against Tristan. Even though it was late, almost 2:00 AM, if the tiny alarm clock on the nightstand could be trusted, she wasn't tired. Her body tingled all over, flush with the pleasure of her orgasm.

"Tell me about your first time," she said.

Tristan shifted and slipped his arm under her head, pulling her up so she was resting on his chest. His heart thumped steadily in his chest.

When he spoke, his voice was a low rumble. "It wasn't good at all. Not as good as this. I'll tell you that much."

He kissed the top of her head.

"You were nineteen…" she prompted him.

When he laughed, her head jostled. "Nothing is very good when you're nineteen. It was a lot of fumbling in the dark, not knowing what to do with my hands or what to do with her. I was a selfish lover."

"You were nineteen," she said, trying to sound reassuring. "Try not to be too hard on yourself."

"Nineteen and horny as fuck. Sex felt like a means to an end. I didn't realize it could be a way to connect to people too. A way to make other people feel good."

Colette had never thought of sex that way either. Until tonight, she'd always thought of sex as transactional. Something gained, something lost. But she realized it hadn't felt that way with Tristan. She didn't feel like she had given up anything to be with him, except her own insecurities and anxious thoughts. And Tristan certainly wasn't acting like he got the short end of the stick with her tonight.

"It's the chemicals in our brains," Tristan murmured. "After an orgasm, we get a rush of dopamine and serotonin and all the other things that make us feel invincible. Do you feel invincible, Colette?"

She ran her hand over his bare chest, toying with his fine, curly blond hairs. "I feel pretty good, yeah."

"I'm glad." He brushed his fingers through her hair. "I want to make you feel good."

He adjusted his arm, and then he was grabbing her around the waist and pulling her on top of him. His dick was fully hard again. She could feel it pressed against her pussy. The heat of it ignited a fire through her center. She lowered her mouth to his. His hands moved down her hips to her ass, spreading her cheeks.

She moaned and broke from the kiss, then whispered in his ear, "Please tell me you brought more than one condom."

He laughed and rolled so she was on her back and he was straddling her. He kissed the tip of her nose, then pulled away, climbing off the bed and scrambling through his suitcase until he found another condom.

After he slipped it on, he grabbed her and rolled her onto him again. He shifted so he was sitting upright with his back against the headboard and she was straddling him. She rocked her hips so her wet folds slipped up and down his shaft. He moaned and took her breast in his mouth.

After a few seconds, he pulled away from her and flashed a wicked grin. "I warned you, didn't I? I tried to tell you that once I get you in my bed, you're not going to want to leave."

"We're in trouble, then," she teased. "Because this isn't even your bed."

He playfully wrestled with her, jostling and spreading her folds until she opened for him.

She gasped as he entered her.

He kept his hands firm on her hips, guiding her up and down the length of his shaft. She bucked and writhed, allowing herself to be swept away again, greedy with her desire, surprising herself with how good it could feel to have a man throbbing inside her. Part of her felt a little stupid that she'd waited so long to do this now that she knew how simple it was, how easily her body came alive with the sensations. Every touch, every thrust awakening new feelings inside her. All her fears about sex unfounded. But as Tristan moved inside her, thrusting deeper, bringing her to the edge of ecstasy, she realized she only felt so good because he made it so easy to feel good.

Now that she'd had him, she knew she wouldn't have wanted anyone else but Tristan Walker to be her first.

WHO WANTS EGGS?

Tristan

Warm light streamed through the window, waking Tristan from a blissful and dreamless sleep. He stretched his naked body beneath the soft, cotton sheets that smelled of salt and sweat and sex and Colette's eucalyptus body lotion. He rolled over to find her face traced in gold, her eyes still closed. The sheet had slipped down in the night, revealing her bare shoulder and the constellation of freckles scattered over her skin.

His cock stiffened at the sight of her naked breasts as he remembered how she writhed on top of him the night before, how she bounced, supple and joyous. God, he wanted to pull her on top of him right now and fondle her until she came again.

He loved the face she made with her head tipped back, her mouth wide open as she gasped and moaned. He loved her moan.

He clambered out of the bed before his thoughts and dick took him any further. He needed a cold shower and a slap in the face. This was nothing, he reminded himself. This was just sex.

She'd made that clear. She wanted him for his experience. Nothing more. He'd done what he could to make her first time good, and considering she came three times last night, he would argue that he'd done more than a satisfactory job.

He turned on the shower and stepped inside, letting the cold water suck the heat of desire from his skin. His dick was still hard, though. Because now he was thinking about fucking Colette in the shower, bending her over and taking her from behind. The water running rivulets down the dimples in her ass.

Snap out of it. It's just sex.

Hot sex.

With the woman of his dreams.

He had to stop thinking of her like that. Sure, from the moment he saw her at the club last week, he'd wanted to bend her over and fuck her senseless. After he found out she was a virgin, he'd wanted to be the one to take her places she'd never been. And now that he'd done that? Well, there was nothing after that. Was there? He rubbed soap over his body and shampooed his hair. When he finished showering, he toweled off and quietly dressed in jeans and a t-shirt.

Colette murmured in her sleep and burrowed deeper into the blankets. They had a few hours before they needed to be out of the rental, so Tristan left her alone. He slipped out of the bedroom and walked to the kitchen where Nick and the others were sipping hot coffee and making plans for which rocks to climb this morning before they went back to Los Angeles.

As soon as Tristan walked in, the conversation stopped. They were all grinning at him like they'd lost their damn minds.

"What?" Tristan reached for a clean cup and poured himself some coffee. "Why are you looking at me like that?"

Jacob grabbed the counter and pretended to hump it as he made moaning sex noises. "Oh, Tristan, give it to me, yeah baby, harder, fuck me, daddy."

Heat rushed to Tristan's face. He tried to ignore them,

focusing on pouring milk in his coffee, scooping in a heap of sugar. But they kept harassing him.

"At least one of us got his knob polished good last night." Carlos snorted a laugh.

"It sounded like she was getting as much as she was giving." Sara bit her lip seductively as she eyed Tristan's crotch. "I wish I could find a man to make me scream like that."

Nick was laughing too hard to pipe in with his own commentary.

Jacob was still humping the counter, making kissing sounds. "Oh! Oh! More, more! You know how I like it, daddy, yeah!"

"Shut up." Tristan tried to hush him, but it only revved him up.

"Ooh, don't stop, don't stop, don't stop. I'm coming!" Jacob slapped his own ass as his voice pitched into a shrill howl.

"I said shut the fuck up!" Tristan rushed across the kitchen and shoved Jacob hard enough to send him stumbling into the table.

"What the hell, man?" Jacob bounced back, rubbing at his hip where it had connected with the table. "What's your problem? We're just having a little fun. It's no big deal, geez. Calm the fuck down."

Tristan jabbed his finger into Jacob's chest. "You calm the fuck down. And you better not say another goddamn word about it. Especially when she comes out here. You better keep your mouth shut. Okay? Don't embarrass her."

"Embarrass her?" Jacob scoffed. "What the hell are you talking about? It's just sex. Who's embarrassed about sex?"

"It's not just sex. It was her first time, okay?" Tristan blurted the words without thinking.

Everyone stopped talking and turned to stare. It was so quiet, he could hear the bacon sizzling in the oven.

Good going, numb nuts. She's going to be thrilled when she finds out you blabbed her business to all your idiot friends.

"Wait." Jacob studied Tristan a moment, then his face cracked into a disbelieving grin. "He's serious. You're serious? Holy shit. He's serious. All that moaning we heard last night was the sound of a virgin's cherry being popped. Hell yeah!" He pumped his hips in the air, gyrating like a horny dog. "Way to go, Tristan! Fucking legendary!"

"She's not a minor, is she?" Nick scrutinized him. "Fuck, Triss, I'm not going to jail because you needed to get some teenage pussy."

"Shut up, Nick. She's not a minor. God! What is wrong with you? You know me better than that. And also, don't be so obtuse. Not every virgin in the world is underage."

"So, she's an old virgin." Jacob nodded with approval. "Hot. Very hot."

"Well, technically, she's not a virgin anymore." Sara's grin was mischievous.

"Ooh! Yeah! That's my boy!" Jacob slapped Tristan on the back.

Tristan shoved him away. "Fuck off. God, I shouldn't have told you idiots anything. Promise you won't make a big deal of it when she comes in here. She'll kill me if she finds out I told you."

Jacob mimed like he was zipping his lip and throwing away the key. The others nodded their agreement to keep their mouths shut, but Tristan knew he'd fucked up big time. His brother's friends could keep their mouths shut for a few hours—maybe—but it was too juicy a piece of gossip to swallow forever. The only way to make sure Colette never found out that Tristan had betrayed her confidence was to keep her as far from these big-mouthed idiots as he could.

The bedroom door clicked open, and Colette shuffled into the kitchen. She was bleary-eyed and a small smile played on her mouth. The glow of sex lingered around her, made more prominent by her halo of ruffled hair and flushed cheeks. She stopped in the doorway when she realized everyone was staring at her.

"What?" She ran her hands over her hair. "Do I have something on my face?"

The entire room broke into a fit of rambunctious laughter.

Colette's cheeks turned bright red. Her eyes locked on to Tristan, who grinned sheepishly as he came toward her. He wrapped his arm around her waist and kissed the top of her head. "You look beautiful. Coffee's fresh if you want some."

She nodded and moved away from him toward the coffeepot sitting on the counter.

Nick winked at Tristan behind her back. Jacob gave a thumbs up.

Tristan shook his head, ignoring them both. He opened the fridge and shoved his head inside to cool his flaming cheeks. "Who wants eggs?"

Later, as they were packing up the cars and doing a last pass through the house to make sure no one forgot anything, Nick pulled Tristan aside.

"So, you really like this chick, don't you, little bro?" he asked.

"I mean, she's cool, yeah." Tristan shrugged like it was no big deal, even though his insides were tied in knots over the thought that in less than three hours, they'd be back in Los Angeles, saying their goodbyes with no idea of when he'd see her next.

"'She's cool?' What's that supposed to mean?"

"We haven't known each other very long."

"So? What's that got to do with anything?"

"It takes time to figure out if you like someone or not," Tristan said. "Right now, we're just... I don't know. Like I said, she's cool, but we're just messing around."

Nick arched his eyebrows. "The way you two have been looking at each other all weekend? This is more than a fling, man. And I'd bet money on that."

Through the front window, Tristan could see Colette by the Jeep, lifting her heavy suitcases into the back. She'd insisted on doing it herself, still embarrassed about how much she'd over-packed.

Nick followed his gaze. He patted Tristan's shoulder. "You know, Troy believed in all that mushy, love-at-first-sight stuff."

"He did?"

"I went to him after a terrible break up." Nick shook his head, remembering. "I mean, it was truly awful. My heart had been stomped. Obliterated. I was sobbing, literally sobbing into Troy's arms, convinced I would never love again. I was going to be alone forever. I didn't want to leave the house, but he told me to stop crying and get back out there. He said my ex was clearly just a stop on the way to something better, that if I didn't keep my head up and my eyes forward, I might miss the person who would change my life forever. They could be anywhere, he told me. Even right around the next corner. You don't want to be so bogged down in your misery that you miss them, do you?"

The two men were quiet for a moment, both lost in their own memories of Troy.

Then Nick slapped Tristan's shoulder and said, "God damn it, I miss that man. Look, Triss, I'm sorry about yesterday. I should have never pressured you the way I did. Troy would have tanned my hide if he was here and heard me running my mouth. I was a dick. I just wanted this weekend to be something special, a new memory for you, but I shouldn't have come at you like that. You're not ready. You need more time. I can respect that."

"Thanks, Nick," Tristan muttered.

But Nick wasn't done. "And I shouldn't have pressured Colette either," he continued. "That was a rough hit she took yesterday, and it was insensitive of me to try to force her back up the wall. I guess I just wanted her to experience that rush of adrenaline, the satisfaction of hitting the top of a route. It seems like you gave her all the thrills and satisfaction she needed later, though, so I should have kept my mouth shut."

Nick elbowed him in the ribs. Tristan shoved him back.

Outside, Colette heaved the last suitcase into the back of the Jeep and dusted off her hands. She stood with her legs spread wide, her shoulders back, her face tilted toward the sun, soaking in the heat and light.

"Don't get bogged down in your misery." Nick grabbed his overnight bag and headed toward the door. "It's the best advice your brother ever gave me, Triss, and I know if he were here right now, he'd be telling you the same damn thing."

DIRTY LITTLE MINX

Colette

Yesterday Colette was a virgin. Today she was—she paused, trying to figure out what the opposite of 'virgin' was. Deflowered? Cultivated? Sexed? Screwed? Horny little devil? She laughed out loud.

Tristan shot her a quick glance before turning his eyes back to the road. "What's so funny?"

"What do you call a virgin who's no longer a virgin?" It sounded like the start of a dirty joke.

"Mine." He reached over the center console and slid his fingers between her legs, rubbing her through her jeans.

She gasped and squirmed and bit down on her lip, but didn't tell him to stop. He pulled his hand away just as she was heating up.

"Tease." She grabbed his thigh, dipping her hand toward his crotch.

"Nope." He pushed her away. "I'm driving. Safety first."

"Maybe you should pull over."

He flicked her a glance, checked his rearview mirror, but ultimately shook his head and kept driving. "Insatiable."

It was funny. She was the same Colette as yesterday, yet she was different. Her skin felt strange wrapped around her bones. Everywhere Tristan's fingers had brushed the night before still flamed with the echo of his touch. She had an important client coming in first thing tomorrow morning and she should have been prepping for that, or at least thinking about it on the two-plus-hour drive home, but all of her thoughts were on Tristan. She couldn't stop replaying what happened between them last night, how blissed-out he'd looked when he was inside her, how they'd moved together, connecting in a way she'd never thought was possible with another person.

She knew this shiny, new feeling wouldn't last, that eventually she'd have to get back to her real life with her real job and the real problem of confronting Scott about his god-awful behavior at Gardenia's on Friday night. She couldn't believe only two days had passed since that dinner disaster.

A disaster that had led to her coming on this weekend trip with Tristan.

A disaster that led to the best sex of her life.

The only sex of her life. So far.

But damn, it had been good sex, and she definitely wouldn't mind if Tristan wanted to go another few rounds with her before the weekend officially ended and she had to drag herself out of this pleasurable sex vacation. She thought they'd have at least one more chance again this morning before they left the rental house, but he was already awake, showered, and in the kitchen by the time she woke up.

She cringed again at the memory of walking into the kitchen that morning and everyone turning to stare at her. She was certain Tristan's friends knew exactly what they'd been up to all night long. It wouldn't have been hard to guess. She and Tristan hadn't exactly tried to keep quiet, and the house, while spacious, wasn't soundproof. But so what? People had sex all the time. There was no reason to be embarrassed that she'd been fucking Tristan last night. They couldn't possibly know that it had been her first time fucking anyone. Tristan wouldn't have told them, not after what happened with Scott.

Still, their stares made her want to run back into the room and hide. If it hadn't been for Tristan intervening, asking if she wanted coffee, she might still be in that rental house, hunkered down in a closet somewhere, refusing to come out until everyone else left.

She stared at the side of Tristan's face as he drove them through the brown desert expanse of San Bernardino County. A smile toyed on his lips. He drummed the steering wheel in rhythm with the rock music blasting through the radio. The wind fluttered his hair. He turned briefly to flash her a warm smile before returning his attention to the road.

She had the sudden urge to tell him to turn the Jeep around, to drive east until they ran out of road. To drive anywhere but to Los Angeles, where they would eventually have to talk about what they were or were not doing together.

It was supposed to be sex. And that's it. He would be her first time, and she wouldn't fall in love. That was the promise they'd made to each other in the Gardenia's parking lot. But the closer they got to Los Angeles, the more Colette's thoughts kept leaping forward to what might come next. What if they kept seeing each other? To have more sex, holy fucking yes please, but also what if they explored their feelings more too? Would that be so terrible?

But she'd promised she wouldn't be clingy after. And relationships were clingy, dating was romance, girlfriend was the definition of attached. It was a bad idea to get emotionally wrapped up with someone who was supposed to be nothing more than a one-night stand. Now, if Tristan wanted to keep this going, if he asked her out again or suggested they keep seeing each other, she would say yes. But she wasn't going to be the one who brought it up first. She wasn't going to be that kind of girl.

The longer they drove in silence, the more she second-guessed herself. They were both adults, weren't they? And she was a liberated, 21st century woman. If she wanted to ask Tristan Walker out on a date, she damn well could. She could express her feelings, and it didn't have to be some huge thing, and if he rejected her, she would gracefully move on. *So do it. Tell him how you feel. Tell him now before you lose your nerve.*

She turned in her seat. The words were on the tip of her tongue. A Christina Aguilera song played on the radio. Tristan shouted, "I love this one," and cranked up the volume. He winked at her as he gyrated his hips and belted out the chorus. He looked ridiculous, and yet Colette would have loved to be sitting in his lap gyrating with him. She laughed and turned her face toward the window again, letting the rush of air cool her suddenly flushed cheeks. As it turned out, sex made you an idiot.

She needed a distraction, something to keep her from opening her stupid mouth and saying words she'd regret. She grabbed her phone to text Brooke.

They'd been texting off and on all weekend. After the disaster at Gardenia's, Colette had called Brooke to tell her that, no thanks to Scott, she did not, in fact, have sex with Tristan Friday night like she thought she was going to. Brooke had acted appropriately horrified when Colette told her the whole story, and was equally excited when she heard about the invitation to Joshua Tree. Her one request was that Colette text her twice a day. *You just met this guy*, she'd said. *I want proof of life at least twice a day or I'm calling the police.* Colette had teased her about listening to too many true crime podcasts, but really, she knew how lucky she was to have a best friend who cared about her well-being as much as Brooke did.

Colette: Hello. My name is Colette. And I am no longer a virgin.
Brooke: What?! Tell me everything! Was it with Tristan?
Colette: Yes. Who else?
Brooke: I don't know, maybe you met some other hottie at a bar while you were there.
Colette: You know me.
Brooke: Well?
Colette: Well, what?
Brooke: How big is his dick? How many times did he make you come? Did he use his tongue? Did you like it?

Colette barked out a laugh. Tristan darted a glance in her direction. She flashed him an innocent smile and texted Brooke that now wasn't a good time to talk.

Colette: I just wanted you to know I'm still alive, that my v-card has been punched, and that we're headed back to LA. Should be home in a few hours.
Brooke: You're still with him? You dirty little minx! I can't wait to hear all the deets! Come over tonight?
Colette: Maybe… I'll keep you posted.
Brooke: Oh my God, oh my God. You're going to take him back to your place and shag his brains out, aren't you? That's my girl! I knew it! There was a sex dragon trapped inside you all along!

Colette shook her head at the dragon emoji Brooke sent her. She closed the messaging app and pulled up the First Timers Group Chat.

She poised her fingers to type, but struggled with what to say. They'd all bonded over the fact that none of them had ever had sex. Now she had, and she wasn't sure what that meant for her in terms of whether she would be welcome anymore. In the time that she'd been a member, no one, as far as she knew, had ever had sex. At least, no one had announced it. Maybe the group only allowed virgins. Maybe once you weren't anymore, you had to remove yourself, but Colette didn't know if she was ready for that. These people, though strangers to her, had been so generous with their time and emotional support. They'd made her feel normal when everyone else around her made her feel like a freak. The group was a safe space, and she wasn't ready to give it up.

She closed out of the app without posting and set her phone in the center console beside Tristan's, then turned her gaze to the landscape whizzing past. Barren hills and desert scrub gave way to housing developments and shopping malls faster than she expected. More cars joined them on the road. Traffic slowed. They would be in LA soon, and Colette needed to think of a way to tell Tristan she wanted to spend more time with him without sounding like his answer mattered to her. She needed to be the cool girl, someone she'd never been able to be in her entire life.

One of the phones resting in the center console buzzed. Thinking it was Brooke texting her again, Colette grabbed without looking. Instead of her phone, she ended up with Tristan's. The text that had come through was still lit up on the screen. Colette wasn't being nosy or jealous or anything like that. The text was right there in front of her. She couldn't help but read it.

Her stomach flipped. She read the text one more time before the screen went dark to make sure she hadn't read it wrong the first time.

"Tristan?" The obnoxious tremble in her voice betrayed her emotions.

Tristan glanced at the phone in her hands and then at her face. He seemed to understand what was happening before she even asked him about it because he grabbed the phone from her, anger sparking in his voice. "Is that mine?"

They weren't dating. Even if they were, she had no right to be snooping through his texts. But she hadn't been snooping, so he had no right to be mad. She'd accidentally picked up his phone, accidentally seen the message from Nick. If anyone got to be mad right now, it was her.

Tristan swiped his finger over the screen.

"You shouldn't text and drive," she said.

He cursed and tossed his phone into the driver's door pocket.

She should let it go, pretend she never saw that damn text, because she and Tristan were nothing to each other, right? After today, she would never have to see him again if she didn't want to. But what if she wanted to? Then she needed to know the truth. "Tristan, what did you tell your friends about me?"

Quick question, the text had read. **Do virgins give good road head?**

Tristan's grip tightened on the steering wheel. A muscle in his jaw twitched. "I didn't mean to tell them you were a virgin. It just slipped out, okay?"

"How does something like that just slip out?" Anger stoked her blood.

"They were teasing me this morning before you came out to the kitchen." His tone stayed even as he explained. "They were being crass, just really crude, and I didn't want them teasing you the same way they were teasing me."

"So, you told them I was a virgin. How is that better?"

"They didn't tease you, did they?"

"Not to my face." She scoffed, remembering how awkward it had been that morning in the kitchen, as if she'd walked in on something she wasn't supposed to. Now she knew exactly what she'd walked in on. They'd been talking about her sex life. Or lack of one. She groaned and buried her face in her hands.

"Colette, come on. It's not that big of a deal." He tried to lay his hand on her knee, but she slapped it away.

"It was a big deal to me."

"I didn't mean us having sex," he clarified. "Of course, *that* was a big deal. I mean, it's not a big deal whether they know you were a virgin before last night or not. I keep telling you. No one cares."

"I care," she said. "Don't my feelings matter at all?"

"I didn't do it on purpose." He made his voice small and contrite.

She wasn't going to give in to his puppy-dog eyes. She crossed her arms over her chest. "Yes, but you knew how I felt about it. How poorly it went for me in the past and yet you still told them? Like what? Some kind of brag? Do you and your friends have some kind of running tally going? Who can bag the most virgins?"

"It's not like that, and you know it."

"It's just so embarrassing," she said. "Now if I ever see your friends again, all they'll be thinking is, 'There's the virgin who wasted all her good fucking years because she couldn't figure out how to get laid.'"

"Trust me. No one's going to be thinking that, and if this weekend was anything to go by, you have plenty of good years left to fuck whoever you want to. They don't call them the dirty thirties for nothing." He flashed her a cheeky grin. "And anyway, you're definitely not a virgin anymore. So the next time you see my friends, the only thing they're going to be thinking is how a screw-up like me landed a hottie with a brain like you."

She could tell he was trying to defuse the situation and get her to loosen up about it, but she was still seething, humiliated, feeling like the entire world knew her business and was laughing at her now.

"I knew this was a bad idea." She turned away from him to face the window.

"What was?"

"I should never have come on this trip with you."

He was quiet for a moment with the wind rushing around them.

Then he said, "I don't think you really mean that," and reached for her hand.

She let him take it, but she stayed quiet for the rest of the drive into LA, not ready to forgive him yet, but also not entirely sure why she'd gotten so angry with him in the first place.

By the time they reached his apartment complex, Colette's initial anger had dissipated somewhat, from seething to simmering. She was still mad at Tristan for telling his friends about her. It wasn't his story to tell. At the same time, she could admit that she was probably making a bigger deal out of it than she needed to. She could admit, too, that some of her anger had nothing to do with the fact that his friends now knew more about her than she would have liked.

Whether she'd meant it to happen or not, having sex with Tristan had made her more vulnerable. She'd used her virginity as a shield for so long, not allowing men to get close to her, but she'd let Tristan inside. *Figuratively and literally*, she thought with a bitter laugh. And now that she'd shown him these most intimate parts of herself, she wasn't sure what scared her more—the idea that he wouldn't want her, or that he would? And that she had no clue what the hell *she* wanted? Well, that was the most terrifying thing of all.

Her car was still parked on the street in front of his apartment where she'd left it.

She got out of the rented Jeep and walked to the back to grab her bags. Tristan met her there. Before she could open the back hatch, he circled his arms around her waist and pulled her into his chest. He buried his face in her hair and planted a row of those delicate, sweet kisses she loved so much along the curve of her neck.

"Come upstairs," he murmured.

"Why?" It was hard not to melt against him and give in to his request, but she needed to know exactly what she was saying yes to, and if this was going to end badly for her, with rejection, heartbreak, and her feeling even more stupid than she already did.

If she went up to his apartment, she would cross into his personal space, and even though it probably didn't mean anything to him, it meant something to her. If she went up to his apartment, she wasn't entirely certain she'd be able to maintain any level of self-control. A closed door. An apartment all to themselves. A full 12 hours before she had to be at the office. Oh, the trouble they could get up to in 12 hours. But no, theirs was a one-night stand, a fling. It meant nothing. Better to cut it off now before she was in too deep.

"I messed up." Tristan stroked her jaw, igniting her desire against her own better judgment. "I should have kept my mouth shut, and I'm sorry. Let me make it up to you? Please."

She locked eyes with him, daring him to look away. She needed him to see the depth of her want, how badly she had fallen for him in such a short time, and how easily he could hurt her. She needed him to know that she wasn't going to be just another booty call he kept in his rotation. "If it's just sex you want, you'd probably be better off calling up one of your club bunnies."

A smile teased his lips, and then he grew serious again, wrapping his hands around her face, leveling with her. "I don't just want sex, Colette. It's you okay? I want you."

He covered her mouth with his, giving her the sweetest kiss so far, somehow both gentle and devouring. She matched his intensity, her body lighting up for him again, the echoes of last night sparking across her skin.

She pulled back from him with a gasp. "So, no sex?"

His eyes bulged and then he laughed, drawing her against him again, murmuring in her ear as one hand cupped her breast, "Oh no, there will definitely be sex. Lots and lots and lots of sex."

She shivered with pleasure, whispering, "I'm still mad at you, though."

"That's okay. Ever heard of make-up sex? It's the second best kind of sex."

"Oh really? And what's the first best kind?"

"How about I show you right now?" He nipped playfully at her neck, then grabbed her hand and led her into the building.

GOING UP

Tristan

Tristan didn't wait until they got to his apartment.

When the elevator doors closed, he pushed Colette against the back wall, his mouth searching for hers, taking pleasure in the sweetness of her lips. He parted her legs with his knee, then slid his hand beneath the waistband of her jeans, unbuttoning as he slid his hand lower. She pushed him back, her eyes sparking wildly with desire but also with uncertainty.

"Here?" She glanced nervously at the closed elevator doors. The buttons lit up slowly as they moved between floors. They were on level 2. His apartment was on level 8.

"You wanted to know what the best kind of sex is." He got on his knees and pulled her pants down over her hips.

His mouth was on her before she could stop him. He parted her with his tongue. She moaned, and her fingers gripped his hair, tugging at the roots. He couldn't get enough of her. His cock pressed against his jeans, aching to be freed, but this time wasn't about him. It was about her pleasure, about making sure she understood how truly sorry he was for fucking up this morning. Making her feel good was his only priority right now. His cock could wait.

Her breathing quickened. She pushed his head harder against her pussy, rocking against him, leveraging her body against the wall, showing him a better angle. He kept one hand on her ass, squeezing it, massaging, as he tucked the other between her legs, slipping his thumb into her hot center. She cried out as she came, pulsing against him.

He kept his tongue against her, tasting her desire, until she was relaxed again, panting and pulling him to his feet. She yanked her pants back up, laughing and blushing in a way that made Tristan want her even more.

"Oh my God," she exhaled, fumbling with her buttons. "I can't believe we just—"

The elevator stopped with a ding on the 6th floor, and the doors slid open. An elderly couple shuffled on to the elevator. The old woman smiled at Tristan and Colette. "Don't you two make a lovely couple?"

Tristan smiled back at her and grabbed Colette's hand, threading their fingers together. Colette looked like she was stifling a laugh. Her face turned beet red as the elevator moved again. A few floors later, the old woman squinted at the panel and said, "Oh dear. I thought we were going down."

Colette couldn't hold it in anymore. She let out a braying laugh that startled everyone. The old man glared at her. The old woman, flustered, started pressing random buttons on the panel. Tristan lowered his face, hiding his own laughter.

The doors opened on the 8th floor, and Tristan led Colette out of the elevators. When the doors closed behind them, they fell against each other, laughing until tears streamed down their cheeks. Just when they pulled themselves together, Tristan said, "Well, one of us was going down," and they crumpled with laughter again.

When they got to Tristan's apartment, the first thing he did was lock the door. The second thing he did was turn on the stereo system. Lo-Fi beats thumped through the speakers. He turned to invite Colette to make herself comfortable, but it seemed she didn't need an invitation.

In the few seconds he had his back turned to her, she'd stripped off her shirt and pants, kicking them to one side. She stood in his entryway in nothing but a lacy pink bra and matching thong, eying him with a desperate lust that made all the blood rush to his cock.

"Well, look at you," he murmured, moving toward her, but she was faster.

She strode across his living room in three long steps, grabbed his shirt collar, and dragged him to the vintage yellow couch in the center of the room. She shoved him down onto the cushion and straddled him. He reached for her waist, but she shoved his hands away with a forcefulness that made him writhe beneath her. The fact that she didn't want him to touch her made him want to touch her even more.

She pulled his shirt off first, tossed it over her shoulder, and ran her hands over his chest, her fingers raking across him like claws. He arched his hips so she could feel how hard he was for her, how turned on by her sudden aggressiveness.

"If this is what you do when you get mad, maybe I'll never say sorry again."

Her eyes narrowed, but a smile toyed on her lips. She said nothing to him in response. Instead, she swayed her hips, grinding against him and shoving her breasts in his face. She was so fucking irresistible. Her lioness was finally unleashed, and he wanted to take her into his possession right now, bend her over, and fuck her from behind. He reached to grab her head and pull her to his mouth, but she backed away from him, slipping from his reach and sliding down the length of his body.

She slid right down to the floor, where she crouched on her

knees in front of him. Seeing her down there, looking up at him with those beautiful brown, hungry eyes, almost did him in. With a coy smile teasing her perfect lips, she unzipped his jeans and tugged them down. She pulled off his underwear, too, tossing everything to one side. His cock sprang free, and she didn't hesitate. She wrapped her fingers around his shaft and guided him into her mouth. He shuddered and groaned with pleasure as she slid up and down his cock, her mouth hot and wet.

He hadn't expected this, but he wasn't about to say no to her. She was a goddess, and he was under her spell. Her lips tightened over his shaft as her hands cupped his balls. He tilted his head back and gripped the pillows. She could do whatever the hell she wanted to him if she made him feel this good. She moved faster, switching now between her mouth and her hand.

He groaned a second time, feeling the throbbing in his cock intensify as he came to the edge. He was on the brink when Colette released him and lifted her head. Her lips were slick and her cheeks flushed red. She gripped his legs and looked him straight in the eyes when she said, "You don't come until I tell you to come."

Fuck. That was hot.

Then she straddled him again and kissed him with her hungry mouth.

The thong she wore was nothing, a slip of fabric he could tear through with his teeth. He writhed underneath her. She groaned and matched his rocking, moving her hips faster. She broke away from him with a gasp and rose on her knees, shimmying out of her thong and tossing it aside. He helped her with the bra, unhooking it and allowing her supple breasts to fall free. Her nipples were hard, and he took one in his mouth, watching out of the corner of his eye as she threw her head back in ecstasy.

She reached her hand down and grabbed his cock, pausing

only long enough for him to slide on a condom, before settling herself onto his shaft. He plunged into her with a sigh of relief.

She was so tight and wet, and he moaned in pleasure, grabbing her waist and holding on as she rode him frantically. She was uninhibited, throwing her head back and gasping with each thrust. She slid her hands over her own body, playing with her breasts, sliding her hands down to her clit. As he moved inside her, she touched herself. When they locked eyes, the movement became faster, more frantic, the need to come rising in him, and he could see it on her face, too, how close she was to ecstasy.

"Not yet," she whispered.

He nodded and grabbed her ass. He would hold himself back for her for as long as she needed. She bounced on top of him, and he loved every ripple of her body, every slick part of her, the way her eyes fluttered and her mouth parted the closer she came to the edge.

She tightened around his shaft. Her whole body stiffened as she gasped, "Now, now, I'm coming."

She let out a wild moan that sent Tristan over the edge. His cock throbbed inside her, pushing, pulsing. Sparks exploded in his vision. For several seconds, there was nothing but waves of pleasure cresting over him and the sound of her voice singing his name. He held on for dear life as her center exploded with heat. She came while he was inside her, and he lost himself in the sensation of it.

She collapsed against his chest with a final pant. "Fuck," she whispered, her breath moving the fine hairs around his face.

"Fuck is right." He pressed his lips to her collarbone.

"Was it good for you?" she murmured.

"It wasn't good, Colette," he answered. "It was unbelievable. You. You're unbelievable."

He shifted her off his lap, took off the condom, and then pushed her down on the couch, snuggling up behind her so they were spooning naked. She relaxed against him, arching her buttocks to meet his cock, which despite having been fully satisfied multiple times this weekend, was already getting hard again.

He traced his finger over her soft curves. A dreamy post-coital wonder filled his voice when he asked, "Where did you even come from?"

She laughed lightly, and the motion turned his cock fully hard.

Colette rolled to face him. She wrapped her fingers around his shaft, stroking it slowly. "Is this how it's always going to be?"

"I can't help that you're so damn fuckable."

"Is that all I am to you?" Her hand stayed wrapped around him, but she stopped stroking. Doubt glittered in her eyes. Then she let go of him and started to ramble, "I mean, if that's all this is, if this is just two adults fucking, then fine, because that's all we said it was going to be. And honestly, the fucking is pretty good, so we should keep that going, but—"

He pressed his mouth to hers before she could say anything else. They kissed for a while. When he pulled away, he tucked a piece of hair behind her ear and said, "The sex is pretty damn incredible, but no, that's not all this is. At least, not for me, it's not."

"It isn't?"

She was so damn cute, naked in his arms, asking him about his feelings. It had been a long time since a woman asked him about his feelings.

"There's a lot I like about you besides your killer body and tight pussy."

"Oh yeah? Like what?" Her cheeks flushed bright red.

He brushed his finger across the apple of her cheekbone. "Like how you wear your thoughts right out in the open. How you don't try to hide who you are and what you want."

"If I could, trust me, I would."

"It's not a bad thing to be yourself in a world full of people trying to be someone else."

"It is when they can use it against you."

"I won't."

"We'll see." She traced her finger over his biceps. "What else do you like about me?"

"I like when you get angry."

She laughed.

He continued, "No, I'm serious. Remember that night at the club?"

She groaned and laid her head against his shoulder. "Please don't remind me."

"You have nothing to be embarrassed about. I was being an asshole. You had every right to put me in my place the way you did."

She hummed but said nothing. Her fingers worked their way down his chest and around to the small of his back. Every place she touched sparked with electricity.

"I like that when I talk to you. It feels like you're listening. Really listening, not just pretending to listen until it's your turn to talk again."

"I have to listen. It's my job. That's what I get paid to do."

He laughed. "I like that too."

"What? That I'm a lawyer?"

"No. You're funny."

"No one else has ever told me that."

"Well, they just don't get your brand of humor, I guess."

"Yes, very dry."

"Smart," he countered.

"I'm a know-it-all."

He thought for a moment and then agreed with her, "That's another thing I like about you, though."

She pretended to be offended and smacked his bare ass. He pretended it hurt.

"Don't be a baby," she said.

"I took care of you when you cracked your head on that rock," he reminded her.

Instead of giving in, she said, "You were the reason I was up on that rope in the first place."

"Admit it." He wrapped his arms around her waist and drew her even closer against him. "You got a little thrill being up on that rock."

She shrugged. "Maybe."

"You like that I'm a little dangerous."

"You're not as dangerous as you think you are, you know." She pressed her hand to his heart. "In here, you're just a big softy."

"How dare you."

"I like soft," she said.

"That's not what your pussy was telling me a few minutes ago." He rocked his erect penis against her.

She sputtered a laugh. "You're filthy."

"So are you." He kissed her shoulder, one kiss for each freckle tracing down her arm. "You know what else I like about you? These freckles. God. They make me so hard."

"Freckles?"

"What can I say? I'm easy to please." He kissed all the way to her fingertips, then laced their hands together and looked into her eyes. "So, do you believe me now? That this isn't just about sex for me?"

"I don't know. I don't think any of your arguments would hold up in a court of law," she teased. "Especially considering we're both still naked and you're—" She stared pointedly at his erection.

"Mmm, excellent point, Counselor. Let's get some clothes on then and see if we still like each other after that." He tried to get up from the couch, but she pulled him back down and slid her hand around his cock.

"Not so fast." Her eyes glinted with desire. "I think we have a few more things we need to work out here first. Don't you?"

God, she was tying him up in the best knots. He leaned in to kiss her, but before things went any further, someone knocked on the door.

CRASHING DOWN

Tristan

Colette and Tristan froze.

"Who's that?" Colette whispered. She let go of his cock and sat up, searching for something to cover her nakedness.

Tristan sat up, too, shaking his head. He had no idea who would knock on his door on a Sunday afternoon. It was a beautiful day, and every person he knew would be outside taking advantage of that. His friends always texted first, never just came over. And he wasn't expecting any packages.

"Jehovah's Witness?" He reached for Colette, pulling her back into his lap, kissing her shoulders, eager to make her moan again. "If we wait long enough, maybe they'll go away."

But the knocking continued, insistent, then his mother's voice rang shrill and curdling through the door, immediately curbing all of Tristan's sexual desire. "Tristan? It's your mother! I know you're in there! I can hear you talking! Open up! I've been calling you all weekend! Have you been getting my messages? Tristan! Helloooo! I'm getting my spare key out!"

The door handle rattled. Tristan would have thrown Colette off his lap, if she wasn't already leaping off herself and scrambling to find her clothes. They both ran around like idiots for a few seconds before Tristan finally got his shit together.

He jabbed his finger at his bedroom door. "Hide in there."

She did what he said, skipping buck naked into his room and closing the door behind her.

Tristan stumbled around the living room, looking for something to pull over his own naked butt before his mom finally figured out how to turn the key in the lock. He scooped up the scattered clothing he and Colette had strewn over his apartment. He separated them as best as he could, opened his bedroom door, tossed her clothes into his room, shut the door again, and pulled on his shorts and t-shirt only to realize too late he wasn't wearing his t-shirt, but Colette's. A pink and white, striped, cotton short-sleeve with a low v-neck that stretched tight over his broad shoulders and muscled chest. He was surprised it hadn't ripped when he pulled it over his head.

The lock clicked, the door opened, and his mom burst into his apartment with an alarmed look on her face. She stopped short when she saw Tristan standing in the middle of the living room wearing a woman's shirt.

"Trissy? Didn't you hear me knocking?" Maureen scanned the apartment, her eyes pausing on the closed bedroom door. "Is someone else here? I heard voices. I could have sworn you were talking to someone."

"Just the radio."

Maureen narrowed her gaze at Tristan. Her nostrils flared. The entire room smelled of sex and sweat and Tristan had overlooked Colette's pink thong, which lay in a crumpled heap beside the couch. He tried to move it out of sight with his foot, but Maureen Walker, though certainly needy and at times vapid, was not stupid.

"Are you entertaining a woman?" Maureen clutched her large

shoulder bag to her chest like it might protect her from all the premarital sex her son was having. She swiveled her head. "Well, don't be rude. Introduce me to her."

"Mom—"

But she wouldn't let him talk. "If my son's dating someone, I want to know about it. I want to meet her."

"We're not dating," Tristan said.

Maureen's gaze dropped pointedly to the thong on the floor.

"It's new," he said, scooting the thong under the couch with his foot. "It's not exactly the best time."

He took a step toward Maureen, meaning to nudge her out of the apartment, but she was already darting toward the bedroom, her hand reaching for the doorknob.

She flung the door open before Tristan could stop her.

"Hello, Mrs. Walker," Colette said from inside the bedroom. "Nice to see you again."

Maureen's mouth dropped open, and she took a step back. Tristan stepped forward, fully expecting to see Colette sitting naked on the end of his bed, but she was—thank God for small miracles—dressed in her jeans and his t-shirt. She smiled nervously at Maureen, who seemed in shock because she stood there, saying nothing, not moving, staring at Colette like she was trying to figure out if what she was seeing was real.

Colette's eyes darted to him and panic flashed across her face.

Tristan stepped closer to his mother, trying to shake her from her stupor. "Mom, you remember Colette?"

"What the hell is she doing here?"

Tristan was stunned. His mother hardly ever cursed.

"She's—"

But Maureen turned on him before he could explain. She jabbed her finger into his chest. "Of all the eligible women in Los Angeles, you choose her? Please, Trissy, tell me this isn't true."

Colette stiffened. Spots of color formed on her cheeks.

"Mom, you don't even know her," Tristan said.

Maureen tilted her chin in the air and sniffed out in disgust. "I know enough about her to know you can do better."

He cringed at her harsh words.

"Mom, come on." But he had never been good at defending himself against her.

"Unbelievable." Maureen shook her head and fussed with the clasp of her purse. "Of all the people to disappoint me, this hurts the most, Trissy. I said it before, I'll say it again. You're just like your father. Never caring about anyone but yourself."

His anger flared hot in his chest. "Mom, you know that's not true."

"No, then what are you doing dating her?" Maureen flung her hand at Colette. "She humiliated me. Kicked me when I was already down. She. Called. Me. Old."

"Mom, don't you think you're overreacting a little? And besides, I told you. We're not dating," he said. "We're just... It's nothing."

He didn't mean nothing, as in *nothing*. He was trying to get his mom to stop freaking out without having to explain to her the nuances of his sex life. But he knew as soon as the words left his mouth that he'd fucked up. Again.

The air left Colette's lungs in a rush. When he looked over at her, she was staring at him in disbelief. She pressed her lips together in a thin line. He shook his head and took a step toward her, but she took a step back. And then his mother was in front of him, shoving something into his hands. He looked down at the brown manila envelope she was trying to give him.

"I need you to give this to your father the next time you see him," Maureen said. "It's the divorce papers. He's refusing to take my calls."

"Mom, I'm not giving him these."

Maureen's neatly plucked eyebrows arched high on her head. "Well, someone needs to."

She snapped her purse shut and turned her hard gaze onto

Colette. There was a split second where Tristan thought the two women were going to fly at each other with claws out. Then Maureen let out a loud snort, spun on her sensible heels, and marched out of his apartment. She slammed the door as she left. Tristan flinched.

He turned to Colette with a contrite smile plastered on his face. "Well, that was embarrassing."

"It certainly was something," she said, her voice as tense as the muscles in her shoulders. "I'd like my shirt back, please."

She grabbed the hem of the one she was wearing, pulled it over her head, and threw it at him.

As he carefully peeled himself out of her too-tight shirt, he said, "Colette, look, I'm sorry. She doesn't normally barge into my apartment like that."

"That's what you're sorry about?" The venom in her voice made him want to get down on his knees and beg for forgiveness.

But before he could do anything even close to that, she grabbed the pink and white shirt from him and shoved it over her head as she rushed to the front door.

"Colette, wait, please. Let me explain—"

"Don't worry, there's nothing to explain," she said, emphasizing the word 'nothing.' She scooped her thong off the floor and stuffed it in her pocket, slipped on her shoes, and barged out the front door. Over her shoulder, she said, "It's really not a big deal, Tristan. We're not dating. So you don't owe me anything, and I don't owe you anything. It's like you said—we're nothing."

She turned her back on him and walked away.

Go after her, dummy. The voice in his head sounded pissed.

Tristan scrambled around his apartment in a panic. He tried to pull on his t-shirt first, but his parents' divorce papers were in the way. His parents' divorce papers? What the actual hell? And what was his mother thinking, asking him to deliver them to his father? Wasn't that what attorneys were for? He threw the manila envelope onto the counter and jammed his shirt over his head. It smelled like Colette.

He couldn't find his shoes. He could have sworn he kicked them off by the door, but they weren't there when he went to put them on, which meant he had to go back into the bedroom to find another pair. God, he was such an idiot. *It's nothing.* Why had he said that? Tristan had experienced a lot of nothings in his life, especially in the past year, and Colette was as far from nothing as a person could get. He just needed a chance to explain to her what he'd meant.

And what did you mean, Triscuit? Exactly?

He paused with his hand stretched under the bed, feeling for his flip-flops. If Colette was more than nothing to him, much more, then why hadn't he said as much to his mom? Because it was too soon. They'd known each other barely a week, and most of that time had revolved around sex. And while Tristan definitely thought there was a lot you could find out about a person while they were naked, there was a lot more that needed to be discovered apart from the distraction of lips and hands and genitals.

Like who she voted for in the 2020 election? Did she like to travel? Had she ever gotten into a fistfight? Did she cry at sad movies? Did she want kids? What were her dreams, goals, aspirations? Where did she see herself in 10 years?

Do you even know where you *want to be in 10 years, Triscuit?*

Last week he would have said no.

Today, he knew one thing at least: wherever he ended up in ten years, he wanted Colette to be with him.

His fingers touched the rubber of his flip-flops. He yanked them out from under the bed and slid them onto his feet.

The elevator wasn't coming up fast enough. It was stuck on the fifth floor. Tristan cursed and shoved through the fire door into the stairwell. He scrambled down all eight levels of stairs, losing his flip-flops at least a half dozen times. His legs were on fire, and by the time he reached the street, sweat poured off him.

Panting, he burst through the fire door into the bright daylight, shouting her name, but he was too late.

Colette's suitcases were missing from the back of the Jeep and her car was gone.

Tristan trudged back upstairs to his apartment. That was it then. The love of his life had walked out the door, and he'd stood there like a total asshole and let it happen.

He plopped down onto the couch that still smelled of her and scowled at the wall. That's when he saw it. Slouched in the corner near the front door was a sad slump of brown leather. Colette had left her purse behind.

Hope fluttered in his chest. She would have to come back for it eventually and when she did, Tristan would apologize to her for real this time. He would tell her what he should have said to his mother: that she was everything to him, not nothing, but his whole damn world. He would do his best to convince her to stay.

ONLY EVER A FLING

Colette

Colette could think of a million and one reasons not to date Tristan Walker.

He wore clothes a teenager would wear.

He enjoyed eating gross food.

He drove a crotch rocket.

He didn't have a job.

He was cocky, and his friends were rude.

Sure, this weekend was pleasant. More than nice. But there was no future with a man like Tristan Walker. Colette laughed bitterly as she sped away from his apartment.

Man was a stretch.

Tristan Walker was a mama's boy with a weakness for pussy. A spoiled-rotten, rich kid with no job and no real ambition, living off his daddy's money. A man-child with an over-inflated sense of bravado and the attention span of a goldfish who only wanted one thing, and once he got it, he moved on to whatever new hot girl caught his attention.

Colette remembered the first time she saw him in the club last week, how presumptuous he'd been, asking if she wanted to join him for a threesome. Her cheeks warmed now at the thought of being in bed with him again, but she clamped down on those feelings.

So he was good in bed. Okay, really good—a fucking rock star with his tongue—but that didn't make him good boyfriend material.

Nope. Colette was done with Tristan Walker. Finished. That's all, folks. Slam, bam, thank you, next.

She reached to grab her phone from her purse, wanting to text Brooke to ask if she should bring over some sushi for dinner and a good cry. But her purse wasn't on the passenger seat where she usually kept it. At the next red light, Colette did a quick scan of the car, but didn't see her purse anywhere.

She remembered having it when she and Tristan first got to his apartment. She'd carried it upstairs, somehow holding on to it as he went down on her in the elevator, but once they'd walked into his apartment, she'd tossed the purse to one side, caring only about getting her hands on Tristan, making him feel as good as she'd felt in the elevator. But she didn't remember grabbing her purse when she stormed out of his apartment. She'd been too caught up in her own humiliation, desperate to get out of there before she—God forbid—started crying in front of him, and in her rush to leave, she'd forgotten her purse.

Colette slammed her hand on the steering wheel and shouted in frustration. At the next intersection, she pulled a U-turn and drove back to Tristan's apartment.

He flung open the door before she even finished knocking, as if he'd been expecting her return. "I thought you might come back."

He leaned his muscular body against the door frame, one arm hidden behind the wall. His serene smile infuriated her.

"I think I forgot my purse." She crossed her arms over her chest.

"Yes, you did." He straightened his body to full height and produced her purse like he was pulling a rabbit from a hat.

She tried to take it from him, but he pulled it close to his chest and took a step back inside his apartment. "I'll give this back to you, but first, you have to come inside and sit down and let me explain what happened. Why I said what I did."

"I don't have to do anything." She stayed in the hallway. "I can scream right now that I'm being robbed, and your neighbors will call the police."

His mouth twitched and his eyes narrowed, but he didn't relinquish the purse.

"Do it," he challenged her. "Scream. I dare you."

She rolled her eyes, then lunged and grabbed the purse handle, trying to yank it from his hands. He tightened his grip, refusing to let go.

"Tristan, this is stupid. Give me my purse."

"You know what's stupid? You being angry with me for no reason."

They stared at each other, neither one of them refusing to let go of the dumb purse.

She couldn't believe him. There were a dozen other things Tristan could have said to his mother that would have explained their situation. We just started seeing each other. It's new. It was unexpected. A surprise. We're taking it slow. We're seeing how this goes. But no. He'd gone with, *It's nothing*. The words spoken so quickly, with such emphasis, that it had been obvious to Colette that he meant what he said. She was no one to him. He'd made that perfectly clear. And now he was holding her purse hostage, trying to convince her that she was the one who'd messed up by walking out.

"I'll tell you what's stupid." She shoved her face close to Tristan, the purse bulging between them. "Getting involved with you in the first place. I knew from the moment you opened your mouth at the club that you are the kind of guy who can't take anything seriously. Sure, you've got all the right moves to get a woman into bed, but then what? You've got nothing to offer anyone long term. You don't have a job. You have no goals, no idea what you're doing with your life. No clue what it means to commit to something. To someone. Before you're even done with one woman, you're already thinking of finding another who's down for a good time, already thinking of how you can talk your way into her panties like you did with me. You're good, Tristan, I'll give you that, but don't for an instant think you had me fooled. I knew exactly who you were when we started. And good news. You met all my expectations."

Tristan's eyes flared wide. For a passing second, he looked genuinely hurt by her comments and the sharp venom in her voice, but then his blue eyes darkened and his expression turned empty.

He shrugged. "Since you knew exactly who you were getting involved with, I don't see what the problem is. You're the one who said you didn't want a relationship. You're the one who said this was just going to be sex. And that's what I agreed to. You wanted me to show you a good time, and I did. So fine. We had sex. Let's leave it at that. You don't want it to mean anything, it doesn't have to mean anything. And you're right, there are a hundred other women out there who are looking for a good time and it'll take a lot less effort on my part to get them into bed. Honestly, it'll be nice to fuck someone who knows what she's doing."

She flinched at his words, surprised at how much they stung, but she refused to let him see how much he'd hurt her.

"Grow up, Tristan." She straightened her shoulders, took a deep breath, and backed away from him, but his arm snaked out.

One hand still gripped her purse, the other wrapped around

her neck, pulling them back together. His eyes locked on to hers, fierce blue and sparking with fury.

"Just tell me one thing, Colette." His voice sounded on the verge of shattering. "If it really was just sex, if that's all I was to you, a means to an end, then why are you so upset right now?"

"I'm not upset." She growled back at him, forcing herself to rise to his anger rather than cower away from it. There was nothing he could do to hurt her any more than he already had. "I just want my purse back."

"Fine." He let go of her neck, but not the purse.

"Fine." She gave another tug.

"Fine," he repeated, before giving one last hard tug and letting go.

She wasn't expecting it and lost her footing, stumbling backward and bumbling her purse so it fell out of her hands.

"Shit, Colette, I'm sorry." Tristan dropped to his knees and started gathering the contents spilled and scattered around their feet.

She dropped beside him, scrabbling to collect lipsticks, pens, hair clips.

Tristan's fingers closed around a piece of pink notebook paper. His eyes skimmed over whatever was written on it, but instead of handing it over to Colette, he pulled the paper close and rocked back on his heels. His scowl deepened as he read aloud the words scrawled in Brooke's handwriting, "Pros for Fucking Tristan Walker…"

Colette realized what he'd found and tried to grab the paper from him before he read anymore, but he pulled it out of reach.

"'He's a stranger, so you never have to see him again after he pops that cherry.'" He kept reading. "'He's rich.'" His laughter was a bitter sound. "'Can probably get us into cool parties.' 'Good sex and no strings equals the perfect fuck buddy.'"

Tristan's eyes skimmed down the rest of the list, which he

thankfully didn't read out loud. He laughed again, shook his head, and pushed up to his feet.

"I'm not the one who needs to grow up, Colette." He crumpled the paper in his fist and dropped it on the floor.

Colette grabbed it, hurriedly shoved it along with all her other scattered items back into her purse, and clambered to her feet.

"It's just this stupid thing I do when I get nervous," she tried to explain, but what was the point? Why bother explaining anything to him when they were so clearly over? But she rambled on despite herself. "And besides, I didn't even write half of these, my best friend did, and I completely forgot about it—"

Tristan held up his hand, stopping her from saying anything else. "It doesn't matter. We're both adults. We both knew what this was before we started. Let's not turn it into something more than it is. We had fun, the sex was good, now it's time for both of us to go back to our real lives. No strings."

He made a snipping motion with his fingers, stepped into his apartment, and closed the door.

Colette stood in the hallway with her mouth hanging open. She didn't know what upset her more—the fact that he'd read her stupid list or that he'd gotten the last word.

She raised her fist to pound on the door, but stopped herself before she actually did. All of this had started with her wanting only one thing from him, and she'd gotten exactly what she wanted, hadn't she? She wasn't a virgin anymore. There was nothing left for her to say and no reason for her to stay.

She marched away from his apartment, taking the stairs because the elevator would only remind her of him. On her way down, Colette texted Brooke.

Colette: Hungry? I can bring sushi.
Brooke: Have I told you lately that I love you?
Colette: At least someone does.

Brooke: Uh oh. I'm not sure I like the sound of that. Everything okay with Tristan?
Colette: If by okay, you mean over, then yes, everything's fine.
Brooke: What a prick! I don't need to know what he did. I hate him already. I'll have the wine and tissues ready.
Colette: Thanks, but really, I meant it when I said it's fine. Things weren't serious between us anyway, right? It was just sex. I'm happy to help with the wine though, regardless.
Brooke: Good, because I've got a bottle with your name on it.

As Colette drove across the city to get to Brooke's apartment, she glanced too often in the rearview mirror, scanning the road behind her. It took a few stoplights to realize she was hoping to catch sight of Tristan weaving his bike through traffic as he chased after her.

But of course, he wasn't there. And he wouldn't be, not now, not in five minutes, not ever. You only went after someone like that if it was true love. And where Colette had doubted before, now she was certain: when it came to Tristan Walker, she had only ever been a fling.

KISS MORE FROGS

Colette

"I'm sorry, Coco," Brooke said as she stuffed the last spicy tuna roll into her mouth. "I know I'm supposed to be on your side here, but honestly, Tristan has a point."

Colette choked on a piece of ginger.

She'd spent the past twenty minutes telling Brooke about her weekend, from when she showed up at his apartment with too many bags to the first time they had sex in Joshua Tree to the awkward text from his friend that led to the hottest elevator ride of her life and finally to the humiliation of his mother barging in on them as they were about to have sex for the fourth time. She had just finished describing the fight in the hallway in excruciating detail, and couldn't believe her best friend was turning traitor.

"And what point is that, exactly?" she asked.

"You were the one who set up the rules of this game, right?" Brooke pointed her chopsticks at Colette.

Colette shook her head, but said, "Yeah, sure, I guess I did. I mean, he approached me first. He asked me out."

"But you said yes," Brooke said. "And if I remember correctly, you said yes only because you thought he'd be an excellent candidate to pop your cherry. Not because you thought he was marriage material."

"I don't want to marry him."

"Good, because that would be a huge mistake."

"I mean, he's nice when he's not being a prick."

"Aren't they all?" Brooke laughed and gathered the empty sushi containers, stuffing them in the takeout bag to throw away later.

"And he's funny. And he smells good. And he—"

"Stop." Brooke held up her hand. "Look, Coco, I love you, but you don't really have a leg to stand on here. You told him you only wanted sex, and that's what you got. Be happy it was really good sex—"

"Great sex," Colette muttered.

"Because I've been with enough men to know it's not always so good. Most of the time, it's actually pretty terrible."

Colette groaned and buried her face in her hands. "Give me something to look forward to, at least."

Brooke laughed and patted Colette's shoulder. "Be grateful, babe. Most of us don't have mind-blowing sex right out of the gate. So you're already miles ahead of the game."

Colette shoved a piece of sushi around on her plate. She'd been doing so much talking, she hadn't gotten around to eating much and now her appetite was gone again, thinking about the look on Tristan's face right before he slammed the door on her forever. Even if she apologized and asked to try again, she doubted he would take her back.

She'd screwed up and there was nothing she could do about it. He'd made it perfectly clear he wanted nothing else to do with her.

Brooke went into the kitchen to open another bottle of wine. When she returned with two full glasses, she handed one to Colette and sank down onto the pile of throw pillows covering the floor. She clinked her glass against Colette's and said, "Cheers to an exciting weekend with a hot guy who treated you like the queen you are! And cheers to finally getting your v-card punched!"

They both drank, though Colette with less enthusiasm than Brooke.

"Really, Coco, it's the best thing that could have possibly happened." Brooke bumped her shoulder. "You had a weekend of no strings attached, hot sex with a guy who wasn't an asshole, mostly, and now you're free to do whatever you want with whomever you want. Oh! I know this hottie from my acting class who would be the perfect next step for you! He's shy, sweet, but he's got this mysterious side. I've tried to get him in my bed more than once, but I think he finds me intimidating. But I think you two would get along great!"

Colette set her plate on the coffee table, wrapped her arms around her legs, and rested her chin on her knees. She didn't want to see other guys; she wanted to see Tristan. But there was no way in hell she was going to admit that to Brooke, or to Tristan, because doing so would be admitting that she'd fallen in love when she promised she wouldn't with a man who had probably fucked half of Los Angeles before they met. A man who was probably in bed with someone right now, even as Colette was here, nursing a broken heart.

But Brooke had been Colette's best friend since elementary school, and could see right through her.

"Trust me, Coco," she said quietly, leaning into Colette's shoulder. "You know what they say. You've got to kiss a lot of frogs to find your prince."

"What's that supposed to mean?" Colette grumbled.

"It means you don't want to fall in love with the first guy you sleep with."

"I think it might be too late for me." Colette tipped her wine to her lips and drained the glass.

"It's definitely not." Brooke shifted on the pillows, pulling one out from under her ass and tossing it onto the couch. "You have a real opportunity here. You and Tristan were together for like a few days? And not even really *together* together, just messing around. He didn't ask you to be his girlfriend or anything, did he?"

Colette snorted a laugh. "We're not in middle school."

Brooke raised her eyebrows. "I'll take that as a no."

"No, he didn't ask me to be his girlfriend. He didn't even ask me on a second date."

"And he didn't say, 'I love you?'"

Colette choked on her wine. "Brooke."

"What?" Brooke gave her a wide-eyed, innocent look. "More than one man has said it to me after I blew their mind, and from what you've told me, it sounds like there was a lot of mind blowing going on this weekend."

"No. He didn't say anything like that."

"Okay, so you're a free agent. You had a taste of Tristan, and now you need to get out there and see what else the world's buffet has to offer. Until you do, you won't truly know if you like Tristan for Tristan or if it's just his dick you want."

Colette sputtered a laugh and bumped her shoulder against Brooke's. "Can't it be both?"

"Of course it can, stupid, but I'm telling you that right now you've got so many chemicals flooding your body that what you think is budding love might be nothing more than a case of good dick. I've seen it happen to plenty of good women. They get involved with a man, thinking he's going to be the one, but it turns out he's a scumbag with a fear of commitment, just like all the rest. If you want my advice, Coco, it's this. One, don't get too attached and you won't end up with your heart broken. And two, play around with whoever you want because you know he's out there doing the same."

"You sound so cynical."

"I'm not cynical. I'm a realist." Brooke tipped back her wine glass and then her expression brightened. "Oh! I know! We should set up a dating profile for you on-line!"

Colette groaned. "You know I hate those apps. They're all about hook-ups and one-night stands."

"Which is exactly what you need right now." Brooke grinned at her. "Give me your phone."

Brooke grabbed Colette's phone where it was sitting on the coffee table. She punched in the code to Colette's lock screen, which was Brooke and Colette's birthdays combined.

"First, let's delete his number." Brooke's fingers moved over the screen.

"What? No, don't do that. What if I want to text him?" Colette grabbed for her phone, but Brooke pulled it out of reach.

"What would you want to do that for?" Brooke swiped over the screen, opening the text app.

"Brooke! Give me my phone. Do not delete his number."

"Too late. Already gone." She tossed the phone into Colette's lap.

Colette scrolled through her contacts and messages and call history, but Brooke had been relentless. With a few swipes of her finger, she erased Tristan's number and all evidence of his existence. Colette stared at her phone screen, already feeling a tug of despair at not being able to text Tristan whenever she wanted.

"If he wants you, he'll find you," Brooke said. "In the meantime, get yourself out there and have some fun! You've been celibate for 30 years, bitch! It's time to let that pussy cut loose!"

Brooke hopped to her feet and danced around her living

room, gyrating her hips and making sharp yipping sounds like a ditzy porn star.

Colette laughed at her, but didn't join in. She checked the time on her phone and said, "I should go. I've got to be in early tomorrow."

"Party pooper." Brooke plopped back down on the carpet.

"Yeah, well, I'm not exactly looking forward to it. After the way Scott treated me on Friday night, it's going to be really awkward at the office from now on. I don't know what I'm supposed to say to him, or how I'm supposed to act."

"Maybe you should fuck him," Brooke suggested.

Colette glared at her. "Don't even joke about that."

"I'm being completely serious. You know what you're doing now. So go into his office, give him a taste of what you can do, and then walk away. Men hate it when you fuck them once and then refuse to do it again. Show him what he could have had if he wasn't such an asshole."

"Sex as revenge?" Colette said.

"There are worse ways to use that beautiful pussy of yours."

Brooke walked her to the door, planting a sloppy kiss on both cheeks. "Promise me you won't spend another minute thinking about this Tristan guy. You got what you needed from him. Now it's time to move on."

Colette tossed and turned in bed for over an hour, replaying her and Tristan's fight and the words she'd said that weren't even her true feelings, just her lashing out in anger, trying to hurt him the way he'd hurt her. To get herself to calm down, she thought of the weekend in Joshua Tree, but that was even worse than thinking about the fight. Remembering the way he'd made her feel, the whisper of his touch lingering on her skin, the way his skin tasted, the way they melted together. She punched the pillow and let out a frustrated scream. No man was worth this agony, but especially not Tristan Walker. Not after the cruel things he'd said to her, not after how dismissive he'd been, brushing her off like the connection they'd shared was nothing. Like *she* was nothing.

Her phone charging on the bedside table lit up, and she rolled over to look at it, hoping that it was Tristan despite herself, hoping that he'd changed his mind and was sending her an apology text, begging her to come over. She wouldn't respond, of course, but it would make her feel better knowing he was in as much misery as she was.

But the text wasn't from Tristan. It was Colette's little sister sending late birthday wishes.

Having so much fun in Rome, I completely forgot! Next time I'm in LA, I'm taking you out on the town!

Colette scrolled through her contacts list even though she knew she wouldn't find Tristan's number there. She spent a few minutes in the First Timers Forum, then checked her text messages again. Still nothing from Tristan. She shoved her phone in the nightstand drawer and rolled over.

She would not think about Tristan. She would not think about his deep blue eyes or shaggy hair. She wouldn't think about his hands or the easy way he lifted her onto his lap. She wouldn't think about how he'd opened up to her about his brother on that hill under the stars, how he cared for her when she hurt herself, how he made her laugh and try new things she would have never tried on her own. No, she wouldn't think about him or any of it.

Maybe he was fresh in her memory now, but in the future, he would fade. He would be no more important than that Irish drummer in her roommate's bed, someone she got off to every once in a while, but not someone who mattered, not someone she ever planned to see again.

She slipped her hand between her legs, closed her eyes, and definitely didn't think about how nice Tristan's mouth felt against hers or how good he was at making her melt. She definitely didn't bring herself to orgasm by imagining him going down on her, and when she finally fell asleep, she definitely didn't dream about him curled up beside her, their hearts beating in unison.

FIRST TIMERS CLUB

Chat Room

NotSoDirty30 (posted 12:23am): I know it's late, or early, but is anyone awake? Something happened this weekend. Something big. I had sex for the first time!!!! It was pretty amazing, but then I went and messed it up–big time. I told myself I wasn't going to get attached, that if I had sex with this guy, that was all it was going to be. Just sex. Just a chance to punch the v-card and move on with my life. If only it had been so simple. It just got so complicated between us so fast. It's hard to explain what happened without writing an entire essay, but I think I'm falling in love with him? The only problem is… He definitely doesn't feel the same way. And we had this huge fight, and I'm pretty sure I'm never going to see him again. I'm not sure why I'm even confessing all of this, or how any of you can help. Honestly, I don't even know if I'm allowed to stay in this group now that I'm not a virgin anymore. But if you have any good ideas for how to get over a broken heart, I'd love to hear them!

2Hawt2Handle: Nice! Way to get some! How did it feel?

HappilyNeverAfter: Was it shitty? Please tell me it wasn't shitty.

NotSoDirty30: No, it wasn't shitty. Awkward at first. It took some time to get comfortable with him, but then after that, it was great. Really. Great.

cherrybomb: Ahh!! You go, girl! Get yours!

LoveConnection (admin): First of all, CONGRATULATIONS! Second of all, developing feelings for someone is perfectly normal when you're sharing that level of intimacy. Time apart could be good to help you figure out whether your feelings relate solely to your physical chemistry or if they run deeper to your soul connection.

TheBoyNextDoor: Soul connection? Isn't that a band?

LoveConnection (admin): And if it is a soul connection, then run toward it, not away. In my experience, physical chemistry is easy, but it's twin beating hearts that are nearly impossible to find. So, if you find someone in this world who lights you up from the inside and out, you owe it to yourself to try to make it work. You at least owe it to yourself to have the conversation.

NotSoDirty30: Thanks, @LoveConnection. That's actually great advice. It might be easier to figure out what I want when I'm not distracted by... Everything.

SexIsOveR-rated: The one-eyed snake's got you in a trance.

Shakespeare-N-Love: Dopamine and oxytocin, man, they're no joke!

2Hawt2Handle: Does that mean you've popped your cherry too @Shakespeare-N-Love?

Shakespeare-N-Love: No. Sadly. Not yet. I just read. A lot.

LoveConnection (admin): As for your other concern—no one is kicking you out of the group. If you want to leave, if you feel your time with us has come to an end, that is your choice. We will send you off with a grand farewell. But you are welcome to continue with this group for as long as you find it useful. That goes for everyone here. We call ourselves First Timers, and yes, our virginity brought us together, but I like to think there is more connecting us than what we may or may not lack in the sex department.

2Hawt2Handle: Sex department—where's that located exactly? I'd like to place an order.

cherrybomb: Hahaha! Always the joker.

2Hawt2Handle: If I don't laugh about it, I'll break down crying.

SexIsOveR-rated: There's no crying in the First Timer's Club.

TheBoyNextDoor: Only shame and self-loathing.

SexIsOveR-rated: None of that, either. We're proud virgins to the very end!

TheBoyNextDoor: Speak for yourself.

HappilyNeverAfter: Don't leave, @NotSoDirty30! At least, not until you decide what you're going to do.

cherrybomb: Yes! We need an ending!

Shakespeare-N-Love: Preferably a happy one.

LoveConnection (admin): No pressure or anything. Whatever you decide is best for you and your future love—that will be the happiest of endings.

HappilyNeverAfter: Amen.

THE NEW ROOMMATE

Tristan

Over the next four days, Tristan wrote and deleted hundreds of texts to Colette, each one more pitiful than the last. He begged, pleaded, cajoled, accused, backtracked, explained, argued, talked himself into a dozen different corners, talked himself back out, apologized—every single word ended up in the digital trash bin. Whenever his phone dinged, he lunged for it, hoping it would be Colette, but it never was.

He stayed out late and slept until noon. He drank too much, drove too fast, and even brought a woman back to his apartment once, but the second she pushed him down on the couch, his thoughts leaped to Colette. His body craved her touch, not the touch of a stranger. He'd pushed the other woman away and ran to the bathroom, pretending to be sick from too much whiskey. He didn't come out again until he heard his apartment door open and click shut.

The awful date was on Tuesday.

On Wednesday, he stayed inside with all the blinds drawn and played video games.

Thursday, he woke up on his couch with a crick in his neck and a thin layer of fuzz on his tongue from the entire bag of Cheetos he'd eaten the night before. He groaned as he rolled over and the muscles in his back tensed. This wasn't like him, feeling so wrecked after a break-up. Even worse was the fact that it wasn't technically a break-up because he and Colette had never been together in the first place. Technically. His heart didn't know the definition of the word.

Well, aren't you a sad, sorry sack of bones?

He pulled his phone from between the couch cushions and checked his messages. Nothing. He started to type another text to Colette that would end up in the trash because no matter what he wrote, it always sounded too snarky or too whiny or too desperate. *Keep it simple, Stupid.*

Can we meet for lunch?

She couldn't possibly say no to lunch, could she? All the rest —the apologies and explanations and begging—could wait until they were together in person and he could look her in the eyes.

I've never known you to beg for anything in your entire life, Triscuit.

The voice in his head was right. Why should he be the one to text first? The one to beg?

It was Colette who'd walked out on him, Colette who used him for his body. Not that he minded the being used part. But it still pissed him off that she walked out on him. And that stupid list that fell out of her purse. He was mad about that, too, about the fact that she'd never seen him as anything more than a fuck buddy, that she'd never taken him seriously. It shouldn't bother him as much as it did. He'd been with plenty of women who only wanted sex. But that was the thing, wasn't it? With Colette, he'd wanted more.

Maybe you should have told her that, dummy.

Maybe he still could.

His thumb hovered over his phone, but a loud knocking interrupted him before he could hit send.

"What now?" he muttered, pissed that his mom was coming between him and Colette yet again. He pocketed his phone without sending the text and went to answer the door.

It wasn't Maureen this time, but his father, Otto, holding a garment bag in one hand and dragging a suitcase in the other. Otto gave Tristan a sheepish grin and shrugged. "Hi, son. Your mother changed the locks on me."

Tristan stepped back from the doorway to let his father inside the apartment.

"Sorry to barge in on you like this," Otto said. "Though, to be fair, I've been trying to get in touch with you since last Thursday."

"I thought you just wanted to talk to me about Mom."

Tristan shut the door and watched warily as his father made himself right at home, laying the garment bag over the back of a recliner and rolling the suitcase to one side so no one would trip over it. Then he walked into the kitchen, took two glasses from the sink, dropped in a few pieces of ice and splashed three fingers of bourbon into each. Otto gave a glass to Tristan, then clinked them together and said, "To bachelor life," and took a sip.

Tristan set the glass on the counter without drinking. "What are you doing here?"

Otto let out a boisterous laugh, the fake one he used when talking to clients and movie people. "I can't very well stay in a hotel for the rest of my life. I'll be broke in six months."

"You're staying in a hotel?"

"I was." Otto raised his glass again and tipped the rest of the bourbon into his mouth. "That's what I've been trying to call you about, son. I can't stay in a hotel anymore. I can't afford it. Not with your mother throwing a fit the way she is, hiring an attorney, trying to come after me for every penny I've got. If I don't want to lose everything, I need to protect my assets."

Tristan's head spun. He reached for the bourbon and tossed it back in one swallow. It burned going down, but was exactly what he needed to get through what his father said next.

"I promise you won't even know I'm here." Otto sniffed the air and his nose wrinkled in distaste. "Though we'll have to do something about that funk. When's the last time you did your laundry? Let's get some windows open, spray some air freshener. I'll call Louisa and have her come over this afternoon."

Louisa was the woman who cleaned the Malibu mansion.

"Dad," Tristan said. "I don't know if living together is a very good idea."

"Don't worry. It's only a temporary arrangement." Otto grabbed his suitcase and dragged it toward the only bedroom in the single-bedroom apartment. He tossed his suitcase on the bed and began to unpack, moving Tristan's clothes out of the dresser and into a pile on the floor.

"Temporary?" Tristan gathered the clothes and moved them into the closet, but his dad took over that space, too, unpacking several three-piece suits from his garment bag and dusting off invisible bits of lint.

"Like temporary until Mom takes you back?" Tristan asked.

"Ah, son," Otto said with a sad shake of his head. He shoved a pile of Tristan's clothes into his arms and moved him out of the bedroom. "I don't think your mother has any intention of taking me back this time. No, this will just be until we find you another place to live."

"Me?" Tristan clutched his clothes against his chest, not sure where he was supposed to put them now. "Why can't *you* find a place?"

Otto smiled patiently at his son. "Remind me again who pays the mortgage on this place?"

"You, but—"

"Me. Exactly. I'm the one who writes the checks, which means I'm the one who gets to live here."

"I don't have anywhere else to go," Tristan argued.

"Neither do I." His father's smile was a hard-edged grimace, and Tristan pitied anyone who got on Otto Walker's bad side.

"Don't worry," Otto's voice boomed cheerfully as he poured more bourbon. "I'm not kicking you out tonight. You can stay until the end of the month."

"That's two weeks away."

"Plenty of time to find a place. And you can sleep on the couch, in the meantime. You know how my back is." Otto dug his fingers into the small of his back, grimacing like he was twenty years older than his spry sixty years.

Tristan stared at the secondhand couch with Cheetos dust staining the cushions. He'd fallen asleep on it last night, which had proved to be the second biggest mistake he'd made all week. The first being Colette.

There was no way in hell he was sleeping on that couch again. He'd been living here for over a year. It wasn't his fault his parents couldn't make their marriage work. That didn't mean he deserved to be kicked out on the street.

He took a breath to tell his father that he wasn't moving out, but his phone pinged, interrupting him. Thinking it was Colette, he yanked it from his pocket. His first reaction was disappointment. It was Nick, texting him about some killer waves breaking at their favorite surf spot. His second reaction was that this was exactly the distraction he needed right now.

His father stood with the fridge door wide open, scowling at the empty shelves. "This is worse than when your mother goes on a diet."

He shut the fridge and took out his cell phone. "I'll order us some pizza."

"I'm going surfing." Tristan grabbed his board and wetsuit, both of which hung on hooks by the front door.

Tristan ignored the hurt look Otto gave him. His dad wanted to come in here and disrupt his living situation? Fine. But Tristan wasn't going to bend over backwards to accommodate him.

As he shut the door, he called to his dad, "Oh, by the way—Mom left some paperwork for you. It's on the counter!"

WIPEOUT

Tristan

Gigantic waves broke at a perfect angle to shore. Tristan stood at the water's edge with his board, watching the swell and picking the perfect spot to swim out to. Nick and the others were already in the water, small black dots bobbing in an endless expanse of blue. One of them—they were too far away for Tristan to say for certain, but he thought it was Carlos—caught a wave, crouched low, angled his board just right and dropped into the barrel. He rode several seconds in perfect harmony with the swell, then the wave bottomed out and Carlos disappeared under the water for a few seconds before popping back up and swimming out to the break again, where the others waited for their own perfect waves.

Tristan zipped his wetsuit, strapped his board to his ankle, and stepped into the ocean. His arms moved with confidence as he swam away from shore. It felt good to be doing something other than sitting on his couch pining after Colette and worrying about his parents' marriage. His muscles warmed as he paddled faster. The swells rocked under his board. His heart pounded with the effort and anticipation.

He got close enough to Nick and Carlos to wave and shout hello. They waved back, gesturing for him to come closer, but Tristan kept his distance. He didn't want to bother with small talk or questions about Colette. He wanted the ocean, the waves, the sun, the wind, and the feel of his body moving inside it all.

Facing the horizon, he bobbed on his board and watched the ocean undulate as a wave began to build. When the wave came close enough, he spun his board to point toward shore. The ocean lifted him; the wave rising as if taking a breath. Tristan paddled furiously to keep up with it. When the wave broke, he was at the perfect drop-in spot. He hopped onto his feet, found his balance, and rode for a few seconds, getting used to the feel of the board beneath him. It had been weeks since he'd been out to surf rather than swim, and it took his muscles a few minutes to remember what they were doing. He bailed off his board before the wave petered out, turned, and swam toward the horizon again to wait for another swell.

Seagulls spiraled above him. The sun sparked across the turquoise water. This was exactly what he needed. Tristan relaxed as he fell into ocean's rhythm. After catching a few small waves, he started looking for larger ones. He fell off his board a few times, but it was nothing he couldn't handle. He was a strong swimmer and could hold his breath for long enough to roll inside the churn for a few seconds before following his board to the surface and breaking free of the wave with a gasp.

Between rides, as he sat on his board to catch his breath, Tristan watched Nick and the others catch their own waves. Carlos was a trick surfer, messing around, trying flips and spins, walking up and down his board. Whatever he thought looked cool. Nick was steady and old school, patient for that strong, perfect wave that rolled on forever. Jacob was the most inexperienced of the trio, but what he lacked in skill, he made up in sheer tenacity. There were other surfers bobbing nearby, people Tristan knew in passing because of Troy.

His chest pinched at the thought of his brother, who would have dropped everything to be out on the waves on a perfect golden California day like this one. He glanced over at Troy's friends again. It wasn't the same without his brother. Troy had always been the cheerleader, giving up the perfect wave more than once so someone else could experience the thrill. Troy surfed because he loved it. Tristan surfed because he loved Troy. When Troy was alive, being out here on the water together were some of Tristan's best days. Now when he came out here with his board, it was to keep his brother's memory alive.

Tristan saw the wave coming from a mile off. It was going to be a big one, the kind you might wait an entire lifetime to catch. He turned his board at an angle and watched over his shoulder as the wave rolled closer. He wasn't sure he could catch it, if he was good enough to ride a wave that big, but he was damn well going to try. Troy would have tried. This would be the last one for the day, he decided. He'd do his best to catch this wave in his brother's memory, and then either ride it all the way to shore or wipeout and swim back to shore. Then he'd grab a beer from Nick's cooler and relax on the beach as the sun went down.

But the wave was bigger than he expected. He caught the crest and dropped in, but the wave kept building. Tristan realized too late that he'd dropped in too early. There was nothing he could do but try to ride it out.

The water churned gray and white, angry and wild, but Tristan held on. Unbelievably, somehow, he was still on his board and thinking he was going to make it. He was going to finish this ride. Then the white foam caught up to him, and with the power of a clenched fist, slammed him off his board, pummeling him beneath the wave.

Tristan spiraled under the water, trying to orientate himself to get back to the surface, but the wave shoved him deeper, churning him dizzy. His board cracked against the back of his skull. His mouth snapped open, expelling a gasp of air. Water rushed in. He clamped his mouth shut again, holding on to what little breath he had, which wasn't much. His lungs were on fire. He kicked and thrashed, squinted against the burning saltwater, trying to fight his way to the light, but everything was a tumult of water and sand.

Tristan couldn't tell which way was up. He stopped fighting. He rolled with the wave, letting it pull him deeper and toss him around like a rag doll.

Just before he passed out, he thought he heard his brother's voice, so faint it might have been nothing more than the ocean's hiss. *I told you, Triscuit. There are two things in this world you'll never be able to escape once you're in it: a killer wave and true love.*

After that, everything went dark.

The heavy weight of hands pumping against his chest brought Tristan back to life.

He bolted upright, coughing and sputtering, confused as hell about what had just happened to him. He remembered being out on the water with his board, the perfect wave inching closer, and then he was spinning in a washing machine, trying not to drown.

"Easy, Triss. Easy does it." Nick kneeled over him. A concerned expression etched deep lines into his face. His hair was wet, his shoulders bare. He was panting hard. "You took quite a beating out there. We thought we'd lost you forever to the great god Poseidon."

Carlos, who stood behind Nick, crossed his hand over his chest. Jacob kneeled on the other side of Tristan, his knees bent under him like a frog. He was frowning. Tristan had never seen Jacob frown in his entire life.

"What happened?" Tristan coughed out the words, tasting salt.

"That wave had your number," Jacob said.

Carlos added, "You're lucky Nick was swimming over to catch it too, or you'd be a goner."

"I saw your board pop up first," Nick explained. "Wasn't sure I'd get to you in time. That wave was killer."

Tristan squeezed his eyes shut. A killer wave and true love. Had he really heard his brother's voice out there? Unlike the other times when he heard Troy's voice in his head, this time he could have sworn he heard it audibly, above the hiss and crash of the wave that had nearly killed him. Yes, he was certain of it now: the voice had come from outside of him, like some kind of guardian angel.

Tristan's stomach twisted. He rolled over and puked in the sand.

The other guys jumped back, shouting in disgust. Then Nick laughed, and Jacob joined in. Then Carlos. Until finally Tristan couldn't hold back anymore, and he started laughing with them. He could have died out there today. If Nick hadn't swam over when he did. If his board hadn't popped to the surface. If the wave had churned him any harder. If he'd swallowed a handful more water. He could have died. But he didn't. He was alive, still breathing, here with his back against the sand and his whole body trembling.

Tristan struggled to sit upright and turned his face to the blue and wild ocean. His board lay beside him. He put one hand on it and stared toward the horizon where the sky was turning a brilliant pink streaked with orange. He wished Colette was here to see this.

Then it all came rushing back to him: the fight, Colette walking out, the terrible words he said to her, the hurt in her eyes when he shut the door in her face.

Nick patted Tristan on the shoulder, breaking him from his thoughts. "You got lucky, man. Damn lucky."

"My phone. I need my phone." Tristan scrambled to his feet, swaying a little as if he were still under the wave.

Jacob gave him a quizzical look. "You want us to take you to the hospital, man?"

"Actually, that's probably a good idea," Nick said with surprising urgency.

Tristan shook his head. "No, I'm fine. No hospital. I just—I need my phone. There's someone I need to call."

"It can't wait?" Nick said. "I mean, you almost died, man."

That was exactly why he couldn't wait. Tristan should be dead after being pummeled by a wave like that, but he wasn't. And even though his ears were ringing from the water and the spinning, and his body ached in every joint, he'd never felt more clear, more certain about anything in his life.

Every failure, every misstep and wasted minute, everything he'd ever screwed up in his life—it didn't matter anymore. What mattered was now. Today. Tomorrow. And all the precious days that came after.

He'd been given a second chance, and this time he wasn't going to screw it up.

TWO-TIMING TACO TRUCK

Colette

The hottie from Brooke's acting class was a dud. Colette met him at a hip whiskey bar near Santa Monica Pier, where he spent the entire date pretending to be Matthew Broderick. And not just doing a Matthew Broderick impression while he talked about himself, which would have at least made the date tolerable. No, he insisted on speaking only in quotes from Matthew Broderick movies. His impression wasn't even that good. Colette suffered through one drink and then faked an emergency call from work. Hot shot lawyer, no rest for the wicked, that kind of thing. He believed her excuse and sent her off with a quote about life moving fast, so try not to miss it, which Colette thought might be from *Ferris Bueller's Day Off,* but she'd seen the movie too long ago to be sure.

As she walked to the parking garage where she'd left her car, she texted Brooke about the terrible date. Brooke texted back: **One frog down, a hundred more to go.**

Colette didn't think she could do it. It's not that Tristan had ruined her for other men, except he sort of had. She'd been on dates before Tristan—bad ones and good ones—but she'd never spent an entire date wishing she was with someone else the way she had tonight. Of course, tonight's date was especially obnoxious. Maybe if he'd been himself, Colette would have given him a chance.

She stopped in front of a brightly lit store window. A line trailed out the door. She knew this place. She'd been here with Tristan. A knot formed in her throat. She'd spent all week avoiding two things: Scott, her boss, and anything that reminded her of Tristan.

Avoiding Scott had been easier than she thought it would be. He was in the middle of untangling a very complicated divorce settlement, and when he wasn't locked in his office, he was in court. They hadn't run into each other in the hallways or the parking lot even once, which made Colette think he was probably trying to avoid her as much as she was trying to avoid him. They couldn't steer clear of each other forever, though; the office was big, but not that big. Eventually, they'd have to talk about what happened at Gardenia's.

Avoiding thinking about Tristan, on the other hand, had been nearly impossible. On Monday, she went into the grocery store to grab eggs and milk only to hear a cover of Madonna's *Like A Virgin*, the song she and Tristan sang together at the bar in Joshua Tree, playing over the loudspeakers. On Tuesday, she was driving down Sepulveda Boulevard near the club Mallory had taken her on her birthday and had to slam on her brakes for a woman who darted across the street right in front of her. Colette could have sworn the woman was the same one dancing with Tristan that night at the club. On Wednesday morning, she saw no less than five red motorcycles on her drive to work, and now she was standing in front of the same ice cream store where Tristan had bought her a vanilla cone the day they'd shared their first kiss.

She had never been a person to believe in signs, but there had been so many this week, it felt like the universe was trying a little too hard to get her attention.

She queued at the back of the line and scrolled through her phone while she waited. She wasn't expecting Tristan to call or text, but she wouldn't have been mad if he did. If Brooke hadn't deleted his number from her phone, Colette would have already texted him a half dozen times with the clingy desperation she'd wanted to avoid. At least her best friend had spared her that humiliation.

When it was her turn at the front counter, Colette started to order a vanilla scoop, then stopped herself and said, "Actually, can I get a pint of the blackberry and bone marrow?"

The cashier rang her up and Colette drove home with the ice cream in the passenger seat. She wasn't sure what had possessed her to buy an entire pint when she could have just asked for a taste. Being with Tristan had shaken her from her comfort zone, and she liked the way it felt being with him, the small thrill she got when he convinced her to try something new. So she wasn't with Tristan anymore—that didn't mean she had to go back to the way things had been. She could find her own small thrills.

Back at her apartment, she grabbed a spoon from the drawer and dug into the pint of ice cream. The first bite was so terrible, she spit it out. The second bite was just as bad. It tasted like sweet meat and jam. Who the hell wanted their ice cream to taste like meat? She shoved the rest of the pint into her freezer and poured herself a glass of wine instead, finishing off a bottle she'd opened at the beginning of the week.

Her recycling was full, so she carried it downstairs to the bins everyone in the complex shared. Someone had left a scraggly-looking, yellow couch on the curb with a handwritten FREE sign propped on the cushions. It was the same horrible yellow as the couch in Tristan's apartment. With the same horrible decorative buttons that had pushed into her skin during their post-coital spooning.

The laugh that came out of her mouth was a bitter one.

If the universe wanted her and Tristan together, it was going to have to do better than that.

Thursday Colette was in court all day, so she didn't look at her phone until late in the afternoon. She'd missed two calls. One from her mother, and the other from a phone number not in her contacts list, but with a Los Angeles area code. She stared at the number, trying not to get her hopes up. Her heart hammered as she lifted the phone to her ear to listen to the voicemails.

Her mother called to apologize for missing her birthday. Apparently, Geoffrey had surprised her with a Caribbean cruise. "He feels so bad, darling. He wants to make it up to you by flying us both to Scotland on his private jet. He's going to rent us a castle for the week!"

Living in a Scottish castle for a week could be a pleasant change in pace, though she doubted she could convince Scott to let her take the time off. She skipped the rest of her mother's message, which appeared to be a play-by-play of her fabulous, romance-filled cruise. Colette wasn't sure she could stand another second listening to someone be so fucking happy. Besides, she knew she'd hear a repeat of her mother's adventures the next time she went over for dinner.

The second voicemail started to play, and Colette's heart almost stopped. Tristan spoke to her in a breathless, excited rush, and the sound of his voice sent electricity crackling through every part of her body. He'd called her. He'd actually called her. She thought of the couch she'd seen on the curb last night. This morning it was gone, and she wondered if she'd imagined it. But now, Tristan was rambling in her ear, saying something about a killer wave and true love and being lucky enough to escape one but not the other and how he realized something important out there, how he needed to talk to her, but he didn't want to wait until she came to her senses, he needed to talk to her now, yesterday, as soon as possible.

He spoke so quickly Colette didn't quite understand what it was exactly Tristan was trying to tell her. But she heard enough to know that he wanted to see her. In person. That whatever he needed to tell her, he wanted to do it face-to-face.

"Please, Colette. I know you're pissed, but give me a few minutes. That's all I'm asking for. Remember Eddy's Taco Truck? The one with the chapulines?"

How could she forget? She laughed, thinking of the grasshopper legs poking out from the shell, Tristan teasing her about the legs getting stuck in his teeth, how she wished she'd been brave enough to try a bite when she'd had the chance.

"That's where I'll be tonight," Tristan's voice murmured in her ear. "That's where I'll wait for you."

Los Angeles at night was a string of red and white lights crammed onto freeways, a sinuous bright snake, inching through the city. In the voicemail, Tristan said he would be at the taco truck at 6:30 PM. Thanks to traffic, Colette was running fifteen minutes late. She thought about texting him to say she was on her way, but decided not to since she was almost there, and if the energy in his voicemail was anything to go off of, it sounded like he'd wait all night for her. Fifteen minutes was nothing.

But when she finally got to the taco truck, Tristan wasn't there. A couple stood off to one side, waiting for their food. A woman ordered from the window. Eddy glanced over the woman's shoulder when Colette approached the truck and gave her a brilliant smile.

Colette wasn't sure if he remembered her specifically from when she was here last week, or if he was just the kind of person who greeted everyone like an old friend. Either way, she smiled back at him. When the woman in front of her stepped to one side, Colette approached the window.

"What can I get you?" Eddy asked.

"You know Tristan Walker, right?" Colette responded.

"Sure do. Love that kid. You looking for him? Cause he's over there." Eddy leaned out the window and pointed off to the right.

Colette twisted her head to look. There was a park bench about a half block from the taco truck and that's where Tristan sat now beside another woman.

Behind her, Eddy chuckled. "Kid sure knows how to get the ladies. If I had half his charisma, I'd be set for life."

Colette's heart hitched in her chest, but she pushed away the jealousy because the woman was probably no one, a friend, or a complete stranger, and Eddy didn't know what he was talking about. But then the woman scooted closer to Tristan and traced her hand along his thigh in a way that definitely implied they were more than friends, or quickly headed in that direction.

DON'T LET THE DOOR HIT YOU ON THE WAY OUT

Colette

Colette moved closer to the park bench, realizing with a jolt that she knew the woman sitting next to Tristan.

Brooke tipped her head back and laughed at something he said. It was the laugh she used when she was trying to get a man into bed—flirtatious and full-throated. She tossed her thick, brown hair over one shoulder and angled her body closer to Tristan, keeping one hand on his thigh and trailing the other across the back of his neck.

Colette's mouth went dry. Her thoughts raced. This felt like some kind of test, but she couldn't figure out what she was supposed to do, how she was supposed to react. She tried to sort out how this had even happened, how Tristan and Brooke had ended up on the same bench, but then she remembered she'd told Brooke about the truck a week ago. Brooke, like Tristan, loved strange foods and trying new things and finding the hippest spots to eat. Eddy's taco truck was a diamond in the rough, exactly the kind of place Brooke would want to try.

Her being here could be a simple coincidence, but it didn't explain why she and Tristan were getting so cozy on that bench. Especially after the voicemail he'd left Colette.

She shook her head, trying to piece it together, but all she kept thinking about was that Tristan and Brooke made a perfect couple. They were so much better suited for one another than Colette ever would be.

Brooke laughed again. Tristan laughed with her. He angled his face toward her in a way that was all too familiar. Colette felt sick. She couldn't stand there and watch as Tristan kissed her best friend. She raced away from the taco truck.

She was almost to her car when she thought she heard Tristan calling her name, but she didn't turn around. There was nothing he could say to her now that would change her mind. She'd gotten what she wanted from Tristan. She'd had a good time with him, but he wasn't someone who could be in a serious relationship, and Colette wanted serious.

She got in her car and drove home.

The next morning, Colette showed up to work two hours late. It wasn't entirely her fault. Tristan wouldn't stop calling. She kept declining his calls, but her phone kept ringing. He texted a few times, too, saying things like, **Were you at the taco truck last night? I thought I saw you, but you ran away.** And, **Please, Colette. We need to talk. Call me back.**

Colette didn't respond to any of his texts and finally, at 1:00 AM, shut off her phone. She still didn't fall asleep until almost 2:00 AM. And because her phone was off, she missed her alarm. And because she missed her alarm, she woke up an hour later than normal. And because of that, she got stuck in bad traffic. She hadn't been this late to work since—she'd never been this late to work.

She stumbled into the building, tripping on her high heels and almost spilling her armful of paperwork over the floor. The receptionist gave her a dirty look. As Colette hurried down the hall to her office, she tried to straighten the stack of papers. Distracted, she didn't see Scott Campbell walking toward her until she crashed right into him. The papers she was trying so hard to organize flew in every direction. Scott grabbed her arm, holding her steady, so she didn't go sprawling after them.

Scott looked as startled to see her as she was to see him. He dropped her arm and took a step back.

"Sorry," Colette mumbled as she bent to pick up the papers. "I didn't see you there."

"No, it was me," he said. "I was looking at my phone and not paying attention. Here, let me help you."

He got to his knees and grabbed a bunch of loose papers, shoving them into a messy pile. He clutched the papers to his chest when he rose to his feet again. The smile he gave Colette was timid and uncertain.

"Thanks." Colette held her hand out for the papers. Scott passed them over.

"Listen. About last week." His voice was contrite, his head tucked with embarrassment. "What happened at Gardenia's—"

"Don't worry about it," Colette said through gritted teeth. This was not a conversation she wanted to have. Not now, not ever. *Let's pretend this never happened.*

But Scott shook his head. "No, I need to say this. You deserve an apology. I acted like a complete asshole."

This was a conversation they should have behind closed doors, but now that Scott had her attention, he was desperate to tell his side of the story, so he just kept talking. "It's just, I've liked you for a long time, Colette. A really long time. From the first day you stepped into my office, I was a goner for you. And I thought you were into me the way I was into you. You flirted with me. You wore those tight skirts that drove me mad. And that night at the club, damn. There's just something about you. You drive me wild."

She swallowed down a laugh. Who said things like that?

Scott's hair was more tousled than usual. His tie was loose around his neck, the top button of his shirt unbuttoned. A week ago, she would have found his rumpled look endearing. She would have been happy to hear him say these things to her. But not today. Not after last night, after seeing Tristan with Brooke. She didn't want any more drama. Not in her personal life, and certainly not at work.

But Scott wasn't done talking. He took a small step closer to her. "Then when I saw you with that other guy at Gardenia's, I don't know… I got jealous. After you rejected me that night at my apartment, I was upset."

"You were more than upset," she said.

"I told you, I acted like a complete asshole. I wasn't expecting you to be a…" He lowered his voice, and his gaze darted to her crotch. "A virgin."

"Life's full of surprises." She gave him her best fuck-right-off smile.

He misinterpreted it as an invitation to get closer. He lifted his hand and brushed her hair behind her ear. "You seem different. What's changed?"

Her phone dinged. Saved by the bell. She took a step back, fumbling with the papers in her hand to find her phone, which was shoved in the tight pocket of her skirt. She scowled at the screen. It was a text from Brooke.

I need to talk to you.

"Is that him?"

"What?"

"Is that your surfer boy?" He gestured to her phone.

Colette grimaced and shoved her phone back into her skirt pocket.

"You can do better than him, you know." Scott closed the gap between them, backing her against the wall. "Why waste your v-card on a loser like him?"

"You think I should waste it on you instead?" She glared at him.

He caged her with his arms. His face was close enough she could see the stubble on his chin. His leg brushed against hers. She tensed, but didn't cower under his dark gaze. She lifted her chin a little higher, puffing out her chest, refusing to let him intimidate her.

"I thought you said I was too old to be a virgin," she said. "That you only sleep with women who know what they're doing."

"Well, I've had some time to think about it and I've changed my mind." His mouth twisted into a crooked smile. "You're like a clean slate, a blank page. It will be so much fun to teach you what I like."

He traced a single finger up the side of her thigh.

Colette pushed off the wall and shoved him back. "I don't think this conversation is appropriate for the workplace."

"Let's take it somewhere else, then." He grabbed her elbow to keep her from walking away.

"You're my boss. This conversation isn't going to be appropriate anywhere. It's not professional." She held the stack of papers tightly against her chest, not that the flimsy printer paper could protect her.

"Oh, now you're worried about what's professional?" Scott's calm smile switched to a tense scowl. His grip tightened around her elbow. "You wave your ass in my face for months. You tease me. You let me between your legs. You really are a cock tease, aren't you?"

"Scott, look, you and me, whatever that was… Well, it isn't anymore, okay? But we still have to work together, right? So let's not do this. Let's stop this conversation before you dig yourself into a deeper hole and I have to file a complaint with HR."

Scott's eyes flashed with anger. "Now you're threatening me?"

"I didn't mean to lead you on," she said. "Neither of us should have let it get that far, but now it's over, okay? Whatever it was, it's over."

"It's that loser, isn't it?" His nostrils flared as he scraped his gaze over the length of her body, lingering a second on her ass. "You had sex with him, didn't you? I can smell it on you. That fresh popped cherry. You dirty girl. Now there's nothing stopping us, is there?"

Colette reeled back from him. She yanked her elbow free and tightened her hold on the papers in her arms. "Leave me alone, Scott. I mean it. If you say another word to me—"

"You'll what?" He loomed over her. "You'll go to HR? And what? What are you going to tell them? We fooled around outside of work? What are they going to do to me? This is my father's firm. In a few years, it'll be mine." He reached to brush her cheek. "I could make you a partner. You'd like that, wouldn't you? A nice pay raise. A bigger office. I can give you that with the snap of my finger. All you have to do is ask nicely."

His hand drifted from her face to her breasts. Colette shoved the papers into his chest, knocking him back with the force of it. "I quit."

"You quit?" He looked as startled hearing her declaration as she felt saying it.

She spun on her heels and marched toward her office.

"Think about what you're doing, Colette," he called after her. "Where are you going to go? I'll tell my father not to give you a recommendation. No one will hire you. Not after they found out you seduced the managing partner's son."

Steps from her door, she whirled to face him. "You wouldn't dare."

His mouth twisted into a smirk.

"Do it." She flung her hands in the air. "Say whatever you want. No one will believe you, anyway."

Colette didn't know if that was true, but she wasn't going to let this asshole blackmail her into staying here. She liked this job, but it was still just a job. She would find another.

She stepped into her office for a moment, trying to catch her breath, as she listened to Scott storm down the hallway to some other part of the building. When she was certain he was gone and not coming back to harass her more, she exhaled and slumped against the closed door.

"That could have gone better," she muttered, and began collecting the few belongings she kept in the office. There wasn't much. A picture of her and Brooke on a vacation in the Bahamas. A novel she'd been reading during her lunch breaks. A small paperweight her mother had given her when she first got hired here.

She could carry it all out in one trip. She didn't even need a box.

She stared at the stack of paperwork on the corner of her desk and the laptop that belonged to the firm. The logistics of leaving baffled her. Should she go to HR? Talk to Archer Campbell, the managing partner? Who also happened to be Scott's dad? No, that was a terrible idea. Could she just walk out? Leave everything behind and let Scott clean up the mess? It was tempting. After how Scott treated her, it would be exactly what he deserved.

Someone knocked quietly on her office door and then opened it. Colette was relieved to see it was her assistant, Mallory, not Scott, standing on the other side.

"What's going on?" Mallory looked concerned. "Scott just came through raging like a bull with a hornet up his butt." Her eyes flicked over the personal items Colette clutched in her arms. "Where are you going?"

"I just quit?" This time, she didn't feel so confident when she said it.

Surprise lit Mallory's eyes. Then she squared her shoulders and said, "Well, if you're quitting, I'm quitting."

"Mallory, don't," Colette said, but then shook her head

because even though she was certain Mallory could hold her own against a prick like Scott, she shouldn't have to. "No, you know what, do what you want. There are better firms out there than Campbell and Sons."

"Maybe we should start our own," Mallory said.

It wasn't the worst idea Colette had heard today. The words tumbled in her head as she gathered the rest of her personal items from her desk and when she walked out of the office for the last time and stepped into the bright Los Angeles sun, the idea had started to stick.

She could do it. She could hang her own shingle, help women like her mother, women who didn't have a lot of money to spare but needed to start over. She was tired of rich people fighting over luxury yachts. She wanted to do something good with her experience. She wanted to help people who really needed help, not just make rich people richer.

"Now what?" Mallory asked as they walked across the parking lot.

Colette flashed her a smile. "I think we should go out dancing."

MISSED CONNECTION

Colette

Salsa music thumped through the speakers. Colette and Mallory danced together for a while in the middle of a crowd of strangers. It was a different club than the one they were at for her birthday. Some things were the same: the loud music and dim lights, the flash of a disco ball, the bodies writhing and twisting together on the dance floor. But this club was in a different neighborhood, tucked in the basement of a fancy restaurant, with gold-trimmed, velvet curtains hanging from the walls and bar top tables made of dark wood. Several women wore fluttering skirts and tapped out rhythms in high-heeled dance shoes. Almost every man wore a cowboy hat and a silver belt buckle. Colette and Mallory were underdressed in jeans and sparkling tops, but no one seemed to care. They were all just here to dance and have a good time.

Colette swayed her hips to the music, laughing at something Mallory said. She wasn't thinking about her job situation or her man situation or her best friend situation. She was here to cut loose and have fun. She was here to forget.

Mallory grabbed Colette around the waist and spun her toward the bar. She pressed her mouth close to Colette's ear to be heard over the music. "That cute guy over there? The one in the mint-green shirt? He hasn't taken his eyes off you all night."

Colette scanned the row of men hanging off the bar. Her eyes caught on one near the end, who was staring straight at her. His lips curled into a smile when they made eye contact, and he tipped his head in a silent greeting. He pushed away from the bar and swaggered over to where she and Mallory were dancing.

"Mind if I cut in?" His deep voice sent a rush of pleasure through Colette's body. He was handsome, with a rugged cowboy look and flecks of silver showing in his thick, dark hair. Fine lines creased his eyes and mouth, deepening when he smiled.

Mallory bumped her hip against Colette's. Colette bumped her back. Mallory twirled away, leaving Colette alone with the strange cowboy from the bar. One hand grabbed hers, the other slipped around her waist. He spun her in a quick circle, then dipped her low. When he pulled her up again, she was laughing, her head spinning.

At the bar, Mallory was chatting up a young blonde woman with a pixie cut and a tattoo of a mushroom on the back of her neck. Mallory glanced over at Colette, checking in with her. Colette gave her a thumbs up. Mallory's smile widened as she turned back to the woman and leaned in close to whisper something in her ear.

Colette and the cowboy danced for an hour without a break. Then he bought her a drink, and they danced more. He whispered his name in her ear, and she smiled. When he asked if she wanted to ditch the club and go back to his place, she nodded. He took her hand and led her outside.

In the passenger seat of his no-nonsense, four-door sedan, Colette texted Mallory not to wait up for her. Mallory texted back a winking emoji.

Colette rolled down the window and stretched out her arm,

tracing the LA skyline with the tip of her finger. A city crawling with four million people, four million beating hearts, every single one a breath away from shattering—how did anyone find true love here and keep it?

She looked over at the cowboy, who smiled back at her.

No, this wasn't ever going to be love, but it was exactly what Colette needed tonight.

Colette woke in a bed that wasn't hers next to a cowboy who wasn't hers either. She smiled, remembering the night before, the guy from the club who brought her back to his apartment and spent the rest of the night making her feel good. Really good.

She stretched her naked body beneath his green flannel sheets and rolled over to look at him. He was as handsome in daylight as he was in shadowed moonlight. The stubble on his powerful jaw had grown thicker. His muscled shoulders peeked out from under the sheets. She traced the line of his body down to his narrow waist, blushing as she remembered what he'd done to her under these sheets, how she'd moaned for him.

She rolled back over and swung her legs out of the bed, trying not to wake him.

He stirred and reached for her, his fingers finding her hips and trying to pull her back to the bed. She looked over her shoulder.

He smiled. His eyes reflected tilled soil and wide-open spaces.

"Where are you headed off to so soon?" His voice was even deeper when he was still half-asleep. "I was thinking I could make us some breakfast, then we could spend the day getting to know each other a little better."

He trailed his finger along her bare shoulder.

"That sounds nice." She pulled the sheet closer to her body. "But I really should get going. I'm meeting some friends today.

And I've got a list of things…" She trailed off when she realized she was rambling.

She rose from the bed, letting the sheet fall from her naked body and reaching to grab her clothes off the floor. She pulled her shirt on, then her underwear and pants.

"Well, can I at least have your number before you go? I had fun with you last night." He propped himself up on the bed. He was still smiling at her, and she felt herself blossoming like a flower under that smile, but for all the wrong reasons.

The sex had been good. More than good, it was great. He'd been a perfect gentleman, and she'd been able to let herself be free with him, uninhibited. They'd ordered pizza and watched some trash reality TV, then they had sex again, slow and sleepy, and after, fell asleep and it really had been a great night with a great guy.

"I'd like to see you again," he said.

"I'm sorry." She flashed him a smile over her shoulder as she laced up her shoes. "I had fun last night, too, but I'm not looking for anything serious."

She kissed him, said goodbye, and let herself out the front door.

Rather than waiting for an Uber, Colette walked. A crisp hint of fall hung in the air, and because it was Saturday morning, traffic was light. She didn't know how far she'd get in her kitten heels, but it felt good to stretch her legs.

She'd told the cowboy a small lie when she said she wasn't looking for anything serious. The truth was, she wasn't looking for anything serious with *him*. She was sure that he was a perfectly nice man who would make a perfectly nice boyfriend, but he wasn't Tristan.

Something had clicked for Colette last night. As she tangled in the sheets of another man, Tristan's face flashed through her mind. But what she thought of wasn't Tristan in bed, Tristan between her legs, Tristan taking pleasure in her. No, it was

Tristan with his head tipped back laughing; Tristan before he jumped into the pool, looking over his shoulder and daring her to follow; Tristan seconds away from punching Scott in the face, protecting her; Tristan edged in moonlight, vulnerable and missing his older brother.

Sex with Tristan had been good. There was no doubt about that. When Colette was a virgin, she used to try to imagine what sex would feel like. It was never as good in her mind as the way Tristan made her feel. Not even close. He'd awoken something inside her that she hadn't even known existed. He'd drawn sensations from her body that she didn't think were possible. Two bodies meeting in time and space, brief and explosive—it could mean nothing, or it could mean everything.

She thought about what Tristan had said when they were lying in bed after their first time together, how sex was a way to connect with someone else, how it didn't have to be a frantic, selfish coupling, but something slow and meaningful, something that drew people closer together. And maybe that was true with some people, but for her, she realized the connection with Tristan had come before the sex. It had come in the small moments shared, the way he shook up her routine, the way he made the world feel edged in wonder. He made her come alive outside of the bedroom too.

If it really was just sex, he'd asked her seconds before she walked out on him, *then why are you so upset right now?*

But it had never been just sex, had it? She was lying to herself by saying that all she'd wanted from him was sex and none of the rest mattered. All of it mattered. Tristan mattered. Not just what he could do to her in bed, but what he could do to her heart. He wasn't perfect. He was conceited and impulsive, but she could use a little more impulsiveness in her life. She could use a little more Tristan Walker.

Two nights ago, this realization would have made her ecstatic. Two nights ago, she would have run straight to Tristan's apartment and told him everything she was thinking. She would have told him she was falling in love. Two nights ago, she could have changed the course of her own destiny. But now, remembering how close Tristan and Brooke had been at the taco stand, the way they'd touched, Brooke leaning in for the kiss—Colette knew she was too late, that her insecurities had once again cost her a chance at true love.

She pulled her phone out of her purse to call an Uber. Her feet hurt, and she was still at least five miles away from her apartment.

As she waited, she pulled up the text Brooke sent yesterday about needing to talk. Colette hovered her fingers over the screen as she tried to figure out what to write back. She already knew what Brooke wanted to talk about: meeting Tristan, kissing Tristan, how one thing led to another.

One thing always led to another with Brooke.

And Brooke, who loved Colette like a sister, would believe her honesty was a kindness. She wouldn't exactly ask Colette's permission to date Tristan, but she would be carefully watching Colette's reaction, and if Colette gave so much as a lip curl, Brooke would call the whole thing off. But who was Colette to stand in the way of her best friend's happiness?

Colette had ended things with Tristan. She had no claim on him. She never did. Not really. They had never been serious. If Brooke liked Tristan and Tristan liked Brooke, well—Colette shoved her phone back into her purse.

She wasn't in the mood to sit and listen to her best friend rehash the details of whatever happened with Tristan that night at the taco truck. Brooke was the actress, not Colette. She wouldn't be able to hide her feelings, but she could avoid them.

With enough time, Tristan would become nothing to her but the fondest of memories. Maybe one day she would even learn to be okay with that, maybe better than okay. One day, she promised herself, she would fall in love with someone new.

THE BACHELORS AND THE BOOMBOX

Tristan

Otto Walker yanked open the curtains. "Wake up, son! The early bird catches the worm!"

Tristan groaned and smashed a pillow over his face to block out the blinding light now flooding the apartment. He hadn't exactly gotten a good night's sleep on the ugly, yellow couch. Cushion springs jammed into his back. His legs were too long, and he either had to keep them tucked against his chest or stretched out over the couch arm. Both positions ended with one of his legs falling to sleep and him being jolted awake from excruciating pain. His only plans for Saturday had been to sleep in, which his father had now ruined.

Otto clapped his hands and jerked the pillow off Tristan's face. "Enough moping. It's time to seize the day!"

"I'm not moping, I'm sleeping." Tristan covered his eyes with his arm, but his father pulled on his shirt sleeve, insistent.

"It's half-past seven. Half the day is gone," Otto said. "And you are moping. I've barely seen you leave this couch since Thursday night."

"Where else am I supposed to sit?" Tristan grumbled. "Your shit is everywhere."

He sat up and rolled his neck, relishing the popping sounds. He massaged his shoulders, then stretched his calves long in front of him.

Otto, who was dressed in a matching blue tracksuit, stood over him with an annoyed look on his face. "I think what you mean is *your* shit is everywhere."

The apartment looked like a tornado had blown through. Clothes and shoes were strewn all over the floor. Half-full glasses, empty beer bottles, and dirty plates littered the coffee table. Takeout bags crowded the kitchen counter. It was surprising how quickly the two of them had trashed the place in the brief span of two days.

"My shit's everywhere only because your shit's taking up too much space." Tristan rose to his feet and cracked his lower back with a grimace. "How's my bed? I trust you're sleeping well?"

"Like a king." Otto slapped Tristan's back. "Get dressed. We're going out."

"Dad—"

"Don't 'Dad' me. We're going apartment hunting."

"You know, Mom's got that big house in Malibu with all those rooms…"

"For you, son. We're going apartment hunting for you." Otto pointed at Tristan and winked.

"Dad, come on, it's really not a good day for me." Tristan shuffled into the kitchen, looking for coffee. There was half a pot sitting in the coffeemaker. "Is this from today?"

"Fresh this morning. Help yourself." Otto checked his watch. "But hurry. I told Jane we'd meet her at the first spot at eight-thirty, and it's all the way out in the valley."

"Seriously? Dad, I don't want to live in the valley." Tristan poured himself a cup of coffee. "And who's Jane?"

"My realtor. And the valley is all you can afford on a personal assistant's salary."

Tristan jerked his head around. "What are you talking about? Last time I checked, I wasn't anyone's personal assistant."

"You're mine, starting Monday," Otto said with a 'what are you gonna do about it' shrug.

Tristan choked on the sip of coffee he'd just taken. "I'd make a terrible assistant. But I think you already know that. Besides, I don't know the first thing about handling actors."

"Don't worry. You won't be going anywhere near my clients. I just need someone to file some paperwork and pick up my coffee." He flashed Tristan a grin. "I've spoiled you, son. It's time for you to grow up and start taking some personal responsibility for your life. Like paying your own rent. And cleaning up after yourself."

He swung a judgmental gaze around the messy apartment.

Tristan swallowed down a string of curse words. He was tired of people telling him to grow up. First Colette, now his father. His mom would probably say it, too, if she were here. She'd wave her hand at the takeout containers and unwashed dishes, and say something like, *You're twenty-eight and still need your mother to pick up after you.* Then she'd start cleaning, even if he told her not to.

"Half this mess is yours, remember?" Tristan barked out the words. "And I can be responsible. I've been going through some things, Dad, that's all. I will find a job. Something that fits me. I've already got something in the works, actually. I just need a little more time."

All Tristan had was the inkling of an idea about what he wanted to do with his life, something that had popped into his head after the ocean tried to kill him, but it was too new of an idea to share with his father who would ask if he'd crunched the numbers, worked out a business plan, talked to any investors, if he had any idea at all what it took to open a small business.

Otto scowled. "All this moping you've been doing lately. Is it about that girl?"

"What girl?" Tristan pretended he had no idea what his father was talking about.

"That attorney woman your mother fired? The one hiding out in your bedroom wearing your t-shirt when your mother showed up here unannounced the other day?"

"How did you hear about that?" Tristan took a second sip of coffee, managing not to choke on it this time. It was bitter, but when he opened the fridge, there was no milk, and when he dug into the cupboard everything had been moved around and he couldn't find the sugar. Bitter coffee it was.

"Your mother called me yesterday."

Tristan almost spit out his sip. "Mom called you?"

"She wanted to know if you gave me the divorce papers." His fingers brushed over the manila envelope that had been sitting on the counter untouched for three days, since Otto had taken over Tristan's apartment on Thursday morning. Otto sighed and shook his head, turning away from the envelope and going to sit on the yellow couch.

"She told me I needed to have a talk with you about the poor choices you've been making lately." Otto rolled his eyes. "She said that it was my fault you weren't settled down, my fault you didn't have a job, that you're so unhappy."

"I'm not unhappy," Tristan muttered.

Otto let out a loud, disbelieving laugh. "Well, I certainly am, so it wouldn't surprise me if some of that's rubbed off on you."

Tristan carried his coffee into the living room and joined his father on the couch. "You're unhappy?"

"Son, I'm fucking miserable." He reached to grab a picture frame sitting on the side table next to the couch.

Inside was a picture of the four of them—Otto, Maureen,

Tristan, and Troy—in front of Sleeping Beauty's castle at Disneyland. They had taken it years ago when Tristan was a freshman in high school. Troy was a graduating senior and his one request had been to spend the day at the Happiest Place on Earth with the people who made him happiest. Such a cheeseball thing to do, but it had been one of the best days of Tristan's life, and he thought Troy had felt the same.

Otto traced his finger over their faces. "I miss him."

"Yeah." A flood of emotions jammed in Tristan's throat, keeping him from saying anything else.

"God, but I miss your mother too." Otto returned the photograph to its spot on the side table. He ran his hand through his hair and stared at the ceiling. "Everything changed after Troy's accident."

Tristan squeezed his hands around his coffee cup. He had never talked about Troy's death with either of his parents. Not directly. They talked around it, discussing facts like what had happened, how he'd died, what kind of coffin to buy, what kind of music to play at the funeral, what to do with all the stuff in his bedroom. But they never talked about the emotional side of things, like the grief, the nights they cried themselves to sleep, the guilt, the nightmares, the what-ifs that beat like a drum in their hollowed-out chests.

"I wasn't there for your mother the way I should have been," Otto admitted. "I was dealing with my own feelings, and seeing your mother so shattered, well, it nearly broke me. I wasn't there for her. I wasn't there for either of you. Honestly, I'm surprised she didn't leave me sooner."

"Don't say that."

Otto's laugh hinted at sorrow. "Ah, but it's true. Your mother and I, we stopped trying. Even before Troy died, we weren't making enough time for one another. But after, it just seemed so much easier to spend more time at the office. I thought she needed space to grieve. I thought we both did, but what we really needed, what we should have done, was throw ourselves into one another. Grieved our beautiful boy together." His voice flooded with emotion. His eyes glistened with tears. He shook his head as if trying to shake off the sadness. "There were so many things I should have done differently. If I could go back, I would fight harder for her, for us. That's what love is, son. It's sticking with someone even when it feels impossible, especially when it feels impossible. Love isn't for quitters."

Otto tilted his head when he looked at Tristan and asked, "Do you love her?"

"Who?" Tristan played dumb, even though he knew exactly who his father was talking about, could picture the constellation of freckles on Colette's shoulders, the way her nose wrinkled when she got mad at him, the way her voice sounded when she whispered her secrets into his ear.

Otto didn't buy his act, though, because he said, "I've never seen you mope this long over a girl before, so you must love her."

Tristan sighed. "I think I do, but it doesn't matter."

"What do you mean? Of course, it matters. Love is all that matters."

"There might have been something between us at one point," Tristan explained. "But now, I'm not so sure. I said something stupid. No, I said a lot of things stupid. We had a big fight, and now she wants nothing to do with me."

"Do you know how many stupid things I've said to your mother, and she forgave me?" His smile fell away as he shook his head. "I might not be the best person to be giving you advice about love right now, but let me just say that if you love this girl, if you think there's a chance, even the smallest one, that she might love you in return, then you have to go out and get her. Fight for her." Otto grabbed Tristan's hand and squeezed. "Fight for love. That is one thing in this life I can promise you will never regret doing."

They sat a moment in silence, then Tristan asked, "Dad? Do you still love Mom?"

Otto heaved a sigh that was weighted with decades of disappointment. "Of course I still love her. From the first time she walked into my office, my heart belonged to her. And, no, I haven't always been there for her the way she needed me to be. I've let her down time and time again. But I never stopped loving her. My heart never stopped being hers."

"You haven't signed the papers yet," Tristan pointed out.

Otto glanced over his shoulder at the manila envelope. "Yes, but she has."

"A wise man once told me love isn't for quitters." Tristan flashed his dad a wide grin, then set his empty coffee mug on the table and hopped to his feet. "Come on, Pops, if it's not too late for me, then it's not too late for you and Mom."

"I appreciate what you're saying, Tristan. I really do, but it's not the same. Your mother and I have a lot of baggage. We have history."

"All the more reason to fight for her, right?" Tristan disappeared into his bedroom.

"What is that for?" Otto asked as Tristan reappeared carrying an old boombox he'd saved when his parents cleared out Troy's apartment. His brother would sometimes go out to Venice Beach, lay down a piece of cardboard, set up the boombox, and break dance for tourists. It was throwback cool and so stupid-cheesy, but that was Troy. He didn't care what other people thought of him, and he wasn't afraid to look stupid if it made other people happy.

"Get dressed," Tristan said to his father.

Otto looked down at his tracksuit. "I am dressed."

"No, something nice. Something Mom likes."

"Why?" Otto eyed him with suspicion.

Troy dropped the boombox into his father's lap. "You're going to win her back."

YOU'LL NEVER REGRET FIGHTING FOR LOVE

Tristan

"I don't know if this is going to work," Otto Walker said, adjusting his tie and smoothing his hand over his hair.

"Won't know until you try." Tristan shoved the tape into the boombox and pressed play.

Then he shoved the boombox into his father's arms and ducked behind the car so when his mother looked out, she would see only Otto. His father seemed unsure what to do with the boombox. He held it awkwardly against his stomach, like he was about to let it slide from his arms onto the asphalt. Tristan waved at his father and lifted his own invisible boombox high in the air, demonstrating.

"Hold it over your head," he whisper-shouted.

Otto looked confused, but did what Tristan said. He bobbled the boombox until he had a good grip on either side, then he pushed it into the air above his head. Just in time, too, because at that moment the front door opened and Maureen Walker appeared on the front steps with a startled look on her face.

"Otto?" She wrapped her pink cardigan tighter around her shoulders. "What on earth are you doing out here? The neighbors are going to think you've lost your mind!"

Otto darted Tristan a glance. He looked ready to throw the boombox into the bushes and flee, but Tristan smiled and flapped his hands, gesturing for him to do what he'd come here to do: confess his undying love.

Maureen exhaled an impatient sigh and folded her arms over her chest. The song playing over the speakers was one of Maureen's favorites, a song Tristan remembered his parents dancing to in the kitchen anytime it came on the radio. He realized he hadn't seen them dance together in years.

"What do you want, Otto?" Maureen's voice had lost its high-pitched indignation. She just sounded tired now.

"I miss you, Maureen. I miss the way you hum when you're lost in thought. I miss the way you laugh at my stupid jokes. You're the only one who laughs because you think I'm funny. Everyone else laughs because they want something from me. I miss our quiet mornings together, reading the news and drinking coffee. I miss fighting with you about where to go for dinner. I miss that mole on the small of your back."

Maureen blushed and looked at the ground. When she lifted her face to Otto again, there were tears in her eyes.

"I miss us, Maureen. I miss how we used to be together. Us against the world, remember?"

"Oh, Otto." It was a sigh, a prayer. She gave a small shake of her head, and Tristan watched as his father's face sank.

It wasn't working, Tristan realized. His father had put his heart on the line, and it wasn't going to change anything. Maureen had already decided, and nothing Otto said or did would make a difference. If thirty years of a life together wasn't enough to keep two people together, then what hope did Tristan have after just one week with Colette?

But then Maureen did something unexpected. She stepped

off the porch and walked to where Otto stood in the middle of the driveway. When she reached him, she took the boombox from Otto, set it in the grass, took one of his arms and wrapped it around her waist, then grabbed his other hand and began to dance with him, a slow sway that didn't match the rhythm of the song at all, but somehow looked perfectly right. For several seconds, they stared into each other's eyes. Then he pulled her closer, and she laid her head against his chest. They danced like that until the song ended.

Otto was the one who stopped. He cupped Maureen's chin and tilted her head so he was looking into her eyes when he said, "I'm so sorry, Maureen. I stopped fighting for us. I stopped fighting for you. I should have never—"

She pressed her mouth to his in a passionate kiss.

Tristan looked away, giving them a few seconds of privacy.

His thoughts swirled. Maybe there was still a chance for him and Colette after all. Maybe that's all life was: a series of mistakes and second chances and sacrificing for what's important.

He rose from his hiding place behind his father's car. Maureen let out a startled laugh.

"Tristan? Have you been here the whole time?" She leaned away from Otto slightly and eyed her son suspiciously. "Wait, was this your idea?"

"No, this was all dad's idea," Tristan said. "I just provided the music."

Maureen relaxed into Otto's side again, leaning her head against his shoulder and letting out a dreamy sigh. "I've never been able to resist that song."

Otto tightened his arm around her waist, as if he would never let her go.

"Why don't you both come inside?" Maureen slipped her hand into Otto's and turned toward the house. "I was just getting the coffee started and I have some baked goods and fresh fruit. We could have a nice family brunch."

"Sorry, Mom, I can't. There's something I have to do."

A small frown tugged on Maureen's lips, but Otto winked at him and said, "Hopefully, some of my luck will rub off on you."

"What are you talking about?" Maureen squinted at him.

Otto kissed the top of her head. "I'll tell you all about it over coffee and then I'm going to—" He leaned in and whispered something Tristan couldn't hear. The way his mother's cheeks flushed, he was glad he couldn't.

"Otto!" Maureen swatted playfully at her husband.

He laughed and nuzzled her neck.

"Well, dinner, then," Maureen said to Tristan. "You'll come for dinner."

"Leave the boy alone, Maureen," Otto said. "You'll see him again soon enough. Tonight, I want you all to myself."

Maureen huffed, but if the smile on her face was any indication, she was delighted by Otto's possessiveness.

"I'll call you tomorrow, Mom." Tristan stepped forward to kiss Maureen's cheek. He gave his father a grin and thumbs up.

Otto flicked his hand at the boombox, still sitting in the grass playing the next track on the tape. "You can take that with you if you think it will help."

Tristan smiled, but shook his head. The magic of the boombox would only work on his parents. To win back Colette, he would need something different. He wasn't sure what, but he was certain he could figure it out in the time it took him to find her.

"Boombox is all yours," Tristan said. "Mind if I borrow your car, though?"

Otto tossed him the keys. "Go get her, son."

Tristan was on the freeway before he realized he didn't know where he was going. He didn't have the first clue where Colette lived. He'd never been to her house, never even been invited. There was no way in hell he was going to text her for her address. That was next-level stalker, and she probably wouldn't respond even if he did. He'd seen enough romantic movies to know that letting the girl know you were coming to confess your undying love was not nearly as romantic as showing up announced.

Undying love now, is it? I never thought I'd see the day.

Tristan wound up at the one place he could think of where he knew Colette spent a significant amount of time: Campbell and Sons, Family Attorneys. Her car wasn't in the parking lot, but that didn't surprise him. It was Saturday. Of course she wouldn't be here. He laid his forehead on the steering wheel, at a complete loss.

He'd been so revved up to find Colette and confess his feelings that he hadn't stopped to think about what to do if he couldn't find her. Drive circles through the city, shouting her name out the window at the top of his lungs? Sleep in his car in this parking lot until she eventually showed up for work? The most obvious thing would be to call her office and set up an appointment, but that was so the opposite of romantic, and there was no guarantee she'd even agree to see him.

A young woman in cut-off shorts and a chartreuse tank-top walked out of the building carrying a box filled with what looked like plants and picture frames. Tristan recognized her from the day he was here with his mother. He had a vague recollection that the woman worked with Colette, or maybe for her, as an assistant or junior attorney or something like that. He got out of the car and walked over to where she was struggling with the box as she looked for a set of keys in her purse.

"Can I help you with that?"

The woman flashed him a dazzling grin and shoved the box in his arms. "Sure, thanks."

He fumbled with the box, almost dropping it. A picture fell

out and clattered onto the asphalt. Lucky for him, the glass didn't break.

"Oh, sorry, let me…" Tristan bent to pick up the picture at the same time as the woman.

They cracked heads, then straightened, laughing.

"This is just not my day." The woman rubbed her forehead. Her dazzling grin never once slipped from her face, and it appeared to be contagious because Tristan found himself smiling back at her.

"Please tell me you didn't just get fired." Tristan gestured to the box he was still holding.

She shook her head, then went back to digging in her oversized purse, looking for keys. "I quit," she said. "But I'm not sure that's much better. At least if they'd fired me, I could have applied for unemployment. Shit! Where the hell did I put them?"

The office doors flew open, and the pompous, asshole prick who'd harassed him and Colette at Gardenia's last week came trotting over. He rattled a set of keys in the air. "You forgot something, Mallory."

Her dazzling smile drooped into a scowl. She swiped at the keys, but he pulled them out of reach. "You can still change your mind, Mal."

"Give me my keys, Scott." Mallory swiped for the keys again, and again Scott pulled them out of reach. "I wouldn't keep working for you if you paid me a million dollars. Not after what you did to Colette."

Tristan shifted the box in his arms.

Scott looked over at him, and his eyes widened in recognition. "Surfer boy? What the hell are you doing here?"

"What did you do to Colette?"

A smirk twisted Scott's pompous face. "Wouldn't you like to know?"

Mallory used the distraction to grab her car keys from Scott. But Scott didn't care anymore about what Mallory was doing.

He turned his full attention to Tristan. "Did you come here looking for her?" He snorted a laugh. "So it didn't work out between the two of you? Why am I not surprised?"

"You're one to talk, Scott." Mallory took the box from Tristan and dropped it into the trunk of her car.

"This isn't any of your business, Mal." Scott glared at the young woman, then he turned back to Tristan. "You were never going to be anything to Colette but a quick fuck, a one and done to get it over with. You know that, right? Once she got what she needed from you, she was always going to move on to someone who has more to offer."

"Someone like you? Is that what you mean?" Tristan took a step closer to Scott.

Scott puffed out his chest. One eyebrow quirked up. "You're too late, dude. That's all I'm saying. You had your chance. You blew it. Colette needs a real man, and you don't even come close."

Tristan wanted nothing more than to lift this pompous asshole up by his tie and swing him around a few times, but honestly, what was the point? Colette clearly wasn't here, and this asshole wasn't worth any more of his energy. He stepped away from Scott and turned to go back to his car.

Mallory stopped him with a hand on his arm. She had her cell phone in one hand. "You want me to text her? Tell her you came by looking for her?"

"Don't bother." Scott's lips curled with smug victory. "I'll give Colette his regards next time I've got her tight ass bent over my desk, showing her what it feels like to be with a real man."

You're not going to let him get away with that, are you, Triscuit?

Tristan wasn't sure what was more satisfying—the feel of his knuckles plowing into Scott's stupid, smug face or the scream that came after.

"You fucking prick!" Scott clutched both hands to his face. Blood dripped onto the asphalt. "You broke my fucking nose!"

Then he turned to Mallory, who had her phone raised in front of her, recording the whole thing. "Mal! You saw that, didn't you? You saw him attack me? Call the fucking cops!"

But Mallory just shook her head, laughing. "I saw you get exactly what you had coming."

She lowered her phone, ducked into her car, and with a flip of her hand out the window, drove out of the parking lot, tires screeching.

Tristan flexed his fingers as he hurried back to his car. He didn't think he'd broken anything, but damn, his hand hurt like hell now. He laughed, imagining how Scott's stupid face felt.

I didn't think you had it in you, little bro.

Turned out his dad was right: fighting for love felt good.

But it had done nothing to help solve his original problem of how to find Colette and what to say to convince her to take him back.

One thing at a time, Triscuit. First, let's get some ice on those knuckles before they swell up like a balloon.

Tristan cranked up the radio and belted love songs out the open window the entire drive home.

WAFFLES DRESSED UP IN A BERET

COLETTE

Colette slid into her favorite booth at Calamity Janes. Before she could even open a menu, the server, a young woman with purple hair and a nose ring, was at her table, pouring coffee. "Waffles with extra syrup, right?"

Colette started to nod, then stopped and reached for a menu. "Actually, I think I want something else today."

The purple-haired server looked surprised.

"I'll give you a minute to decide." She left Colette to pour coffee at another table.

When she returned, Colette handed her the menu and said, "I'm going to have the French toast today, thank you."

The server cocked her head to one side, studying Colette. "You know, that's pretty much just waffles dressed up in a bow tie, right?"

"I think you mean waffles dressed up in a beret," Colette said, trying to make a joke. "Because it's French. Get it?"

Unimpressed, the purple-haired server said, "French toast,

extra syrup. Got it." She tucked the menu under her arm and walked away.

Colette hadn't said anything about wanting extra syrup, but of course she did. She was all for adding new things to her life, but some things were perfect just the way they were. Like extra syrup.

She settled back into the booth to wait for her food. As she sipped her coffee, she scrolled a list of attorneys' offices who were hiring. The longer she scrolled, the less enthusiasm she had for the task. She would need a new job sooner rather than later, but maybe sooner didn't have to be now. She set her phone screen down in the center of the table. Her thoughts drifted to Brooke and Tristan. It was turning out to be much harder than she thought it would be to stop thinking about him, but it had only been a few days. Time healed all wounds, but not today—today she was going to indulge her broken heart and then drown it in maple syrup.

Were Brooke and Tristan together right now? Were they fucking on his awful yellow couch? Was he whispering dirty things in her ear? Had they even given Colette a single moment's thought before they started doing whatever the heck they were doing? Were they happy?

As if summoned, Brooke walked through the front door of Calamity's right at that moment. She scanned the room, locked eyes on Colette, and marched straight to her table.

Colette stiffened in the booth, like a kid caught doing something she wasn't supposed to be doing, even though Calamity Janes was her spot and she had every right to be here on a Saturday morning alone, feeling sorry for herself. "How did you know I'd be here?"

"Saturdays are waffle days." Brooke slid into the opposite booth without an invitation.

The purple-haired server chose that moment to bring Colette her plate of French toast.

Brooke's mouth dropped open. "I think they gave you someone else's order."

"No, this is mine." Colette unwrapped the fork from the napkin, pulled the plate close to her, poured on the extra syrup, and took a bite.

Brooke's wide eyes glinted with delight. "Who are you? And what have you done with my best friend?"

"It's just breakfast," Colette muttered around a mouthful of sticky, sweet toast.

Brooked laughed, then grew quiet again, her face turning serious. She twisted a strand of hair around one finger, something she did when she was nervous.

"Listen, Coco, we need to talk. I've been texting, but you haven't texted back." She grabbed the extra set of silverware and unwrapped it from the paper napkin.

"Yeah, I've had my hands full." Colette took another bite of French toast. "I quit my job."

"What?! When? Why?" Brooke snatched a small bit of French toast from the plate and popped it in her mouth.

"And I slept with a hot cowboy who I met at a club."

Brooke choked on the French toast. She coughed and sputtered, her eyes bugging wide. Colette nudged her coffee across the table. Brooke grabbed it and took a sip. After she'd gotten herself under control again, she said, "No, seriously, what have you done with my best friend?"

Colette sighed and pushed away her plate. She'd eaten half of the French toast, and actually enjoyed it, too, but her appetite was gone now. She knew why Brooke was here. There was no more avoiding this conversation.

"Why are you here, Brooke?" Colette wiped syrup from her fingers with a napkin.

Brooke shifted uncomfortably on the bench. She tucked a chunk of hair behind her ear. "I don't know how to say it other than to say it straight. Something happened the other night.

Between me and Tristan. I didn't plan it. You need to know that. I didn't go looking for him."

"I saw you," Colette said.

Brooke's neatly plucked eyebrows rose.

"At the taco truck on Thursday," she continued. "I saw the two of you together."

"Okay, but let me explain." Brooke spread her hands over the table.

"I saw you kissing. That seems pretty self-explanatory to me."

"Except, hold on, Coco, it's not. It's not what you think." Brooke pointed her fork at the plate of uneaten French toast. "Are you going to finish that?"

Colette nudged the plate closer to her.

Brooke shoved a piece in her mouth, talking as she chewed. "You told me you broke up. I mean, you weren't even really together, but you told me it was over. So when I saw him at that taco truck, I mean, I didn't go there intending to run into him, I swear to God. You told me how good the tacos were, and I was hungry. I just wanted to see for myself, but then he was there, and what was I supposed to do? Not go over and talk to him? I didn't know he was there waiting for you. He didn't tell me until after, until I tried to kiss him."

Brooke scraped up the last bite of French toast and dropped her fork onto the plate with a loud clatter. She sat back in the booth, stretching her belly. "God, that was good."

Colette was trying to process all the words flying from Brooke's mouth. Finally, she said, "Wait. What do you mean, *you* tried to kiss him?"

Brooke groaned and laid her head down on the table. "I know I'm a terrible friend." Then she whipped her head up again, her eyes taking on that doe-like appearance, wide and innocent and filled with regret. "But it's okay, right? I mean, you're not mad because you slept with that hot cowboy from the club, so you've clearly moved on, and we can still be best friends? Even though I made this one tiny mistake?"

"But you didn't know I'd slept with someone else until right now," Colette pointed out. "You knew I was confused about my feelings, but you told me to forget about him. You deleted his number from my phone."

"I thought I was helping!" Brooke reached across the table and grabbed hold of Colette's hand. "If it helps, he pushed me away."

"He pushed you away..." Colette felt like an idiot repeating everything Brooke was saying, but her head was spinning and she didn't understand what her friend was trying to tell her, if it even mattered who kissed who first and who pulled away. Their lips touched. They shared an intimate moment. But if it wasn't mutual? If Tristan hadn't wanted to kiss Brooke? That changed everything, didn't it?

"Like, he wasn't a jackass about it or anything," Brooke said. "He just pulled back from the kiss and said he was seeing someone else. Well, the exact words he used were, 'I'm sorry, I can't. You seem like a nice person, but I'm in love with someone else.'"

Colette's heart fluttered in her chest. Brooke squeezed her hands.

"Coco? Did you hear what I said? He said he was *in love* with someone else. You. He's in love with you. After he broke off the kiss, he told me the whole thing, how he met this beautiful woman at a club and knew from the moment he saw her—saw *you*—that he was going to spend the rest of his life with you."

"There's no way in hell he actually thought that," Colette said with a laugh, but her heart was racing now, as she listened to Brooke.

"He told me about your fight. He said he'd been a complete idiot, letting you walk away, and that he'd asked you to meet him at the taco truck because it's where you had your first date."

"It wasn't technically a date," Colette said, but with no real enthusiasm and only because she felt like she needed to say something, to defend herself for jumping to the worst conclusions when she saw Tristan and Brooke on the bench together Thursday night.

"Well, he thought it was," Brooke said with a quirk of her eyebrow. "But do you hear what I'm saying, Coco? I've met guys like Tristan before. Hell, I've fucked guys like him. Too many to count. And none of them have ever done anything as romantic as Tristan was trying to do that night before I showed up and ruined everything. None of them would have given a second thought to coming home with me. Those other guys? They would have jumped into my bed, no questions asked, girlfriend or no girlfriend. But not Tristan. He's a good one, Coco. I don't know if he's good enough for you, but he's pretty damn close."

Brooke tilted her head, giving Colette a half smile and squeezing her hands one last time before letting go. She rummaged through her purse until she found lipstick, which she dabbed onto her lower lip.

"Well?" Brooke capped the lipstick tube and dropped it back in her purse. "Don't you have anything to say? Or are you just going to keep staring at me like that?"

Colette's thoughts were spinning, and no matter how much she tried to wrangle them, they kept slipping her grasp.

"Why are you telling me this?" she finally asked.

"I saw you at the taco truck," Brooke said. "I saw you running away."

Colette stared at the dregs of coffee left in her cup, feeling both stupid and furious. Stupid because instead of giving Tristan the benefit of the doubt when she saw him sitting on the bench with Brooke, she'd assumed the worst. She'd walked away from what could have been the best relationship of her life, and all for nothing. Which made her furious. Furious at herself for not being brave enough to walk up to him and tell him exactly how she felt. But furious at Brooke, too, for being at the taco truck in the first place, for sitting down on that bench next to Tristan and kissing him with no thought of how it might affect Colette.

"You saw me leaving, and you didn't call me to come back?" Colette asked.

"By the time I realized it was you," Brooke said. "You were already around the corner."

"Did you tell Tristan?"

"What?"

"Did you tell him you saw me?"

"No, I—"

"You didn't tell him you knew me? That we're best friends? Or used to be." She tacked on the last part with a bitter curl of her lip.

Brooke pulled back, hurt. "Used to be? What's that supposed to mean?"

"Friends don't go around kissing each other's boyfriends."

"He isn't your boyfriend. Technically, you weren't even together that night."

Colette rolled her eyes. "Give me a break, Brooke. That's your excuse? I don't get to be mad at you for kissing Tristan because of a small technicality?"

Brooke slouched in the booth with her arms crossed over her stomach. "Coco, I'm sorry. I told you, I didn't plan it."

"Right. You just tripped and fell onto his lips." Colette fumbled with her wallet, hoping she had enough cash to throw on the table so she could storm out of the diner without having to wait for a check, but all she had was a one-dollar bill and a coupon for a free sub sandwich.

She looked around Calamity's trying to catch the server's attention, but the girl was nowhere to be seen.

"Coco, please. If I could take it back, I would." Brooke leaned forward again, trying to bridge the gap between them.

Then she scooted off her bench and moved to the other side of the table, sliding in beside Colette, trapping her in the booth.

"What do you want me to say?" Brooke pleaded. "What can I do to make it up to you? If I'd known you were coming to meet him, I would have never—Coco, please. We've been friends since we could tie our shoes. I messed up. But you were the one who ran."

"Oh, so now it's my fault you kissed him?" Colette tossed her hands in the air.

"No, of course not," Brooke said. "I'm impulsive, you know that. I act before I think, every damn time, and I know it's not great. I kissed him because I wanted to kiss him, and I wasn't thinking about you. But I should have been. I'll say I'm sorry a million times if I have to." Brooke laid her hand on Colette's leg. "I'll keep saying it until I'm blue in the face. But you also have to ask yourself why you ran when you saw us together? If you like him, if you want to be with him, why walk the other way?"

Colette stared at her hands in her lap and shook her head. "I don't know. It seemed too good to be true. I guess seeing you together confirmed the doubts I was already having. I was scared, and when I saw the two of you kissing, I guess it was the excuse I was looking for."

"Love is terrifying," Brooke said. "Why do you think I don't date anyone for more than a few weeks? But Coco, if you find someone who lights you up the way Tristan does, you shouldn't run from that."

"Now you tell me," Colette said with a sad laugh.

Brooke bumped her shoulder. "So, do you forgive me?"

"I don't know…" Of course Colette had already forgiven her, but she didn't want to seem like a complete pushover.

"You could always make a pros and cons list," Brooke said. "Pros to forgiving Brooke… She'll thank you in her Oscar speech.

"Cons of forgiving Brooke," Colette said. "She'll never stop talking about the Oscar she won."

The two of them laughed together, the familiar joke easing the tension.

Colette's phone vibrated. She picked it up to check the incoming message and frowned at the screen.

"What is it?" Brooke asked her.

"A text message from this woman I work with, or used to work with," Colette said, swiping to read the rest of the text. "It says, 'Karma, bitch,' and then there's a link to a video."

"Well, watch it already." Brooke leaned in as Colette pulled up the video and pressed play.

The video was unsteady, obviously recorded on someone's phone. Probably Mallory's, since she was the one who had forwarded the video and it was her voice in the background, first crying out in surprise, then laughing and saying, "I saw you get exactly what you had coming." The image cut out after that.

Colette sat stunned, staring at the phone in her hand, her mind trying to make sense of what she'd just watched.

"Oh my God!" Brooke's hand flew to her mouth. "Was that...? Play it again, Coco."

Colette pressed play.

They watched a second time as Tristan Walker hauled back and punched Scott Campbell in the face.

FIRST TIMERS CLUB

Chat Room

NotSoDirty30 (posted at 11:37 am): I would love to hear all your brilliant ideas for how to proclaim your undying love to someone. Okay, it might be a bit too early in the relationship for undying love, so how about ideas for how to proclaim that you're falling hard and fast?

HappilyNeverAfter: Ooooo! Looks like someone found their love connection!

2Hawt2Handle: Please tell me it's the guy who punched your v-card.

HappilyNeverAfter: And if it isn't?

2Hawt2Handle: I mean, I'm over here just trying to get one guy interested in me, and she's already had two? Good for her, but come on universe, throw a bitch a bone!

TheBoyNextDoor: When it rains it pours?

LoveConnection (admin): Don't worry @2Hawt2Handle. Your time will come.

NotSoDirty30: It's the same guy. It turns out I was feeling insecure for no reason. I think he might actually have genuine feelings for me, too, but after the way we left off, I'm not sure what would be the best way to reach out to him. A text just doesn't feel special enough, you know?

SexIsOveR-rated: Just go over to his house and tell him how you feel.

HappilyNeverAfter: Boring. She needs a grand gesture.

SexIsOveR-rated: What's that?

ShakespeareNLove: In the movies, they always do something big and impossibly romantic.

TheBoyNextDoor: You know, like when the hero goes chasing the heroine through the airport? That's a grand gesture.

SexIsOveR-rated: Is he going on a trip soon?

HappilyNeverAfter: You can't really run through an airport anymore. Not the way you used to.

cherrybomb: How about showing up at his apartment with a bottle of wine wearing nothing under your coat but an apology?

TheBoyNextDoor: Sexy.

HappilyNeverAfter: Not big enough.

SexIsOveR-rated: What about a flash mob?

2Hawt2Handle: No one does flash mobs anymore.

SexIsOveR-rated: Too bad. I would fall hard for someone who organized a flash mob for me.

LoveConnection (admin): Go big or go home, that's what I always say.

HappilyNeverAfter: Hire a skywriter.

TheBoyNextDoor: Call in to one of those late-night radio shows and dedicate a song to him.

SexIsOveR-rated: Do those shows still exist?

TheBoyNextDoor: I DJ for one, so I'd say, yes, they do still exist.

2Hawt2Handle: Bring him food. Bake him a cake or make him a fancy dinner. The way to a man's heart is through his stomach.

TheBoyNextDoor: Write him a song.

ShakespeareNLove: A love letter.

HappilyNeverAfter: Recreate that scene from Say Anything!

SexIsOveR-rated: Hire a marching band.

NotSoDirty30: These are all such fun ideas! Thank you everyone! This group is a lifeline!

LoveConnection (admin): Whatever you decide, grand gesture or something else, the important thing is to speak plainly, from your heart. Tell him the truth. It's hard to go wrong with honesty.

TheBoyNextDoor: Let us know how it goes.

HappilyNeverAfter: We're all rooting for you!

CHASING AFTER LOVE

Tristan

Tristan couldn't stop thinking about Colette. When he looked at his bruised knuckles, he thought about Colette. When he passed a taqueria, he thought about Colette. When he saw the ocean, he thought about Colette. She was there when he closed his eyes. She was there when he opened them too. He would catch glimpses of her on the street outside the grocery store, the coffee shop, the bar, his favorite surf spot. It was never actually her, just some other woman with dark flowing hair and stern features, but his heart would still catch in his throat.

What are you waiting for? Just text her already.

He would pull up her number and his mind would go blank looking at the last message he sent four days ago asking her if she'd been at the taco truck, then begging her to call him back. He sounded so desperate in that text, so obnoxious, and she must have felt the same because she never texted him back. Four days since the taco truck and one day since rushing to her office hoping to find her and profess his feelings, only to end up punching her ex-boss in the face, and he'd heard nothing from her. So maybe it wasn't meant to be, and he should let it go. So maybe she had made up her mind about him, and the answer was a resounding hell no.

His father had told him to fight for love. Which worked out well for Otto and Maureen, who had years and decades of love to bring them back together. But how did one fight for almost-love? How did two people make it through the beginning when everything felt weightless and untethered? When it was so easy to walk away and never look back?

Sunday morning, Otto showed up at Tristan's apartment around noon to pack up the rest of his things and move back home with Maureen. He slapped $20 into Tristan's hand and told him to go grab them some coffee from the cafe at the end of the block. It was close enough to walk. When he got there, the line was out the door. It took almost an hour for him to get the coffees and walk back to the apartment.

He was approaching the entrance to the building's parking lot, with two hot coffees balanced in his hands, when he saw her. A woman with long, dark hair and oversized sunglasses steered her turquoise Chevy Aveo out of the driveway. The car stopped at the curb, waiting for traffic to clear so she could turn right. There were thousands of women with long, dark hair and oversized sunglasses. And there had to be plenty of turquoise Chevy Aveos driving around LA too. Tristan wasn't close enough to see if this one had only one hubcap the way Colette's did. He walked faster, trying to catch the car before it made the turn, but he wasn't fast enough. At the next break in the oncoming stream, the woman in the Chevy Aveo made the turn and drove off.

Tristan had been seeing Colette everywhere, so it made sense he would see her here too. But what if it really was her this time? But no, it couldn't have been the real Colette. Why would she make all this effort to come to his apartment only to leave without talking to him? It didn't make sense. Certainly, if it had been Colette, his father would have invited her inside to wait until Tristan returned.

Tristan was too impatient to wait for the elevator. He took the stairs two at a time up to his apartment. He burst inside to find his father dragging two more suitcases from the bedroom to the living room to add to the small pile growing near the front door.

"Did I miss anything?" Tristan asked, his mind still on the woman in the Chevy Aveo, still hoping that maybe today his luck would change.

Otto set the suitcases down with the others and scratched his head.

"Did someone come to the door, I mean?" Tristan said, knowing how desperate he sounded and not caring. "I thought I saw—"

"Well, now that you mention it," his father interrupted. "A woman was here, but I sent her away."

Tristan set the coffees down on the entry table. "What did she look like? Did she say what she wanted?"

Otto frowned. "Pretty. Rather serious expression. Brown hair. Nice eyes. She asked if you were home, and I told her you weren't and she looked awfully disappointed. She was carrying a sack of tacos, I think."

"Tacos?"

"Yes, Eddy's Taco Truck." His father snapped his fingers. "That's what the bag said."

"You didn't invite her in? Did you tell her I was coming right back?"

"Well, no. I told her you were in love and that you were off the market, that you weren't seeing anyone right now." Otto's brow furrowed. He clearly thought he'd been helping Tristan by sending the woman away.

"Dad." Tristan sighed. "Please tell me you didn't."

"What's the problem? You don't want to date other women, do you?"

"Dad! That was her! That was Colette!"

"That was—" Otto's eyes widened as they darted to the door. "Oh dear. She didn't tell me her name."

"You could have asked her!"

Otto nodded slowly and stroked his chin. "Yes, I suppose that would have been a smart thing to do. I'm sorry, son. I had no idea. Surely, you can call her?"

Tristan ran to the window that overlooked the street. Traffic backed up at a red light, and there in the middle of the cluster was the turquoise Chevy Aveo. If he hurried, he might catch up with her.

He grabbed his motorcycle keys and helmet, bolted out of the apartment, and sprinted down the stairs. By the time he turned his Ducati onto the street, the light had turned green and traffic was flowing again. He wove between the lanes, trying to catch up to the Chevy Aveo. A large pickup truck cut him off. He slammed on his brakes, narrowly avoiding a collision. By the time the pickup truck moved out of his way again, the distance between him and Colette had widened significantly.

He chased her through the city, darting in and out of traffic, running stale yellow lights, once even blasting through a red light to stay on her tail. Just when he was about to catch up to her, another car would cut him off. But he kept her in sight and even closed the distance. The garish turquoise color of her car made it easier to keep track of her on the crowded roadways.

About five miles from his apartment, Colette took the freeway on-ramp headed west. Tristan followed. Now that they were on the freeway, he wasn't sure what he would do if he caught up to her. It wasn't like they could pull over on the shoulder so he could profess his love with cars and semi-trucks whizzing past at 80-miles an hour. But she had to be headed somewhere. Eventually, she'd have to get off the freeway.

A few minutes later, the Chevy Aveo took the off-ramp toward Venice Beach. Tristan followed. His heart slammed in his chest the closer they got to the boardwalk. He had taken Colette here on their first unofficial date. They'd kissed for the first time on the boardwalk. His lips still remembered hers and ached to rediscover her soft sweetness. He was lost in this memory when he lost sight of the Chevy Aveo.

One second it was right in front of him, the next it was gone. She'd turned a corner, and he hadn't noticed. He drove in slow circles near the Venice Beach Boardwalk, hoping that his instinct was right and she was finding a place to park, that she had come here to reminisce about that day when the spark between them ignited. His hope faded the longer he drove in circles, but then he turned a corner and almost ran right into it. Colette's turquoise Chevy Aveo with the single hubcap was parked in front of a clothing store—a bright pop of color among the drab tans and silvers—but Colette was nowhere to be seen.

Tristan maneuvered his bike into a small parking space a block away from the Aveo. Colette was somewhere nearby. He could feel it in his bones—how close he was to finding her. He reached into his pocket for his cell phone, intending to text her to wait for him near the pier, but his pocket was empty. He'd left his cell phone at his apartment.

Guess you're doing this the old-fashioned way, Triscuit.

It was Sunday afternoon, a beautiful, blue-sky day with warm sun beating down on bare shoulders. Tourists and locals alike packed the boardwalk. Tristan pushed his way through the slow-moving crowd, twisting his head side to side, trying to find Colette. People laughed and talked loudly to one another. Musicians and street performers stood at the periphery, doing their best to draw the attention of passers-by. Young people carried surfboards and skim boards toward the water's edge. Bikini-clad women stretched out on beach towels in the sand. Tristan's gaze skimmed over it all, his eyes seeking Colette.

Just as he was thinking he should return to the Aveo and wait for her there, the crowd in front of him parted and he saw her walking along the boardwalk a few steps ahead of him.

"Colette!" he shouted her name, but she kept walking.

A trio of young men drummed buckets nearby. A man with a parrot on his shoulder walked by and the bird squawked loudly. Tristan called out to Colette again, but it was too noisy for her to hear him shouting. The gap in the crowd closed again. Tristan pushed his way through. He was steps away from catching her when a man on roller blades cut across the boardwalk in front of him.

"Rollers coming through! Clear a path!" The man flung his arms in front of him and did a fancy spin, parting the crowd so a large group of what appeared to be newbie rollerbladers could cross to a different part of the boardwalk. They stumbled and clattered, grabbing on to one another to keep from falling.

The long line of skaters blocked Tristan's view of Colette. He stood on tip-toe trying to keep her in his sights, while he waited for the group to pass, but they were a chaotic mass of waving arms and jostling bodies. There was no good way to go around the group, and he didn't dare go through for fear of causing a mass pile-up. By the time the last rollerblader had cleared the boardwalk, Tristan had lost sight of Colette again.

This was getting ridiculous.

He'd just go wait by her car. Or hell, maybe he'd go home, get his phone, and call her the way he should have from the beginning. She'd shown up at his apartment with tacos from Eddy's Taco Truck. That had to mean something. He'd call her and tell her to come back. He craned his neck, scanning the crowd one last time before giving up.

"Tristan?" Her voice cut through the noise.

He was afraid to turn around for fear that he was imagining her again, that he would find the man with the parrot instead, the bird imitating Colette's stern voice. A voice with the power to shatter him and put him back together again. He had to look. He was Tristan Walker; he wasn't afraid of anything.

He took a deep breath, turned, and almost burst out laughing. Because there she was, standing right behind him as if she'd been the one looking for him all along. She clutched a paper bag in one hand, Eddy's Taco Truck printed in red on the side. A light breeze fluttered the dark strands of her hair around her face. She looked as shocked and delighted at seeing Tristan as he felt seeing her.

Colette shook her head, confusion furrowing her brow. "Tristan? What are you doing here?"

TACOS BY THE OCEAN

Colette

It had to be fate, right? That Tristan was standing right in front of her, smiling at her, walking toward her—it had to be a sign from the universe that they were meant to be together, didn't it? Colette's heart pounded in her chest, and she kept thinking she would blink and he'd disappear. He had to be a figment of her imagination. Los Angeles was a big city. What were the odds of the two of them ended up in the same exact spot at the same exact time?

"What are you doing here?" Colette asked him.

"Looking for you." He grabbed the hand that wasn't holding the bag of tacos and squeezed.

"Looking for me?" she repeated, her head spinning to have him this close to her again, touching her.

"I followed you here." The grin on his face widened.

"Followed me?"

She sounded like a broken record, but she couldn't seem to bridge the distance between his apartment where the man who answered the door had told her to leave because Tristan didn't want to see her anymore and this moment, here on the boardwalk, where Tristan was staring deep into her eyes and gripping her hand so tightly, it felt like he would never let her go.

"I saw you leave my apartment complex," he said.

"Yeah, I brought you tacos." She lifted the bag. "Chapulines. Your favorite. But there was some man there? He told me you were off the market and I should just go. That you didn't want to see me anymore."

Tristan ducked his head, embarrassed, but kept tight hold of her hand. "That was my dad. Sorry. He doesn't know what he's talking about."

A woman on stilts and juggling oranges walked past them.

Colette watched her for a moment, then returned her attention to Tristan. "So, are you?"

"Am I what?"

"Off the market?"

He tilted his head, studying her. "I could be."

"What does that mean?"

Three teenage boys zipped by them on skateboards. The wheels clattered noisily over the sidewalk. One of them held a Bluetooth speaker blaring music for the entire boardwalk to hear.

Tristan leaned close to Colette, brushing her hair from her neck and speaking softly into her ear. "Can we go somewhere else to talk about this? Somewhere quieter?"

He led her off the boardwalk and into the sand. They walked parallel to the water for a few minutes until they came to a spot where the people thinned out and you had to go out of your way to bump into someone. The ocean's hiss drowned out the nearby chatter and screams of children playing in the water.

Tristan found them a flat, dry spot to sit. Colette sank into the sand beside him and set the bag of tacos between them.

"What were you going to do with them?" Tristan gestured to the bag. "After my dad told you to get lost?"

Colette shrugged. "Eat them, I suppose."

There was an uncomfortable beat of silence, and then they both spoke at the same time.

"Colette, about what I said last week—it's not how I really feel."

"I came to the taco truck on Thursday night."

He twisted his head to look at her. Surprise colored his cheeks. "You were there?"

She nodded.

"I thought I saw you leaving," he said. "But then I thought I'd imagined it. Why were you running away?"

Before she could answer, understanding swept across his face. "You saw me with that other woman. You saw her kiss me."

Colette shifted her gaze toward the ocean. Sun glimmered brightly across the waves. Several yards from shore, surfers bobbed, waiting for the perfect swell. She turned to look at Tristan again, smiling at him when she said, "It doesn't matter. I'm not mad, I mean. It's not like we were together or anything."

"No, but I was there to meet you." His fingers crept across the sand, reaching for hers.

"I know the whole story." She met him halfway. Lacing her fingers through his, she told him about Brooke, the smallness of the world, the strange way life plays out. "I shouldn't have run. I should have stayed and told you how I was feeling."

"And how are you feeling?" He smiled at her, and she couldn't help but smile back.

It was odd how suddenly shy Colette felt in his presence. All the words she'd been prepping crammed against the back of her teeth, and all she had to do was open her mouth and let her heart spill out, but it was harder than she thought it would be. She'd never been in love before.

She traced her thumb over his knuckles.

"How about I tell you how I'm feeling first?" Tristan kissed the back of her hand. "That day when my mom interrupted us at the apartment, when I said all those stupid things about you not meaning anything to me, I was being an idiot. I was scared, and I said that first thing that came to my mouth, but it's not really how I feel. It's never been how I feel."

Then he turned his face toward the ocean and told her about trying to ride a killer wave, how he'd been knocked off and churned underwater until he almost died. "When I was under, when I thought I would never see the sunlight again, you were the person I thought about. Yours was the face I wanted to see one more time."

He shifted in the sand to angle his body toward her. He brushed his hand over her cheek, leaving little flecks of sand on her skin. "You are the best thing that's ever happened to me, Colette, the best and most beautiful, and nothing makes sense when you're not around."

He stared into her eyes, and she felt her fear dissolving. His words were a wave washed ashore, knocking down her sandcastle walls.

"I want this to mean something." He leaned his forehead against hers. "The two of us. I want this to be more than sex. I want strings."

"You want to be tied down?" She couldn't help herself.

A smile tugged on the corners of his mouth as he said, "Only if you're the one holding the ropes." He clutched her tighter. "I'm serious, Colette. These feelings I have for you, they're not nothing. They're everything. You're everything."

And then he was kissing her, lighting her body and soul on fire with the heat of his lips. His fingers tangled in her hair as he pulled her even closer. He kissed like he was making up for lost time, and she kissed him back just as eagerly.

After a minute, she broke away with a gasp. "Wait, before you decide you really want to be with me... Before we do this for real... There are some things I need to tell you too."

The words came spilling out then. How she never meant to fall for him, but now that she had, she couldn't think of any other way this could have turned out. How the weekend in Joshua Tree had been the best twenty-four hours of her life, but she'd been so afraid that her feelings weren't real, that sex had only complicated matters.

"It's called chemistry." He dragged his finger along her jawline, sending a pleasurable tingle through her whole body.

"I just wasn't sure if I could trust my feelings." She put her hand on his knee. "I can't think clearly with you around."

"And that's a bad thing?" He kissed her nose, then the corners of her mouth, then both sides of her neck.

She was already having a hard time holding back. Her whole body wanted him. She ached to feel his skin against hers, to have him inside her once more. But she needed to tell him everything first. If they were going to be more than fuck buddies, she needed to be able to have a full and honest conversation before stripping off each other's clothes and hopping into bed. Although, having conversations while naked sounded appealing too.

She pulled back from him and grabbed both of his hands so he couldn't run his fingers over her and drive her slowly insane.

"There's something else." She told him about the man from the club, the cowboy who took her home. She didn't tell him every detail, just enough for him to get the idea.

His jaw tightened, then relaxed again. He shook his head and smiled. "That's okay. I don't care what happened. I mean, like you said, we weren't together, and honestly, if it took you being with another man to realize that I'm who you really want to be with, then fine. That's worth it to me."

He eyed her lips hungrily, and she couldn't take it anymore. She lunged for him, knocking him back in the sand as their lips found each other once more. She straddled him and deepened her kiss. His hand roamed over her back and then down to her ass. He moaned, and she felt his cock harden between her legs.

She pulled back and flashed him a predatory smile. "We could get in trouble for this."

There were families on the beach, lifeguard towers within sight, a children's surfing lesson happening steps from where they were sitting. Whatever they wanted to happen would have to wait until they were alone. Colette rolled off of Tristan and reached for the bag of tacos. The paper crinkled as she removed two wrapped tacos and handed one to Tristan.

His eyebrows shot up in surprise when she unwrapped her taco. He watched her take the first bite.

"Well?" he asked. "What do you think?"

The chapulines were better than she thought they'd be, nutty and spicy, with a delectable crunch she wasn't expecting. She eyed the bug legs sticking out of the corn tortilla, then took a second bite.

"I guess that means she likes it, folks." Tristan laughed and chomped into his taco, eating the whole thing in three bites.

He flashed his teeth at her. "Any legs in my teeth?"

She laughed and shoved his shoulder, then spread her lips in a wide grin. "What about me?"

He shook his head. "You're perfect."

His words moved under her skin, flooding her with warmth. She leaned her head against his shoulder and together they watched as the group of kids learning to surf moved their boards from the sand into the rolling waves. The kids paddled furiously over the small swells, following their lean, tanned instructor farther and farther into the ocean until they were tiny black dots bobbing against a clear-blue sky. They were pretty cute, chasing waves, trying to balance on their boards, falling into the water with yips and howls, resurfacing with smiles on their faces, ready to get back up and try again.

Tristan held his breath as he watched, as if he were the one out there, the one invested in their successes and failures. After a few minutes, he turned to Colette, his expression tentative, but hopeful. "What if I did that?"

"Surf?" She smiled. "You already do that, don't you?"

"No, what if I taught other people? Kids, or adults, whoever wanted to try it. What if I opened a surf shop with rentals and lessons and gear and…" He trailed off, turning his eyes back to the water. "Never mind, it's a dumb idea. I don't have the first clue how to get started doing something like that."

Colette squeezed his hand. "It's not a dumb idea at all. In fact, I think it's a great one."

"I'd probably kill someone on my first day." He tried to play it off as a joke, but she could see by the tension in his shoulders and the clench of his jaw, how much he really cared about this idea, and how afraid he was of failing.

"Hey." She placed her hand on his cheek, turning his head so they were looking into each other's eyes. "What was it you told me about your brother? What was it he used to say to you?"

"Don't ever order crickets on a first date?"

She smiled at his answer, and Tristan smiled back at her, relaxing into her touch.

"Life's too short to waste time being afraid." She ran her thumb across the ridge of his cheekbone, thinking of how close she'd come to missing this, missing him because of her own fears and insecurities. Tristan had shown her how to be brave; she hoped she could do the same for him now and always. "If this is what you want, if you're serious, then you should do it. Dive in with both feet. I can help you figure out the business stuff, but I have to tell you, I don't know the first thing about surfing."

"Well, we're definitely going to have to change that." Tristan drew her closer, rearranging her so that she was sitting between his legs with her back against his chest and his arms wrapped around her in a bear hug. She sighed and nestled into him.

They stayed like that until the sky turned rose and lavender, and the sun dipped beneath the waves. The surfers came out of the water and peeled off their wetsuits. The beach emptied. Twilight deepened, and the first stars appeared above them. Still, neither of them moved, neither wanting to break the spell.

When they were the only ones left on the beach, nothing more than shadows in the dark, Tristan leaned down and whispered into Colette's ear, "Pros for fucking Tristan Walker tonight?"

She lifted her eyes to meet his, smiling mischievously when she answered, "I'll probably fall in love."

His eyebrows shot up. "And the cons?"

She thought a minute before answering, "I might never leave your bed."

"Now that's a con I think I can live with." His grin widened.

"Me too." She tilted her face, and his mouth found hers in the dark.

Colette lost herself in the kiss, pushing aside every pro and every con, mentally shredding every list she'd ever made. She didn't need them anymore. When it came to Tristan, she knew exactly what she wanted.

EPILOGUE

Three Months Later

Tristan covered Colette's eyes with one hand and guided her along the boardwalk with the other. "No peeking."

"I'm going to trip and break something." But she played along, clinging to his waist, trying not to think about how easy it would be for her stilettos to get caught in a crack, sending them to the hospital instead of the vow renewal ceremony they were already running late for. But Tristan had been adamant about stopping by the boardwalk on the way to his parents' house. *Trust me*, he'd said. And she did. Clearly, since she was willing to walk with her eyes closed down a busy sidewalk with no clue where they were headed.

She clung to him as he led her through a maze of tourists, vendors, and street performers. A dog barked. Somewhere a low bass thumped and rattled cheap speakers. People laughed and talked and bustled around them. Above it all came the steady roar of the ocean, the hiss of the waves chasing over the sand. The air tasted sweet of waffle cones, the scent drifting from the ice cream shop near where they'd parked.

"Almost there," Tristan said. A few steps later, he stopped her and spun her around. "Okay. Are you ready?"

"For you? Always," she teased.

He placed a tender kiss on the back of her neck before lifting his hand from her eyes and sweeping his arm in the air, the gesture filled with pride and nervous anticipation.

"Well? What do you think?" He watched her closely as she swept her gaze over the empty storefront, which faced a bustling section of the boardwalk just steps from the sand.

The place looked deserted with the windows covered in brown construction paper and a For Lease sign hanging in the door, but Colette could imagine it fixed up, repainted, the smudges shined from the glass, colorful displays drawing customers inside, a row of surfboards lined on the sidewalk outside, beckoning adventure.

"I don't think you could find a spot better than this, even if you tried." She flashed him a grin. "Really, Tristan. It's great. It's perfect."

"Good, because I already signed the lease." He took a key from his pocket and waved it in front of her face. "Do you want to see inside?"

"Do we have time?"

"I'm officiating," he said with a wicked grin. "They can't start without me, right?"

"I'm trying to stay on your mother's good side, remember? I don't think making her son late to her wedding is going to win me any points."

Over the past three months, Maureen Walker had done little more than tolerate Colette's presence in her son's life. More recently, though, ever since Colette had opened her own practice and started doing pro bono work for women who couldn't afford a high-profile divorce attorney, Maureen had seemed to warm up to her, even asking her to a girls' brunch last weekend.

Colette didn't know if any woman Tristan brought home would ever be good enough for Maureen, but she didn't want to erase what little progress had been made between them by ruining today's festivities. Maureen might still believe Colette was just a passing phase, someone Tristan needed to get out of his system before he found someone better, but as far as Colette was concerned, Tristan was her forever, and she knew he felt the same. So she really needed to stay on Maureen's good side.

"You're not making *me* late. I'm making *you* late." Tristan unlocked the door and dragged Colette into the building.

He shut and locked the door behind her and even though they'd had sex this morning, twice, he was all over her again, grabbing her and spinning her, pressing his lips to hers, letting his hands roam. When he pushed her up against the wall, all thoughts of the ceremony and being late and pissing off Maureen vanished from Colette's mind.

There was only Tristan, biting her lip, caressing her breasts, heat spreading between her legs, the hammer of her heart, the taste of him, the hardness of his cock pressed against her thigh, desire flashing sparks between them, threatening to burn the place down.

When Tristan's hand slid under her skirt, Colette worried for a second about the windows, if people could see inside, but paper spanned every inch of glass, and even if there was a way for someone to peek in, let them look, because what Tristan's fingers were doing to her now was too good to stop.

"Why didn't you tell me you weren't wearing any underwear?" He growled low against her neck and nipped her skin.

She smiled and tugged on the skinny black tie knotted around his neck, pulling his mouth back to hers. As she worked her tongue over his, she unbuttoned his dress shirt and tugged the tails loose from his pants, running her hands over his chest.

She moved to his belt, sliding it out from the loops before unzipping the fly of his pants and reaching to grab his cock. He moaned when her fingers wrapped around him. She stroked him, building the intensity slowly, making him gasp and shudder with pleasure.

Before she could bring him all the way, he grabbed her wrist and lifted it above her head, pressing her hard against the wall, pinning her with his weight. Now he was the one with his hands between her legs, rubbing her and making her wet with desire. She arched against him, wanting more.

He spun her around and pushed her against the wall, positioning her hips at an angle. She let out a quiet gasp as he hiked up her skirt, spread her legs and entered her from behind. He kept one hand on the wall for balance and the other he slipped down the front of her dress, fondling her breasts.

"No bra either? Naughty girl." He growled in her ear and thrust harder.

She bit her lip, swallowing down the loud moan that was rising for him. It came out as a whimper, and she felt him throb with desire.

"That's it, Colette. Tell me how you like it."

She arched her hips back at a sharper angle, taking him in deeper. He moved his hand from her nipples to her clit, which he rubbed tenderly, making soft noises in her ear, telling her how good she felt, how much he wanted her. "Come for me, beautiful."

He pumped faster, rocking her to the edge. She took him along with her, the two of them climaxing together. He throbbed as she tightened around him. Then they both relaxed. He stayed inside her for a second longer, holding her up, his breath slowing again. When he pulled away from her, there was a reluctance, a contented and wistful sigh. He hitched his pants back around his waist, grabbed his belt off the floor, and slipped it through the loops. She adjusted her dress, straightening the skirt, fixing the scooped neck of her dress so it covered her cleavage.

"That was a pleasant surprise." She flashed him a coy smile.

He leaned close to her, brushing his finger over her cheek. "Do you know how much I love you, Colette Harris?"

"I think I have some idea, yes." She arched up to kiss him on the tip of his nose. "And I love you too. But I don't think love is going to be a good enough excuse for Maureen if we ruin her special day."

"Okay, okay." He stole one more kiss from her before grabbing her hand and hurrying her out of the store.

Twenty minutes later, they pulled up to the Walker's Malibu mansion, handed the keys to the valet, and headed toward the backyard. Soft notes from a string quartet filled the air. Beneath that were the murmurs and quiet laughter of the waiting guests. Just before they rounded the corner, Colette pulled Tristan to a stop. She wiped a smudge of lipstick from the corner of his mouth and fussed with his tie, then tugged on the hem of her skirt one more time and tousled her hair.

"Is it obvious?" she asked.

His brow furrowed in a question.

"Can you tell we just had sex?" she clarified.

His expression softened, though his eyes sparked with desire. "The only thing that's obvious to me is that I'm the luckiest man in the world."

He grabbed her around the waist and was about to pull her in for another kiss when Maureen Walker's frantic voice interrupted them. "Tristan! I've been looking everywhere for you. It's time to start the ceremony. Where have you been?"

She fluttered around her son, brushing invisible lint from the shoulders of his jacket, then her hands stilled and she frowned at his chest. "Your shirt buttons are crooked. Why is your shirt crooked?"

Colette swallowed a laugh as Maureen reached to fix Tristan's shirt. He swatted at her hand. "Mom, leave it. I'll fix it. Don't get yourself all worked up. I'm here now. We're here. Let's get you married."

He fixed his buttons, took Maureen by the elbow, and led her toward the backyard where friends and colleagues waited in folding white chairs. Colette trailed after them, ducking away at the last minute to find her seat in the front row beside an elderly aunt who clutched a tissue in her lap and wept openly when the music started and Maureen appeared at the end of the aisle.

Draped in a creamy cloud of tulle and lace, Maureen was a vision. As she walked toward a large, wooden archway covered in pink roses where Otto waited to take her hand and repeat his vows, her gaze stayed fixed on her husband's, her eyes glistening with tears, her wine-red lips pulled back in a blissful smile. Colette had never seen her look so happy.

The ceremony itself was short, but sweet. Tristan read a poem about second chances and soulmates. The string quartet played a cover of an Elvis Presley song. A trio of doves were released from a cage in a flutter of chirping wings. It was sunny, but not too warm, with a kiss of a breeze blowing through the yard. A perfect California day, a perfect day for love.

They held the reception in the lower section of the mansion, which was decorated in chic whites and creams with pops of red and pink. The guests grabbed beer and wine and bacon-wrapped dates from the kitchen then moved into the grand living room where they perused photographs of Otto and Maureen and their two boys, before eventually ending up outside on the back patio where a DJ played upbeat jazz music and several people pawed through the karaoke catalog looking for favorite songs.

Colette helped the elderly aunt get settled in a comfy wing-backed chair in the center of the action and went to find them both a drink. She grabbed a wine spritzer for the aunt and a mojito for herself. An arm slipped around her waist as she was stepping back from the bar.

"Please tell me one of those is for me?" Tristan's voice melted across the back of her neck, sending shivers through her.

Colette smiled and turned to plant a playful kiss on his lips. "Sorry, darling, I have a new date now."

She sashayed out of the kitchen to deliver the spritzer to Tristan's aunt. Tristan asked for a beer and followed Colette. When he caught up to her, his arm slipped around her waist again, his fingers squeezing her hips in a proprietary way. Colette settled against him, marveling at the perfect way she fit inside his arm.

The elderly aunt eyed them with a knowing look, a smile curling her lips. She waved her spritzer in the air, gesturing at them. "You two are going to be next. I can see by the way you look at each other that what you two have is true love. The kind that lasts forever. Mark my words, we'll be back here in another few months toasting Tristan and his beloved."

"We'll see, Aunt Irene. We'll see." Tristan laughed and tightened his hold around Colette.

"I was right about your parents." She clucked, tipping her head to where Maureen and Otto had just entered the room. "Trust me, I know genuine love when I see it."

At that moment, Otto grabbed Maureen around the waist and dipped her into a passionate kiss while the guests clapped and cheered. When he pulled Maureen upright again, she laughed, breathless, and he drew her close, whispering something in her ear that no one else could hear. Maureen blushed as she smiled, her entire face lighting up with pleasure.

"They really do love each other, don't they?" Colette leaned her head against Tristan's shoulder.

"They do," he said, smiling. "But I'm glad that for a minute they didn't."

"What do you mean?"

He turned to face her. His eyes glinted mischievously, drawing her in like they always did. "If my mom wasn't so adamant about divorcing my dad, she would have never gone attorney hunting," he said. "And we wouldn't have ended up in the office of Campbell and Sons, and I wouldn't have gotten my second chance with you."

"Oh, I don't know." Colette's lips curled into a smile. "Fate can be surprisingly stubborn."

"Is that what we are? Fated?" He nuzzled her hair. Before she could answer, Tristan sighed and said, "Troy would have loved today, you know. He was such a sucker for all this 'and they lived happily ever after' stuff."

"I wish I could have met him." Colette slipped her hand into Tristan's. "He sounds like a great brother."

"He was." Tristan squeezed her hand. "He would have liked to meet you too. Though he probably would have told everyone that you are too good for me."

"I am too good for you." She laughed and bumped her hip against his.

"Dance with me?" He put their drinks down on a nearby table and swirled her in a circle, drawing her onto the dance floor despite her protests.

As they swayed in each other's arms, Tristan stared at her with such adoration, such intensity, Colette lost her breath. He looked like he was seconds away from dropping to one knee and asking her a question she wouldn't have to think twice about before answering. Because she knew, with Tristan, the answer would always be yes.

If he asked her to move in with him tomorrow, she'd say yes. If he asked her something else, too, something involving a ring and a dropping onto one knee, she wouldn't even need a minute to think about it. Yes and yes and yes. Yes to Tristan. Yes to her life with him. Yes to big adventures and great sex and taking risks and falling in love again every day, knowing that the pros would always outweigh the cons.

ACKNOWLEDGMENTS

I'm going to make this quick and dirty. French kisses and a strip tease for my truest love, first and last, for always making me feel like the hottest, smartest, most important woman in any room (even when I'm definitely not). Exes and ohs to E for pointing out the obvious and saying don't you dare stop (not a direct quote). Cuddles and a snog to K for showing me what was possible and doing it for free (for now)—if our corporate takeover plans don't work out, we'll just keep doing this. I must also raise a glass of bubbly rosé to the Unchurched Sluts. Here's to finding ourselves, finding each other, and finding a better way—here's to US (I don't expect you to read this book, but I do expect you to tell me it's the best thing I've ever written even if it's not). And finally, with the deepest love and gratitude to the people who let me belt karaoke at the top of my lungs even when I'm singing off key—thank you for being my reason to wake up in the morning and write. Muah!

ABOUT THE AUTHOR

Loni Hansen believes in love at first sight, laughing until she cries, and that a freshly baked chocolate chip cookie can end almost any argument. She likes her coffee hot, her women complicated, her men good-hearted, and her endings satisfying. Once a champion of purity culture and a devout virgin, Loni now fully supports embracing vulnerability and exploring life's most carnal desires with gusto, curiosity, and humor.

Her debut romantic comedy, *First Time Lucky*, is the first in a standalone series about older virgins whole-heartedly going after the three most important things in life: true love, belly laughs, and great sex. Though not necessarily in that order.

To stay up to date on upcoming releases, discounts, and more sign up for Loni's Love Letters.

CPSIA information can be obtained
at www.ICGtesting.com
Printed in the USA
LVHW052327110623
749469LV00003B/251

9 781954 815087